the Boss

A sensual takeover bid she can't refuse!

**Three glamorous office romances from
three favourite Mills & Boon authors!**

In January 2009 Mills & Boon bring
you two classic collections, each
featuring three favourite romances
by our bestselling authors...

TAKEN BY THE BOSS

His Very Personal Assistant
by Carole Mortimer
In the Banker's Bed by Cathy Williams
The Takeover Bid by Leigh Michaels

A PASSIONATE AFFAIR

The Passionate Husband
by Helen Brooks
The Italian's Passion by Elizabeth Power
A Latin Passion by Kathryn Ross

Taken by the Boss

HIS VERY PERSONAL ASSISTANT
by
Carole Mortimer

IN THE BANKER'S BED
by
Cathy Williams

THE TAKEOVER BID
by
Leigh Michaels

MILLS & BOON®

Pure reading pleasure™

Harlequin Mills & Boon Limited,
Eton House, 18-24 Paradise Road, Richmond, Surrey TW9 1SR

TAKEN BY THE BOSS
© by Harlequin Enterprises II B.V./S.à.r.l 2009

His Very Personal Assistant, In the Banker's Bed and *The Takeover
Bid* were first published in Great Britain by Harlequin
Mills & Boon Limited in separate, single volumes.

His Very Personal Assistant © Carole Mortimer 2005
In the Banker's Bed © Cathy Williams 2005
The Takeover Bid © Leigh Michaels 2004

ISBN: 978 0 263 87122 7

05-0109

Printed and bound in Spain
by Litografia Rosés S.A., Barcelona

HIS VERY PERSONAL ASSISTANT

by

Carole Mortimer

Carole Mortimer was born in England, the youngest of three children. She began writing in 1978, and has now written over one hundred and forty books for Mills & Boon. Carole has four sons, Matthew, Joshua, Timothy and Peter, and a bearded collie called Merlyn. She says, 'I'm happily married to Peter senior; we're best friends as well as lovers, which is probably the best recipe for a successful relationship. We live in a lovely part of England.'

Don't miss Carole Mortimer's exciting new novel, *Bedded for the Spaniard's Pleasure,* **available in March 2009 from Mills & Boon® Modern™.**

For Peter

CHAPTER ONE

'I WOULD like to strangle that woman with one of her diamond necklaces!'

Kit looked up as her outer office door opened, inwardly wincing as it was thrown back with such force that it slammed against the wall. Inwardly, because outwardly she always remained the calm and efficient personal assistant that she was...

She raised enquiring brows as her boss, Marcus Maitland, strode purposefully across the room to his own office, receiving a narrow-eyed glare for her efforts, his handsome face harsh and grimly set.

'I don't want to be disturbed,' he bit out gratingly as he wrenched open his own office door. 'By anyone,' he added forcefully, slamming that door behind him with equal force.

Kit breathed out slowly, turning to Lewis Grant, the lawyer for Maitland Enterprises, as he entered the room. 'I take it the meeting with Angus Gerrard didn't go as planned?' she prompted softly.

'Not exactly.' Lewis grimaced as he sat on the edge of her desk to look across at the blankness of the door so recently closed in both their faces. He was tall and blond and in his early thirties.

Marcus and Lewis had set out earlier for their meeting with Angus Gerrard believing the takeover of the other man's newspaper empire was only a formality; a mere signing of the papers was to be performed. But, from Marcus's comment when he'd come in, and his obvious fury, Kit had a feeling that it had been far from a formality!

'Nothing that you did or didn't do, I hope?' Because she also knew, from six months of working as Marcus Maitland's personal assistant, that he worked so hard himself he was not a man to accept incompetence or compromise in others.

Not that she could blame him; as a multimillionaire, involved in numerous diversified companies and holdings, he had little time to spare for other people's mistakes.

'No—thank goodness!' Lewis gave a rueful grin.

'The lady he wants to strangle with her diamond necklace?' Kit prompted knowingly.

Lewis nodded. 'Catherine Grainger.'

Exactly whom Kit had thought Marcus was referring to. But had hoped that he wasn't.

She hadn't known of it when she'd started working for Marcus Maitland, but there seemed to be some sort of long-running competitiveness between Maitland Enterprises and Grainger International. Catherine Grainger was the major shareholder and head of the latter. In the six months that Kit had worked for Marcus Maitland this was the third time the two of them seemed to have locked horns over a business acquisition.

Kit grimaced. 'What happened this time?'

Lewis shrugged. 'She outbid and outmanoeuvred us. Angus Gerrard signed a contract with her yesterday,' he enlarged as Kit continued to look at him.

'Oops!' she breathed slowly.

'Oops, indeed,' Lewis acknowledged as he continued to stare at the door Marcus had closed so decisively behind him minutes ago. 'You know, Marcus mentioned this is the third time this has happened in the last few months,' he said slowly.

Kit looked up at him enquiringly as his words echoed her own recent thoughts.

'It's probably nothing,' Lewis dismissed briskly as he stood up. 'There's obviously no point in my hanging around here—' he smiled wryly '—so I may as well get back to my own office—if only to shred these defunct contracts!' He picked up his briefcase from beside Kit's desk before leaving for his own office further down the carpeted corridor.

Kit was still frowning as she watched him go. Surely it was all a coincidence that Marcus Maitland had lost yet another deal because Catherine Grainger had outmanoeuvred him…? To attribute the blame to anything else was surely to bring into question the integrity of everyone who worked closely with Marcus Maitland. Including herself.

'Daydreaming, Miss McGuire?' a female voice queried nastily. 'Does that mean that Marcus isn't back yet?' Andrea Revel added as she strolled into Kit's office completely unannounced, bringing the aroma of her heavy perfume with her.

Kit kept her expression deliberately bland, knowing that it wouldn't be her secretary, Laura's, fault that this woman had managed to get in here without interference. The latest in what appeared to have been a long line of women in Marcus Maitland's life, Andrea Revel seemed to think she was a law unto herself when it came to Marcus.

The other woman was astoundingly beautiful, with

her pale blonde hair, slanted green eyes and a figure that had all the men in her immediate vicinity turning to admire her, especially as she usually wore some stunning creation or another. As a fashion buyer for one of the most prestigious stores in the city, Andrea had no problem finding or buying such clothing.

But Andrea also had to be one of the most unpleasant women Kit had ever met, and hard as nails with it. At least, away from Marcus Maitland she was. When in his presence, Andrea somehow contrived to look small, vulnerable, and completely feminine.

However, Kit refused to rise to the bait about sitting around daydreaming while her boss was out of the office. 'Actually, he's back—'

'Oh, good.' Andrea smiled as she turned towards Marcus's office, showing even white teeth behind the glossy red lipstick she wore, which matched her short, fitted dress.

'But he doesn't want to be disturbed,' Kit added firmly as she stood up.

Andrea gave her a dismissive glance. 'He'll want to see me,' she said confidently, reaching for the door handle. 'Go away,' she bit out impatiently as Kit tried to move smoothly in front of her. 'You take your duties as Marcus's PA too seriously, as far as I'm concerned,' she added scathingly. 'In fact, I've told Marcus as much on several occasions.'

Kit drew herself up to her full height of five feet ten inches and looked at Andrea down the length of her nose as she breathed deeply in an effort to stop a cutting reply from leaving her lips. Andrea might be gone from Marcus's life in a matter of months—in fact, to Kit's disapproval, the secretaries in the company were taking bets as to how long this particular relationship was going to last!—but in the meantime she had to attempt to be polite to her. Even if sometimes she did inwardly feel like wiping that superior smile off the other woman's face!

'It doesn't seem to have affected my current employment,' Kit finally returned in a pleasant voice—not quite succeeding in hiding her resentment, after all.

Green eyes narrowed venomously. 'Why, you—'

'I'll just ask Mr Maitland if he is free to see you now,' Kit continued lightly, opening the door to Marcus's office and closing it firmly behind her. After all, this was nothing personal, just part of her job.

But that certainly hadn't been her most successful attempt at handling Andrea Revel, she inwardly berated herself as Marcus raised his head to look scowlingly across at her for her intrusion.

At the age of thirty-nine, Marcus Maitland had to be one of the most handsome men Kit had ever seen, with that midnight-dark hair and deep blue eyes. His nose was a straight slash, his lips sculptured, his chin square and determined. But she made sure always to regard him with cool impassivity.

Because she had been warned by Angie Dwyer, this man's previous PA, when she had come for her interview for the job seven months ago, that the worst possible thing she could do was to fall for Marcus—that he *never* fell in love with any of the women he was involved with, his relationships with them only ever lasting a couple of months.

Considering the circumstances that had forced Kit to leave her last job—her boss seemed to have considered it normal policy to be involved with his assistant—

she'd had no intention of falling in love with Marcus. Until she had actually met the man himself. Then she'd had trouble believing that any woman within a twenty-mile radius could actually stop herself from being attracted to him!

The term 'tall, dark and handsome' definitely applied to Marcus Maitland, but there was so much else that was attractive about him too. For one thing—when he wasn't furiously angry, as he was this morning, he was capable of charming even the hardest heart, and his wealth and success had given him a self-confidence that made him stand out in any crowd.

In a word, Marcus Maitland was *gorgeous*!

But Kit took great care never to let him see what she really thought of him.

Besides, having taken account of Angie Dwyer's warning, Kit played down her own looks when at work, wearing her copper-coloured hair in a French pleat, keeping her make-up minimal, discarding her contact lenses for thick-rimmed glasses during the day in an effort to lessen the effect of the deep grey of her eyes and surrounding dark lashes. The jackets of the dark business suits she wore were shapeless, the skirts always discreetly knee-length and her shoes low-heeled.

There was no way, she had decided, after looking at her reflection in the mirror that first morning she had come to work here, that any man seeing her like this would consider it part of her job to keep his bed warm if they should happen to be away on business together!

Kit had spent too long running round desks, and hotel bedrooms, trying to avoid her previous boss's less-than-welcome advances, to want a repeat of it in her new job.

Although once she had actually met Marcus Maitland she hadn't been quite so sure about that…!

Still, she had deliberately chosen her role as demure, plain, featureless, figureless Kit McGuire, and so far she had stuck to it.

But a few more conversations like the one just now with Andrea Revel, and she might just decide to throw caution to the wind and—

No, she wouldn't, she gently rebuked herself; she enjoyed her work here, the people she worked with, the man she worked for, and most important of all— she needed the job! Besides, how would it look on her c.v. if, when she applied for another position, she had to own up to being dismissed for insubordination to her boss's girlfriend?

But it would be nice, just for once, if Marcus could see what she looked like when away from the office, with her hair loose, no glasses to hide the luminous depths of her eyes, a pair of denims that fitted snugly to—

'Well?' Marcus snapped harshly, tapping his fingers impatiently on his desk top as he continued to wait for an explanation for her intrusion after he had explicitly told her he didn't want to be disturbed.

At the same time completely bursting Kit's bubble of illusion where, as in Hollywood movies, Marcus saw her change from a moth into a butterfly and instantly fell in love with the way she really looked. A fairy tale!

She straightened. 'Miss Revel would like to see you,' she told him briskly.

'When?'

'Now. She's waiting outside in my office,' she explained as he continued to scowl.

His brow cleared. 'Then why didn't you tell me that when you first came in?' He stood up to move impatiently around her and open the inter-office door himself. 'Come in, Andrea,' he invited. 'I was going to call you in a few minutes anyway; I have something I need to discuss with you.'

Kit stiffened as the other woman gave her a triumphant look in passing, her hands closing at her sides, her jaw clenching. Andrea deliberately went to link her arm with Marcus's, before standing on tiptoe to kiss him lingeringly on the mouth.

Kit felt her stomach turn as Marcus bent his head with the intention of returning the kiss, quickly turning on her heel and leaving the room, closing the door behind her to lean weakly back against it.

So much for Angie Dwyer's warning!

Kit had known by the end of the first week of working with Marcus that she was deeply attracted to him. Not the cleverest thing she had ever done in her life, but probably not the worst either. After all, Marcus had no idea how she felt, so at least her pride was still intact. It was only her heart that went AWOL every time she looked at him!

Only…!

She gave a self-deriding shake of her head as she moved back to sit behind her desk. It was probably as well that she could laugh at her own stupidity, because over the last six months Andrea Revel was the third woman Kit had seen Marcus get involved with—and they had all, without exception, been aged in their mid-thirties, petite, blonde, and curvaceously feminine—not twenty-six, tall and slim, with red hair.

In other words, even without the severe hairstyle, no make-up, and the shapeless business suits she wore, she just wasn't Marcus Maitland's type. It was—

'Give me a call when you get back,' Andrea Revel snapped as she suddenly stormed out of the inner office. 'I may decide to see you again—but then, I may have something else more important to do!' she ended before slamming the door behind her. Her face was an ugly, angry mask as she leant over Kit's desk to thrust it inches away from Kit's. 'You think you're so clever, don't you?' she hissed furiously as Kit could only blink her surprise at the attack. 'But we'll see who has the last laugh,' she scorned as she straightened and, with one last flounce of her rich blonde hair, swayed provocatively from the room.

Now what on earth had all that been about? Kit wondered dazedly as she watched her leave, slightly shaken by the vehemence behind the woman.

The door to Marcus's office opened again, gently this time. He stood framed in the doorway. 'Has she gone?' he enquired.

'Are you referring to Miss Revel?' Kit prompted innocently.

His gaze narrowed as he looked at her assessingly, a smile tugging at the corners of that sensuously curved mouth. 'Yes, I'm referring to Miss Revel,' he confirmed dryly, his earlier fury seeming to have abated as his normal good humour asserted itself.

Kit gave a slight inclination of her head. 'She appears to have gone, yes,' she confirmed evenly, still feeling totally stunned by Andrea's verbal attack.

Marcus's eyes gleamed deeply blue as he looked at her consideringly. 'You know, Miss McGuire, sometimes I'm not sure you're altogether quite what you seem…'

She remained outwardly composed, but inwardly her stomach was clenched, her thoughts were racing. What if he knew…what if he had guessed at her connection to…? But there was absolutely no reason why he should have done, she instantly consoled herself.

'Miss Revel seemed—upset, when she left just now?' she said briskly, deliberately changing the subject.

Marcus smiled more openly now, leaning against the doorframe to fold his arms across his chest. 'Furious, you mean?' he drawled.

'Well…yes,' Kit confirmed coolly.

He gave an acknowledging inclination of his head, his hair gleaming blue-black in the overhead light. 'Your fault, I'm afraid,' he derided.

Her eyes widened. 'Mine? But—I was only doing my job just now,' she defended. 'Besides, she was rude to me first,' she added quietly.

Marcus raised dark brows. 'She was?'

'Yes, she—' She broke off, her frown deepening as she realised from his curious expression that he had no idea what she was talking about. 'Exactly why is Miss Revel furious with me?' she asked slowly.

He shrugged broad shoulders beneath the white silk shirt and dark tailored jacket he wore. 'She's taken exception—and I very much doubt we will see each other again—to the fact that you're the one coming away with me this weekend rather than her.'

Kit stared at him blankly.

When had he—
When had they—
When had she—
What on earth was he talking about?

CHAPTER TWO

'WELL, Marcus's last PA did warn you that you might have to go away on business with him occasionally,' Penny, Kit's flatmate, teased her later that evening as the two of them prepared a meal together.

Yes, Angie Dwyer had told Kit that travelling with Marcus Maitland on business was part of her job description; it was just that it hadn't been an issue over the last six months because, until this weekend, Marcus had preferred to take Lewis with him when he went on a trip.

Not that going away on business with Marcus Maitland was actually a problem. It was just the way he had told her and then chuckled at her stunned reaction that had thrown her slightly.

In fact, a lot!

'Don't look so worried, Miss McGuire,' Marcus had grinned as she'd stared across the office at him after his announcement that he and Andrea Revel had parted company, and that he was taking Kit away for the weekend with him. 'I'm not suggesting that I'm about to make indecent advances upon your person,' he'd told her mockingly. 'I just happen to need your capabilities more this weekend than I do Andrea's rather more obvious charms!'

Kit hadn't been too sure she found that an altogether flattering summing-up of the situation, but as she had made a point of deliberately playing down her own

looks there wasn't too much she could say in her own
defence.

What would Marcus say if he could see her now?
she wondered. Her hair was loose like silken flame past
her shoulders, her skimpy tee shirt and fitted denims
clung to her slender curves and there were no heavy
glasses, either, to hide the large deep grey eyes that
were surrounded by thick dark lashes. She looked a
good ten years younger than the primly efficient Miss
McGuire!

But knowing Marcus's preference for tiny blondes,
he probably still wouldn't be impressed, she allowed
ruefully.

'So where exactly are the two of you going this
weekend?' Penny enquired with deliberate innocence
as she sliced up tomatoes to go in a salad.

Kit paused in opening a bottle of wine to wince at
her friend's teasing. 'We aren't going anywhere,' she
corrected irritably. 'Marcus has accepted an invitation
from Desmond Hayes—'

'The airline tycoon, Desmond Hayes?' Penny cut in
speculatively, blue eyes glowing interestedly.

'Is there another one?' Kit came back evenly—
briefly enjoying her moment of glory as she could see
that her friend and flatmate was impressed by the name
of their host for the weekend.

'None that matter,' Penny acknowledged. 'Wow. So
you're going to be spending the weekend with
Desmond Hayes,' she admired enviously.

Kit pursed her lips. 'I am no more spending the
weekend with Desmond Hayes than I am with Marcus
Maitland; this is simply a working trip,' she stated
firmly.

'Yes, but you're still going to be there, alone, with two of the most gorgeous men—'

'There's apparently going to be a few other people staying too over the weekend,' Kit quickly interrupted.

'Stop bursting my bubble!' Penny exclaimed disgruntledly, taking a sip from her glass of wine before looking sharply at Kit. 'Don't, for goodness' sake, tell me that you're going there as Miss McGuire, the PA from No-Nonsenseville? You are, aren't you?' she accused incredulously as she saw Kit's raised brows. 'Oh, Kit, you can't—'

'Of course I can,' Kit said a little crossly. 'This is a *working* trip, Penny, in case you've forgotten—'

'I haven't forgotten anything,' her friend assured her seriously. 'And, after the shenanigans with Mike Reynolds while you worked for him, I can't exactly blame you for being more cautious where Marcus Maitland is concerned. But you've been his assistant for six months, Kit; surely you know what sort of man he is by now?'

Oh, yes, she knew exactly what sort of man Marcus Maitland was: clever and shrewd where business was concerned, a fair but demanding boss. But, as Angie Dwyer had warned her, he changed his women almost as often as he changed his shirt.

'You're going to meet Desmond Hayes this weekend,' Penny said impatiently. 'Desmond Hayes, Kit; one of the wealthiest men in the country!'

Kit gave a faint smile. 'He may be, but the last I heard he was on his third marriage!'

'No, that's been over for some months,' Penny dismissed.

Kit gave a firm shake of her head. 'Then he's in the

middle of a messy divorce,' she persisted. 'In either case, I'm not interested. Neither,' she continued firmly as Penny would have spoken, 'do I intend changing a single thing about my appearance for what is, after all, a work commitment.' If she kept repeating that phrase enough, she might even start to believe it herself!

Because a part of her was secretly excited at the thought of spending this time with Marcus away from the office—safely behind the façade of the PA from No-Nonsenseville, of course!

Penny gave an exasperated sigh. 'Well, for what it's worth, I think you're insane!'

Kit gave a smile. 'I'll try to bear that in mind.'

'Insane!' Penny repeated disgustedly before picking up the salad bowl and sweeping over to the kitchen table, leaving Kit to follow slowly behind her with the plates of baked salmon.

Maybe, feeling as she did about Marcus, she was mad to keep up this charade of efficient primness, but having started it she now had no idea how to finish it…

'I beg your pardon?' Kit looked at Marcus incredulously when he called for her the next afternoon, having allowed her to leave the office earlier so that she might be ready for the two of them to make the journey to Desmond Hayes's home.

He gave a sigh. 'I said, could you change into something a little less—formal?' he repeated tersely, eyeing her cream linen suit and flat shoes with obvious distaste. 'Desmond is expecting my partner for the weekend to be the current woman in my life, not my PA,' he explained with the deliberate patience of an adult talking to a recalcitrant child.

'But—but—'

'Now you sound like a broken record,' Marcus drawled derisively, moving past her into the flat's hall-way.

Penny was, thankfully, still at work; otherwise there was no knowing what she might have made of what Marcus was asking.

Kit wasn't too sure of that herself! Exactly what did he mean, she was supposed to be the current woman in his life and not his PA? Surely he wasn't suggest-ing—?

'Calm down, Miss McGuire,' Marcus ordered as he stood in the hallway looking down at her—a novelty in itself: at five feet ten inches tall, Kit usually found she was taller than most men. 'I only said Desmond Hayes is expecting you to be the woman I'm involved with—not that I am expecting it too!'

She could feel the warmth of colour enter her cheeks at his taunting tone and mocking expression. But how else could she react after what he had just said?

Marcus gave another sigh. 'It's quite simple, Miss McGuire, I look on this weekend as purely business. Desmond may see it a little differently, hence—'

'Hence you want me to appear to be your girlfriend,' Kit finished dazedly.

'There you are.' Marcus smiled teasingly. 'I knew you would get it in the end!'

She hadn't got anything!

This was the very first time Marcus had mentioned anything about this particular aspect of the weekend.

Deliberately so? she wondered as she looked at him suspiciously.

His smile turned to a scowl. 'As I told you yesterday, I'm not about to make indecent advances on your person!' he told her disgustedly.

But Kit hadn't needed him to repeat it, knew that he didn't find her in the least attractive; she just couldn't make too much sense of what he was saying. It appeared that Marcus had originally intended going with Andrea to Desmond Hayes's for the weekend—the woman's vehemence yesterday at being told she wasn't going after all was proof of that!—so why was he now taking Kit, but still leaving his host with the impression it was his girlfriend who was accompanying him?

'It's simple enough, Miss McGuire—'

'You keep saying that,' she cut in tensely.

'But you don't find it so,' Marcus replied through gritted teeth. 'I swear, I want your experience as my PA this weekend, not as a woman.'

'That part you've made abundantly clear!' she snapped back, slightly disconcerted as Marcus gave her an assessing look for her vehemence. 'And quite rightly so,' she added hastily. 'But what is it you want me— as your PA—to do?' she persisted, desperately trying to claw back some of the credibility she was sure she had lost just now when she had sounded almost disappointed that Marcus wanted her services professionally but not personally.

Idiot, she chided herself. As if Marcus could ever have any personal interest in her.

'Observe and listen, mainly,' he answered in a casual voice. 'There are rumours that Desmond Hayes is in trouble—financially, for a change, as opposed to the mess he's made of his personal life. Three wives!' he added with a disgusted shake of his head.

'I suppose you think he shouldn't have married those women at all but just—er—what I meant—' Kit broke off abruptly, wincing awkwardly as she realised what she had been about to say, the colour once again hot in her cheeks.

'But just bedded them—like me,' Marcus finished for her. 'Was that what you were about to say?'

It was. Though it had dawned on her just how unwise she was being before she had even finished saying it. Although that didn't stop Marcus from being completely aware of what she had been about to say, anyway!

'You know, Miss McGuire,' he murmured, the humour once more lighting the deep blue of his eyes, 'perhaps this weekend will serve another purpose, after all. You've been working for me for six months now, and it's time I got to know you a little better,' he enlightened her as she looked at him warily.

Having Marcus get to know her a little or, indeed, a lot better, was not something she particularly wanted!

She deliberately avoided his gaze now. 'What do the rumours have to say about Desmond Hayes's financial problems?' she prompted, determined to take the conversation onto a more businesslike footing.

'So far, only that he's in trouble. I want to see if we can't find out a little more about that over this weekend.'

'And you don't think Miss Revel would have been able to help you with that better than I?' Kit replied, sure that the kittenish Andrea would be much more successful at persuading Desmond Hayes, a man with an obvious weakness for beautiful women, into talking about himself and his problems.

Poor Penny, too; she would be most disappointed to hear that Desmond Hayes might no longer be one of the richest men in England!

Marcus's mouth thinned. 'My relationship with Andrea is over,' he bit out decisively. 'Besides, I've always made it a rule to keep my personal and my private life completely separate.'

'Strange, I'd heard differently—' Kit gave an uncomfortable wince as she realised what she had just said.

'From whom, may I ask?' he demanded.

'Someone mentioned it. I forget who,' Kit said firmly as he gave her a disbelieving look.

His smile was humourless. 'Angie always did have a big mouth,' he ruminated. 'It's one of the reasons she didn't work out too well as my previous PA. Whereas you…'

Kit arched dark brows. 'Me?'

Marcus gave her an appreciative smile. 'You're so discreet that even your own personal life is a closed book! This is a nice apartment, by the way.' He looked around them admiringly. 'Very minimalistic,' he approved. The bare wooden floors were adorned with brightly coloured scatter rugs rather than a carpet, and there was just a cream sofa, chair and bookcase in the sitting-room, which he could see from the hallway. 'Very nice,' he repeated slowly. 'Perhaps I'm paying you too much.' He eyed her with challenging amusement.

Kit had been reeling from his comment about her personal life being a closed book, but this comment about her apartment, coming so close on its heels, made her frown darkly. 'I happen to share this apartment,' she told him sharply. 'And you certainly do not pay me too much!'

Marcus laughed, his teeth very white and even against his tanned skin, his eyes gleaming deeply blue. 'I thought even you might have something to say about that,' he responded.

'Even me?' she rejoined, wondering exactly what he had meant by that remark.

'Well, as I've already said, you've worked for me for six months or so now, and I still know very little about you.'

And he wasn't going to know anything about her either, if she had her way! Most of it was pretty boring, and what wasn't boring was pretty damning—as far as Marcus was concerned, she intended her life should remain a closed book!

'I see nothing wrong in that,' she told him tartly. 'The only things I know about your personal life would be better left unknown—' She broke off abruptly, realising she had yet again overstepped the line she had drawn between them when she had first started working for him. 'Sorry,' she muttered, looking away.

Marcus eyed her assessingly. 'No, you're not,' he said comfortably. 'You said you share this apartment?' he continued.

One of the things she most admired about this man was his intelligence—though she wasn't quite so sure about that when it was directed towards her! She had thought he hadn't paid any particular notice to her comment about sharing the apartment, but he had simply been saving his curiosity for the right moment. Like now.

'Yes,' she answered unhelpfully. 'Now, what is it you want me to wear this weekend, if not my business clothes?' She noted his own casual black denims and dark blue shirt open at the throat.

'Anything but,' he responded. 'What you have on is okay—if you were going to pay a visit on an aged relative! And I'm sure those suits you wear to the office are very smart—'

'But?' Kit interjected guardedly, already stung by his comment about the cream linen suit she was wearing. Though the four dark suits that she usually wore to work were sensible, they were smart of their kind—and had been expensive too.

'But they aren't suitable for a summer weekend in the country,' Marcus persisted unapologetically. 'For instance, have you packed a bikini?'

'Certainly not!'

'Well, Desmond has a full-sized outdoor heated swimming pool. Plus a stable if you happen to ride—'

'I don't.' Kit did her best to repress a shudder just at the thought of getting on a horse; they were truly magnificent creatures to look at—from a distance!—but too unpredictable for her taste. 'I like to go for walks, though,' she said lightly, starting to wonder if this weekend might not be fun, after all.

'Then you'll need a pair of walking boots, and so do I,' Marcus informed her happily. 'And a pair of jeans and some tops to relax in during the day, plus something a bit more glamorous for dinner in the evenings—'

'Okay, okay.' Kit held up her hands in self-defence. 'I get the picture.'

'Good.' Marcus nodded his satisfaction. 'Off you go and change, and repack your suitcase, then. I'll just sit in here and look through your book collection while I'm waiting,' he informed her arrogantly, before strolling into the sitting-room to do exactly that.

Kit stared after him frustratedly. She might, as she said, get the picture, but how on earth was she supposed to keep up the prim Miss McGuire role wearing denims—or worse!—a bikini?

CHAPTER THREE

'THAT'S better!' Marcus voiced his approval when Kit rejoined him in the sitting-room fifteen minutes later.

Fifteen *agonizing* minutes later. Kit simply hadn't known what to do for the best once she was in her bedroom. If she did as Marcus asked, and dressed and behaved as casually as he was himself, wasn't that going to make a nonsense of the working relationship she had gone to such lengths to establish the last six months? But on the other hand, if she didn't fulfil her role as his PA, Marcus wasn't going to think she was of much use to him, and maybe he'd decide, as he obviously had with Angie Dwyer, that she wasn't working out too well.

Besides, as he had gone to great pains to point out, he had no designs upon her body!

Not sure whether she felt relieved, chagrined, or just plain disappointed about that, Kit had taken a quick inventory of her wardrobe and had picked out the clothing she thought might do for the occasion, without compromising herself too much. From the look on Marcus's face as he looked at her now in a black tee shirt and fashionable fitted black trousers, he obviously approved of the transformation.

'At least,' he said as he slowly stood up, 'the clothes are. Can't you do something with your hair?' He glowered at the severe style she still wore. 'And the glasses?'

he added with exasperation. 'Desmond is going to think my taste has turned to the studious!'

'As opposed to dumb blondes!' Kit was stung into retorting, the colour swiftly entering her cheeks as Marcus turned to look at her beneath lowered lids. 'I'm so sorry!' she gasped. 'I really shouldn't have said that. I just— You were being extremely personal about me, and so—'

'You felt the freedom to be extremely personal about me, in return,' Marcus drawled.

She grimaced. 'Yes.'

'Fair enough,' he agreed.

Her eyes widened in surprise. She had expected a verbal setting-down, if nothing else. 'It is?'

'Of course,' he said. 'Although I wouldn't advise you to do it too often!'

Kit stared at him for several seconds, and then she gave a laugh as she saw the glint in his dark blue eyes.

Marcus tilted his head as he looked at her consideringly. 'Is that really how you see the women I've been involved with?' he asked quizzically.

In truth, yes. Oh, they were beautiful enough, but Kit very much doubted that their conversation had run to much more than fashion and social chit chat. Not exactly scintillating to a man of Marcus's intelligence. Although she very much doubted it was intellect that had attracted him to them!

'Perhaps,' she answered noncommittally. 'Although I really don't know them well enough to comment, do I?'

'That doesn't seem to have stopped you doing exactly that, anyway,' Marcus pointed out dryly.

No, it hadn't, had it? Kit realised, the colour once

more in her cheeks. And it really wasn't any of her business, was it…?

She put up a self-conscious hand to her hair, aware that its vibrancy of colour was mostly muted by its severe style; that it glowed like flame when released, sometimes deeply red, sometimes that red hinting at gold, at other times just pure gold. As for discarding her glasses…!

'Which brings us back to your hair,' Marcus said firmly as he saw her nervous movement. 'It looks like okay hair to me.'

'It is,' she confirmed awkwardly.

'Then why not let it down for a change? Just your hair, Miss McGuire,' he added as he recognized his choice of words could be misinterpreted. 'And do you really need those glasses?' He reached out as if to pluck them off her nose. 'The lenses don't look very strong to me—hey, I was only going to look at them!' he protested as she swung away from his hand.

'You might break them,' she said stiltedly, reaching up herself to remove the glasses; she had her contacts with her, could put them in later. 'I really only need them for reading,' she excused, her face turned away as she put the glasses carefully into their case and into her handbag.

'Miss McGuire…?'

'Yes?' she replied distractedly.

'Would you mind looking at me when I talk to you?'

'What—?' She broke off as she turned and saw the look on Marcus's face. He was staring at her, which sent the colour once more to flush her cheeks.

And she knew what he would see too; eyes of deep gun-metal grey, but with the softness of velvet, her lashes long and dark, those eyes emphasizing her high cheekbones, the perfect bow of her lips.

Marcus blinked. 'Could you take down your hair, too?' he pressed huskily.

She gave an irritated groan. 'Look, I really don't think this is at all necessary—'

'Please,' he pushed gently.

Kit shot him an uncertain glance before looking away again, reaching up to remove the pins from her hair, its straight, silky softness falling gently about her shoulders, the sunlight streaming in through the window giving it the texture of living flame.

'There.' She raised her chin as she looked at him, flicking her hair back over her shoulder as she did so. 'Satisfied?'

Marcus put a hand up to absently stroke the roughness of his chin as he continued to look at her with enigmatic eyes. 'As a matter of fact—no, I'm far from satisfied!' he replied. 'What I am, though, is curious as to why you've been walking around my office the last six months masquerading as someone's maiden aunt, when, in actual fact, you really look like this!'

Kit continued to look at him with steady grey eyes. 'Like what?'

He looked ready to explode. 'Like—like—'

'Yes?' she prompted curiously.

'You know exactly what you look like, Miss McGuire,' he bit out coldly. 'What I want to know is why?'

She avoided meeting his gaze. 'If you really must know—'

'Oh, I think I really must,' he assured sarcastically.

Kit took a deep breath. 'My previous boss thought

it part of my job description to go to bed with him. And after Angie Dwyer's comments about you, I— well, I thought it best not to draw attention to—to my femininity,' she concluded awkwardly.

'In other words, you didn't draw my attention to it!' Marcus rasped furiously. 'Damn it, have I so much as looked at you in a way that could be called personal in the last six months?'

'No,' she acknowledged with a pained grimace, knowing his anger was justified.

'You—I—oh, to hell with this,' he suddenly said impatiently. 'If you're ready, let's just go, shall we?' He turned on his heel and walked out of her apartment.

Kit breathed a sigh of relief at being released from his domineering company for a couple of minutes at least, the tension relaxing from her shoulders. Marcus obviously wasn't a happy man at what he saw to be her transition from moth into butterfly, or the reason for it. As she had known he wouldn't be...

Oh, well. She gave a philosophical shrug of her shoulders as she picked up her bag and followed him out to his car; he had asked for it, hadn't he? He could hardly sack her just because she had turned out to be more attractive without her hair confined and not wearing her glasses than he had actually bargained for!

'Where, exactly, are we going?' she asked after ten minutes of silent driving on Marcus's part—and, she admitted, a certain amount of discomfort on hers!

'Worcestershire,' he supplied economically.

'Really?' She brightened. 'I've never been there, but I believe it's supposed to be a very pretty county—'

'Would you mind not chattering?' Marcus cut in hardly. 'I need to concentrate while I'm driving.'

He needed to learn some manners too—but somehow Kit didn't think he would appreciate having her point that out to him!

But if he didn't want to talk, she was quite happy to look out the window at the countryside as they left London far behind them, the Jaguar sports car Marcus drove quickly eating up the miles.

She'd had all too few opportunities to get out of London since selling her car six months ago, driving and parking in the city simply weren't worth the nightmare. Her parents lived in Cornwall, and it was easier to get on the train when she went to see them than it was to struggle through all the tourist traffic that constantly clogged the roads down there.

'Okay, I apologize for my brusqueness,' Marcus said suddenly beside her, startling her out of her reverie.

Kit tilted her chin up as she looked at him. 'Which time?'

His hands tightened on the steering wheel as he glanced back at her.

'Both times,' he acknowledged. 'I admit, I was initially a little—startled, by the change in your appearance—even more so by the reason for the subterfuge in the first place.' He looked darkly at the road ahead. 'Talk if you want to,' he commanded.

Kit continued to watch him for several long seconds, finding that, now he had invited her to talk, she actually had nothing to say!

'Well?' he persisted tersely at her continued silence.

She gave a rueful laugh. 'Isn't it strange, that when someone invites you to talk, there's really nothing to talk about? But if I think of anything, I'll certainly say it,' she amended hastily at the frown line remaining between his eyes.

Marcus gave a small smile. 'I'm gratified to hear it!'

'No, you aren't,' she said with certainty. 'And I'm really quite happy just looking out of the window,' she assured him. 'It's easy to forget, living in London, just how beautiful England really is.'

'Yes,' he answered shortly. 'Tell me a little about yourself, Miss McGuire,' he invited. 'I ought to know something about the woman I'm spending the weekend with, don't you think?'

'I suppose,' she acknowledged reluctantly, not sure how much she wanted this man to know about her. Always a private person, she now found it more important than ever to keep personal information to a minimum—considering this man's connections...

'You suppose?' he echoed slightly incredulously. 'Miss McGuire, I'm not asking for intimate details; just a general outline will do! Things like parents and siblings; after all, your résumé has already told me about your previous employment, educational qualifications and marital status!'

'Oh, good,' she said sarcastically. 'Well, I have two parents: a mother and a father—'

'I'm glad to hear it!' he drawled with derisive patience, 'why is it I get the feeling you really don't want to talk about your private life?'

'Probably because I don't,' she answered candidly. 'But I'm quite happy for you to tell me about yours, if you feel so inclined?' She looked at him expectantly.

He flicked her another glance with those deep blue eyes. 'You know, I think you might be a lot less trouble as the supremely efficient Miss McGuire; she tends not to answer back!'

Kit grinned self-consciously. 'Sorry.'

'No, you're not. And, for the record, I have a mother and a father, too,' he continued wryly.

'Well, at least we have that much in common, Mr Maitland—'

'Marcus,' he insisted. 'I think that might sound a little less—formal, for the benefit of this weekend, don't you?' He raised mocking brows.

She hesitated for a moment. 'You know, I really don't think you thought the consequences of this weekend through enough before deciding on your plan of action—'

'You don't?' His brows rose higher.

'No, I don't.' Kit turned fully in her seat to look at him. 'For one thing,' she continued determinedly as he would have interrupted, 'how are we supposed to go back to being Mr Maitland and Miss McGuire when we return to the office on Monday morning? And for another—'

'Tuesday morning,' Marcus corrected. 'We aren't leaving until Monday afternoon,' he explained as she looked at him enquiringly.

So now, attracted to him as she was, she had three torturous days in his company instead of two!

Great!

'But you're right about the Miss McGuire bit,' Marcus continued thoughtfully. 'Looking at you now, I'm not sure I will ever be able to think of you in that guise ever again!'

Hadn't she tried to tell him that—?

'Or for you to return to that coolly efficient role, either,' he said pointedly.

Kit winced as she inwardly acknowledged that her change in appearance had also resulted in certain subtle—and some not so subtle!—differences in her personality. Dressed in her casual clothes, her hair loose, and no heavy-framed glasses, she certainly felt, and behaved, differently from the coolly capable Miss McGuire!

'All in all—Kit,' he paused briefly before deliberately using her first name, 'I have a feeling that being away on business with you is going to be altogether a completely different experience to going away with Lewis!'

That was what she was afraid of!

Marcus glanced at her, chuckling huskily as he saw the woebegone expression on her face. 'Cheer up, Kit,' he encouraged. 'What's the worst that could happen?'

Attracted to him as she was, feeling about him the way that she did, she would rather not think about that, either!

'After all,' Marcus went on lightly, completely relaxed now as he drove effortlessly along the country roads, 'you're going to be chaperoned by several other guests. And don't forget, my taste runs to dumb blondes.'

She gave a pained groan. 'I wish that I had never made that remark!'

Marcus was grinning, obviously enjoying her discomfort now. 'Well, it's a sure fact you aren't blonde.' He gave her hair an admiring glance. 'And I can personally vouch for the fact that you aren't dumb, either!'

She gave a heavy sigh. 'Mr Maitland—'

'Marcus,' he reminded her firmly. 'Is Kit short for something else?' he mused. 'Kitty or Kathryn, something like that?'

'It's short for Kit,' she told him woodenly. 'Plain and simple Kit.'

'Okay.' He shrugged broad shoulders. 'You were going to say something before we got into this discussion about names…?'

'Before *you* got into the discussion about names,' she corrected flatly. 'And I was just going to apologize—' once again! '—for my remarks about your personal life. They were rude, and intrusive, and altogether—'

'True,' he finished happily. 'But I'm sure it isn't too late for my tastes to change—to tall, outspoken redheads, for instance.'

Kit was almost afraid to look at him now, sure he was just teasing her to get his own back for her earlier remarks—but at the same time she wasn't sure of any such thing!

It was difficult to tell what he was thinking from the blandness of his expression. Deliberately so? Probably, she acknowledged heavily. One thing she had learnt over the last couple of days: Marcus had a wicked sense of humour when he chose to exert it.

'Very funny,' she scorned, choosing to err on the side of caution. 'Do you have any idea who any of the other guests will be this weekend?' She deliberately changed the subject onto something less personal. And disturbing!

'The usual hangers-on and social bores a man like Desmond Hayes attracts, I suppose. Never mind, Kit, we'll have each other for company.'

Now she knew he was deliberately teasing her. Because he knew she found him attractive? Because he had guessed that, against all the warnings, she had fallen into the trap of being half in love with him? That would be just too awful! Well, in this case, lack of interest was the best form of defence...

'How nice.' She made her reply deliberately saccharine-sweet.

Marcus gave an appreciative laugh. 'Well, I can assure you, Kit, *I'm* certainly not expecting to be bored!'

While he kept teasing her like this, no, she didn't expect that he would be...

She gave a weary yawn. 'I'm feeling rather tired. Would you mind if I had a short nap before we arrive?' Not waiting for his reply, she settled herself down in her seat and closed her eyes.

Shutting out his image along with it.

But not her full awareness of him. Of the lean strength of his hands as he drove with such easy assurance. Or, the sprinkling of dark hair that ran the length of his arms. And further. The determination of his jaw. The full sensuality of his lips. The dark blue of his eyes. The way those eyes crinkled at the corners when he smiled or laughed. The potent, slightly elusive smell of his aftershave.

Face it, Kit, she told herself derisively; you stand about as much chance of relaxing around Marcus Maitland, of really going to sleep, as you do sitting next to a tiger poised to spring!

But that didn't stop her giving every appearance of dozing during the rest of the journey, only making a pretence of waking as Marcus touched her arm lightly and told her that they had arrived.

'You had a good nap,' he told her admiringly as he brought the Jaguar to a stop on the gravel driveway in front of what looked like once having been a stately home. Huge pillars supported its entranceway, the stonework old and mellowed. Noise seemed to flow from every open window as the two of them stepped out onto the gravel driveway, where there were a dozen or so other cars already parked outside.

'"Come and spend a peaceful weekend in the country" was how Desmond described it to me!' Marcus gave a hint of his distaste for the loud music and chatter as he moved to get their bags from the boot of the car.

Although not normally one for crowds of people on a superficial basis, Kit found herself smiling, quite happy to make this weekend the exception; the more people there were around them, the less likely she was to be so aware of Marcus. Or to spend too much time alone with him.

'It sounds like fun,' she responded lightly.

Marcus gave a disgusted snort, leading the way up the stone steps that fronted the house. Its massive front door was thrown open and the large entrance hall inside was filled with what looked like dozens of people.

'Are you sure you have the right weekend?' Kit questioned of Marcus.

'I'm sure,' he replied grimly. 'You—'

'Kit? Hey, Kit, is that really you?' called out a familiar voice.

A voice that made her freeze in her tracks and caused the smile to fade from her lips as she looked frantically around the entrance hall for its source.

And then she saw him, making his way purposefully

towards her, a smile of amused recognition on his over-confident, too-handsome face.

Mike Reynolds.

Her ex-boss from hell.

But he wasn't the sole reason her cheeks paled and her breathing seemed to stop. There was also another person whom she could see standing a short distance behind Mike Reynolds. Someone Kit wanted to see even less than she did Mike!

Catherine Grainger…

CHAPTER FOUR

KIT was so stunned that she stood totally immobile as Mike Reynolds took her in his arms and gave her a bear hug.

It was as if he had totally forgotten that the last time the two of them had met she had told him exactly what he could do with his job—and his sexual harassment!

But Kit hadn't forgotten, stiffening in his arms and trying to push him away, panic setting in as she wished herself anywhere but here. Mike Reynolds was bad enough, but she could handle him. She just hadn't been prepared for that other, much more disturbing guest.

Mike stepped back, his hands gripping the tops of her arms as he held her in front of him. 'You're looking good, kid,' he said, his bold blue gaze moving slowly down the length of her body.

Kit's mouth tightened at his familiarity, her eyes glowing deeply grey as she glared at him. 'It's a pity—'

'—that we haven't seen each other for so long,' he completed smoothly.

She had been going to say something much more insulting! Which was totally unlike her. But after the shock she had just received, politeness—especially to Mike Reynolds!—was the last thing on her mind.

Mike nodded appreciatively, apparently completely impervious to her less-than-enthusiastic response as his arm slid lightly across her shoulders as he moved to stand next to her. 'Aren't you going to introduce me to your friend, Kit?' he prompted lightly as he looked curiously at Marcus.

Marcus!

It was testament to the shock she had received in the last few moments that she had completely forgotten Marcus had entered the house with her. In fact, she had completely forgotten everything else but that disturbing female presence standing only metres away from her!

She shrugged off the arm Mike had draped about her shoulders, moving deliberately away from him to stand next to Marcus. She shot a glance at her boss; he was watching her and Mike, his expression unreadable, his gaze hooded.

'Yes, do introduce us, Kit,' he encouraged now in a voice that sounded as if it came after walking over broken glass.

Kit winced at the sound of it, knowing that the last thing she wanted to do was introduce these two men. Yet it seemed that was the one thing she was going to have to do if she was going to escape from this hallway any time soon. And she most certainly was going to have to escape, to find somewhere she could be on her own for a while, if only to give herself time to decide what she should do next.

Because she couldn't stay on here. Not now.

'Marcus Maitland. Mike Reynolds,' she introduced stiffly, seriously wondering if this weekend could get any worse than it already was. Not only Mike Reynolds, of all people, but—

'Marcus! Darling…!' suddenly greeted an all-too-familiar voice.

It just had, Kit acknowledged with an inward groan.

Andrea Revel's heady perfume enveloped them all as she moved into their group and stood on tiptoe to kiss Marcus lingeringly on the lips.

'And Kit, too.' Andrea turned to her, the light of triumph in those cat-green eyes before she gave Kit the merest peck on the cheek. 'How nice,' she added with dismissive insincerity before turning back to Marcus. 'Derek Boyes was kind enough to invite me to come with him this weekend,' she told him with glee as she linked her arm companionably with his.

Kit looked at Marcus beneath lowered lids, but it was impossible to tell from his enigmatic expression just how he was taking that particular piece of news. Although he had to feel something; after all—despite Marcus's claim that the relationship was over—he and Andrea had been something of an item for at least the last couple of months.

'How nice,' he finally answered with the same insincerity Andrea had used towards Kit a few minutes ago.

Causing Kit to look at him with a new appreciation; perhaps he wasn't as blind to this woman's bitchiness as she had thought that he was…?

'Well, if the two of you will excuse us…?' He deftly removed his arm from Andrea's clinging grasp as he bent to pick up his and Kit's cases. 'Kit and I have only just arrived, so I think it might be appropriate if we find our host and say hello, don't you?' Without waiting for a response from either Mike Reynolds or Andrea, he motioned Kit with an urgent inclination of his head to move further into the house.

Further into the lion's den, as far as Kit was concerned. This weekend was just going from bad to worse. And she had thought the only thing she would have to worry about during the next couple of days was keeping her feelings towards Marcus hidden from him!

A glance at his face as they walked away from the other couple was enough to tell Kit that he wasn't quite as calm as he wanted to appear: his mouth was set grimly, his eyes narrowed to icy blue slits.

'Stop looking so worried, Kit,' he bit out between clenched teeth. 'I'm not the type to make a scene.'

She hadn't for a moment thought that he was—it was that he had just thought about making one that bothered her!

But perhaps the fact that Andrea was here with another man had made him realise he didn't want the woman out of his life, after all? What other possible reason could there be for him making a scene...?

But Marcus's attention seemed to become distracted as he looked around them, that frownline back between his eyes. 'There's something odd going on here,' he muttered harshly.

Surely he hadn't just noticed! Her ex-boss was here, someone she had hoped never to see again, and the current woman in his life was here with another man, and as for—

'Look around you, Kit,' he said.

She gave him a startled look. 'Look—?'

'Just look,' Marcus encouraged gruffly.

Kit looked, seeing twenty or so other guests: all of the men looked rich and confident, the women beautiful and glamorous.

But when she looked closer, at individuals, she realised that she recognized quite a number of the men, that several of them had either met with Marcus on business, or she had actually seen their photographs— including Mike Reynolds's!—in the business newspapers in connection with one successful deal or another.

'Exactly,' Marcus pronounced as he saw the dawning realisation on her face. 'It seems I'm not the only one to have heard the rumours. Or that Desmond isn't averse to actually using those rumours to his own advantage,' he added knowingly.

Kit instantly saw what he meant by that remark. Bring together a group of a dozen businessmen, supposedly on a social basis, but with the real object of picking up a bargain on a business deal—like sharks circling one of their own injured species!—and the price on those deals was sure to go higher than if business had been done with those individuals on a private basis.

She gave a rueful smile. 'He could even have started them.'

Marcus turned to give her an admiring look. 'You're turning out to be amazingly astute, Kit,' he said appreciatively.

She felt the blush in her cheeks at this unexpected compliment. 'It was just a guess,' she admitted. 'I could be completely wrong.'

He gave her a teasing smile. 'I'm not sure that— well, well, well,' he said consideringly as something over her left shoulder caught and held his attention, his expression once again enigmatic.

Kit stiffened. 'What is it?' she asked as he continued to look at something—or someone!—behind her.

'Hmm?' he murmured distractedly. 'Let's go and say hello to our esteemed host, shall we?' He didn't wait for her reply before grasping her arm with his free hand and directing her across the hallway.

Kit almost came to a full stop again as she saw their host chatting amiably with a number of people, easily recognizing several of them; Mike Reynolds had joined them, since she and Marcus had left him a couple of minutes ago.

Marcus turned to give her a curious glance as he sensed her reluctance to join the group. 'How about we have a little chat about—your friend, later, hmm?' he suggested.

She gave him a sharp look before replying, 'Mike Reynolds is no friend of mine!'

'I already gathered that,' Marcus replied. 'But I have a feeling that he was once,' he added speculatively.

'No way!' Kit denied heatedly. 'Mike Reynolds is nothing but a—'

'Later, Kit,' Marcus advised tersely as they reached their host. 'And don't forget what I told you: observe and listen.' He turned a socially bright smile on Desmond Hayes. 'Quite a crowd you have here, Desmond,' he greeted the other man jovially, releasing Kit's arm to shake the other man's hand.

'Marcus!' The other man's face lit with recognition. 'So glad you could make it,' he welcomed with the smooth charm for which he was renowned. He was a tall, attractive man in his late fifties, his dark hair sprinkled with silver, his lined face handsome, his smiling blue eyes sharply intelligent.

Kit stood slightly behind the two men as they greeted each other, trying to make herself as inconspicuous as possible. 'Observe and listen,' Marcus had told her—when all she really wanted to do was blend in with the velvet-embossed wallpaper, disappear into it if that were at all possible!

How much longer was this torture to go on before she could escape to the bedroom she had been allocated and actually give herself time to think—and breathe? Because she was sure she had all but stopped doing the latter a good five minutes ago!

'And this is Kit. Kit…?' Marcus called sharply, having turned to introduce her only to find her lurking behind him.

She moistened dry lips, keeping her gaze down on the carpeted floor as she held out her hand to the other man. 'Mr Hayes,' she greeted shyly.

'Desmond, please,' the older man encouraged with warm invitation, holding onto her hand to pull her slightly forward as she would have released it. 'And just where has Marcus been hiding you?' he queried.

Kit swallowed, still not looking up, but very much aware that the group around them had grown silent now as they listened to the exchange. Exchange? It could hardly be called that when Desmond Hayes was the one doing all the talking! In a flirtatious way he had. And, to add to her confusion, he still hadn't released her hand!

She moistened her lips once again. 'I—'

'Careful, Desmond,' Marcus told the other man with lazy derision, his arm moving casually about Kit's shoulders as he did so.

'Private property, eh, Marcus?' the older man said regretfully.

Kit found this whole conversation distasteful—and attention-drawing. Which was what she most certainly didn't want at this particular moment!

'Something like that,' Marcus returned noncommittally.

'Can I offer the two of you glasses of champagne?' Without waiting for their answer, Desmond Hayes plucked two flutes off the tray that a passing waiter was carrying.

Kit accepted the glass he held out to her, taking a much-needed sip of the bubbly liquid it contained. Getting drunk certainly wouldn't help this situation, but hopefully she would become too numb to care!

Marcus held up the two bags he was carrying. 'Are you going to tell us where the two of us are to sleep so that I can get rid of these, or do we just go upstairs and take our pick of bedrooms?' he prompted.

'I'll have Forbes take your luggage upstairs,' Desmond Hayes murmured apologetically, giving Kit's hand one last familiar squeeze before releasing it to turn and signal to the butler standing unobtrusively down the hallway. The elderly man immediately came over to relieve Marcus of the two bags.

Not that Kit was taking too much notice of these proceedings, still caught up in Marcus's last comment, especially the part about, 'where the two of us are to sleep'!

Surely Marcus wasn't expecting them to share a bedroom? That would be taking her supposed role as the current woman in his life a little too far. In fact, as far as she was concerned, much too far!

'Catherine,' Marcus was greeting lightly now as their host disappeared to instruct Forbes on where to put their luggage, turning to smile coolly at the woman who stood slightly apart from the other guests.

Almost as if, like Kit, she were trying to remain

unobtrusive. And yet Kit knew that couldn't be true. It was more likely that the older woman was watching them all with the contemptuous amusement for which she was so well known.

The woman's height only added to her imperiousness, her smooth, shoulder-length hair completely without adornment, or any pretence of hiding its silver colour, confirming her sixty-seven years, though her figure was still youthfully slim in the plain black dress she wore, and the unlined beauty of her face dominated by hard silver-grey eyes.

Kit had never actually met her before, and yet she would have known her anywhere.

Catherine Grainger.

Marcus's arch business enemy...

But also the very, very last person of whom Kit wanted to be within one hundred miles!

CHAPTER FIVE

'WILL you stop pacing up and down like that?' Marcus said as he lay back on the bed watching her. 'I feel exhausted just watching you!'

Kit spared him an annoyed glance, but didn't hesitate in her pacing. This whole situation was intolerable, and all he could do was lie there looking—looking—utterly desirable!

His dark hair was ruffled, his eyes sleepily sensual—and the fact that he was completely relaxed as he lay on the bed certainly didn't help to allay that impression!

'Look on the bright side, Kit—'

'Is there one?' she groaned, moving to stand next to the bed. 'And will you please get up?' she demanded. 'This is where I have to sleep tonight.' Something that was going to be virtually impossible for her to do now she had the image of this man lying back on her pillow!

'Sorry!' Marcus sat up slowly, eyeing her with amusement. 'But surely that is the bright side?' he encouraged. 'At least we have adjoining bedrooms rather than having to share one.'

Oh, yes, that was really comforting! The connecting door between the two bedrooms stood wide open at the moment, with no key on either side to lock it even when it was closed. Kit knew this, for she had already looked for one!

The half an hour or so of torture Marcus had spent

downstairs socializing with the other weekend guests before coming up to change for dinner was nothing compared to finding that they had been given connecting bedrooms.

'Personally, I think it was pretty decent of Desmond not to have just assumed that we—well, that we—'

'Are lovers?' Kit finished forcefully, way beyond being reasoned with.

Marcus shrugged. 'Well, you have to appreciate that it's good of him, given the circumstances, and the amount of other people here for the weekend. After all, this isn't a hotel; I could hardly phone on ahead and book two single rooms!'

She didn't have to give Desmond Hayes anything. Or Marcus Maitland, either, for that matter!

'You wouldn't have done it anyway—I would!' She sighed, her nerve endings feeling so frayed she wanted to scream.

The hour since they had arrived at Desmond Hayes's home had been filled with one shock after another, so much so that all Kit wanted to do right now was lock herself in the *en suite* bathroom and stay there until it was all over. She certainly wasn't in the mood to be teased and cajoled!

She glared at Marcus, her hands clenched at her sides, so agitated that she felt as if she wanted to hit someone, if not physically then verbally would do. 'Is this the usual practice when you're away with your PA? Was that the reason that Angie Dwyer told me about you, the reason she decided to leave? Did she object to—?'

'Careful, Kit,' Marcus cut in with quiet intensity, his eyes narrowed. 'I may be feeling pretty mellow at the moment, but I would advise you not to forget exactly what the two of us are doing here.'

She breathed deeply. 'That's the problem; I'm no longer sure what I'm doing here. If this really is a working weekend, then that's okay. But if you expect me to—to—' she made an agitated gesture towards the rumpled bed that he still sat on '—then I'm afraid you're going to be sadly disappointed, because I—'

'Stop right there,' he commanded harshly, standing up so abruptly that Kit took an involuntary step backwards. He gave a humourless smile as he saw the movement. 'To put the record straight, the reason Angie Dwyer decided to leave had nothing to do with my behaviour—and everything to do with her own!' He grimaced. 'To be ungentlemanly about it—'

'Oh, do!' Kit invited agitatedly.

He gave her a warning look. 'To be ungentlemanly about it,' he repeated tautly, 'Angie was the one who decided our relationship could be a little more—intimate, shall we say? I don't get involved with employees. For goodness' sake, Kit,' he implored as she still looked unconvinced. 'Need I remind you that until a couple of hours ago you looked as desirable as someone's maiden aunt. I certainly didn't give you the job because of the way you looked!'

Of course he hadn't, she realised self-disgustedly. She was just so upset by whom she was expected to spend this weekend with that she had gone completely off on a tangent. As if Marcus would ever find her attractive, even without the severe hairstyle and glasses, when there were women like Andrea Revel falling all over him.

And that was something else…!

'Okay,' she dismissed tautly. 'I suggest we forget about that side of things for the moment.'

Especially as she had been completely wrong in her conclusions about his relationship with Angie Dwyer. She should have known from her conversation with Angie that she'd had some sort of chip on her shoulder about Marcus. From the other woman's catty remarks about his private life, namely the women who populated it, perhaps it should have been obvious what that chip had been.

'Big of you,' he muttered.

Her eyes glowed deeply grey. 'You have no idea how big.' She sighed, remembering only too well those awful months she had spent working for Mike Reynolds. 'But what are you going to do about Andrea Revel?' she challenged.

Marcus raised dark brows. 'Do about her?'

Kit gave him a frowning glance. 'As in her being here this weekend at all.'

'But she's not here with me, is she?' he reasoned. 'You are.'

'Yes, but—but—'

'We're back to that broken record again. The fact that Andrea is here has absolutely nothing to do with me,' he told her clearly. 'She came with Derek Boyes; she's his problem.'

Kit couldn't agree with him, on either statement; he and Andrea had ended their relationship because he had told her he was bringing Kit instead of her, and if Andrea was anyone's problem, then she was definitely Marcus's!

'Mr Maitland—'

'I thought we had agreed that, for this weekend at

least, it's to be Marcus and Kit?' he reminded her dryly.

'But that's my whole point!' she said frustratedly. 'Andrea—Miss Revel—knows that the two of us aren't a couple.'

'Does she?' He looked at her with steady blue eyes.

Kit blinked. 'Doesn't she?'

He shrugged. 'A little hard to tell, wouldn't you say, considering the changes in your appearance, and the fact that we're sharing a suite?'

'Yes, but—okay, let's just forget the broken-record remarks,' she offered. 'Until yesterday the two of you were—well, you were!' she accused.

'And now we're not,' he dismissed unconcernedly. 'Life moves on very fast sometimes, doesn't it? And at other times…' he stood up, moving purposefully towards her '…it moves very slowly…' Before Kit even had time to gauge what he was doing, his head lowered and his mouth claimed hers.

There was no thought of denial on her part as she melted into his hardness, her lips parting beneath his.

She had longed for this all those months of working beside Marcus, had lain awake at nights wondering what it would be like to be kissed by him. And now she knew.

It was wonderful!

His arms moved about the slenderness of her waist as he moulded her body against his, his tongue moving in exploration of the sensuous warmth of her bottom lip, her groan of capitulation all the encouragement he needed to deepen the kiss.

Kit felt like liquid fire in his arms, her body pressed

against his, groaning low in her throat as she felt the caress of his hand against the curve of her breast.

Quite what would have happened next, Kit had no idea, if a door banging noisily shut further down the corridor hadn't made her start back guiltily to stare up at Marcus with disbelieving eyes.

His expression was unreadable, his blue eyes shuttered as he looked back at her.

Kit swallowed hard, her tongue moving to moisten her lips as she searched for something to say. What could she say? Except the obvious!

'Didn't you just violate your own rule where employees are concerned?' she ventured—desperately hoping to divert his attention from the fact that she had very definitely responded to him!

His mouth quirked. 'I read somewhere once that ''rules are made for the guidance of wise men and the blind obedience of fools''!'

Kit raised auburn brows. 'And which are you?'

'At this moment? Anybody's guess!'

She couldn't help it—she laughed. A light, relieved laugh that seemed to release some of the tension that had surrounded them.

Marcus's smile was sheepish as he ran a hand through the dark thickness of his hair. 'I apologize, Kit. I suppose it's no good asking you to forget it ever happened?'

Well…she could try. But did she really want to? As regards the two of them continuing to work together, she knew that she had to, but as Kit McGuire…she had enjoyed the kiss too much to ever really want to forget it had happened.

'We could try,' she answered as noncommittally as

she could, her gaze not quite meeting his now. 'But for the moment,' she added briskly, 'shouldn't we be changing for dinner?'

Marcus sighed heavily. 'That was the plan.'

'Well…?' she prompted as he made no effort to go to the adjoining bedroom.

He gave a perplexed frown as he looked at her. 'Incredible!' he exclaimed. 'And after my self-righteous claim of never becoming involved with my employees…'

'I promise not to tell anyone if you don't!' Kit's cheeks burned with embarrassment.

'Kit—'

'I really do need to change,' she reminded him firmly before turning away.

But she could sense his presence in the room behind her for several more long seconds before he moved away, the adjoining door closing softly behind him and telling her when she was at last alone.

What had they done?

What had she done?

Her obvious course of action should have been to have stopped the kiss before it had even started. If she hadn't been enjoying it so much she might just have done that!

But it had been wonderful. All she had ever thought kissing Marcus would be. And she had spent quite a few hours during the last six months wondering exactly that.

Besides, the kiss had certainly taken Marcus's mind off discussing her 'friend', Mike Reynolds!

She paused from unpacking the black dress she intended wearing this evening. Mike Reynolds, of all people. And he'd had the cheek to greet her as if the two of them hadn't parted on such bad terms seven months ago!

And just how much longer was she going to delay thinking of that other—even less welcome!—guest? Kit asked herself candidly.

The rest of her life, she could have hoped. But it was no good trying to deny the fact that Catherine Grainger was also a weekend guest here.

But would the lady have a clue as to who Kit was? If she did, Kit knew only too well that the other woman wouldn't be interested.

Kit's mouth tightened. Irrational though it was, how she disliked Ms Grainger! Her arrogance. Her coldness. Just her complete air of superiority.

But what would Marcus say if he were to know Kit's secret? Especially since there seemed to be a security leak in his company where Catherine Grainger was concerned... He could think it very odd that Kit hadn't told him the truth in the first place. But other than telling Marcus everything—something she had no intention of doing unless forced—there was no way she could explain away her knowledge of the older woman. She would just have to keep hoping—and praying!— that Catherine never guessed the truth.

If only she could avoid so much as talking to Catherine for the brief time they were here!

Something she didn't look like doing when the first person she saw as she came down the stairs twenty minutes later was—Catherine Grainger, who was standing in the entrance hall talking on her mobile telephone.

Kit had knocked on the adjoining door between

Marcus's room and her own a few minutes earlier, only to find that he had just come out of the shower, wearing nothing but a towel wrapped about his waist.

After a first glance Kit's eyes had remained fixed on the picture on the wall behind him, wings of colour burning in her cheeks. 'And they say women take a long time to get ready!' she joked weakly.

'I was delayed by a telephone call,' he came back swiftly.

Kit glanced at him. 'Andrea?'

He gave an acknowledging inclination of his head. 'How very astute of you!'

'Not really,' she assured him; Marcus might have calmly dismissed Andrea's presence here as being none of his business, but it was a certainty that Andrea, having had time to think about the abrupt end of her relationship with him, wasn't going to do the same where he was concerned. 'I'll wait for you downstairs, shall I?'

'Unless you want to sit down and wait while I get dressed?' he taunted, dark brows raised in invitation.

'No, thank you,' Kit came back stiffly, already turning towards the door as she heard him chuckle under his breath.

Which accounted for why she was completely on her own now as she descended the stairs to meet Catherine Grainger, the only other person in the huge entrance hall…

CHAPTER SIX

'I DON'T believe we were introduced earlier...?'

Kit froze two steps from the bottom of the staircase as Catherine spoke to her. No, they hadn't been introduced, deliberately so, as far as Kit was concerned; she was determined to avoid Catherine Grainger as much as was possible.

'Have the two of us met before...?' Puzzlement edged the older woman's clipped tones as she spoke again.

Kit's chin rose and she looked down at the other woman, schooling her features into polite disinterest. 'I'm sure not,' she replied, only the whitening of her knuckles as she tightly gripped the banister beside her demonstrating that she wasn't quite as composed as she might appear.

There had been a time in her life when she had imagined a moment like this, when she and Catherine Grainger would come face to face. But that had been when she was still young enough to believe in fairness and justice. Reality was something else entirely.

Catherine was so tall and slim that she looked elegant in whatever she wore, tonight a dress of sparkling midnight blue. Her silver hair lightly touched her bare shoulders, and her throat sported a simple necklace of sapphire and diamonds—her only jewellery.

One of those diamond necklaces that Marcus had wanted to strangle her with only yesterday!

60

But despite the elegance of her dress, the understated simplicity of the jewellery, everything about this woman spoke of wealth and power.

'You seem familiar somehow,' Catherine persisted, her silver-grey gaze focused assessingly on Kit now.

Kit's own black dress was nowhere near as expensively tailored as Catherine's, and her only jewellery was a small gold locket suspended between her breasts by a delicate gold chain.

What would Catherine Grainger have to say if she could see the two people photographed inside that locket?

Not a lot, Kit sadly hazarded a guess.

'Doubtful,' she answered Catherine, finishing her descent of the stairs, standing only feet away from her now.

Catherine's gaze remained on her. 'You arrived with Marcus Maitland, didn't you?' she probed.

Kit smiled slightly at the slight edge in Catherine's voice. 'I did,' she confirmed, inwardly pleased to be able to make that claim; the obvious dislike between this lady and Marcus was one sure way to keep her, and her curiosity, at bay!

Catherine's mouth curved derisively. 'No accounting for taste, I suppose,' she drawled scathingly.

Kit stiffened. 'Please don't let me keep you from the other guests,' she replied, hearing the distinctive murmur of voices coming from a double-doored room to their right.

'You aren't,' the other woman countered. 'In fact—'

'There you are, Kit!' Marcus greeted from the top of the stairs, both women turning to look at him as he descended.

Marcus looked devastatingly attractive in a black dinner suit and snowy white shirt, more so than Kit had ever seen him before.

Catherine Grainger's expression remained impassive, confirming that there was no love lost between the two of them.

'Catherine,' Marcus greeted smoothly as he reached the hallway, his hand moving possessively on the slenderness of Kit's waist.

Kit turned to him, groaning inwardly as she saw the hard glitter in his eyes.

'Marcus,' Catherine returned dryly. 'Your—young friend, and I were just keeping each other company while she waited for you to come downstairs.'

'Really?' he drawled sceptically. 'Well, I'm obviously here now, so please don't let us delay you any further.' He looked at the older woman challengingly.

A challenge she was only too pleased to meet, mocking humour to her smile now. 'I'm in no hurry.' She shrugged her elegant shoulders. 'Perhaps the three of us could go to the library and have a quiet drink togeth—'

'I wondered what was keeping you, Catherine,' Desmond Hayes called out reprovingly after flinging open the double doors to the sitting-room to find the three of them standing there. 'Now I see that it was Marcus—' he strolled over to join them '—and his charming companion, Kit,' he added with obvious intent, his eyes flirting shamelessly as he took in her appearance.

Kit winced as Marcus's grip on her waist tightened; was she going to do anything right at all this evening?

She knew from Marcus's response to finding her

downstairs with Catherine that he wasn't pleased to see them together—well, he could join the club, because Kit wasn't pleased about it either! But he had no right at all to be annoyed with her because Desmond Hayes kept flirting with her—she certainly wasn't encouraging the man!

'Kit...' Catherine repeated consideringly, once again eyeing Kit speculatively. 'Would that be short for—?'

'It would be short for nothing,' Kit cut in firmly. 'And I'm sure the three of us have already delayed dinner for long enough,' she finished with a pointed smile in Desmond Hayes's direction.

'You two go ahead,' Marcus suggested tautly.

'If you're sure,' Desmond Hayes accepted as he tucked Catherine's hand snugly into the crook of his arm.

'I'm sure,' Marcus confirmed. 'Kit and I will join you in a few moments.' His grip on her waist held her back now as the other couple moved towards the noisy sitting-room.

Kit should have felt relieved at their departure—and she did feel a certain amount of tension ease out of her—but the anger she could still feel emanating from Marcus as he watched Catherine and Desmond was enough to tell her he was far from finished talking to her. In fact, he probably hadn't even started yet.

He moved away from her as soon as the sitting-room doors closed, looking down at her with accusing eyes. 'How long have you known Catherine Grainger?'

Kit felt her cheeks pale. 'I—but I don't know her!' she claimed dazedly.

His mouth twisted humourlessly. 'The two of you

looked friendly enough when I came downstairs a few minutes ago.'

Kit scowled as she gathered her wits. 'How can you say that? We had barely got past the civilities when you appeared—'

Marcus eyed her scathingly. 'Kit, I had been watching the two of you for several minutes before making my presence known.'

Her eyes widened. 'You were spying on us?' she realised incredulously.

'Of course not,' he dismissed irritably. 'I was merely on my way downstairs when I—'

'Saw the two of us talking together and decided to listen in!' Kit finished disgustedly, just thankful that he couldn't possibly have heard anything in the least damning—simply because there hadn't been anything like that for him to hear!

Marcus drew in a deep, controlling breath. 'Kit, are you aware of the—rivalry, between Maitland Enterprises and Grainger International?

'And the fact that they seem to be stealing the march on us lately with several business deals?'

'Well, of course I'm aware of it. I'm your PA—now just a minute.' She drew herself up to her current full height of six feet—in the two-inch-high-heeled shoes she was wearing—and was almost able to meet Marcus eye to eye. 'Exactly what are you implying?'

'I've suggested to Lewis that there may be some connection between the last three deals that Grainger International have stolen from under our noses.'

'Yes?' she prompted slowly, remembering all too well Lewis Grant's remarks on the subject on Thursday. And the implication behind them. 'When you said lately just now, did you really mean to say in the last six months?' she pressed resentfully. 'The exact amount of time I've been working for you?'

'Calm down, Kit.' Marcus sighed. 'I didn't mean to imply—'

'Oh, yes, you did!' Kit bit out indignantly. 'How dare you? How dare you even think such a thing about me and that—that woman?' she finished for want of something better to say.

The things he was implying about her, that she might possibly have leaked information to Catherine Grainger—presumably, he thought, for some monetary reward to herself?—would be laughable if they weren't so insulting!

'For your information, I wouldn't offer to help that woman—in any way—if she and I were the last two people on the planet!' Kit was breathing so hard in her agitation that her creamy breasts were clearly heaving beneath the low neckline of her dress.

Not that she was too concerned about that, realising as she saw the sudden change in Marcus's expression that she had said too much; Marcus was far too intelligent a man to believe she could possibly have come to that conclusion about Catherine Grainger after only five minutes' acquaintance!

Which she obviously hadn't. No, her knowledge of Catherine went back much further than that. Too far back to even give Marcus a hint at the reason she felt the way she did.

She made a dismissive movement of her hand. 'What I meant to say was—'

'I believe you made yourself more than clear, Kit,' Marcus assured her dryly. 'And I apologize if my remarks just now were less than—well, trusting.' He grimaced. 'All I'm saying is that I'm inclined to think the only explanation for those three lost deals is that there is someone in my employ who is revealing details of my business interests to Grainger International. But just because you and Catherine were talking together just now is really no reason for me to think that you—'

'That I'm the disloyal employee,' Kit completed tautly, having already known—and dreaded—the connection he could make concerning her and Catherine Grainger. 'Maybe you should try looking a little closer to home for your leak?' she suggested, still smarting from the fact that he might have thought it could have been her.

He blinked. 'Such as where?'

Kit gave him a smile of completely insincere sweetness. 'Did it ever occur to you that maybe you talk in your sleep?'

Marcus looked momentarily stunned by the suggestion. But then his good humour, which had been such a welcome surprise to Kit the last few days, took over, and a wry smile started to curve his lips. 'I think maybe I deserved that,' he acknowledged.

She gave an accepting inclination of her head. 'I think maybe you did.'

'Hmm,' he murmured ruefully, still smiling. 'Am I forgiven?' His expression was cajoling.

She was still annoyed with him, but at the same time knew how ludicrous were his suspicions that she could have betrayed him to Catherine Grainger. But Marcus couldn't know that. And she would rather it remained that way.

'You are,' she returned lightly.

'In that case—' he reached out to take a courteous hold of her arm '—shall we join the others, Miss McGuire?'

'Certainly, Mr Maitland,' she instantly accepted, knowing that if he had overstepped a line where she was concerned, then she had certainly done the same thing to him with her inference about pillow talk with women like Andrea Revel—and got away with it, thank goodness!

She had no idea what had prompted her to make that completely personal remark, except that it had disturbed her to have him accuse her of somehow being in cahoots with Catherine Grainger, of all people. She would rather ally herself to a rattlesnake!

'But don't be under the misapprehension,' Marcus murmured close to her ear as they entered the noisy sitting-room, 'that because I made a mistake about Catherine Grainger, I've forgotten our need to discuss your—acquaintance, with Mike Reynolds.'

Kit turned sharply, the high colour back in her cheeks. 'I don't feel such a need!' she assured him quickly.

He raised dark brows at her vehemence. 'Like that, is it?'

'Exactly like that!' If she never saw Mike Reynolds again it would be too soon!

Marcus gave her a considering look. 'There really is a lot more to you than meets the eye, Kit McGuire—'

'I thought that for this weekend it was to be Marcus and Kit?' she reminded him, preferring not to have her surname bandied. Especially in Catherine Grainger's hearing…

'Oh, it is,' he replied. 'Have I told you yet this evening how beautiful you look?'

If anything that colour in her cheeks deepened. 'There's no need to keep up the pretence when we're on our own,' she informed him awkwardly.

'It's not pretence,' he assured her softly, blue eyes laughing warmly as she gave him a puzzled look. 'You really are a very beautiful woman, Kit,' he told her seriously. 'I had absolutely no idea.'

'Perhaps it might be better if we left it that way,' she said stiffly.

'Too late,' he responded. 'I think simply coming in to the office might be a pleasure in future!'

Kit didn't feel the same enthusiasm, not if it was based on the fact that he now found her an attractive woman. Considering the short amount of time his interest in a specific woman usually lasted, that could mean that her days as his PA were numbered...

'Especially...' he looked at her intently '...if you really have forgiven me for my remarks of a few minutes ago?'

Kit gave an abrupt nod of her head. 'I said I had.'

Marcus grimaced. 'It's been my experience that women don't always mean what they say.'

'Well, this one does!' she assured him firmly.

Oh, she had forgiven him. Of course she had. But she wouldn't forget. Couldn't forget.

Because if Marcus knew the truth about her acquaintance with Catherine Grainger, she was sure he wouldn't have Kit anywhere near him, let alone working in his office!

CHAPTER SEVEN

'I THOUGHT the man was never going to leave your side!' Mike Reynolds complained as he joined Kit beside the buffet table and a mouth-watering array of desserts.

Because of the amount of people staying at the house this weekend dinner had necessarily been a full buffet affair, which actually suited Kit much better than being seated formally at a dinner table and stuck between two men she would probably rather not spend the time of day—or evening!—with.

Which pretty much covered most of the men here this weekend. With the exception of those wealthy businessmen—and women!—Kit had noted earlier, she had so far found them exactly as Marcus had earlier described them, a lot of 'hangers-on and social bores'. And Mike Reynolds came even further down the social list as far as she was concerned!

'Marcus will be back in a few minutes,' she informed Mike frostily, her expression one of utter contempt as she looked unflinchingly into his too-handsome face. 'He's just slipped upstairs to collect some cigars he brought with him for our host.'

'So I noticed,' Mike responded comfortably, as usual not affected by her obvious dislike. 'I also noticed Andrea Revel slipping out to join him a few seconds later,' he added. 'So if I were you, I wouldn't count on your boyfriend being back any time soon!'

Kit tried very hard not to show her surprise—and chagrin—at being told that Andrea was upstairs with Marcus. Not that she really was that surprised that Andrea hadn't given up on Marcus; she had been extremely visible during the last hour or so as they had all stood or sat around eating their sumptuous dinner, her loud laughter ringing out often at something her companion—presumably Derek Boyes—had said to her.

Not that Marcus had seemed to be taking too much notice, but then Kit didn't know him well enough to really say whether he had been or not. But other than telling her briefly earlier that he had been delayed getting ready for dinner by a telephone call from Andrea, he hadn't mentioned her again. The fact that he had left the room ten minutes ago, quickly followed by Andrea if Mike was to be believed, and hadn't returned yet, seemed to mean that he had been...

'For your information, Marcus isn't my boyfriend,' she snapped, giving Mike a withering look. 'And don't presume to project your own moral failings onto other people!'

He gave her an admiring glance. 'You've grown up in the last seven months, Kit.'

'Oh, please!' Her look of disdain intensified. 'Haven't I already made it obvious that you hold absolutely no charm for me? To the point where I actually walked out on a very well paid job just to avoid being anywhere near you?'

The handsome face grew dark with anger. 'You always did consider yourself superior—'

'I did not!' she cut in indignantly, more stung by the

remark than he could possibly imagine. 'I simply didn't—and still don't,' she continued heatedly, 'find you in the least attractive!'

He appeared unmoved by her outburst. 'Well, you're wasting your time as far as Marcus Maitland is concerned.'

'It's my time to waste!' she came back tartly, turning away from the array of desserts, having suddenly lost her appetite.

She already knew how stupid it was for her to be attracted to Marcus, didn't need this obnoxious man to tell her so!

Mike shook his head, a taunting smile curving his lips. 'You're way out of your depth, Kit.'

Her eyes flashed deeply grey. 'I would much rather have depth than be shallow!' Like you, her words obviously implied.

So much so that even the thick-skinned Mike Reynolds couldn't help but know exactly what she meant, his handsome face once again flushed with anger as he grated, 'As long as you don't mind being just another pretty face.'

Kit gave him a pitying look. 'You're just being pathetic now,' she dismissed contemptuously, knowing that in a woman his behaviour would have been classed as bitchy rather than pathetic!

'"The truth always hurts",' he quoted nastily.

Kit wasn't about to give up. 'You wouldn't recognize the truth if it jumped up and bit you on the nose!'

To her surprise Mike laughed at this insulting remark.

But his next move surprised her even more as he

reached out to pull her against him to kiss her on the mouth. Hard.

She jerked away angrily, totally bewildered by his action. 'What on earth—?'

'You always were a lot of fun, Kit,' he told her cheekily, a maliciously triumphant gleam in his eyes now.

'Yes, that's Kit, all right.' Marcus spoke from just behind her. 'Fun and laughter all the way!'

Kit's face paled as she turned to look at Marcus, feeling slightly sick as she saw the contempt in those deep blue eyes of his as he looked back at her.

Deservedly so, she acknowledged heavily, knowing that Mike had done this on purpose, that he must have seen Marcus's return and had deliberately kissed her.

She pulled sharply away from Mike, uncaring that his fingers bruised her arms as she did so. 'You can't possibly believe I was enjoying that?' She turned to Marcus disbelievingly.

He looked at her searchingly for several long seconds before turning back to Mike, his expression grimmer than ever. 'I believe you owe Kit an apology,' he said tersely.

'Do I?' Mike came back aggressively.

'Is there a problem?' Desmond Hayes enquired as he approached them, having obviously already seen that there was and moved smoothly away from the group he had been conversing with.

'Nothing I can't handle,' Marcus assured him tightly. 'I suggest that in future—' he turned back to Mike Reynolds '—you save your less than obvious charms for someone who is more interested in them than Kit appears to be!'

'And if I don't?' the other man challenged.

'That's up to you, of course.' Marcus shrugged. 'But I should warn you that I have no intention of letting you upset Kit.'

Kit could have wept at the scene that was unfolding in front of her eyes, couldn't believe this was happening.

'I believe that at the moment both you gentlemen are upsetting Kit,' Desmond intervened, at the same time putting a protective hand on her shoulder. 'I suggest we leave the two of you to sort this out in private.'

'That's fine by me,' Marcus snapped, his icy gaze not leaving Mike's angrily flushed face.

'And me,' Mike concurred, looking at Marcus with intense dislike. 'If anything, you're even more arrogant than your girlfriend,' he told Marcus.

Kit gasped. 'I told you, I'm not—'

'Leave them to it, my dear,' Desmond advised, turning her away from the other two men and back into the throng of the party. 'Don't you know better than to try to come between two males fighting over territory?' he chided, reaching out to take a glass of champagne from a passing waiter and hand it to her. 'Drink some of that,' he encouraged. 'It will make you feel better.'

Kit didn't feel anything was going to succeed in doing that as she saw Marcus and Mike leave the house by the French doors. Doors that very firmly closed behind them!

'They'll be fine,' Desmond assured her laughingly. 'I believe Marcus was a champion boxer when he was at Cambridge. Unless, of course, it's Mike Reynolds you're worried about?' He raised amused brows as the idea suddenly occurred to him.

'Not in the least,' Kit told him firmly, sipping her champagne agitatedly. 'Tell me, does hitting another man actually ever solve anything?'

'Not usually, no,' Desmond confirmed. 'But it makes you feel a hell of a lot better!' he said with relish.

Kit laughed too. It was impossible not to, this man's expression was so full of boyish mischief. In fact, it was easy to see, when he was amusingly charming like this, exactly why Desmond had been married three times.

'All the things you've heard about me are true,' Desmond said, those shrewd blue eyes seeming to read her thoughts exactly. 'Except one of them,' he added softly, suddenly serious. 'I don't intend letting my third wife divorce me. She's the love of my life,' he told Kit quietly as she looked at him enquiringly.

It was too much on top of everything else that had happened to her this evening; Kit's eyes filled with sudden tears at the utter desolation she detected in the gentleness of his voice.

'It does happen, you know,' Desmond told her candidly. 'The so-called biggest of womanizers, when they find the right woman, will never look at another one.'

'I'm sorry.' She bowed her head, searching through her small evening bag for the tissue she had placed in there earlier. 'I know I'm being silly. It's just—'

'You're falling in love with Marcus,' he said knowingly.

Kit raised her head to look around them worriedly, concerned that someone might hear their conversation, reassured when she saw that no one was listening. She turned back to Desmond. 'Of course I'm not falling in love with Marcus—'

'Of course you aren't,' Desmond echoed her words teasingly. 'In the same way I'm not still in love with my wife.'

Kit gave a rueful smile. 'No, I really mean it—'

'So do I,' Desmond encouraged sympathetically. 'Ah, the victor returns,' he said with satisfaction after a glance over her shoulder. 'No doubt battle-scarred but victorious!'

Kit was almost afraid to turn round and see which one of the two men had just re-entered the house, Marcus or Mike. Not that she thought for a moment that it wouldn't be Marcus; there was just no comfort in it, knowing how furious he was with her.

She sighed, the tingling sensation she felt down her spine telling her that it was indeed Marcus who had just re-entered the house. And that he was making his way across the room to where they stood talking. 'I shall have to leave, of course—'

'You most certainly will not,' Desmond told her firmly, his hand once again clasping her shoulder. 'You're the only thing that's making this whole weekend bearable!'

'How touching,' drawled that all-too-familiar voice. 'Really, Kit,' Marcus said with hard derision as he moved to stand beside her, his shrewd gaze having taken in Desmond's proprietary hold on her, 'you're turning into quite the *femme fatale*!'

'She *is* a *femme fatale*,' Desmond told him happily. 'Beautiful. With a delightful sense of humour. Sensuous. Deliciously—calm down, Marcus,' he ordered as the younger man made an impatient movement. 'You can't go around fighting every man Kit so much as talks to, you know.'

Poor Desmond had this all so wrong, it would have been laughable if it weren't so tragic. She was falling in love with Marcus. But he certainly didn't feel the same way about her, despite his defence of her just now. And she very much doubted that he appreciated the suggestion that he did!

'Ah, to add to the intrigue, the lovely Andrea returns,' Desmond observed speculatively as Andrea Revel came back into the room.

The beautiful, sensuous, delicious Andrea Revel, Kit acknowledged heavily, knowing that the other woman really was everything that she wasn't herself. Andrea also looked stunningly attractive this evening in a bright red silk sheath of a dress that clung to her voluptuous curves. A fact she was obviously completely aware of as she strolled across the room to rejoin Derek Boyes.

Frankly, Kit had had enough of all of them for one evening!

'I'm afraid I have a headache.' She spoke to Desmond Hayes, deliberately keeping her gaze averted from the broodingly silent Marcus, one quick glance having shown her that, despite what Desmond had said, he showed no visible battle scars. But the fact that Mike Reynolds hadn't reappeared seemed to say that Desmond was right about which man had been the victor. 'If you will excuse me?' she added for politeness' sake only, not waiting for a response from either man before she turned and hurriedly left the room, looking to neither left nor right as she did so. She certainly didn't want to see Catherine Grainger again before she went to bed!

What a disaster of a weekend this was turning out

to be! There wasn't a single person here that she wanted to be with. Although Desmond Hayes had been something of a surprise these last few minutes, not at all what she had expected. Surprisingly, she actually found herself liking him. He—

'Oh, no, you don't!' Marcus grated gruffly, grasping the bedroom door as Kit would have closed it behind her.

Kit turned to look at him apprehensively. She had been completely unaware of him following her up the stairs—not surprising really, when her thoughts had been so full of the misery she had endured the last couple of hours!

'Let's go inside,' Marcus said, not waiting for her answer before moving past her into the bedroom.

Kit followed slowly, shutting the door quietly behind her, sensing his reproving gaze on her before she even looked at him. But once she had looked at him, she wished that she hadn't, the grimness of his voice more than reflected in his harshly set features!

'Well, you've certainly made a spectacle of yourself this evening, haven't you?' he said scornfully, thrusting his hands into his trouser pockets as he stared across the room at her.

'I have?' She gasped her indignation, feeling her anger starting to rise. 'I'm not the one who spent fifteen minutes out of the room with one woman and then came back and started acting all proprietorial about another one!' She glared at him accusingly, well past the mood of caution. And if Marcus sacked her for her outspokenness—fine! She really wasn't sure how they were going to continue to work together after this weekend, anyway.

'I'm flattered that you actually took note of the time,' he drawled.

'I didn't,' she told him swiftly. 'Mike was the one who noticed Andrea following you out of the room, and Desmond remarked on her return.' She threw her evening bag down on the bed. 'I couldn't give a damn what you do!' Her eyes sparkled deeply grey in her anger. 'Or, in fact, who you do it with!'

Marcus was very still, only a nerve pulsing in his jaw to tell of his own fury. 'Couldn't you?' he prompted softly.

'No!' she assured him decisively. 'As for going outside with Mike Reynolds—! Did the two of you actually have a fight?' She still found that whole scene unbelievable.

'Nothing so crude, Kit,' Marcus responded tersely. 'There are far subtler ways of dealing with a man like Mike Reynolds than resorting to physical violence. But how the hell do you even know a man like him? He said something about the two of you being involved seven months ago?' His eyes had narrowed to blue slits.

Kit gave a frustrated shake of her head. 'I thought you said you had read my résumé?'

'So I have,' Marcus confirmed with a perplexed frown. 'But what does that have to do with—?' He broke off abruptly, grimacing self-derisively as he momentarily closed his eyes.

'Exactly,' she bit out disgustedly, knowing the truth had finally dawned. 'Mike Reynolds is a prime example of what is meant by sexual harassment in the workplace. I utterly detest the man,' she finished with a shudder of distaste.

'Perhaps I should have hit him, after all,' Marcus muttered.

'Not on my account, no,' Kit assured him hastily.

He gave a ragged sigh. 'It seems I owe you an apology.'

'Accepted,' Kit said gruffly. 'Now would you please leave my bedroom?' She really had had quite enough for one day!

He drew in a harsh breath. 'One way or another, this has been—quite an enlightening evening, hasn't it?'

For whom? It certainly wasn't anything that Kit would want to live through again.

'Perhaps,' she returned noncommittally. 'But in the circumstances, I think it might be best if I were to leave here tomorrow.'

Before anything else disastrous happened!

'Because of Mike Reynolds?' Marcus queried. 'I believe he's leaving himself in the morning.'

Her eyes widened. 'Your doing?'

'My doing,' Marcus confirmed levelly.

Okay, so the Mike Reynolds problem might have been dealt with. But that still left Catherine Grainger…

'I would still rather leave,' Kit told him determinedly, knowing it was for the best.

Marcus paused for a moment. 'Because of my behaviour this evening?' He grimaced. 'First I accuse you of disloyalty, then I question your friendship with Mike Reynolds!'

'Partly because of that,' she answered cautiously.

He looked at her directly. 'But also because…?' he prompted.

Because a part of her had felt pleased at the way he had defended her against Mike Reynolds, and the fact that he hadn't seemed to like Desmond Hayes talking to her, either. But, ultimately, she had known it wasn't real, that it was only male pride on Marcus's part. To remain here for the rest of the weekend, posing as the woman in his life, would only give her false hopes.

She forced a smile. 'I just think it's for the best. Besides,' she went on, 'I'm sure Miss Revel will be only too pleased to keep you company.'

'And if it isn't Andrea that I want to keep me company?'

He was suddenly standing much too close for comfort, and Kit was easily able to feel the heat of his body, the warmth of his breath stirring the loose tendrils of hair at her temples.

She swallowed hard, at the same time forcing herself not to take a step backwards, determined not to let him see the effect his closeness was having on her. 'But we both know that it is,' she persisted.

'Do we?'

'Yes,' she said firmly, her eyes meeting his steadily. 'You said as much when we arrived here and you mentioned not making a scene.'

'What makes you think I was referring to Andrea…?'

Well, he certainly couldn't have been referring to her because of the friendly way Mike Reynolds had talked to her—could he…?

Marcus continued to look at her for several long seconds, finally taking a step backwards. 'How about we discuss this again in the morning?'

'How about we don't?' she came back heavily.

To her surprise, Marcus grinned, a completely humorous grin that warmed his eyes and curved his lips over even white teeth.

'It certainly is different being away on business with you rather than Lewis!'

Kit's own mouth quirked, relieved that the tension between them seemed to have broken. Although that didn't change her resolve to put as much distance tomorrow between herself and Desmond Hayes's house as was possible. As much distance between herself and Catherine Grainger as was possible...

'I would think it would be,' she conceded dryly.

Marcus chuckled now, his bad humour obviously dissipated. 'No borrowing his aftershave when I forget my own, for one thing,' he teased.

'Or socks and underwear,' Kit came back playfully.

'I draw the line at the underwear!' Marcus assured her dryly. 'The socks at a pinch, maybe, but—'

'Please go back downstairs and join the party!' Kit cut the conversation short.

Marcus sobered, looking at her intently now. 'You'll be okay up here on your own?'

'Of course,' she assured him easily.

A few more hours and she might be able to get away from here completely.

Away from the possibility of finding herself alone with Catherine Grainger again...!

CHAPTER EIGHT

THERE was someone in her bedroom!

Kit wasn't sure what had woken her: an unexpected noise, a sixth sense? But something had certainly disturbed her sleep and now she was aware of another person in the room with her—even though she couldn't see them in the dark shadows of the room, she could hear the soft sound of their breathing.

'Marcus?' she called tentatively.

She had no idea what he would be doing creeping about her bedroom during the early hours of the morning. But there again, he certainly hadn't seemed to have too much hesitation about walking into her bedroom unannounced yesterday evening!

The fact that she received no answer to her query convinced her that she was right in thinking it wasn't him...

'Who is it?' she said sharply, sitting up as she desperately tried to see into the shadows. 'Who's there?' she demanded as anger started to replace her apprehension.

If someone was trying to frighten her, then they were succeeding, and if they were trying to frighten her, then they deserved her anger!

'I said—' She broke off abruptly, her wrist grasped between tight fingers as she reached out to turn on the bedside light.

'I heard you, Kit,' came the unmistakable voice of Mike Reynolds.

'What are you doing in my bedroom?' Kit gasped disbelievingly, moving frantically across to one side of the bed as she felt him sit on the other side of it. 'How dare you—?'

'Be quiet, Kit,' he rasped, maintaining that steely grasp of her wrist. 'And don't be naïve; you know exactly why I'm here.'

'No, I—'

'Yes,' he cut in forcefully. 'To be honest, I couldn't quite believe my luck, when, instead of coming in here to join you when he came up to bed half an hour ago, I saw Maitland go into the room next door.'

Kit's eyes widened as she once again tried to see Mike's face in the darkness. 'You've been outside watching my bedroom?' Somehow just the thought of that made her skin crawl.

Mike gave a disgusted snort. 'What else did I have to do with my time after Maitland's threatening behaviour earlier?'

'Marcus didn't threaten you,' she defended, wishing now that Marcus had actually hit Mike—the verbal warning alone obviously hadn't worked!

'I thought your delicate sensibilities might prefer that description to the arrogant bastard he really is!' Mike said contemptuously.

'Isn't it a little late for you to be thinking of my delicate sensibilities?' she suggested, her vision having finally adjusted to the dim moonlight. She was able to see Mike's face now, if not his actual features. 'You have to leave, Mike,' she told him.

'And if I don't choose to?'

'Then I'll scream,' she informed him determinedly. 'Marcus is in the bedroom next door,' she added as a deterrent, knowing that Mike was a coward at heart.

He gave a humourless laugh. 'Poor little Kit,' he taunted. 'So naïve. So trusting. Your boyfriend is no longer in his room next door!' he informed her with hard satisfaction. 'Maitland only stayed a couple of minutes before leaving again. And he hasn't come back. Now, I don't know about you, but considering how thick he and Andrea Revel have been the last few months, I would say it's pretty easy to guess exactly whose bed he's in right now! Wouldn't you?'

Yes, she would, Kit accepted heavily, angry with Marcus for putting her in such an embarrassing position, but even more upset that he had left her an easy target for Mike Reynolds!

'Will you just leave?' she said stiffly. 'Before you do something we're both going to regret,' she added warningly.

'Oh, come on, Kit,' Mike cajoled. 'For goodness' sake, lighten up, will you? After all, we're old friends.' His tone was persuasive as his hand moved caressingly up her arm.

'Are you totally thick, or just plain stupid?' she challenged, annoyance easily overcoming her fear. 'I do not find you attractive. I have no intention of becoming involved with you. In fact, I'm sure I've made it perfectly plain that I don't even like you!' she finished frustratedly.

'Do you realise your boyfriend has persuaded Desmond to throw me out of here first thing in the morning?' The cajoling tone had turned to fury, and his hand tightened about her arm.

'Not soon enough, as far as I'm concerned!' Kit came back heatedly.

'Now just—'

'Or me!' rasped an authoritative voice that Kit easily knew belonged to Marcus. At the same time she felt Mike's hand release her arm as Marcus landed a punch on his jaw, which threw him off the bed.

'Get your things together now, Reynolds, and just leave!' Marcus was standing gloweringly over Mike as Kit at last managed to reach the switch for the bedside light. 'And I would advise you not to show your face anywhere near me in the next decade!'

Mike got slowly to his feet, the slight discolouration on his jaw already visible. And, despite her earlier protests about physical violence, Kit knew that she felt no regret at Marcus's action. In fact, she felt like hitting Mike herself!

'Playing musical beds, Maitland?' Mike sneered. 'One woman won't play, so you've come back to try the one in reserve?'

Marcus's eyes narrowed dangerously. 'I have no idea what you're talking about, Reynolds,' he rasped. 'Neither do I have any wish to know. Just go!'

'What do you think, Kit?' Mike turned to her tauntingly. 'Second-best about your limit, is it?' He gave a derisive smile as she wasn't quick enough to hide the flinch his hurtful words inflicted.

She knew he was being deliberately nasty, knew he was enjoying her discomfort, but there was so much truth behind his words that for the moment she couldn't think of anything to say.

'Go,' Marcus repeated in carefully controlled tones.

Mike went, slowly, nonchalantly, as cockily sure of himself as ever.

Kit's shoulders slumped once he had left the room, reaction starting to set in as she began to shake. Amazingly, she had no doubts in her mind that if Marcus hadn't come in when he had Mike really would have tried to force himself on her.

What made someone behave in that way? She had made it more than obvious that she disliked him, that she didn't find him attractive, that she certainly didn't want any sort of relationship with him, and yet he had still persisted. Maybe she had led a sheltered life, but she didn't understand that sort of behaviour…

'What on earth possessed you to let that man into your bedroom—?'

'I beg your pardon?' Kit rounded on Marcus disbelievingly, her eyes widely accusing as incredulity took over from the near-collapse she had felt coming on.

His mouth was a grimly set line. He was dressed only in the white silk shirt and trousers to his black dinner suit, having discarded the jacket. 'You knew what sort of man he was, so what on earth—?'

'Possessed me to invite him into my bedroom?' Kit finished through gritted teeth, getting out of bed, perfectly respectable in her coffee-coloured satin pyjamas, but reaching out to pull on the matching robe anyway. She hadn't thought that she would have her bedroom invaded in this way, not by one man, but two!

'Exactly,' Marcus agreed.

Kit gave an indignant sigh, at the same time tying the belt to her robe securely about the slenderness of her waist. 'It's all your fault,' she began.

'My fault?' he echoed as his head rose incredulously.

'And just how do you account for that, when I did everything in my power earlier this evening—apart from actually hitting the man!—to dissuade him from coming anywhere near you again?' His mouth twisted scathingly.

'He said you threatened him,' Kit accused.

'Obviously not strongly enough,' Marcus responded. 'I'm just surprised at you for inviting him into your room after that.'

'You just don't get it, do you?' she rejoined impatiently. 'I didn't invite Mike in here; he broke in while I was asleep. After first ascertaining that you had crept off to Andrea's bedroom, of course.'

'That I had—! What do you mean, he broke in?' Marcus seemed to think this part of her conversation was much more important than answering her other accusation.

Kit didn't agree with him, knew that if Marcus hadn't gone off to Andrea's bedroom Mike would never have dared to enter her bedroom in the way that he had.

She was also aware that this might be misdirected anger—but she had to blame someone, didn't she?

'Exactly what I said.' She moved away impatiently. 'The man needs locking up!'

Marcus remained silent for several nerve-racking moments and then he slowly nodded. 'We can do that,' he murmured harshly. 'If what you say is true—'

'Of course what I say is true!' Kit turned on him indignantly. 'I don't tell lies.'

'Look, Kit,' Marcus's expression softened slightly as he seemed to take in her agitated, wide-eyed appearance, 'I don't think losing your temper with me is going to solve anything—'

'Why isn't it?' she exclaimed. 'If it wasn't for you I wouldn't even be here. And if it wasn't for that, I wouldn't have been subjected to Mike Reynolds's unwanted advances! Neither would I have had to meet—' She broke off then, realising—almost too late!—exactly what she had been about to say.

The last thing she wanted to do was introduce the subject of Catherine Grainger to this already explosive situation!

'Yes?' Marcus prompted, dark brows raised enquiringly.

'Desmond Hayes,' she substituted defensively, only too aware of the seriousness of the slip she had almost made. 'Although, of the three of you, I think I prefer his company!'

Marcus's brows rose even higher. 'I noticed that the two of you seemed to be getting on well together, but—' He gave an incredulous shake of his head. 'Kit, you'll only end up getting hurt if you fall for Desmond,' he warned darkly.

'Oh, for goodness' sake!' She glared at him, two bright spots of angry colour in her cheeks. 'I said that, so far this weekend, his is the company I prefer, not that I'm attracted to him! Does everything have to come down to this male female attraction thing?'

His mouth twisted wryly. 'No, of course not. Although, it's usually a relevant factor.'

'Not to me,' she sighed. 'For your information, the only thing I've been able to learn this weekend by observing and listening, as you put it, is that Desmond is still very much in love with his wife!' She was breathing hard in her indignation, her chin raised challengingly, nipples roused beneath her robe.

A fact Marcus seemed very aware of as his gaze moved slowly over her.

Making Kit aware at the same time, the flush in her cheeks caused by something else entirely now, a wild fluttering in her chest, her breath seeming constricted in her throat, every inch of her tingling skin seeming as aware of Marcus as he was of her.

Not the most ideal situation to find oneself in at almost three o'clock in the morning when alone with a man you already knew yourself to be half in love with!

Although he had certainly done little to encourage those feelings this evening!

Kit straightened, her hands thrust defensively into the pockets of her robe. 'I think it's time you left, Marcus,' she told him, instantly wishing she had sounded more convincing.

'Yes,' he acknowledged with as little conviction.

She swallowed hard, her tongue moving nervously across her bottom lip, instantly knowing that had been the wrong thing to do as Marcus's gaze darkened, a nerve pulsing in his jaw.

After the noise and bustle of the evening, it was all so quiet about them, the house itself seeming asleep. Only the beat of Kit's heart, it appeared to her, sounded loudly in the silence.

Her eyes widened as Marcus slowly took two steps towards her. Her throat felt constricted so that she couldn't speak, not when he stood in front of her, not when he took her into his arms, not when his head lowered as his lips took gentle possession of hers.

His kiss deepened as passion exploded between

them. Marcus's tongue moved questioningly against her lower lip and Kit's response was to draw him deeper inside her.

He felt so right against her, their bodies moulded together as if two halves of a whole, Marcus's hands moving caressingly the length of her spine before tightening on her lower back to pull her into his hardness.

Warmth spread through her lower body at this evidence of his own arousal, her neck arching as Marcus's lips moved down its length to the sensitive hollows beneath.

Kit could only groan longingly as he pushed aside her robe and pyjama top to take one hardened nipple into the moist warmth of his mouth, sucking her deep inside him as his tongue lathed that sensitive tip.

Kit felt as if she were on fire, the centre of that fire situated at the very heart of her, her hands clinging to the broad width of his shoulders as his hand moved caressingly to her other breast, his thumb moving delicately, oh, so delicately, over the hardened tip.

She had never known such pleasure in her life, felt her control rapidly slipping away from her, her response to his caresses instinctive, as if her body had always known his touch, his caress.

A sob caught in her throat as she realised she was in love with this man, a part of her knowing this was just too much on top of everything else that had happened to her.

Marcus instantly pulled back slightly, raising his head to look at her with concerned blue eyes. 'I won't hurt you, Kit,' he promised.

It wasn't him she was afraid of—it was her own newly realised emotions!

Because she was already in love with Marcus. Deeply. Irrevocably. Knew it as surely as she knew her name.

And he was making love to her in such a way that she knew there could be only one way of this ending. Unless she put a stop to it—now!

Offence was her best form of defence... 'Marcus, haven't both of us had enough—excitement, for one evening?' she ventured.

'What do you mean?'

'Me, by having Mike invade my bedroom in the way that he did. And you, because—Andrea Revel,' she concluded, able to ease out of his arms now as his hands fell back to his sides, straightening her robe back into place as she moved even further away.

'Andrea?' Marcus repeated in a puzzled voice. 'What does she have to do with us?'

'Us?' Kit repeated, feeling more in control now that she had put some distance between them. Although she had no doubt that the memory of their closeness would haunt her dreams—day as well as night!—for a very long time. 'There is no "us", Marcus,' she responded quietly.

'Exactly what are you accusing me of where Andrea is concerned?' Marcus demanded, his expression stormy now.

'I'm not accusing you of anything,' she returned with more bravado than she really felt. If Marcus were to so much as touch her again, she knew she would be in his arms, with no thought of what tomorrow might bring! 'I told you, Mike only came in here earlier because he saw you go off to Andrea's bedroom.'

'He might have seen me leave my bedroom,' Marcus

conceded. 'But what makes either of you think it was in order to pay Andrea a nocturnal visit?'

Kit gave a shrug. 'It's obvious the two of you are still involved.'

'Says who?' he came back.

'Says anybody who looks at the two of you, apparently,' she returned, remembering all too easily how even the insensitive Mike Reynolds had taunted her about the relationship.

Marcus drew in a harsh breath. 'For your information, I went downstairs to enjoy a cigar with Desmond,' he explained. 'He was kind enough to invite me to join him. But for the record,' he continued coldly, 'as I've already told you, Andrea and I are finished. Totally. Irrevocably.' He walked purposefully to the adjoining bedroom door to wrench it open. 'I've told Desmond we shall be leaving tomorrow. He would prefer that we make it after lunch; is that going to be okay with you?'

'Fine,' Kit accepted numbly, just wishing he would go now and leave her alone to try and regain some of her shattered defences.

He paused in the open doorway. 'You know, Kit, I don't know what I've done to give you this—unflattering opinion you seem to have of me, but I can assure you that I do not make love to one woman while being involved with another!'

She swallowed hard, easily able to discern the scorn in his tone. But she was just too tired, too emotionally raw from her newly realised love for him, still too physically aware of him, to try to make any sense out of what had been a disturbing, confused evening.

'Goodnight, Kit,' Marcus said gruffly when it became obvious she had nothing else to say.

'Goodnight,' she echoed shakily, managing to remain standing upright until he had left the room.

When she collapsed shakily back onto the bed, at last allowing the tears that had been threatening for the last hour to overflow and cascade hotly down her cheeks.

Was this nightmare never going to end?

CHAPTER NINE

'I UNDERSTAND there was some sort of—situation, in your bedroom last night?'

Kit forced herself not to move on the sun lounger on which she lay beside the swimming pool, even though the sound of Catherine Grainger's voice had been enough to bring her eyes wide open behind the sunglasses she wore.

Unlike Kit, Catherine was fully dressed, albeit in a cool green linen sundress that showed her overall suntan to advantage. Kit, on the other hand, was wearing the black bikini she had bought for her holiday last year, her skin colour still creamy magnolia; she hadn't gone away on holiday yet this year.

Despite receiving no response to her question, Catherine Grainger made herself comfortable on the adjacent lounger, as beautifully composed as she had been yesterday; her hair was perfectly styled and her skin smooth, despite her being in her late sixties.

In fact, Kit knew *she* wouldn't mind being in this prime condition at the age of sixty-seven!

Which admission was enough to make her sit up a little straighter on her lounger, totally, she instantly realised, giving away her wakeful state.

'I thought you were awake.' Catherine Grainger nodded her satisfaction, her own sunglasses hiding silver eyes that Kit nevertheless knew to be totally shrewd and calculating.

'Did you?' Kit returned with cool uninterest.

'Oh, yes.' The older woman nodded again. 'It was the tapping of your fingers on the arm of your lounger that gave you away.'

Something Kit instantly stopped doing. Not that she was surprised to learn she had been doing something so mind-numbingly repetitive; after last night she was having trouble stringing two thoughts together, let alone making any sense of them!

It had been impossible for her to sleep after Marcus had left her room last night, because of a combination of anger towards Mike Reynolds and sheer frustration where Marcus was concerned—her body still remembered his kisses and caresses even if her mind was trying desperately to shut them out!

All in all, she'd not had a good night's sleep, and she had come outside early this morning to claim a lounger beside the pool, pushing the barrier of sunglasses onto the bridge of her nose in the hope of avoiding having to speak to any of the other people at this weekend party. Marcus, in particular!

Not, it appeared, that she need have worried about him too much; a maid cleaning beside the pool had informed her that Marcus had gone horse-riding with their host early this morning and wasn't expected to return until mid-morning.

A pity she hadn't been as fortunate where Catherine Grainger was concerned.

'So...' Catherine removed her own sunglasses to turn those penetrating silver-grey eyes on Kit '...why is it, when you assure me that we have never met before, I have the distinct impression we know each other?'

Every defensive bone in Kit's body cried out to tell this woman the truth, to tell Catherine Grainger exactly why she had this feeling of familiarity, of who and what it was that gave her that feeling!

But another part of her knew she couldn't do that; she had no intention of betraying a confidence given to her, and to do so would hurt other people as well as herself.

Kit turned her head to look at Catherine. 'I can assure you—once again!—that the two of us have never met before,' she said with complete honesty.

What would Marcus think, what would he say or do, if he could see Catherine Grainger talking to Kit now? It would no doubt arouse his suspicions all over again about where those leaks from his office were coming from—when, in point of fact, Kit wouldn't tell this woman the time of day!

'So you've said,' Catherine acknowledged distantly, but still looking intensely at Kit with those piercing silver-grey eyes. 'So what did happen last night?'

Kit gave a start. Although why she was surprised was beyond her; Catherine Grainger was a woman who always got what she wanted, and that included answers to the questions she asked.

Except, not this time... 'I have no idea what you're referring to,' Kit dismissed.

And, in point of fact, she didn't, not specifically. Was Catherine referring to Mike Reynolds's unexpected visit to her bedroom, or Marcus's appearance following that? Whichever it was, it was none of Catherine's business!

'Oh, come on, Kit.' Catherine gave a hard laugh. 'A man pays an unwelcome visit to your bedroom in the middle of the night and you have no idea what I'm referring to? My dear, if that really is the case, then what an exciting life you must lead!'

Catherine's reference to an unwelcome visitor to her bedroom didn't help to enlighten Kit in the least; she could still just as easily be referring to Marcus's visit as Mike Reynolds's!

'Not particularly.' She answered the other woman tersely. 'As you say, it was unwelcome and, as such, I think it better to forget it ever happened.' In both cases. As far as Mike Reynolds was concerned, she hoped she never saw him again. With regard to Marcus's visit, she had to forget it if she intended to continue working for him.

'Just pretend it never happened, you mean?' the older woman mused. 'My dear, you certainly have spirit!'

And Kit had to stop herself from visibly gnashing her teeth at having Catherine Grainger, of all people, refer to her as 'my dear', not once, but twice. She wasn't Catherine Grainger's 'dear' anything, and never would be!

'Thank you,' she accepted briskly.

'I'm not sure that Desmond intends treating the situation as lightly as you seem able to,' Catherine announced.

Kit gave her a sharp look. 'What do you mean?'

Catherine shrugged. 'It happened in his home, my dear; not exactly pleasant. Especially if you decide to press charges later on.'

She had to be referring to Mike Reynolds's unwanted visit to Kit's bedroom, couldn't possibly think

Kit would press charges against *Marcus* for what had, after all, been a mutual passion.

'I won't,' Kit denied. 'The Mike Reynoldses of this world are, as you say, unpleasant, but hardly worth disrupting one's life for.'

'That's very commendable,' Catherine replied graciously. 'By the way, that's a really nasty bruise you have on your arm.'

Kit felt the colour flush her cheeks; she had put foundation cream on the discolouration caused by Mike clasping hold of her arm so tightly the night before, but unfortunately she hadn't quite managed to hide the colours-of-the-rainbow effect in the shape of fingers!

Kit found herself disliking this woman more than ever for drawing attention to her bruising. Was it any wonder that—?

'My fault, I'm afraid,' Marcus remarked easily as he dropped down onto Kit's lounger, bending forward to kiss her bruised arm. 'A little over-enthusiasm on my part. Sorry, darling,' he told her throatily.

Kit, having dreaded seeing Marcus again after what had happened between them last night, suddenly found herself very pleased to see him. Especially as he seemed to have summed the situation up at a glance— well…some of it!—and come to her rescue.

She had been so caught up in her conversation with Catherine Grainger that she hadn't even noticed his approach. But now she could only admire how handsome he looked in his riding jodhpurs and a loose white shirt.

'Marcus,' she greeted warmly, her relieved smile telling him how grateful she was for his interruption.

'Well, it seems I must leave you two lovebirds alone,' Catherine Grainger murmured as she stood up.

'A word of advice, though, Marcus…' She paused beside them. 'Kit's skin is far too delicate and fair for such rough lovemaking!' She strolled away towards the house.

'Why, that interfering old—'

'Now, now, Kit, let's not be bitchy,' Marcus interrupted her with amusement, his blue eyes reflecting his smile. 'Catherine is such a cold person herself she's probably forgotten what lovemaking is like, rough or otherwise!'

Kit grinned. 'Now who's being bitchy?'

He straightened to look at her critically. 'Did Reynolds really do that to you last night?' His mouth had thinned as he inspected the marks on her arm.

'Yes—but it doesn't matter,' she quickly dismissed as Marcus's expression darkened even more. She reached out to pick up her towelling robe and pull it on, hoping that hiding the bruises might take Marcus's mind off their existence. She should have known better. Marcus was nothing if not single-minded.

'Oh, yes, it matters,' he assured her softly.

'Please leave it, Marcus.' She put a pleading hand on his arm. 'He's gone now.' Mike's departure was the first thing she had checked on when she had come downstairs this morning. 'It's enough that as many people know about it as they do.'

Marcus looked at her searchingly. 'I owe you an apology for last night—'

'Couldn't we just forget about that too?' she said self-consciously.

'Can you forget about it?' he replied huskily.

Forget Marcus kissing her? Forget Marcus caressing

her? Forget the way he had aroused her? Forget the way he had been aroused by her?

No—of course she couldn't forget about it. But the alternative, of leaving his employment and never seeing him again, wasn't acceptable, either.

She couldn't quite meet his searching gaze now. 'I can try,' she told him slowly.

Marcus gave a shake of his head. 'I don't know what the hell came over me, talking to you in the way that I did! And as for—'

'Please!' Inwardly Kit cringed; the last thing she wanted was to hear his regrets about kissing and caressing her.

'Perhaps you're right,' he allowed heavily, standing up too. 'Incidentally, what were you and Catherine Grainger talking about before I arrived? Besides Reynolds, of course.'

Kit gave him a darting look, unable to read anything from his bland expression. Deliberately so? She wasn't sure. But it was obvious from Marcus's question that he was still uneasy about her conversations with his arch business rival, that maybe he did still suspect her in some way.

She actually had no idea why Catherine Grainger kept singling her out in this way.

She only knew the reason she would rather the other woman didn't do so!

She gave Marcus a narrow-eyed look. 'You still don't trust me, do you…?'

'Kit, I have no idea who to trust any more,' he answered truthfully. 'I only know that when I do find the traitor in my camp, they are going to wish they had never been born!'

She swallowed hard, not doubting for a moment that he meant what he said. Should she tell him now of her past connection to Catherine Grainger, of the reason she disliked the woman so much she couldn't possibly be the one who was passing her information?

She shuddered just at the thought of doing that, at the contempt she would see in his face if he knew the truth. Besides, it wasn't her secret to tell...

She gave an abrupt shake of her head. 'Then it's just as well it isn't me, isn't it?'

'Isn't it?' he returned hardly.

Their gazes locked in mutual challenge, Kit determined not to be the one to back down.

Marcus finally gave in. 'I think I'll just go upstairs and take a shower. I've finished talking to Desmond, so we can leave before lunch if you would—'

'Oh, yes!' she accepted quickly. 'I can't wait to get away from here,' she admitted abruptly.

'Believe me, it isn't the most successful twenty-four hours I've ever known, either. Oh, and by the way, you were right about Desmond.' He paused.

Kit gave him a curious look. 'About his still being in love with his wife, you mean?'

'That—' Marcus nodded '—and the fact that the rumours concerning his financial problems did originate from him.'

'They did?' She had merely been guessing when she had made that comment yesterday, hadn't really thought there would be any truth in it.

'Yes,' Marcus went on. 'Although not for the reason we supposed. He's actually in no financial difficulty at all, but he thought that if his wife believed he was she might come back to him.'

Kit's expression was perplexed. 'Isn't it usually the other way around…?'

'That's very cynical of you, Kit,' he teased. 'Obviously you've never met the latest Mrs Hayes.'

'Well, of course I haven't met her! I don't usually mix in such exalted company as I have this weekend,' she shot back.

'The exalted bit is certainly a matter of opinion!' Marcus responded wryly. 'I can think of several people here this weekend who certainly don't come under that heading!'

Mike Reynolds and Catherine Grainger being two of them, Kit easily guessed.

'So can I,' she agreed dully.

'I'm sure you can,' he allowed flatly. 'Anyway, the bottom line is that Jackie wants children and Desmond is terrified at the thought. But as he also loves his wife to distraction…'

'He came up with the idea of starting a rumour that he's in financial difficulties in the hopes of winning Jackie back,' Kit realised.

'Yes,' Marcus confirmed.

'But didn't they discuss having children before they got married?'

'I have no idea,' Marcus told her lightly. 'Having only just started my career as a marriage guidance counsellor, I didn't think to ask that question!'

'And you're so highly qualified too!' She instantly felt the colour warm her cheeks at her unthinking outspokenness. 'What I meant to say was—'

'I know what you meant to say, Kit,' he assured her. 'As for Desmond, I felt quite sorry for him, actually.'

'Who did you feel sorry for, darling?' Andrea Revel

cut smoothly in on their conversation, moving to stand next to Marcus as she linked her arm loosely with his to look up at him.

Instantly making five-feet-ten-inches-tall Kit feel like a giraffe—and with about as much grace of movement!

The other woman looked gorgeous, of course, the skimpy green bikini she wore moulding to the perfection of her voluptuous curves, the tiny pieces of material leaving little to the imagination.

Not that Marcus needed imagination where this woman's curves were concerned, Kit reminded herself crossly.

Or that it was any of her business, she rebuked herself.

'Surely not Mike Reynolds?' Andrea persisted when she received no answer, green eyes glittering maliciously as she looked across at Kit.

'No, not Reynolds,' Marcus rasped, obviously having no intention of breaking Desmond's confidence by enlightening Andrea as to exactly whom he had been talking about.

Andrea arched blonde brows. 'I believe you had a little trouble with the man last night, Kit…?'

Did everyone here know what had happened in her bedroom last night? Although she didn't need to look far to know who had been Andrea Revel's informant!

She gave Marcus a glare before answering Andrea. 'Nothing that couldn't be sorted out,' she said tightly.

'Lucky for you that Marcus came back when he did,' Andrea drawled pointedly.

'Very,' Kit acknowledged tautly, knowing from the taunting glint in the other woman's catlike eyes that she was enjoying her discomfort thoroughly. 'If you'll both excuse me, I would like to go inside and dress?' she said stiltedly. 'You said we're leaving shortly, Marcus?'

'In about an hour,' he confirmed.

It couldn't be soon enough for her, Kit knew as she turned away from the sight of Andrea Revel leaning her curves into Marcus's body as the two of them whispered together.

Her heart ached as she acknowledged that Marcus wasn't exactly pushing Andrea away. Oh, she believed him when he said his relationship with Andrea was over before the two of them had come away together for the weekend, but that didn't mean that it couldn't be rekindled, did it? She didn't doubt that if Andrea Revel had any say in it then it certainly would be!

Just as she didn't doubt her own love for Marcus. Or that that love was of the everlasting variety.

What an idiot she was.

She had spent the last six months hiding her own attractiveness from Marcus, only to fall in love with him and wish that he would feel the same way about her.

What a futile hope…!

CHAPTER TEN

'YOU'RE very quiet?'

'I was under the impression you preferred it that way when you're driving.' Kit didn't even glance in Marcus's direction as he sat behind the wheel of his Jaguar, remaining relaxed back in her seat, her sunglasses once again perched protectively on the bridge of her nose.

'*Touché,*' he allowed. 'What are you going to do with the rest of your weekend?'

'What do you mean?'

'Well, you must have cancelled all your original plans in order to come away with me this weekend, and now we're returning early. And I won't expect you to come in to the office until Tuesday—after all, you've given up most of your Saturday.'

'Yes?' she acknowledged guardedly.

'I just wondered what you were going to do with all this sudden free time?'

She gave a puzzled smile. 'Whatever I usually do with my weekend, I suppose.'

'Which is?' he persisted.

'Marcus—er—Mr Maitland,' she corrected hastily.

'Marcus will do,' he told her dryly. 'After all, we're still out of the office,' he qualified.

'Okay,' she agreed slowly. 'But where is all this questioning leading?'

'It isn't leading anywhere.' He grimaced. 'At least—

I wondered if perhaps you would like to have dinner with me this evening?'

Kit became very still, slowly turning her head to look at him, glad that the surprise that must be in her eyes was hidden by her sunglasses. Was Marcus inviting her out on a date? But he couldn't be. Could he...?

'Why?' she finally said bluntly.

'Well, it's logical that you have to eat, and I have to eat, so I thought perhaps we might eat together,' he supplied.

Kit opened her mouth to answer him in the negative, and then closed it again. Logic, as far as she was concerned, had absolutely no place in any suggestion that the two of them have dinner together this evening!

But even so, she was tempted. What would it be like to actually go out for the evening with Marcus? To take her time getting ready for the evening, to be collected by Marcus and swept off to an exclusive restaurant for a meal, possibly even a club later.

She had no doubts that he would prove an interesting and charming companion. Or that she would absolutely love to spend the evening with him. What didn't make any sense was why he was asking her in the first place!

Unless it was just as he had said: he had to eat, she had to eat—and why not eat together?

'If it takes you this long to decide, maybe you should just forget I asked!'

'Maybe we should,' Kit agreed stiffly. 'I was thinking of going to see my parents,' she added lightly as she realised how rude she must have sounded.

'Really?' He gave her an interested look. 'Do they live in London?'

'No. Cornwall,' she replied awkwardly as she realised she was being rude again. 'I thought I would go down by train later this afternoon.'

'That's quite a way.' Marcus nodded. 'I could drive you there, if you would like?'

'Why on earth would you want to—? No,' she amended hastily, not even wanting to give him that particular opening. He was far too curious about her private life already, without trying to wheedle his way into meeting her parents; she could hardly accept such an offer from him without inviting him to stay the weekend too. Something she had absolutely no intention of doing! 'It's much quicker by train,' she dismissed, deliberately turning away to look out of the side window.

'So, no dinner this evening? Either in London or Cornwall,' he persisted.

'I'm afraid not,' she answered with a breeziness she didn't feel.

'What do your parents do in Cornwall?'

She gave him a sharp look. 'Do...?'

'As in work.'

'Oh.' She nodded. 'My mother looks after the house—cottage, really,' she amended. 'And my father paints.' She wished she had never mentioned her parents. And she wouldn't have done if it hadn't seemed like the ideal way of getting out of his dinner invitation without being rude.

'As in walls or canvases?'

'Marcus, I really don't think this is a line of questioning we should be pursuing.' She straightened uncomfortably in her seat.

'Line of questioning? Pursuing?' Marcus was incredulous. 'You sound like a lawyer defending her client. I was only showing an interest, Kit.'

'I know you were.' She sighed, her cheeks blushing warmly. 'I just—canvases. My father paints canvases,' she explained reluctantly.

'Really?' Marcus raised dark brows. 'Do I know him? Is he famous?'

'Would you expect him to be living in a cottage in Cornwall if he was!' Kit responded, knowing that she wasn't being strictly honest. There was plenty of money now for her parents to move to a larger, more comfortable home; they just preferred to stay at the cottage where they had lived since they had first married. 'I believe my father is what is usually known as a starving artist.'

'But not in a garret?' Marcus returned lightly.

'No.' She laughed, relaxing slightly. 'But the cottage is certainly—rustic.' She remembered that, until a few years ago, the cottage hadn't even had running water, her mother having to get water from a well in the garden until they had had the main water supply connected.

'Sounds wonderful.' Marcus smiled.

'It sounds it,' Kit conceded. 'And actually it is. If you don't mind roughing it a bit.' She had enjoyed a completely carefree childhood amongst the rugged hills of Cornwall, roaming for miles; it was what had given her her love of walking.

'I'm ashamed to say I've never tried,' Marcus admitted.

Was he still trying to persuade her into allowing him to drive her to Cornwall?

What would her parents make of him? Her father,

she knew, would find him the complete antithesis of himself, but somehow she still had a feeling that he would like the younger man. As for her mother—she would just be pleased to see Kit with a man, her hints of wishing to be a grandmother having increased during the last year or so.

Which was a very good reason for not giving into Marcus's persuasive tone.

The last thing she needed was her parents thinking she was actually involved with Marcus!

'I'm sorry.' She shook her head firmly. 'The cottage is simply too small to accommodate all four of us.'

'We could share,' he suggested.

'I said my father is an artist—not that he's an advocate of— Well, the fact that he married my mother within weeks of meeting her should tell you something about him,' she amended awkwardly; her parents were far from being prudes, would probably accept the idea if she brought a man home for the weekend. It was Kit who had a problem with it!

Marcus gave an appreciative nod. 'It tells me he's an astute man. They have obviously been married for some time, so I presume it's a happy marriage?'

'Very,' Kit confirmed unhesitantly.

'Then that's all that really matters, isn't it?'

She gave him a searching look. 'Is it?' Somehow it had never actually occurred to her, in light of his own brief relationships with women, that Marcus believed in love and marriage...

'Of course. Look at Desmond,' he reminded her. 'He made two serious errors in his first marriages, and now he's in love with and married to a woman thirty years his junior. He's making a bit of a mess of it at the moment, I grant you, but I have complete confidence in him seeing, before it's too late, what an idiot he's being.'

'Did you tell him as much?' Kit chuckled.

'Of course,' he confirmed unrepentantly. 'He *is* being an idiot. Second to actually finding the woman you love, having a child with that woman has to be the most wonderful experience of any man's life. Wouldn't you say?'

She would, yes. But she wouldn't have thought that Marcus would say so, too...

He gave her a glance, noting her thoughtful expression. 'You just didn't think I would say so, too, did you?' he guessed shrewdly.

Kit glared at him. 'Well, you hardly give the impression that marriage and a family are high on your list of priorities!'

'You have to meet the right woman to even begin to think in that vein.'

And he expected to find that 'right woman' by going out with women like Andrea Revel? Somehow Kit didn't think so.

But if Marcus did, who was she, a complete outsider, to say otherwise? Even if she did love him to distraction!

'I suppose so,' she conceded noncommittally. 'I had rather a disturbed night's sleep, would you mind if I had a little nap now?'

'Just as the conversation was getting interesting...' he murmured speculatively.

'Maybe to you,' she shot back, settling down comfortably in her seat. 'It's a matter of complete indifference to me.'

'Of course it is.'

Kit turned sharply at what she felt was a completely patronizing tone. 'Not every woman wants to get married and have children, you know,' she snapped.

'You do,' he insisted softly.

She gave him a frustrated glare. 'Maybe,' she finally accepted tersely. 'But if Mike Reynolds is an example of what men are like, then I would rather not bother, thank you!'

'He isn't,' Marcus assured her. 'At least, I hope he isn't!' he added frowningly. 'You don't think I'm like Mike Reynolds, do you?'

This conversation had taken an extremely strange turn as far as Kit was concerned—one she would rather not pursue!

'I've never thought about it,' she responded airily.

'I bet you haven't,' he returned, obviously not at all happy with the conversation himself now.

Kit closed her eyes, a little smile playing about her lips, as her last vision of Marcus was a most disgruntled expression as he struggled with the concept of there being any sort of comparison between himself and a man he obviously despised.

Not that there was, of course. But it wouldn't hurt to leave Marcus with that thought, anyway. It was certainly better than discussing her personal life!

As it was she had told him a lot more about herself, and her parents, than she had really intended doing. But, with any luck, that was the end of the subject...

'Sure I can't persuade you into letting me drive you to Cornwall?' Marcus pressed once he had parked his car outside her apartment building.

'Positive.' She pushed open the car door and got out.

'If I get a move on I'll be able to make the afternoon train,' she told him as he got out of the car too in order to take her bag out of the boot.

'This is goodbye, then.' Marcus stood beside her on the pavement.

Kit gave an incredulous laugh. 'Hardly, when I'll be seeing you in the office on Tuesday morning!'

'Not the same,' he said. 'I very much doubt you'll be strolling around the office in a bikini!'

'Very funny!' she replied, not at all happy with the way her cheeks flushed fiery red at his teasing.

'I wasn't trying to be funny, Kit,' he said quietly, dark blue gaze staring intently into hers.

'Well, you succeeded, anyway,' she told him, wishing she could break the intensity of that gaze, but knowing she couldn't, that it was simply beyond her at this moment.

How she loved this man! How she would love to accept his invitation to dinner, to drive her to Cornwall; anything to spend more time with him.

But ultimately she would only end up hurting herself more than she already had; despite the attraction that had flared up between them briefly this weekend, she knew she simply wasn't Marcus's type, and never would be.

'Kit, you have the most amazingly beautiful eyes I have ever seen,' he murmured gruffly, his gaze even more intense. 'Dark and soft, like grey velvet.'

Kit moistened her lips nervously, wishing—

'Don't do that!' he ground out suddenly, his gaze focused on her mouth now. 'Do you have any idea how provocative that is?' he groaned before his head bent and his mouth took fierce possession of hers.

She hadn't, no. But she did now!

Once again she melted as soon as Marcus's lips touched hers, both his hands cradling the sides of her face as he kissed her with searching passion, sipping and tasting, plundering, possessing.

Kit was aware only of Marcus as she clung to him, of the thrust of desire coursing through them both as her fingers tightly gripped the warm strength of his shoulders, of—

'Wow!' came an amused voice. 'Is that really you, Kit?'

Kit pulled sharply away from Marcus as she easily recognized that voice, turning to look at Penny as her flatmate came down the steps of their apartment building, dressed for her usual Saturday afternoon game of tennis with her fiancé, Roger.

'Penny!' Kit greeted lightly, almost afraid to look at Marcus after the desire that had blazed between them so suddenly.

And completely. How was she going to be able to work with Marcus day after day after this, when all she really wanted was to lose herself in his arms, to forget everything else but the fierce attraction they seemed to share?

'Penny…?' Marcus looked at Kit enquiringly.

'My flatmate,' Kit revealed with a certain amount of reluctance, knowing by the slight smile of satisfaction that suddenly curved his lips that Marcus really had nurtured the idea that her flatmate might be male! 'Penny Lyon. Marcus Maitland,' she introduced stiffly, knowing that Penny needed no explanation as to who and what Marcus was.

Although her friend could just be wondering what

Kit was doing kissing her boss out in the middle of the street! Could just be wondering? Penny would no doubt demand the full story as soon as she had Kit on her own again!

The problem with that was that Kit had no idea what the full story was where she and Marcus were concerned. Marcus seemed to be acquiring the habit of just taking her in his arms and kissing her whenever he felt like it. And it would be useless to deny that she responded to those kisses. But was there any more to it than that? As far as Kit was concerned, there was, but she had no idea what Marcus's motivation was.

Except that he seemed to like kissing her...

'I had a feeling that's who you were,' Penny told Marcus as the two of them shook hands. 'You're back early.' She looked enquiringly at Kit. 'I was expecting you to be away the whole weekend...?'

'Change of plan, I'm afraid,' Marcus was the one to answer Penny smoothly. 'We aren't delaying you from an appointment, are we?' he prompted with a pointed look at the tee shirt and the long display of bare leg beneath the shorts Penny was wearing in preparation for her game of tennis.

'Not in the least—but I can take a hint!' Penny replied laughingly.

'My dear, Miss Lyon—Penny?—I can assure you that if I wanted to be alone with Kit then I would just say so,' Marcus said.

'I had a feeling you might,' Penny acknowledged wryly. 'I'll see you later, Kit?'

She gave a thankful shake of her head; she needed to get her own thoughts about this weekend into some sort of order before subjecting herself to Penny's obvious interest in finding her kissing Marcus! 'I'm going to see my parents this afternoon,' she explained economically. 'I'll be back late tomorrow.'

'I'll look forward to it,' Penny assured her. 'Nice to meet you, Mr Maitland,' she added warmly.

'Marcus,' he insisted. 'Nice to meet you too, Penny.'

A smile remained on his lips only long enough for Penny to get into her car and drive away with a friendly wave of her hand.

At which time he looked down at Kit with accusing eyes. 'Yesterday you deliberately let me think your flatmate was a man.'

'I did not,' Kit defended. 'I simply didn't say one way or the other.'

'Exactly,' he sighed impatiently. 'But you knew I had assumed it was a man.'

'I knew no such thing!' she denied calmly. 'If you chose to think that, then—'

'Kit, why are we arguing again?' He winced. 'The last thing I want to do at this moment is argue with you!'

One look at his face, at the glitter of intent in his blue gaze as it fixed on the pouting softness of her mouth, was enough to tell her what he did want to do with her!

But they simply couldn't continue to behave in this way, not if they were to continue working together. A break away from each other, to get things back into perspective, was exactly what they needed.

'I really do have to go, Marcus,' she told him after a glance at her wrist-watch. 'My train leaves in just under an hour,' she added pointedly.

He drew in a sharply disapproving breath at her haste. 'I had better let you go, then, hadn't I?'

That urge to ask him to come to Cornwall with her after all returned with a vengeance, the words actually on the tip of her tongue. A tongue she bit with sharp purpose, deliberately saying nothing.

'Fine,' Marcus said abruptly. 'Thank you for your help this weekend, Kit. I appreciate it.'

She gave a rueful smile. 'I don't think, with the situation that developed with Mike Reynolds, that I was much of an asset!' More of a liability, really!

He shook his head. 'Forget Mike Reynolds,' he dismissed. 'Desmond was the main reason for going this weekend, and he liked you very much.'

Her eyes widened. 'He did?'

'Oh, yes,' Marcus confirmed. 'I believe you had a word with him yourself before we left…?'

Actually, she had had several words with their host before leaving earlier, having decided she would probably never see Desmond Hayes again, so she might as well tell him exactly what she thought about his separation from his wife, and the reason for it. But she hadn't realised he had mentioned that conversation to Marcus…

She gave a self-conscious grimace. 'Did he say that I had?'

'He did.' Marcus nodded approvingly. 'On your advice, he's going to call Jackie this afternoon and hopefully meet up with her to discuss having half a dozen kids or so!'

'Half a dozen—!' Kit gasped. 'I don't think I said anything about six children…!'

Marcus grinned. 'Whatever you said, it was the right

thing. I have a feeling that Desmond and I are going to have quite a healthy business relationship in future.'

Then Kit had fulfilled her role as his personal assistant. Because that was all she was to him, no matter how much she might wish it were otherwise.

'What did you say to him to make him act so quickly?' Marcus looked at her searchingly.

'I think it was something along the lines of life being too short, and love being too hard to find to let it go because sometimes the commitment of that love might frighten us.'

Marcus's gaze became guarded. 'You sound like someone who has had experience of the emotion…?'

Only as regards her own parents. If her mother hadn't been so determined to be with the man she loved, if her father hadn't been that man, then Kit knew she would never have been born.

'Maybe,' she answered noncommittally.

Marcus stepped back from her. 'I'll let you get off, then.'

'Yes,' she agreed, knowing that one of them had to make a move. But also realising that neither of them seemed to want to do that. 'I have to catch my train,' she reminded Marcus firmly, giving him a quick smile before turning to run lightly up the stairs to open the door to her apartment building, determined not to look back, knowing it could be her undoing if she did.

All the time feeling as if she were leaving the biggest part of her standing outside on the pavement…

CHAPTER ELEVEN

'GOOD weekend?'

Kit looked up at the sound of Lewis Grant's voice. 'Not particularly,' she answered honestly.

'Oh?' He leant against the side of her desk, obviously in no hurry to go to his own office down the corridor.

She put aside the papers she had been working on for the last half an hour to give him her full attention. 'Those sort of house parties aren't really my scene.'

Lewis grinned understandingly. 'Lots of glitz and glamour on the surface—and knives being wielded behind the backs!'

'Something like that,' she said noncommittally.

To be perfectly honest, she really wasn't quite with it this bright and sunny Tuesday morning, was wishing herself anywhere but here.

Luckily, Marcus hadn't arrived in the office yet. Kit usually arrived half an hour or so before he did so that she could deal with any urgent correspondence and put it on his desk.

Lewis chuckled. 'I quite enjoy them, actually. But I can understand why some people wouldn't,' he sympathized.

Especially someone like her, Kit silently added. Prim Miss McGuire, the PA from No-Nonsenseville, was back in place this morning; after the intimacy that seemed to have developed between herself and Marcus over the weekend, she had thought it for the best. Not that she for a moment thought she would have Marcus chasing her around the desk at every opportunity; no, prim Miss McGuire was for her own protection—from her feelings towards Marcus!

'It was okay.' Kit returned her attention to Lewis.

'Any success with Desmond Hayes?' he enquired with interest.

'Not particularly,' she returned. 'I'm really not being a lot of help this morning, am I?'

'Probably tired after the weekend.' Lewis smiled understandingly.

'I still don't understand why Marcus didn't take me with him,' he mused. 'But there you are. I suppose—'

'Don't you have any work to do, Lewis?' Marcus barked as he came into Kit's office, dressed in one of the dark business suits and snowy white shirts he usually wore to work, briefcase in hand. 'Kit,' he added in tight acknowledgement.

'M—Mr Maitland,' she hastily corrected her initial slip of going to call him by his first name.

'Come through to my office, will you?' he instructed her curtly, his gaze cold as he looked at Lewis. 'Anything I can do for you?' he grated.

'Nothing at all,' the younger man said easily, not seeming too concerned by Marcus's mood.

'Then don't let us keep you,' Marcus responded, looking straight at Kit as he held his office door open.

Kit got up slowly to move across the room and enter Marcus's office, very aware of his brooding presence as he closed the door behind them with a firm click.

She turned to look at him. 'Don't you think you were a little rude to Lewis just now?'

'Was I?' he replied unconcernedly. 'I'm sure he'll get over it.' He placed his briefcase down beside his desk before sitting down in the high-backed leather chair behind it, resting his elbows on the desk as he looked at her over the top of the pyramid of his fingers. 'Why the hell are you dressed like that again?' he suddenly exclaimed.

Kit felt herself pale as she stared at him through her heavy, dark-rimmed glasses, her breath catching in her throat, in no doubt as to Marcus's annoyance; his face was grim, a nerve pulsing in his jaw.

'I thought it best,' she offered, moistening her lips with the tip of her tongue.

'And I thought I warned you about doing that,' Marcus snapped, his gaze focused on her mouth now.

Kit instantly clamped her lips together, the colour flooding back into her cheeks as she remembered what had happened the last time she had moistened her lips in that way in front of Marcus.

'Well?' he prompted harshly.

She flinched at his attack. 'Well, what…?'

He rose quickly to his feet, as if his mood was too big to be contained in a sitting position. 'Exactly what sort of man do you think I am? Don't answer that. The fact that you're back to wearing that ridiculous disguise tells me exactly what you think of me!'

What she thought of him? It was herself, the love she felt towards him, that she was trying to protect!

'I don't see how,' she said wearily.

'No?' He moved out from behind his desk to pace the room restlessly. 'I think I should warn you that I don't care for being put in the same category as your last boss!'

'Mike Reynolds…?' Kit repeated dazedly. 'But I—' She broke off, frowning across at Marcus now. 'I never for a moment thought that you were in the least like him…' But she could hardly explain that it was herself she was trying to protect by once again becoming Prim Miss McGuire from No-Nonsenseville!

'Oh, give me a break, Kit,' Marcus came back. 'You've already told me exactly why you started wearing those ridiculous glasses and unflattering clothes. The fact that you're back to wearing them today implies you still think you need some sort of protection from my obviously unwanted advances!'

What would he say if she were to tell him that what she really wanted to do—not just now, but all the time!—was throw herself into his arms and have him make love to her? Here. Now.

'And just when did you intend telling me about your father?' Marcus continued.

Kit blinked at this sudden change of subject. 'My father…?'

Marcus nodded tersely. 'Your father is Tom McGuire!' he accused.

'I know who he is,' she answered levelly.

'So do I—now.'

Kit looked at him curiously. 'How do you know?'

Marcus's mouth twisted self-derisively. 'Because I have one of his paintings hanging on my apartment wall. I sat there in my apartment all weekend—'

'We didn't come back to town until Saturday afternoon,' Kit reminded him.

Marcus gave her a scathing look. 'I sat there all weekend,' he repeated, 'when I suddenly realised that the painting I was staring at was by Tom McGuire. It was just too much of a coincidence for it not to have been painted by your father!'

Kit didn't even attempt to deny the connection— how could she? 'His paintings are considered a very sound investment nowadays—'

'I didn't buy the painting as an investment!' he replied. 'I've owned it for twelve or thirteen years now.'

She nodded. 'It's only the last ten years he's suddenly become quite famous—'

'Quite famous!' Marcus echoed with an incredulous note in his voice. 'Each of his paintings are worth thousands of pounds!'

'And do you know how old he was when he suddenly became famous?' she returned exasperatedly. 'Sixty-two,' she continued without waiting for him to answer. 'Before that he and my mother lived on the little they could make selling the odd painting and some of the vegetables my mother grows—in—in their huge—garden.' Her voice began to falter as the façade she had kept up so far this morning slowly began to crumble and disintegrate. 'It was a—a happy life,' she defended huskily. 'But it certainly wasn't—wasn't—' She simply couldn't go on any more, her throat clogged with the tears she was trying so hard not to shed.

She had tried so hard to appear normal this morning, to come to work as normal, to sit at her desk as normal, even to carry out this ridiculous conversation with Marcus as normal—when in reality her whole world felt as if it were falling apart. Every certainty, every stability in her life, suddenly no longer seemed that way...

*   *   *

She had travelled down to Cornwall on Saturday, totally ignorant of the bombshell that was about to be dropped on her.

'Kit!' her mother cried out excitedly, absolutely thrilled to see her getting out of the taxi, running over to hug her, and then promptly bursting into tears.

'Hey…' Kit said gently once she had paid off the taxi, looking affectionately at her tall, slender, still-beautiful mother.

Heather McGuire had been a noted beauty in her youth, with her long auburn hair and classical features. She was still a very striking woman.

She linked her arm with Kit's as the two of them strolled over to the cottage. 'I'm just so pleased to see you.' She beamed. 'Your father will be too,' she added with certainty.

And he was, taking Kit up in his arms and hugging her.

He was tall and handsome, his hair and beard snowy white now; his blue eyes twinkled at her merrily as he said, 'You're looking lovelier than ever, Kit; new boyfriend?'

'No,' she laughingly denied.

He arched white brows. 'Still hankering after that handsome boss of yours?'

'For all the good it's doing me,' she confessed, knowing she never had been able to keep secrets from her father.

'Come along in and let's all have a glass of wine before dinner,' her mother suggested happily, her tears dried now.

Kit hung back as her mother went off to get the glasses for their wine, looking concernedly at her father. 'What's wrong with Mummy?'

'Wrong?'

'Wrong,' Kit insisted, very aware of the fact that her father's voice sounded forced, that his eyes weren't quite meeting hers, or in fact twinkling any more.

'Why, nothing, darling—'

'Daddy,' she rebuked gently. 'I'm not a child any more, you know.'

'I do know.' He sighed wistfully. 'Long gone are the days when I could—'

'Daddy, please,' she encouraged, definitely knowing there was something wrong now from the way he was prevaricating.

Not that her mother wasn't always overjoyed to see her; she just didn't usually cry over it, had accepted long ago that Kit worked and lived in London, that she would come down every four to six weeks to see them. It had, in fact, only been three weeks since she'd last visited, so her mother's emotional outburst just now seemed totally out of character.

Her father hugged her to his side. 'We'll discuss it over dinner, all right, Pumpkin?' he told her gruffly.

No, it wasn't all right, but she knew her father too well to try and push him; he would explain when he was ready and not before.

And he had explained, both he and her mother...

But it wasn't an explanation she intended sharing with Marcus now, here in his office.

His anger this morning was one thing, something, she could deal with; his sympathy would be something else entirely!

'Which painting is it?' she asked, recovering her composure.

'"Tempest",' Marcus revealed. 'The young girl on the rocks? It's you, isn't it?'

'Yes,' she confirmed, knowing exactly which painting he was referring to, of a young girl, red hair swirling behind her, as she sat on the rocks looking out at a storm-tossed sea.

Kit had been thirteen when her father had painted her, no longer a child, but not quite a woman yet, either. That winter, some days she had been so angry with herself, the world, everything, that her only escape had been to go to the beach near their cottage, sit on the rocks, uncaring of how wet she became, and just allow herself to become a part of the stormy sea.

Her father had seen her there one day and captured her on canvas.

And it was incredible to think that Marcus had owned that particular painting for all this time...!

She gave a warm smile. 'It's probably now worth a hundred times what you paid for it.'

Intensity flared in the dark depths of Marcus's eyes. 'I have no intention of selling it.'

'It's a very sound investment.'

'I told you, I didn't buy it as an investment!' he came back impatiently.

'I was only—'

'Kit, I know what you were "only",' he cut in forcefully. 'And I don't appreciate it!'

Kit could see that he didn't. But if she were to have any pride left at all she had to try and keep up the barriers between them. And if that meant alienating Marcus, then that was what she would have to do.

Besides, she had other, much more pressing things to think about at the moment...

She met his gaze unblinkingly. 'I'm not sure this is the right moment to ask this—but do you think I could have a little longer for lunch today?'

'A little longer—!' Marcus looked momentarily nonplussed by this sudden change of subject, and then his gaze narrowed speculatively. 'Why?'

Her eyes widened. 'I don't think that is any of your business,' she told him stiffly. 'Of course, if it's going to interfere with anything here, then I—'

'It isn't,' he responded flatly. 'As it happens Lewis and I have to go to a meeting early this afternoon. I merely wondered if you were seeing someone for lunch.'

Kit felt perplexed now. This was the first she'd heard of any meeting arranged for this afternoon. 'Again, I don't really think that is any of your business...'

'You're asking me for extra time off—'

'I'll work later this evening to make up for it!' she came back heatedly, hands clenched at her sides. The extended lunch break she was requesting really wasn't up for negotiation—it was too important for that!

Besides, in the last six months she hadn't been off sick once, had never asked for any time off other than her allowed holiday. As far as she was concerned Marcus was being totally unreasonable.

'That won't be necessary,' he told her icily.

It might not be necessary, but she was going to do it anyway. No matter what the outcome of her lunch-time appointment...

It wasn't a meeting she was looking forward to, and that was without Marcus being so difficult about it.

'Kit?' Marcus's voice softened slightly, his gaze searching now on the paleness of her face.

She swallowed hard, straightening defensively. 'Will that be all, Mr Maitland?'

'No, it will not be all, damn it!' he barked once more, taking a determined step towards her to grasp her by her upper arms, once again taking in her businesslike appearance with obvious displeasure. 'You look totally ridiculous in that get-up.'

Her mouth tightened at his deliberately insulting tone. 'Thank you!'

'You know very well what I mean!'

'Do I?' Kit eyed him challengingly, very aware that she was playing with fire, but unable, at that moment—later might be a different matter!—to resist.

Besides, the mere touch of his hands, even when he was bad-tempered like this, had rekindled her yearning to be in his arms, to know the thrill of his lips on hers, to lose herself in the passion the two of them seemed to ignite in each other.

Some of that yearning must have shown in her eyes, because Marcus, giving a groan low in this throat, bent his head and his lips moved to possess hers.

Kit returned the kiss as all of the emotions of the last few days washed over her, losing herself in the fierceness of the desire that flared so intensely between them. Marcus's arms were about her now as he moulded the length of her body against his, making her fully aware of his arousal.

He felt so good to touch, his back hard and muscled against her restlessly caressing hands beneath his suit jacket, his warmth heating her body, her breasts aching heavily, her nipples hard and ultra-sensitive against his chest.

She had been waiting for this man all her life, it

seemed; that young girl on the rocks in her father's painting, who'd dreamed of the man she might one day fall in love with, who during the years since had waited for that man to appear—only to have him do so now, in the guise of Marcus Maitland.

How she loved this man! How she longed to just lie down beside him and make love with him, to become lost in the—

Kit looked up at Marcus unseeing as she suddenly found herself thrust away from him. 'What—?'

'Come in!' Marcus called out, his gaze not leaving hers.

Someone—Lewis, it seemed as the other man opened the door and entered the office—had knocked on the door, a knock Kit hadn't heard in her total awareness of Marcus. Her cheeks blushed scarlet as she saw the knowing look harden Marcus's eyes.

'I have the papers here I thought you should look at,' Lewis told Marcus slowly, obviously sensing the tension in the room as he looked at the two of them questioningly. 'But if you're busy, I can always come back later…?' He seemed aware that he had interrupted something—although, hopefully, not actually what that was!

'I was just leaving, anyway,' Kit assured him, deliberately avoiding meeting Marcus's eyes as she turned away.

'Kit…?' he called out as she reached the open door.

She stiffened, turning slowly back to look at him, wishing he would just let her escape.

'That extended lunch break you requested…'

'Yes?' she replied warily, very aware of Lewis as he

studied the papers in his hand in an effort to try looking as if he weren't listening to their conversation.

'It's fine with me,' Marcus told her.

She drew in a sharp breath, wanting to make a cutting reply back, but unwilling to add to Lewis's curiosity by doing so. 'Thank you,' she accepted tersely, at last able to escape to the relative sanctuary of her own office.

She had known it was going to be difficult to come in today and just continue working with Marcus, as if nothing had changed between them over the weekend. That was one of the reasons—despite what Marcus might have thought!—she had returned to her guise as efficient, prim Miss McGuire. But the fact that Marcus had kissed her in the way that he had showed he had no intention of forgetting the intimacy they had shared over the weekend. How much longer, Kit wondered miserably, would she be able to continue working for him…?

CHAPTER TWELVE

'Kɪᴛ…isn't it?'

Kit stared at the woman sitting behind the wide oak desk, hoping the trembling of her legs wasn't visible as she stood on the thickly carpeted floor in front of that desk. The last thing she wanted was to appear in the least lacking in self-confidence.

'You asked to see me,' Catherine Grainger reminded at Kit's continued silence.

Yes, she had. She had telephoned Catherine Grainger's office first thing this morning; lunchtime was the only time the other woman was available to see her. But now that Kit was here she had no idea what she was going to say to her!

Her hands were clammy, she felt alternately hot and then cold—and she seemed to have forgotten how to talk!

The older woman gave an impatient sigh. 'I'm sure my secretary has already explained to you that I'm very busy today, so if you have something to say then I really wish you would get on with it—'

'My name is Catherine McGuire!' The words burst out starkly before Kit even had time to formulate them in her mind.

Catherine Grainger remained unmoved, her face hard and unyielding. 'I believe my secretary did mention that was the name of my one o'clock appointment, yes.'

'Doesn't that name mean anything to you?'

Catherine Grainger lifted elegant shoulders in dismissal. 'Should it?' she returned coolly.

Kit drew in a sharp breath, her face deathly pale now, her hands clenched tightly into fists at her sides. 'I'm your granddaughter!'

Catherine Grainger continued to look at her, her expression impassive, not showing so much as a flicker of her eyelids to demonstrate that what Kit had said meant anything to her.

Kit stared back, still amazed that this woman, so cold, so hard, could possibly be her mother's mother!

She had always known who her grandmother was, of course, had been told the truth by her parents at a very young age, after she had asked them why she didn't have grandparents like the other children at school. But actually coming face to face with her the previous weekend, knowing exactly who and what she was, had been something of a shock.

A shock, now she had been told the truth, Catherine Grainger didn't seem to share...

Catherine gave a gesture of acknowledgement. 'Yes,' she agreed.

It wasn't a question, or an exclamation, just a simple statement of fact!

Kit was startled. 'You already knew...?'

'I guessed. You look remarkably like your mother did at this age,' she explained unemotionally.

'You haven't even seen my mother since she was nineteen!' Kit exclaimed, stunned beyond measure that this woman had known all the time exactly who she was. And had said nothing...

'True,' Catherine Granger confirmed. 'But you're

still very like her to look at. The likeness was enough for me to—ask certain questions, in order to find out exactly who you were.'

Kit's eyes widened. 'Of whom?'

'Does that really matter?'

'What questions did you ask?' Kit persisted.

'Your surname was enough to tell me all that I needed to know.' Her grandmother's top lip turned back scornfully.

'And yet you said nothing?' Kit said incredulously.

Catherine Grainger's eyes narrowed icily. 'What was there for me to say? So you're the daughter of Heather and that man—'

'That man is my father!' Kit interjected. 'And he has a name. Tom McGuire,' she announced proudly.

Her grandmother's mouth thinned. 'He's old enough to be Heather's father, and your grandfather!'

Kit stared at her disbelievingly. 'And is that the only reason you objected to their relationship all those years ago? The reason you made my mother choose between the two of you?'

Heather had explained to her daughter that her own mother didn't approve of her choice of husband, that it had come to a choice between the two, and that Tom had easily won.

Having met Catherine Grainger at the weekend, and looking at her now, Kit could easily understand why Heather had chosen to be with the man she loved, and who loved her, rather than this cold, unemotional woman. What Kit couldn't understand was why Catherine had forced Heather to make that choice in the first place...

'Isn't that reason enough?' Catherine came back derisively.

'Not to me, no!' Kit denied.

Catherine gave a humourless laugh. 'I don't really think this is any of your business, do you?'

'None of my—!' Kit gasped disbelievingly. 'What sort of woman are you?'

Those grey eyes—like Kit's own, only hers were warm as velvet rather than cold as ice!—hardened glacially. 'Heather was nineteen years old, hardly more than a child herself—what did she know about love?'

'Enough for that love to have lasted twenty-eight years!' Kit told her grandmother triumphantly.

Catherine looked unimpressed. 'They're still together, then?'

'Of course they're still together!' Kit had wondered how she was going to feel when she confronted this woman today, but now she knew exactly how she felt—furiously angry! This was Catherine's own daughter they were talking about, a child this woman had presumably nurtured until she was nineteen years old. And yet, Catherine could have been talking about a stranger.

Catherine grimaced. 'More from luck than judgement, I'm sure.'

Kit could feel her emotions building. 'What absolute rubbish! If anything my parents love each other more now than they did twenty-eight years ago.'

'Love!' the other woman scorned.

Kit had once asked Heather why she hadn't tried to see her mother over the years, to try and make up the quarrel between them, to show Catherine that years later she was still happy with the man of her choice.

Her mother had looked bleakly unhappy as she had assured Kit that would never be possible.

Looking at Catherine's expression of contempt just at the mention of the word love, Kit could now understand her mother's reticence. Heather had already been hurt once; why put herself through the risk of a second rejection…?

'Yes—love,' Kit told her grandmother heavily. 'Something you obviously know nothing about!'

Kit had come here today because she had felt compelled to do so, because after talking with her parents at the weekend, and knowing who this woman was, she felt she owed it to Catherine.

'And you know absolutely nothing about me, Kit McGuire!' her grandmother spat the words.

'Then tell me! Explain to me why it is a mother disowns her own daughter, doesn't even see her for the next twenty-eight years, just because she dared to fall in love with a man her mother doesn't approve of! Because I certainly don't understand it. My mother would never do that to me,' Kit added with absolute certainty.

She didn't care about this for herself, had lived without a grandmother for the last twenty-six years, was sure she could live without one for the rest of her life. But she cared for her mother's sake…

Catherine gave a cynical laugh. 'No, I don't suppose innocently trusting Heather ever would.'

The heat flooded Kit's cheeks as she heard the contempt in Catherine's voice. 'My mother is seriously ill! She could die,' she explained in a pained voice, still too shocked by that knowledge herself to be able to soften or lessen the terrible enormity of what her parents had told her over the weekend.

Her mother had begun to have headaches a few months ago, which had become worse as time went on. A visit to a doctor was followed by one to a specialist, who diagnosed that those headaches were being caused by a brain tumour. A tumour that needed to be operated on straight away in order for Heather to stand any chance of living out the year.

Kit had cried brokenly when told the news, absolutely devastated at the seriousness of her mother's illness. But as far as she could see, that same news had elicited very little reaction from Catherine Grainger.

A nerve pulsed briefly in her grandmother's creamy cheek, there was a flicker of something in her eyes, though it was too brief for Kit to be able to tell what it was. But other than that, Catherine gave no outward response to the announcement.

'Did you hear me?' Kit snapped angrily. 'I said—'

'I heard you,' the older woman cut in softly.

'And?'

Catherine's chin lifted slightly. 'Exactly what is the nature of Heather's illness?'

'She has a brain tumour,' Kit told her frankly. 'They're going to operate on Thursday, but—' She broke off as her voice trembled emotionally. 'They're operating on Thursday,' she repeated flatly once she had herself back under control.

'Who is?' Catherine demanded.

'Does that really matter?' Kit sighed heavily. 'Don't worry, my father now has enough money to pay for the best, and that's what my mother has.'

Catherine stood up, looking haughtily down her nose at Kit. 'Does Heather know you've come to see me?'

'No,' Kit confirmed. 'In fact, my mother has no idea I've even met you.'

'I see.' Her grandmother breathed out slowly. 'Well, now that you've told me, what do you want me to do about it?'

Kit stared at her incredulously. 'Isn't it obvious? I thought you would want to know. Thought I owed it to you to tell you. So that—so that—'

'So that Heather and I can have some grand emotional reconciliation before her operation?' Catherine Grainger guessed. 'I hardly think so, Kit.'

Kit didn't understand her grandmother, couldn't relate to her at all. 'Why not?' she asked hesitantly.

Catherine stood ramrod straight before her, tall, elegant and imposing in a navy blue business suit and white silk blouse. 'Heather made her choice twenty-eight years ago. I no longer have a daughter.' Her expression hardened as she looked at Kit. 'Or a granddaughter. Even one apparently named after me.'

Kit was shocked into retaliation. 'Don't worry, I have absolutely no wish to be your granddaughter, either! In fact, I've done what I came here to do. Said what I came here to say. So now I can leave. Except...' She paused before turning to walk to the door.

'Yes?' Catherine replied stiffly.

Kit gave her a pitying glance. 'I would hate to be you, with no love in my life, no one who cares for me, or for me to care for. Oh, you're obviously very wealthy.' She looked around at the expensive furnishings of Catherine's office, evidence of her success in her business life. At the sacrifice of all else... 'But by being the way that you are, so hard and unforgiving, you've missed out on so much.'

'Having you as my granddaughter being one of them, I suppose?' Catherine shot back.

'Not at all,' Kit answered levelly. 'My mother is such a lovely woman, so undeserving of—of you, or her illness!'

Silver brows rose over cold grey eyes. 'Have you quite finished?'

Kit took a steadying breath. 'Yes, I've finished.'

'In that case—' Catherine looked quite deliberately in the appointment book on her desk top '—I have another meeting in two minutes.' She dismissed Kit with a wave of her hand.

'You really are very sad,' Kit finished.

'And you have taken up enough of my time for one day!' Catherine slammed back.

'So I have,' Kit accepted, adding nothing more, but turning on her heel and walking out of the office, closing the door carefully behind her.

She managed to stay calm as she walked down the corridor and into the lift, determined to hold onto her emotions until she was well away from here.

Away from Catherine Grainger. Her grandmother...

She didn't care for herself, had lived all these years without a grandmother, could live the rest of her life without one.

But what she didn't understand was how a mother could behave in that way.

Even knowing of Heather's illness, of the operation she would go through on Thursday, Catherine seemingly had no forgiveness in her, no softening of the resolve that had made her a stranger to her own daughter for the last twenty-eight years.

The only positive thing about this morning, as far as Kit could see, was that Heather knew nothing about her visit to Catherine, or of her mother's lack of compassion—

Kit came to a sudden halt as she stepped out of the lift and found herself face to face with both Marcus and Lewis.

A stunned Lewis.

And a *furious* Marcus!

CHAPTER THIRTEEN

'I HAVE another meeting in two minutes,' Catherine Grainger had told her so dismissively a few minutes earlier.

Obviously, that appointment was with Marcus and Lewis!

It had to be. It was just too much of a coincidence for it not to be.

'What the hell are you doing here?' Marcus exploded, apparently no more pleased to see Kit than she was to see him.

Kit moistened dry lips, but as quickly stopped the instinctive movement as she saw Marcus's eyes narrow ominously. 'I—I—' What could she say in answer to that question? How could she explain what had just taken place in Catherine Grainger's office?

'Would you leave us for a few minutes, Lewis?' Marcus instructed.

This was awful. Kit's worst nightmare. But how could she have known—how could she have guessed? Catherine Grainger hadn't said anything about *Marcus* being her next appointment, and Kit hadn't had any idea about whom he was going to meet today.

Which was curious in itself...

Of course, as Marcus's PA normally she dealt with all his appointments, had never known him to make his own arrangements like this before—with Catherine Grainger, of all people.

'Of course,' Lewis agreed, a little flustered, shooting Kit a questioning glance before moving away to stand over by the glass front doors of the building.

Marcus grasped hold of Kit's arm and pulled her away from the lifts and round the corner of the reception area, away from the curious eyes of both Lewis and the receptionist.

He released her from his grasp. 'Well?' he demanded forcefully, blue eyes boring into hers.

She swallowed hard. 'I—I—'

'You lied to me, Kit,' he said quietly, that nerve pulsing angrily in the rigid line of his tightly clenched jaw.

Her eyes widened in dismay as she realised what he must think: having found her here, he'd concluded that *she* must be passing on information to Catherine Grainger about his business transactions.

And who could blame him for thinking that? She *was* here. Clearly on her way down from Catherine's office. What other possible conclusion could Marcus come to but this?

Even so, she had to at least try to defend herself.

'No, Marcus, I didn't—'

'Oh, yes,' he interrupted, 'you did. Why, Kit? That's what I don't understand.' His expression was bleak. 'What did I ever do to you to make you do such a thing to me? Or are you just paying me back for the way Mike Reynolds behaved towards you—' he looked at her searchingly '—on the premise that all bosses are bastards?'

'But they aren't! You aren't!' Kit told him desperately. 'Marcus, you can't really believe I would behave like that? Do something so vicious?' She looked at him pleadingly, tears swimming in the smoky depths of her eyes.

'I don't know what to think any more,' he admitted, running an agitated hand through the dark thickness of his hair. 'And I really don't have the time to discuss this just now, either,' he said after a glance at his wrist-watch. 'But we will discuss it later, Kit. At length, in fact.'

Kit was sure that they would. But admitting to him now that Catherine Grainger was her grandmother wasn't likely to convince him that she wasn't his disloyal employee, now was it?

What a mess. A complete, unmitigated mess!

She looked at the floor. 'Maybe it would be better if I just went back to the office, packed up my things, and left...?' She really didn't want to do that, but in the circumstances she couldn't see what option she had.

'Oh, no, Kit,' Marcus assured her. 'You don't get away that easily. I want to know the who, what, when, where and why—most of all why!'

And she didn't have answers to any of those questions!

'I have to go,' Marcus announced after another glance at his watch. 'But I shouldn't be too long,' he warned. 'In fact, I'm no longer sure this meeting is even necessary.'

Kit gave him a questioning look, a look he totally ignored as he walked away to join Lewis, the expression on his face more than indicative of his mood.

And who could blame him? Kit thought sadly.

Lewis shot her another enquiring glance as she walked past the two men on their way to the lift, but it was one Kit chose to ignore, looking neither left nor right as she walked across the lobby, her head held high. Even though tears threatened to fall at any moment.

Her meeting with Catherine Grainger, in order to tell her of her mother's illness, had been a complete waste of time. Walking straight into Marcus on her way out had been nothing short of a disaster.

She had never felt so totally miserable in her life before, felt sure that Marcus, when he did return to the office, would demand answers, and when he got none would tell her to leave and never come back.

What other choice did he have? She looked guilty. Her behaviour appeared guilty. The fact that she wasn't was totally irrelevant.

Except…if she wasn't the one guilty of betraying Marcus, then who was?

'I thought I told you to stay at the office!' Marcus barked as soon as Kit opened her apartment door to him later that afternoon.

She knew exactly what he had said, appreciated why he had said it, but there was no way, having returned to the office, that she had been able to just sit there and wait for him to come back and sack her. So she had packed the few personal things she had about her office, left her set of keys on Marcus's desk, and made her weary way home.

She had known, after what he'd said earlier, that Marcus wouldn't let her get away that easily. But she'd decided that she would rather their confrontation took place on her home ground rather than in the formality of Marcus's office.

At least if he dismissed her here he couldn't actually have her thrown out of the building!

'I know what you told me, Marcus.' Blow 'Mr Maitland', she decided heavily. 'But I could see little point in my remaining there.'

Waiting for him to fire her!

'What's in the box?' she prompted as she noted the flat cardboard box he had beneath one arm.

'The rest of your things,' he stated flatly. 'Nothing of any importance. Aren't you going to invite me inside, Kit?'

She sighed, her hand clinging tightly to the door. 'Is there any point in my doing that?'

'Every point.' He gave a terse inclination of his head. 'Unless you want to have this conversation overheard by some of your neighbours?'

She would rather not be having this conversation at all, but, as she had known when she had left the office so precipitously that Marcus wouldn't just leave things as they were, it was a conversation she had been expecting to happen.

Even though she was no more prepared for it now than she had been earlier!

'Yes, do come in.' She stepped back to let him pass, almost able to feel the chill he emanated as he swept past her into the sitting-room beyond.

Kit followed more slowly. In order to put off the dreaded moment? There was little point in doing that. Reluctance to hear all the verbal abuse she was sure Marcus was going to rain down on her head? Possibly, she allowed. But mostly it was because she couldn't bear that look of contempt in his eyes now when he looked at her.

The cardboard box he had carried in now sat recriminatingly in the middle of the coffee table that stood in front of the sofa. Marcus looked tall and imposing as he stood in front of the unlit fireplace.

Unable to look at the accusation in his face any longer, Kit moved to pick up the box, opening its lid, the tears welling up as she looked at its contents: the fluffy yellow toy chick that had resided on top of her computer screen, her collection of pens—including the pot she kept them in!—that had stood on top of her desk, and lastly the card that had accompanied some flowers Marcus had sent to her a couple of months ago after he had concluded a very successful business deal, claiming her hard work had contributed immensely to that success. 'With many thanks, Marcus Maitland', the card read—as if she knew anyone else called Marcus, anyway!

'Nothing of any importance,' he had commented about the contents of the box. And perhaps to him that card wasn't important, just a thank you to an employee for a job well done, but Kit had kept it for secret sentimental reasons: it was something that Marcus had sent to her.

As she looked at it now that card brought her only pain.

The hand holding that card trembled slightly as she looked up at him. 'Didn't this mean anything to you?'

'Catherine Grainger wasn't involved in that particular deal. As you well know.'

Grainger International had never been interested in the acquisition of hotels, and this particular deal had involved Marcus buying a small chain of them, very exclusive, very up-market.

'I don't suppose there's any point in my saying I didn't know?' She sighed, putting the card back in the box and firmly closing the lid.

His mouth twisted scornfully. 'No point at all.'

'I didn't think so.'

'I'm glad to see you've discarded the disguise,' Marcus said sardonically.

'It wasn't a disguise,' Kit protested, having changed into denims and white tee shirt on arriving home earlier, her hair loose about her shoulders, contact lenses in place now instead of her dark-framed glasses. She was dressed in stark contrast to Marcus's formality, the dark business suit, snowy white shirt and grey tie he still wore.

'No?' Marcus taunted sceptically. 'I wonder…'

Kit was needled. 'I think that at the moment you're adding two and two together and coming up with six!'

'Am I?' he countered. 'Then why don't you enlighten me as to what two and two really add up to?' He moved over to the armchair, sitting down to look up at her with expectancy.

What was the point when he had already judged her, tried her, and found her guilty?

She took a deep breath. 'I know meeting me as I came down from a meeting with Catherine Grainger looked bad—'

'"Looked bad"?' he repeated, sitting forward in the chair. 'It *was* bad, Kit,' he stated. 'And damning!'

'But only if—if—' She broke off.

She had decided, as she'd waited for Marcus to turn up on her doorstep, that she had no choice but to tell him the truth about her relationship with Catherine—mainly on the basis that her grandmother could well have already told him that, anyway!—and the real reason for which Kit had been to see her. But actually doing it, she was discovering, was something else entirely.

Once Kit had admitted to Marcus her connection with Catherine, she would then have to go on and tell him about her own mother, about how ill she was, about how Kit had pleaded with Catherine to go and see her daughter, to heal the breach between them before—before—

The seriousness of her mother's illness was still so raw to her, so devastating, that if she once began to talk about it she knew she would start crying and never stop!

Kit swallowed hard, her throat already clogged with tears. 'What did Catherine Grainger tell you about my visit to her?'

Marcus gave a humourless smile. 'You really think I asked her?'

Kit's eyes widened incredulously. 'Are you telling me that you didn't?'

'Of course I didn't!' He stood up, his size seeming to fill the room. 'Isn't it bad enough that my PA has been passing the woman confidential information, without giving her the satisfaction of gloating over it?' His eyes were so dark now they looked almost black.

'But—but—didn't she mention it either?' Kit gasped, having been sure that Catherine would very much enjoy telling Marcus about Kit's visit, if not the actual reason.

'No.'

Kit stared at Marcus, not quite open-mouthed, but not far from it. 'Are you telling me that the two of you went through the whole of your meeting without so much as mentioning the fact that I had been there a few minutes earlier?'

'I'm not telling you anything any more, Kit,' Marcus grated. 'You no longer work for me, remember?'

She inwardly flinched at the starkness of that statement. It was one thing knowing it, something else entirely when put into words.

'If you really must know, Kit,' Marcus went on harshly, 'I didn't ask Catherine Grainger, and she didn't volunteer the information, because after seeing you there I had no reason to continue with the meeting; Lewis offered to go up alone and cancel it.'

She gave a dazed shake of her head. 'I don't understand.'

'I'd grown tired of the game, had decided it was time to confront Catherine. Meeting you there cancelled out any need I had to do that.' He paused. 'I trusted you, Kit.'

Her breath caught in her throat at the total disillusionment in his tone. 'I thought you would have talked to Catherine, that she would have told you—! It never occurred to me—' she broke off, totally unsure as to what to do next. 'Marcus, I know you aren't going to believe me, but I'm not your mole!'

His mouth twisted mirthlessly. 'You're right—I don't believe you!'

She had an ache in her chest that was like no other pain she had ever known. Was it really possible for a heart to break? It certainly felt like it!

She took a step towards him. 'Marcus, please—'

'Please what?' He stood only inches away from her now as he towered over her ominously. 'Do you know the worst of this as far as I'm concerned, Kit? I actually liked you,' he said bitterly.

Liking was better than nothing, she supposed. Although Marcus had used the past tense...

'I wanted you, too,' he continued candidly, his dark gaze fixed on the trembling of her mouth now. 'I still do!' he muttered self-disgustedly. Then he reached out, pulled her into his arms and his mouth claimed hers.

It was a kiss of anger, of sheer, frustrated fury, his mouth hard and unyielding against hers, bending her to his will, with absolutely no allowance given to her feelings.

Kit didn't fight him, at that moment had no strength left in her to fight anything or anyone.

Finally Marcus wrenched his mouth from hers. He held her mere inches away from him, his face a mask of emotion as he stared down at her.

She loved this man. How she loved him!

His expression softened slightly. 'How could you do it, Kit?' His voice was flat now, his anger abating.

She shook her head. 'I didn't.'

He closed his eyes briefly. 'Don't lie to me! After the shock I've already received today, I don't think I can take any more of your lies!'

She drew in a sharp breath, more hurt than she cared to think about. 'I'm not lying, Marcus. Not now or in the past,' she told him quietly. 'I know you don't believe me. But maybe when the betrayals continue after I've left the company, then you'll know I'm telling the truth.' That was her only hope.

She knew the evidence against her was damning, that to Marcus there could be only one explanation. But Kit also knew that if she had told him the truth about her relationship to Catherine Grainger it wouldn't have helped convince him that she hadn't betrayed him. The woman was her grandmother, for goodness' sake! Only finding the real culprit was ever going to do that.

Marcus made a frustrated movement. 'I think I can forgive anything but the lies, Kit.'

'But there's nothing to forgive—'

'Stop it. Just stop it!' He groaned low in his throat before pulling her back into his arms, his mouth once again taking possession of hers.

But his kiss was no longer angry as his mouth explored hers with searching thoroughness. His hands moved restlessly down the length of her spine, cupping her thighs to pull her against the increasing hardness of his body.

Despite everything he believed—in spite of everything he believed!—Marcus still wanted her!

Kit sobbed low in her throat as she gave herself up to the love she felt for this man, to the desire he obviously felt for her. For the moment it was enough. It had to be. Because there was nothing else.

Her arms moved up as her hands grasped his shoulders, feeling his tension beneath her fingertips, before she moved to entwine her fingers in the dark thickness of the hair at his nape. She felt his quiver of pleasure as she touched him there, his mouth moving erotically against hers now, the tip of his tongue searching on her bottom lip, her top lip, before moistly entering her.

Kit felt her senses soar, her body engulfed in sudden heat, straining against his as she wished herself a part of him.

'Kit...!' he whispered as his mouth left hers to travel the arched length of her throat. 'You taste so good!'

he murmured achingly, his lips and tongue now searching the hollows of her throat.

His hands were hot against her flesh now as he explored beneath her tee shirt, holding her arms above her head as he peeled it from her body, his eyes dark as he looked down at the thrusting softness of her breasts in their lacy white bra and then back up to her flushed face.

Kit held his eyes as she stepped back to slowly reach behind her and release the catch to her bra, sliding the straps from her shoulders to throw the garment to one side.

Marcus froze, his gaze once again shifting to her breasts, bare now to his scrutiny, their rosy tips firm and aroused.

'You're beautiful…!' he exclaimed, then, moving forward, his head bent and he slowly, oh, so slowly, took one pouting nipple into his mouth.

Kit's legs buckled beneath her as she looked down at his dark head against her creamy softness, moaning low in her throat as his tongue lathed damply against the rosy tip of her breast, her fingers digging tightly into the hard strength of his shoulders as she clung to him to stop herself falling.

Heat. There was so much heat in her body that she felt as if she were on fire, the flames centred between her thighs, that not even her increasing dampness there could put out.

Marcus's hand moved to cup the breast he'd kissed and sucked so pleasurably, the soft pad of his thumb continuing that caress against the hardened nipple as he turned the attention of his mouth to its twin.

Kit's legs really did give way as dual pleasure ripped

through her body. Marcus followed her down onto the carpeted floor, raising his head to look down to where one large hand still cupped her breast. Then his heated gaze returned to her face as he slowly moved his thumb across the sensitivity of her dampened nipple, holding her eyes as he bent his head to lick that rosy tip once more.

She couldn't breathe, the warmth between her thighs intensifying to an unbearable degree, ripples of pleasure building within her, her eyes widening as that pleasure began to overflow. The orgasm that ripped through her body seemed to last for ever and ever as Marcus kept her nipple in his mouth, and his hand moved down between her thighs so that he could feel the rippling convulsions of her deep satisfaction.

'Marcus!' Kit cried heatedly, her fingers digging into his shoulders now. 'Oh, Marcus!' she groaned brokenly, burying her face against his chest as she slowly began to come back down to earth.

What had just happened to her was completely unprecedented, like nothing she had ever known before, a total loss of control that had left her weak and trembling.

Marcus's hand moved to smooth the hair back from the dampness of her face, his expression once again guarded as he looked down at her flushed cheeks. 'I could take you right now,' he told her evenly. 'Could take the rest of your clothes from your body and take you again and again.'

'Yes,' she confirmed huskily.

'But I'm not going to.'

She swallowed hard, a stillness stealing over her as

she sensed distance moving over and into him. 'Why not?'

He drew in a shuddering breath, giving her one last intense look before rolling away from her and getting to his feet, his back turned towards her.

After only a moment's hesitation, Kit took advantage of his turned back to pull her tee shirt back on, aware that her breasts still thrust barely against the thinness of the material, but needing that barrier nonetheless, very aware of the intense satisfaction she had found only seconds ago in his arms. And the fact that Marcus hadn't reached that same completion.

He turned back suddenly, his face pale but his expression dark. 'Why not?' he repeated harshly. 'Because that would make me no better than Mike Reynolds, that's why not!' He thrust his hands into his trouser pockets.

Kit gasped. 'But you're nothing like Mike Reynolds—'

'No, I'm not,' he agreed. 'And I'll never give you the excuse to say that I am.'

'What happened just now—what happened to me— none of that was like Mike Reynolds, either,' she assured him with sincerity. 'Besides, I no longer work for you, remember?' She felt a chill as she repeated his earlier comment.

Marcus looked at her for several long seconds, and then he gave a determined shake of his head. 'I have to go.'

Sudden tears blurred Kit's vision. Biting down painfully on her bottom lip, she willed herself not to beg him to stay, much as she wanted to. Much as she wanted to once again lose herself in his arms, to take him with her this time.

'I have to go,' Marcus repeated, turning and striding from the room, the door to her apartment closing with controlled violence seconds later.

But Kit's control was completely shattered and she allowed the tears to fall hotly down her cheeks, having no doubts this time that the crushing pain she could feel in her chest *was* her heart breaking…!

CHAPTER FOURTEEN

'HE JUST came here and sacked you?' Penny looked at her disbelievingly.

Kit was loath to tell her flatmate what else had happened when Marcus had come here a couple of hours ago; after all, she did have some pride. Even if that pride completely deserted her whenever Marcus was around!

But Kit had had to give Penny some sort of explanation for the way she'd looked when her friend had arrived home a short time ago; there was just no hiding the puffy redness of her eyes or the deathly paleness of her cheeks.

'He felt he was justified, Penny—'

'Just because he saw you leaving Grainger International?' her friend fumed angrily. 'He can't do that! I'm sure there are laws to say that he can't just sack you without notice—'

'But he has. And he did,' Kit said flatly, one of her hands agitatedly pleating the material of her tee shirt. 'Penny, it really doesn't matter,' she pleaded wearily as her friend still looked outraged. 'There's no way I could go on working in the office with him anyway when he believes I've betrayed him.'

'But why didn't you tell him the truth?' Penny frowned at her frustratedly. 'Surely he would have to believe you—'

'If I were to tell you that I'm not the one leaking

confidential information, but that I was just visiting Catherine Grainger because she's my grandmother, would you believe me?' Kit reasoned; she had never made any secret of that fact to Penny, the two women having been friends for years.

'Well, of course, I—' Penny broke off, a perplexed frown marring her brow now. 'Maybe... But then again, maybe not,' she conceded slowly.

'You see,' Kit said sadly.

'It does sound—a little damning,' Penny allowed with a pained wince.

'A little!' Kit echoed bitterly.

'Don't you have enough—upset, going on in your life at the moment, with your mother's illness, without this?' Penny asked with genuine concern.

'Again, Marcus knows nothing about that,' Kit admitted.

'That isn't the point!' her friend exclaimed. 'And to think I actually liked the man!'

'So did I.' Kit sighed. 'But it's not—' She broke off as the telephone rang, giving Penny a grateful smile as her friend moved to answer the call, turning away to stare sightlessly out of the window, still trying to come to terms with the fact that Marcus had gone completely from her life.

But surely he had to realise at some time that she had been telling him the truth? Surely the next time one of his business deals was sabotaged...? But perhaps the real culprit was intelligent enough to realise that, and would cut their losses before that happened? It was what she would do. If she really had been the traitor...

'What do you want?' Penny demanded, turning to raise her groomed eyebrows at Kit.

Kit immediately tensed, at once dreading—and hoping!—that the caller might be Marcus. But maybe if it was he had already realised he had made a mistake? Maybe—

'Well, she doesn't want to talk to you!' Penny told the caller. 'Haven't you already done enough damage?' she added angrily. 'Kit already has enough to worry about at the moment without being falsely accused by you— Why should I tell you?' Penny exclaimed. 'Oh, give me a break! You have to be the most arrogant man I have ever met in my life! You don't think—! Listen, buster,' Penny continued furiously, 'I'm making it my business, okay?'

Kit had got to her feet as soon as she'd realised it was Marcus, but Penny's side of the conversation held her frozen with dismay.

'I'm glad we understand each other,' Penny went on heatedly. 'For the record, Kit is so honest she even drove back to a supermarket once because she realised she hadn't paid for the newspaper she was reading as she went through the checkout! You're right—it is a waste of time—mainly mine!' Penny fumed. 'And to think, I actually liked you! My only consolation is that you are going to feel like a complete idiot when you finally realise Kit had nothing to do with this!'

Kit was grateful for her friend's championing of her, but it was clear from Penny's reaction to Marcus's responses that it was getting her nowhere.

'I've already told you no,' Penny stated with force. 'She's upset enough already without having you start on her again. Oh, get lost,' she yelled, before slamming the receiver back down in its cradle. 'Arrogant bastard!' she muttered, her face tight with anger when she turned back to Kit.

Kit gave a wan smile. 'I sincerely hope that wasn't our landlord offering to lower our rent!'

Penny grimaced, some of the tension starting to leave her body. 'Very funny!' She smiled ruefully. 'Can you believe the arrogance of that man?'

'Yes,' Kit said flatly. 'But did you ever find out why he was calling?'

Penny pulled a face. 'He said he wanted to talk to you.'

Kit frowned. 'What about?' It was obvious from what she had been able to hear that Marcus hadn't changed his mind about her guilt.

Her friend hesitated. 'He didn't say. Well…to be strictly honest—I didn't give him the chance to.' She put her hand to her mouth self-consciously. 'I guess I told him, didn't I…?'

Kit gave a ghost of a smile. 'I guess you did.'

Penny looked upset. 'I'm sorry—did you want to talk to him? It's just that I can't stand the way he's hurt you. You're already so worried about your mother that you didn't need all this on top of it.'

'No, I didn't want to talk to him,' Kit confirmed. 'He probably just wanted to insult me some more, anyway.'

'Probably,' Penny agreed. 'Can you believe him just phoning up here after what he did to you this afternoon?'

And Penny wasn't even completely aware of what Marcus had done to her that afternoon…!

Kit still blushed to think about the time she had spent

in his arms, of Marcus's response to her, seemingly against all his instincts, as if he totally despised his own weakness.

Which he probably did.

She straightened determinedly. 'Let's forget all about Marcus Maitland and make something for dinner.' It was Roger's evening for going to the gym, so Penny wouldn't be meeting him until much later.

To give Penny her due, she fell in with this plan with a light heart, although when it actually came to eating the spaghetti bolognese, neither woman really had much appetite, picking at the food, enjoying the red wine that accompanied it more.

In fact, Kit was sure it was a relief to both of them when the doorbell rang to announce Roger's arrival an hour later.

'Would you like us to stay in with you this evening…?' Penny paused on her way to answer the door. The engaged couple were due to go to a later evening showing of a recently released film. 'I really don't like the idea of just leaving you here alone.'

Kit smiled her gratitude, but shook her head. 'To be honest, I think I would quite enjoy a little time to myself.' If only to try to come to terms with the fact that she was never again going to see the man that she loved. Marcus…

'If you're sure…?' Penny didn't look convinced.

'Positive,' Kit assured her bravely, standing up to begin clearing away the plates for their meal.

Plates she almost dropped as she turned and found herself face to face with Marcus as he stood in the open doorway.

'What do you want?' she blurted out rudely, too shocked to be anything else.

His mouth twisted humourlessly. 'I'm getting a little tired of people asking me that this evening!' He gave a pointed glance back at Penny as she stood in the hallway behind him.

'Then maybe you shouldn't keep barging in unannounced,' Penny came back tartly. 'Sorry, Kit, but he just walked in.' Her flatmate gave her an apologetic grimace before once again turning to glare at Marcus.

Kit put the plates she held carefully back down on the tabletop—before she dropped them from her suddenly shaking hands!

Telephoning her was one thing, but arriving unannounced on her doorstep like this was—as Penny had already pointed out so succinctly!—totally unexpected.

Marcus looked at her under hooded lids. 'Could I talk to you, Kit? Alone,' he added.

'You really do have a nerve—'

'It's all right, Penny,' Kit cut in reassuringly, though her hands were tightly clenched at her sides. 'I know you have to go out, and I'm sure Mr Maitland won't be staying long.'

'If you're sure…?' Penny looked far from convinced that leaving Kit alone with Marcus was the right thing to do.

But Kit knew that her friend had nothing to worry about; one look at Marcus's face, his expression and dispassionate eyes, and she knew that whatever he had come here to say it had nothing to do with apologising to her, either for his mistaken accusations, or for making love to her.

'I'm sure.' She gave Penny an encouraging smile.

Penny smiled back before turning to give Marcus a hard stare. 'Just don't upset her any more than she already is,' she warned.

'I'll try not to,' he replied. 'And by the way,' he went on as Penny turned to leave, 'I quite liked you too.'

Penny gave him a look that could kill before leaving the room and closing the door softly behind her.

Leaving a painful tension between Kit and Marcus. At least—it was painful to her! She doubted Marcus felt any such awkwardness.

But as the silence continued between them the tension just seemed to get more intense to Kit, so much so that in the end she couldn't stand it any longer. 'Well?' she prompted.

'Well what?' Marcus returned.

Kit raised her hands in frustration. 'You were the one who telephoned me,' she reminded him. 'You're also the one visiting my apartment.'

An apartment he had frequented little more than three hours ago. Although there was no memory of that, it seemed, in his coldly opaque eyes.

'So I am,' he agreed. 'When I spoke to Penny earlier she—well, she gave me the impression that there's something else going on in your life other than—our argument, earlier today...?'

'You have no idea!' she mocked his arrogance. 'Besides, it wasn't an argument; you sacked me!'

His mouth tightened. 'I accepted your resignation, effective imm—'

'That's a lie!' she defended indignantly.

'You cleared your desk and left your keys—'

'Only because you had already made it perfectly obvious that you were going to make me do that anyway!'

'Whatever. The outcome was effectively the same.'

Kit noticed how handsome he looked in the casual black trousers he wore with an open-necked shirt.

'The outcome may have been,' she said, dragging herself back to reality. 'But there is a vast difference between my resigning and your sacking me!'

Marcus quirked a challenging brow. 'Worried I might not give you a good reference?'

Her eyes flared angrily. 'Not in the least,' she snapped. 'Now would you just state your reason for being here and then leave?'

'What's going on, Kit?'

She started nervously. 'Going on…?' she delayed.

'Penny said you were upset—'

'Well, of course I'm upset—I've just lost my job!' Kit reminded him.

'That isn't it,' Marcus said slowly.

'Why isn't it?' she defended. 'You may have so much money lying around that being out a job wouldn't bother you, but some of us need to pay rent and eat occasionally!'

He looked at her steadily for several long seconds, and then he slowly gave another shake of his head. 'That isn't it,' he repeated firmly. 'What happened over the weekend, Kit?' he prompted astutely. 'And don't tell me nothing did—because I won't believe you.'

'What's new?'

His mouth tightened, his eyes dark now. 'I know you're trying to annoy me into walking out of here, Kit, but it isn't going to work,' he told her with certainty. 'I want to know the reason behind Penny's earlier remark—she's a worthy champion, by the way,' he acknowledged sardonically, 'and I'm not leaving until I know what's going on!' As if to add weight to this statement he sat down in one of the armchairs.

Kit watched him silently for several seconds, and then she gave in. 'My mother isn't very well, that's all,' she revealed.

All? It was everything! If anything should happen to her mother—if she didn't come through the operation on Thursday—

But she mustn't think like that, Kit immediately admonished herself. She had to be positive for both her mother's and her father's sakes.

'As in?' Marcus was once again studying her intently.

'As in not very well,' she repeated. 'It's really none of your business, is it?'

'I care about you, Kit—'

'Oh, please!' she derided.

'But I do care, damn it!' He stood up, suddenly towering over her. 'I don't want to,' he admitted, 'but that doesn't change the fact that I do!'

Kit looked up at him, seeing only implacable anger in his face, his eyes cold with the fury of his admission. 'Don't let it worry you, Marcus,' she taunted. 'It's probably just like a summer cold, rather uncomfortable for a few days, but quickly gone!'

'Very funny,' he rasped coldly. 'So you aren't going to tell me?'

'I just did.' She sighed wearily. 'My mother isn't very well, I'm naturally worried about her. End of story.'

'Somehow I don't think so,' he said slowly.

Kit tried to look unconcerned. 'Think what you like—you usually do, anyway! Now, if you wouldn't mind…' She looked in the direction of the door.

Marcus didn't move. 'The reason I telephoned earlier was because I had received a call from Desmond Hayes, inviting the two of us out to a celebration dinner with him and his wife tomorrow evening.'

Her face brightened. 'The two of them are back together, then?'

'It would seem so,' Marcus confirmed distantly.

'I'm so glad! For Desmond's sake,' she exclaimed warmly.

'Yes,' Marcus agreed. 'Well?'

Well, what? He couldn't seriously expect that she would calmly go out to a dinner that included him with the way things stood between the two of them?

'I'm afraid not,' she told him quietly.

'I did tell Desmond that when he called to make the invitation, but he still insisted I ask you anyway,' Marcus said off-handedly.

Kit's hands tightened at the pain he deliberately inflicted by letting her know he had no desire to spend any more time in her company, either. 'Well, now you've asked me,' she said flatly.

'Yes,' he agreed curtly.

'Was there something else?'

'No,' he answered after another short pause, standing up. 'Nothing else. I'll give Desmond and Jackie your good wishes tomorrow evening, then, shall I?'

'Do that,' she agreed.

'Fine,' he bit out briskly. 'I'll say goodnight, then.'

'Yes,' Kit acknowledged dully.

'Kit—'

'Will you please just go?' she snapped at him, her self-control dangerously on the edge of cracking wide open.

He drew in a harsh breath. 'There's something you aren't telling me—'

'There's nothing I need to tell you!' she dismissed hurriedly. 'You're not even my employer any more!'

'No,' he acknowledged heavily.

As if that bothered him. Which Kit was sure it didn't. And they could hardly work together again anyway after the intimacies they had shared this afternoon.

'Okay, Kit, I'm going,' he accepted when she continued to look at him challengingly. 'But I will find out what's going on.'

She gave a disbelieving laugh. 'I have no idea how!' she responded. 'Or why it should interest you,' she added as he continued to look at her with that implacable expression.

'You might be surprised.'

'I doubt it,' she said. 'Now if there was nothing else…?' She folded her arms and looked him square in the face.

No matter what effort of will it cost her to do it! And it took a lot, his being here again at all giving her self-control a battering.

'For the moment,' he allowed. 'But I have a feeling that I'll be back.'

Her chin rose defensively. 'And I have a feeling that I'll be busy if you are!'

He gave a humourless smile. 'Then I'll just have to wait until you aren't busy, won't I?' He turned and left the apartment.

Kit swayed where she stood, totally overwhelmed— and confused—by this second visit from Marcus today.

CHAPTER FIFTEEN

'GET in.'

Kit peered into the interior of the car that had pulled to a halt at the pavement beside her as she waited for her taxi to arrive, her eyes widening with dismay as she saw it was Marcus sitting behind the wheel of the Jaguar—which she should already have recognized!

And maybe she would have done if she weren't already so agitated that she couldn't think straight!

'No, thank you.' She straightened, turning purposefully to look down the road for her taxi.

'Kit.' Marcus had got out of his car now, dark glasses hiding his eyes as he looked across at her over the low roof. 'I'll drive you to the clinic.'

She gave him a startled look. 'How did you—? You said you would find out,' she acknowledged with resignation. 'I don't think so, thank you.'

She was already worried enough. Her mother and father had arrived at the clinic the previous afternoon, and Kit had spent most of the evening there with them. Her father had stayed at the clinic overnight in preparation for the operation later this morning...

Her eyes filled with the ready tears that never seemed to be far away at the moment. 'Go away, Marcus,' she choked. 'I really can't deal with any arguments today.'

'You won't have to,' he said soothingly, having

HIS VERY PERSONAL ASSISTANT

moved around to her side of the car. 'I promise I won't even speak if you don't want me to.' He held the door open for her as he helped her into the passenger seat.

'Oh, yes?' Kit gave him a disbelieving look.

'Yes,' he confirmed evenly. 'Let me help you with that.' He took the seat belt out of her hand as she fumbled with it, one of his hands lightly brushing against her breast as he pushed the catch into the fastener.

Kit immediately felt the heat that washed over her. Even now, when she was so worried about her mother? It would appear so.

She shook her head, knowing he couldn't help but be aware of her response. 'Marcus, I really don't think I can deal with you today,' she told him pleadingly.

'I told you, you won't have to.' He gave her a reassuring glance as he got into the car beside her.

'But what about my taxi?' she wailed.

Marcus shrugged unconcernedly. 'He'll find another fare.'

'Yes, but—I'm keeping you from your work,' she protested. 'Or is Lewis holding the fort today?'

His mouth tightened. 'Something like that.'

'But—oh, never mind.' She could see that her protests were getting her precisely nowhere; if he wanted to waste his morning on her, then that was up to him. 'Just drive me to the clinic, if that's what you really want to do.'

'It's one of the things I really want to do,' he affirmed. 'Most of the others are probably out of the question!' His meaning was more than obvious as his gaze lingered on her mouth.

Kit gave him a baffled look. 'I don't understand you;

you think I gave details of your business deals to Catherine Grainger!'

'Do I?' he shot back, switching on the engine, putting the car in gear, and driving off. 'If I do, it doesn't seem to have made much difference, does it?'

Difference to what? Kit wanted to know. To the fact that he was here? Or something else...?

'How did your dinner go with Desmond and Jackie last night?' She deliberately changed the subject onto something she could understand.

'Very well. Although they both expressed their disappointment that you weren't able to be there. Several times.'

Kit looked down. 'I'm sorry.'

'It's okay.' Marcus reached out and squeezed her tightly clenched hands. 'I understand the reason for your refusal now.'

'But I wouldn't have come even if it wasn't for—wasn't for—'

'Everything will work out, Kit,' he assured her determinedly. 'Your mother's surgeon is the best in his field—'

'How do you know? Never mind.' She knew Marcus well enough by now to realise that what he wanted to know, he would find out.

'Yes, he is,' she agreed. 'But he's still only given my mother a fifty-fifty chance of survival.' Tears filled her eyes again as she thought of her beautiful mother and all she would have to endure over the next few hours.

'We'll be there in a few minutes, Kit,' Marcus said quietly.

Kit still had no real idea of why Marcus was here, but a part of her was very glad that he was. Both she and her father were very supportive in front of her mother, but once alone…! The two of them would have need of Marcus's strength.

'I know.' She wiped the tears from her cheeks. 'It's just—just—'

'I know, Kit,' he gently interjected. 'But whatever happens I'll be there for you, okay?'

But why would he? What was he doing here at all? Kit didn't know the answer to either of those questions, and she was too emotionally upset at the moment to even try to find the answers.

'Now we have to be strong for your mother and father—yes?' he prompted as he parked the car outside the clinic.

He was right, Kit knew he was right, that she had to at least try to present a façade of cheerfulness once with her parents.

'Yes,' she agreed, slowly getting out of the car, drawing in deeply controlling breaths as she looked across at the one-storey private clinic where her mother lay awaiting her fate.

Marcus locked the car before taking a firm hold of her elbow. 'I'll be right here, Kit.'

She no longer questioned his presence, it was enough that he was here. Nothing else mattered—not his accusations, the fact that she no longer worked for him. He was here…

'Kit, before we go in, there's something I—' Marcus ventured. He broke off, at last removing those dark sunglasses. 'I wasn't exactly truthful with you earlier,' he confessed.

She gave him a puzzled glance. 'No?'

'Lewis isn't holding the fort—because as of nine o'clock this morning he no longer works for me!'

Her confusion deepened; what possible interest could it be to her now whether or not Lewis still worked for him? 'I don't understand,' she replied.

'I know you don't,' he responded. 'And now isn't the time for us to talk about it. But for what it's worth, I'm sorry I ever doubted you. I know that isn't enough after the things I said to you, the things I did, but—I really am very sorry.'

The last two days had been awful, and she had barely slept last night, could hardly think straight now, let alone understand why Marcus was apologizing to her.

'Don't worry about it now.' Marcus moved to run a gently caressing hand down the paleness of her cheeks. 'I still have no idea what you were doing at Catherine Grainger's office on Tuesday, but—I'll explain what I do know later, okay?'

Later. When they would all know one way or another how her mother had fared.

Kit had heard nothing from Catherine Grainger since their meeting. Not that she had expected to after the cold response she had received from the other woman on Tuesday. But she still couldn't help feeling hurt on her mother's behalf.

'Fine,' she told Marcus distractedly, eager to visit her mother now.

She saw her father almost immediately as they approached her mother's room, standing outside in the corridor, as handsome as ever, looking very much like a well-matured version of the actor Donald Sutherland.

Her heart ached at the defeated expression on her father's face, his wide shoulders slumped, although his face lit up as soon as he saw Kit, blue eyes warming with paternal love as he took her in a bear hug.

'Everything's fine,' he said as she looked up at him anxiously. 'The doctor is with her now, and then we can all go in.' He turned to include Marcus in his reassuring smile, although there was a question in his eyes as he turned back to Kit.

'Marcus Maitland.' Marcus was the one to introduce himself to the older man, holding out his hand. 'It's a pleasure to meet you, Mr McGuire. Although I obviously wish it could have been under happier circumstances,' he added apologetically.

'Mr Maitland.' Kit's father returned the handshake, the two men obviously sizing each other up.

Not that Kit could tell from either of their expressions what conclusions they had come to, but for the moment that didn't matter, either. 'How's Mummy?' she prompted concernedly.

Her father grimaced. 'Tired. Frightened. Most of all worried about the two of us if—if—'

'She's going to be fine,' Kit told him determinedly, at the same time feeling her hand taken in a firm grasp. Marcus squeezed it reassuringly, and she had to blink back fresh tears as she turned to look at him.

And then she had to blink rapidly again—not only to clear those tears, but also to make sure her eyes weren't deceiving her as something else, some movement, caught and held her attention.

Walking down the carpeted corridor towards them, her face coolly composed, was Catherine Grainger!

Tall. Elegantly beautiful in the perfectly tailored black suit and white blouse. Her expression haughty. Grey eyes icily remote.

But she was here…!

'What the—?' Kit's father gasped at her side, his face stricken as he recognized the woman walking so purposefully towards them. 'What's she doing here?' he demanded. 'How—?'

'It's my fault, Daddy,' Kit told him quickly, her shoulders tensing at the enormity of what she had done. 'I went to see her on Tuesday to tell her about Mummy.' She didn't even glance at Marcus as she felt his hand tighten painfully about hers as the significance of what she had just said sank in; her attention was all centred on her father as he still stared disbelievingly at his mother-in-law.

The older woman came to a halt a few feet away from them, her expression wary now. 'Tom,' she greeted tersely.

'Catherine,' he returned guardedly.

'How is she?' Catherine Grainger enquired in her brisk, no-nonsense voice, seeming to have decided to ignore the fact that Kit and Marcus were there too.

'Resigned but determined too,' Kit's father answered economically.

Catherine nodded, as if she would have expected little else from a daughter of hers. 'Can I see her?'

'That depends,' Kit's father said slowly. 'On what you intend saying to her if you do see her,' he added as Catherine raised haughtily questioning brows.

Kit could see some of the arrogant self-confidence leaving that handsome face as her grandmother paused uncertainly, as if aware that so much rested on what she said next.

'To be honest, Tom...' Catherine finally spoke uncertainly '...I have no idea! Except...I have to say something.'

His expression softened slightly. 'That would appear to be a start!'

Kit found herself glancing at Marcus as he studied Catherine. Then he looked at Kit.

Although she had no time to even acknowledge that questioning look as the surgeon came out of her mother's room, all of them turning to look at him anxiously.

'You can all go in for a few minutes now,' the tall, middle-aged man informed them. 'Although, as we've already given Mrs McGuire her pre-med, you may find her a little sleepy.'

Kit felt the hand still holding hers increase its pressure. Turning to look at Marcus, she saw his own gaze now fixed on the woman he could see inside the hospital room.

Kit's mother...

And Kit could see exactly what Marcus must now be seeing. It was as if Heather were the missing link between Catherine Grainger and Kit, the red of her hair liberally sprinkled with silver, her face nowhere near as haughty as Catherine's, but not as youthfully softened as Kit's.

Marcus turned back to Kit.

She gave him a shaky smile, knowing she would no

longer have to explain to him what her connection was to Catherine Grainger, that it was perfectly obvious to anyone seeing the three women together exactly what their relationship was.

But the important thing was that Catherine was here!

After all her coldness on Tuesday morning, her claims of having no interest in the daughter she had disowned twenty-eight years ago, she was here!

As Kit's father had already stated: it was a start...

CHAPTER SIXTEEN

'I SHOULD have known!' Marcus whispered at Kit's side. The two of them were sitting in the relatives' room, after Kit had gone in briefly to speak to her mother before leaving her alone with Tom and Catherine. The look on Heather's face had been both hopeful and apprehensive when she had seen just who was accompanying her husband.

'Why should you?' Kit responded. 'As far as you were aware, there was absolutely no connection between myself and Catherine Grainger.'

'Except the fact that she's your grandmother!' Marcus returned, obviously still completely poleaxed by that fact.

'Not really.' Kit wrinkled her nose at the thought. 'Never having had a grandmother, I've always thought of them as little old ladies who live in cottages and knit tea cosies and things like that; hardly an accurate description of Catherine!'

'Hardly,' Marcus allowed.

Kit could see by the expression on his face that he was still having difficulty coming to terms with the fact that Catherine was her grandmother. 'Catherine is my mother's mother, yes. But she's denied the fact for the last twenty-eight years.'

'Something you decided to change on Tuesday,' Marcus observed. 'That's why you were at Grainger International that afternoon, isn't it?'

Kit gave a shiver as she remembered that conversation with Catherine. 'She was so horrible. I had no idea a mother could be so hard and unyielding towards her only child!'

'But she's here now, Kit,' Marcus reminded her.

'Yes—and if she says or does anything to upset my mother, then my father is never going to forgive me for bringing her back into our lives!' Kit said with certainty.

Kit was well aware that her father adored her—both her parents had always been wonderful with her. But nevertheless she had always known that her mother and father shared a very special love, the sort of love that needed no one else.

Perhaps that was what Catherine had sensed all those years ago, sensed and resented?

'I don't think Catherine has come here to cause trouble,' Marcus reassured her.

But while he had continued to be supportive since Catherine's arrival at the clinic, Kit sensed a certain remoteness in him now that hadn't been there before, a distancing, as if he wished himself far away from here. And her.

'I hope not.' Kit still felt uncertain about that. 'But— Marcus, I'd never even met her until last weekend at Desmond Hayes's house,' she explained.

'Amazing!'

'Yes,' Kit agreed. 'I have always known she was my grandmother, of course, but—I couldn't believe it when I saw her there!'

'It must have taken a lot of courage for you to enter the lion's den on Tuesday.'

Kit glanced across the corridor to her mother's room.

'What do you think they're saying in there?' she said worriedly, able to hear a low murmur of voices, but not what was actually being said.

'Anybody's guess,' Marcus replied. 'But if Catherine's got any sense whatsoever she will take the second chance she's been given and grasp it with both hands!'

Kit gave him a searching look, wondering if there was any hidden meaning to that statement—after all, he was here too, wasn't he…? But Marcus's expression was as unreadable as ever.

She sighed at the barrier she sensed he had deliberately put up. 'That certainly wasn't the impression Catherine gave me when I left her office on Tuesday. She—' She broke off as the door across the corridor opened and Catherine came out and crossed the hallway to join them in the relatives' room.

Catherine's normally composed face seemed ravaged by emotion; for once she looked every one of her sixty-seven years. Just how had the meeting with Heather gone…?

'Can I get you a coffee or tea, Catherine?' Marcus offered as he stood up.

The older woman looked at him as if seeing him for the first time. 'A whisky would probably be more beneficial!' she answered shakily.

'Sorry.' Marcus grimaced apologetically as he indicated the machine in the corner of the room. 'There's only tea or coffee.'

'Coffee, then. Black. No sugar. Thank you,' Catherine added belatedly, suddenly dropping down onto one of the chairs to bury her face in her hands.

Kit hesitated only fractionally before moving to sit

on the chair beside Catherine and put her arm around her grandmother's shaking shoulders, deciding she didn't care whether or not Catherine welcomed her attention; she was going to get it, anyway!

Marcus placed the coffee on the table beside Catherine before turning to Kit. 'I think it might be better if I go now and leave the two of you alone to talk—'

'No!' Kit instantly looked up to protest. 'You said you would stay, Marcus,' she reminded him, sure now that she hadn't imagined that distance he was once again putting between them.

'I did, yes, but—' He broke off, drawing in a deeply ragged breath. 'I'm sure you and Catherine must have a lot of things you need to talk about. In private.'

Kit felt sure that if he left now, despite what he had said earlier, she was never going to see him again.

'Stay, Marcus,' Catherine was the one to plead with him now as she raised her head to look at him. 'Some of what I have to say concerns you as well as Kit.'

His eyes widened. 'It does?'

'Yes,' Catherine confirmed. 'Strange as it may seem…yes.'

'Please do stay, Marcus.' Kit added her own plea to Catherine's; she couldn't imagine what the older woman might have to say that involved Marcus, but she wanted him to stay, anyway; *they* still had a lot to say to one other!

'Okay.' He dropped down into a chair on the other side of the room from the two women, his expression guarded as he looked across at them.

Kit could have cried for the ever widening gap that

seemed to be growing between them, but could think of nothing to say that might close it.

'Very well.' Catherine straightened in her chair, composing her features into their usual calmness. 'You may have wondered, Marcus, why over the years I have attempted to subvert certain business deals that your father, and subsequently yourself, have been interested in…?'

'You mean this has been going on for longer than the last six months?' Kit gasped, at the same time giving Marcus a frowning look.

'Well…to give Marcus his due, he may not have been aware of it until the last six months or so,' Catherine allowed. 'His father and his uncle Simon ran the company until his uncle's death ten years ago.'

Then she spoke to Marcus once again. 'After that, it was your father and yourself, and since your father's retirement just over a year ago you have managed the company alone.'

'Yes…' Marcus confirmed warily.

'Forty years ago I was in love with your uncle Simon,' Catherine told him flatly.

Marcus looked stunned. 'But—but forty years ago he would have been married to my aunt Stella, with a young daughter.'

'Yes,' Catherine acknowledged emotionlessly. 'And I was a young widow, with my own daughter, and my dead husband's ailing business to run. But Simon and I fell in love, anyway.'

Marcus was listening intently. 'What happened?'

Catherine smiled humourlessly. 'What usually happens; Simon decided to stay with his wife and child!'

'And you have carried on some sort of vendetta

against Marcus's family ever since…?' Kit guessed, incredulous.

'It wasn't quite like that,' Catherine told her. 'But—yes, I suppose that's more or less what I have done. I really loved Simon, you see, but it wasn't enough to hold him. Maitland Enterprises was already a very successful business, and Simon was sure that if he left his wife and child to be with me that James—your father…' she gave an inclination of her head in Marcus's direction '…would cut him out of the business, as well as the family.'

'Forty years ago he probably would have done,' Marcus conceded softly.

'Yes,' Catherine sighed. 'So after Simon left me, I put all my time and energy into bringing up my daughter and making a success of my business. It thrived—and at the age of nineteen my daughter decided she was madly in love with a man old enough to be her father!'

'More to the point,' Marcus was the one to put in quietly, 'a man who loved her as deeply?'

'Yes,' Catherine acknowledged shakily. 'Tom McGuire was a penniless, middle-aged artist—and anyone with eyes in their head could see that my daughter loved him, and he loved her, with a love that transcended any obstacle that might stop them being together!'

'They still love each other in that way,' Kit told her huskily, the tears once again swimming in her eyes.

'I know.' Catherine reached out tentatively and touched Kit's hand briefly. 'And I, my dear—as you pointed out so clearly on Tuesday—am a silly old woman,' she said tremulously.

'Oh, but—'

'No one has ever spoken to me in the way that you did on Tuesday.' Catherine gave a rueful smile. 'Maybe if they had I wouldn't have been so stupid as to allow that one unhappy love affair to sour the rest of my life, to deprive me, not only of my daughter for twenty-eight years, but also my—my granddaughter.' She drew in a shaky breath. 'Kit, I told you on Tuesday that I had no need of a granddaughter, but I was wrong. So very wrong!'

Kit looked into eyes so like her mother's now they were softened with emotion, so like her own, that it was impossible to withstand the pleading for forgiveness she could see there.

She moved tentatively towards this woman, her grandmother. Catherine seemed to move at exactly the same time, and the two of them were soon in each other's arms.

'She will be all right, won't she, Kit?' Catherine murmured brokenly some time later. 'All these years I've missed, all this time, and now—'

'She will be all right,' Kit said with much more certainty than she actually felt, knowing Catherine needed to hear that at this moment.

'Ladies,' Marcus intervened. 'I think it's time for you to go back in to see Heather.' He indicated Tom standing in the doorway waiting for them all to accompany him back into Heather's room.

It wasn't all settled between her mother and her grandmother—Kit wasn't naïve enough to be believe that it was—but she felt certain that the two of them had made a lot of headway towards an understanding today.

If only she and Marcus could do the same…!

'If you'll all excuse me…?' Marcus stood up, his expression once more remote.

Kit stood up. 'Do you have to go?'

His eyes were darkly unfathomable as he met her gaze. 'Yes, I really do have to go,' he confirmed, turning away before hesitating and turning back again. 'You'll let me know? How things go?' he asked.

'Yes, of course,' she confirmed breathlessly, wishing she could persuade him to stay, wishing he would stay; if she needed anyone today it was the man she loved. 'I'll call you later, shall I?' she said stiffly.

'Do that,' Marcus accepted. 'Catherine. Tom.' Then he left without a backward glance.

Kit's eyes instantly burned with the tears that were so near the surface of her emotions today. Marcus had said he would stay, that he would be here for her, but all that had seemed to change once he had realised Catherine was her grandmother.

But why? Why was he here at all today? He hadn't explained anything!

But it was time to go in and talk to her mother now, to offer the love and support she knew she needed. There would be time later for her to think of the pain of Marcus's abrupt departure.

'Go after him, Kit.'

She turned to look at the woman who was her grandmother, the two of them back in the waiting room. Her father was by the bedside of his beloved wife, last seen kissing her hands with all of the pent-up emotion of the last five hours as Heather came round from her operation.

It had been a success! A complete and utter success. Heather was still incredibly sleepy, but out of danger, so the surgeon had told them all a short time ago.

In fact everything looked so much more positive to Kit than it had this morning, her mother and grandmother reconciled, the operation over and successful. The only thing keeping her from jumping with joy was the fact that Marcus had left them without a backward glance.

'Sorry?' She turned to Catherine blankly.

The older woman smiled encouragingly. 'I said go after him, Kit. Don't make the same mistakes I did. Maybe if I had put up more of a fight for Simon...'

'It isn't the same.' Kit smiled as she tried to hide the misery that was consuming her.

She shouldn't feel like this; her mother had survived the operation, was going to be completely well again, and that was all that really mattered, not her foolish love for Marcus.

Catherine gave a rueful smile back. 'You're right, it isn't—I believe Marcus really is in love with you!'

'No—'

'Oh, yes,' Catherine persisted. 'I knew it when I saw him here with you this morning.'

Kit shook her head. 'He just felt sorry for me—'

'Now you're being silly, Kit,' Catherine rebuked with some of her old sharpness. 'You're beautiful. Accomplished—'

'Your granddaughter,' Kit put in.

Catherine's eyes widened. 'And what does that have to do with anything?'

'Everything, I would have thought!'

'Don't be ridiculous,' Catherine bridled. 'Okay, so I accept that was probably a bit of a shock for him—'

'"A bit of a shock"!' Kit echoed. 'You have no idea!'

'Oh, but I think that I have—'

'Kit.'

She turned sharply at the sound of Marcus's voice, completely surprised to find him standing in the open doorway.

'I think I can take it from here, Catherine,' he told the older woman, although his expression was once again guarded as he turned back to Kit. 'I had the surgeon's secretary inform me as soon as the operation was over. I'm so glad everything turned out well.'

Kit swallowed hard, her head still spinning from the fact that he had come back. 'Thank you,' was all she could manage.

'If you'll excuse us for a few minutes, Catherine?' Marcus spoke briskly. 'I have a few things I need to say to Kit.'

'More than a few, I should have thought,' Catherine commented derisively.

'Perhaps,' he allowed coolly. 'Kit?' his voice softened noticeably.

It was that very gentleness in his tone that persuaded her into going with him. 'You'll explain to my father when he comes back?' she prompted Catherine. 'I shouldn't be long.'

'Of course,' Catherine agreed. 'Oh, and by the way, Marcus...' She stopped them as Kit would have followed Marcus from the room. 'I had a visit from your lawyer this morning—'

'Ex-lawyer,' Marcus put in harshly.

Catherine gave a gracious inclination of her head. 'He seemed to be of the opinion that I might offer him a job.'

'An opinion you quickly disillusioned him of, I'm sure,' Marcus rejoined.

'Of course,' Catherine confirmed graciously. 'I only ever employ people whose loyalty I can be completely sure of.'

'So do I,' Marcus returned sardonically.

Lewis. They had to be talking about Lewis. And if Lewis had gone to Catherine for a job after Marcus had sacked him—!

It suddenly all became clear. In fact, Kit could kick herself for not having realised before. And maybe if she hadn't been so agitated this morning then she might have done! Lewis had to have been the one passing confidential information on to Catherine all the time!

And Marcus had to have known that this morning in order to dismiss Lewis…

Marcus hadn't been with her today because he cared about her, he had just felt guilty for having wrongly accused her.

'I think this is far enough, don't you?' she said woodenly once they stood outside in the car park. 'Just make your apology and then I can go back inside. I take it you are going to apologize again for the mistake you obviously made?'

Marcus closed his eyes briefly. 'It isn't the way you think, Kit—'

'Isn't it?' Her eyes flashed deeply grey. 'I thought you cared, really cared, and instead you're just feeling foolish for having made a mistake. Well, you can take your apology and—'

'Kit…!' he groaned throatily.

'I'm sorry if that isn't ladylike enough for you—but it's the best you're going to get!' She was shaking with anger now, feeling utterly foolish herself for ever harbouring any hopes where this man was concerned. 'Yes, it's true that Catherine Grainger is my grandmother. It's also true that until last weekend I had never met her. But even if that weren't the case, I worked for you.' She glared at him. 'I would never have betrayed your confidence in me. Never!' She inwardly cursed herself as her voice broke emotionally.

Marcus's hands were clenched at his sides. 'It's also true that when I came to your apartment Tuesday evening I still didn't know Lewis was the one responsible for those security leaks; I didn't find that out until I confronted him with it first thing this morning,' he told her directly. 'It's what I thought on Tuesday when I arranged that meeting with Catherine, had hoped to see the two of them together and then confront them with it. Instead I found myself face to face with you…!'

Kit already knew how damning that had looked; hadn't her heart been breaking ever since?

'I didn't know what to think any more,' Marcus continued. 'I wanted to believe you, but the evidence against you was so damning. But I came back on Tuesday night anyway, Kit. I couldn't have stayed away, not once Penny had told me you were upset— and not just because of me,' he added firmly as Kit would have spoken. 'Kit, I came back,' he repeated determinedly.

She looked at him searchingly now, that barrier no

longer there, all his emotions, everything he was feeling reflected there in his eyes. 'Why?' she finally breathed, hardly daring to move as she waited for his answer.

'You know why, Kit,' he said.

She knew the reason why she wanted him to have come back; she just wasn't sure it was his...

'I love you!' he groaned as he saw the continuing doubts in her eyes. 'I've loved you since I first saw Kit McGuire as she really is and not as she wanted me to see her. Before that I knew you to be a capable and efficient PA, but without the disguise—'

'I told you, it wasn't a disguise!' she defended, but not with the same heat as before, her own barriers starting to crumble.

'Without the defences, then,' he amended. 'You were beautiful, and desirable, and completely adorable. I love you, Kit. I left the clinic earlier because I thought—I realised, once I had seen your mother and Catherine, that I should get out of your life, get out and stay out, that I don't deserve to have you forgive me. My only excuse is that it's because I love you that I reacted as strongly as I did. I know that's no excuse, not really, but— No matter what happens between us in the future, you deserve to know that I love you more than life itself.'

'"No matter what happens between us"...?' she repeated.

'If you tell me to go away, to stay away—' He broke off. 'If you turn me away, Kit, I will still love you. And go on loving you. Always.'

In the same way that her parents had always loved each other...!

She looked at him, deliberately holding his gaze as her tongue moistened her lips. 'And if I don't tell you to go away?'

His gaze was fixed on the moistness of her mouth now. 'Then I'll ask you to marry me. And pray,' he added.

Marcus loved her? Wanted to marry her?

Her eyes began to glow, the ice that had settled about her heart quickly melting. 'Well?' she prompted huskily.

His dark gaze held hers. 'Kit, I know I don't deserve your forgiveness—'

'Skip that bit.' She gave a shaky smile. 'In future I promise not to keep secrets from you, particularly damning ones,' she vowed.

'But I should have believed you—'

'Why should you?' she interrupted. 'Even I know how bad it must have looked.' She tilted her head. 'I'm still waiting, Marcus,' she reminded him, encouraged by the love she could see burning in his eyes.

Marcus took hold of her hand, his fingers tightening about hers before he went down on one knee in front of her. 'Kit, will you marry me?'

'Get up!' she told him hurriedly, aware, even if he didn't appear to be, that it had rained some time during the last few hours, and that the pavement was wet beneath the knee of his expensively tailored trousers.

'Not until you answer me,' he told her stubbornly.

Marry Marcus? Spend the rest of her life with him, loving him, and being loved in return?

'Marry me, Kit.' He looked up at her intensely. 'Marry me and I swear I will never again doubt a single word you ever say to me!'

She could see that he meant it too, for the first time noticing the evidence of his own pain the last two days, lines etched beside his eyes and mouth that hadn't been there before.

'I do love you, Marcus,' she declared.

His eyes flared with emotion, his hand tightening on hers. 'Then say you'll marry me!'

She gave a choked laugh. 'If you get up from the pavement I promise I'll marry you,' she bargained.

'Good enough.' He rose to his feet, his arms moving about the slenderness of her waist, his eyes blazing with love as he looked down at her. 'As soon as your mother is well enough to attend we'll be married, yes?'

'Yes,' she agreed unhesitantly before his mouth claimed hers and she lost herself in the wonder of his kiss, knowing that, like her mother before her, she had found the one man she loved and wanted to spend the rest of her life with.

And who, despite their rather shaky start, loved and wanted to spend the rest of his life with her.

Love.

It really was the only thing that mattered.

IN THE
BANKER'S BED

by

Cathy Williams

Cathy Williams is originally from Trinidad but has lived in England for a number of years. She currently has a house in Warwickshire which she shares with her husband Richard, her three daughters, Charlotte, Olivia and Emma, and their pet cat, Salem. She adores writing romantic fiction and would love one of her girls to become a writer, although at the moment she is happy enough if they do their homework and agree not to bicker with one another.

CHAPTER ONE

ELLIOT frowned as he stared out of the window. The spacious, minimalist room had a particularly pleasing view over one of the few areas of greenery in London and, basking in the full light of a summer day, one would be forgiven for thinking that they were somewhere in the Med, and not, in fact, standing in a private room in a posh gym in central London.

Elliot glanced impatiently at his watch and swung round to face the door, leaning against the window-ledge.

Waiting was something Elliot Jay didn't do. It was something other people did. He expected his summons to be obeyed immediately without him having to hang around for…twenty minutes so far, according to his watch.

With mounting frustration, he stalked across to one of the chairs and sat down, wishing that he'd had the sense to bring his laptop with him so that he could at least do some work, wishing even more that he wasn't now in the position of having to do what he was doing, but he had no choice. Circumstances beyond his control had brought him to this juncture.

With a discipline born of experience, Elliot closed his mind off from those particularly unwelcome circumstances and instead allowed his eyes to roam around the room, to take in its harmonious lack of clutter, its sanitised impersonality. This was one of the reasons he had joined this particular gym when it had opened its doors eighteen months ago. That and the fact that it was a stone's throw from his massive penthouse apartment in

Kensington. Vigo was a health club that didn't waste time trying to be cosy. There were no chummy sitting-room-style bars where the weary could unwind with gossip over cups of tea, no lounging chairs around the pool or wavy slides for the kiddies. Instead the bars were all kitted out just like this room, in black and chrome with sensible newspapers on the tables. There was an internet café for anyone inclined to stay longer than was strictly necessary and the exercise machines were of the highest specification. Not that he used them. He unwound twice a week over a brutal game of squash and then swam it off in the giant-sized pool which, at eight in the evening, was usually empty.

As in every area of his life, Elliot applied himself to his exercise with focused, ruthless concentration. As a teenager, his skills on the rugby field had been formidable enough to warrant encouragement from his coach to turn professional, not that being a professional sportsman had ever presented itself as a practical possibility. His intellect could never have been contained by something as physically demanding as a sport, however talented he might have been at it. His finely tuned brain required enormous mental challenge. As the youngest ever chairman of a prominent investment bank, not only did he get this challenge, but he also earned the phenomenal sums of money associated with the job, which meant that by the age of thirty-two he could afford to begin indulging in his own private ventures, which brought their own financial rewards. The intense workload, which most men would have found crippling, Elliot found invigorating. His days were charged with adrenaline and mapped out with the precision of military campaigns. Meetings followed meetings and his name was synonymous with thrusting success in the financial world.

But Elliot didn't work for the money. He worked because he was driven. Even his hours of relaxation had a purpose.

Right now, he had a task at hand and hanging around wasn't something he found relaxing. In fact, he had to curb his annoyance and remember that in this one instance, he was actually in the unfamiliar terrain of the supplicant asking a favour.

Which didn't mean that he liked it.

But Melissa Lee had been personally recommended to him by the manager of the gym, a shrewd businesswoman and someone he trusted to give him clear-headed, impartial advice. Of course, he had been sparing with the actual details, merely told her that he required someone who could assist someone slightly overweight and a bit off-key. The Lee woman fitted the bill to the detail. She was twenty-four, a nutritionist and physiotherapist by training, although more than capable of mapping out a successful exercise routine, and she was fairly new to the gym, so had not yet acquired a string of regulars who needed her attention on a regular basis.

Keen though he was to employ Melissa Lee for the task at hand, he still could not resist looking pointedly at his watch when she finally entered the room.

'I've been waiting for forty minutes, Miss Lee.'

Melissa looked at the figure casually reclining on the chair and stopped abruptly in her tracks.

'One of our clients is interested in seeing you about a personal job,' Samantha had told her, interrupting the session which Melissa had only just started. 'Right now, if you could possibly make it.' Samantha had failed to elaborate on either the nature of the job or the nature of the client in question, and the *right now* command in the sentence Melissa had chosen tactfully to ignore.

The blood now rushed to Melissa's face as she took in the physically striking specimen in front of her.

Working in a gym was a passport to seeing impressively built men. Every morning, when Melissa went in for her light workout on the machines at seven-thirty, before she began her daily routines, they were there, suits waiting for them in changing rooms while they primed themselves for the day ahead on rowing machines and treadmills and other vicious-looking instruments of torture. From the relatively relaxed safety of an exercise mat, she absentmindedly watched them as she did her sit-ups, knowing herself to be unobserved because it had to be said that most of them had eyes only for themselves in the floor-to-ceiling mirrors that dominated the massive rooms.

But she had never seen the man sitting in front of her before. She would have remembered if she had. He had a memorable face. Glossy raven-black hair contrasted vividly with his eyes, which were a pure, cold blue, and his bone structure was perfect enough to make her do a double take. He was a sensationally attractive male, and even in that split second of taking him in she knew that he possessed the kind of presence that most women would have buckled at the knees at.

His expression, however, did not encourage that reaction in her. In fact, Melissa felt her smile rapidly fade away and she became aware that she was hovering by the door, like a student called in to see the headmaster for cheating in class.

She drew in her breath and took a few assertive steps into the room, holding out her hand, noticing that, although he politely extended his to briefly take hers, he didn't budge from his position on the chair, instead gesturing for her to sit down, as though he owned the place.

'I take it you are Miss Lee?' Blue eyes roved at a leisurely pace over her.

'That's right,' Melissa answered, disconcerted by his

scrutiny. 'I'm sorry if I've kept you waiting but I was in the middle of a session when Samantha told me that you wanted to see me.' She found no smiling acceptance of her apology, rather, silence and those ice-blue eyes appraising her, as though committing how she looked to memory. It was destabilising. Was he aware of that? 'She said that you wanted to see me about a job of some kind.' Whatever job it was, she decided on the spot that she wasn't going to take it. The man was positively intimidating. He also didn't look as though he needed any extra help with working out. Even dressed as he was in casual trousers and short-sleeved shirt, she could see that his body was well-toned and muscular with a slightly bronzed hue that gave him an exotic, compelling beauty. If he did want extra help working out, then it would be to a calibre that she, for one, was not trained to supply.

'That's right, although, of course, should you get this particular job, then showing up late would be out of the question.'

'I *did* apologise,' Melissa muttered in self-defence. 'You could hardly expect me to cancel Mrs Evans without notice just because I had to suddenly dash over here to see you. Mrs Evans is one of my few regular clients and she really needs the physiotherapy sessions she has with me twice a week. She was in a car accident a few months ago and—'

'Enough.' Elliot held up one hand impatiently. 'I'm not here to waste time talking about perfect strangers. I'm here to put forward a proposal which I think you will find financially very rewarding.'

Still smarting from having effectively been told to shut up, Melissa drew herself up and surveyed him loftily. 'I'm employed by Vigo, Mr...Mr...I don't know your name...'

'Jay. You can call me Elliot.'

She preferred not to call him anything. 'I don't think I would be allowed to take on outside work. I'm sure there must be something in my contract about that. Besides, I have a pretty hectic schedule at the moment and it's increasing by the day. I may only have been here a few months but...'

'You needn't worry about taking time off for this job. No objections will be raised, I assure you.' He was beginning to wonder what had possessed Samantha to sing the praises of this woman. She certainly wasn't what he had expected. For one thing, he hadn't expected to have to argue his case. He didn't know how much newcomers earned at a gym, but he would bet his bottom dollar that it wasn't a fortune, and London was an expensive place to live in. The prospect of some extra money should have been greeted with howls of delight.

And for another thing, Melissa Lee wasn't physically what he had expected either. He couldn't see very much under her shapeless dress but what he did see didn't accord with someone in the business of the body beautiful. She clearly wasn't fat but neither was she whipcord-slender with the muscles to match. She also didn't look the sort who thrived on putting people through their paces. He suppressed a sigh of pure frustration.

'I expect you want to know about the job I have in mind?'

'I don't think I can help you,' Melissa informed him up front. 'You're obviously a regular here at the gym and, whatever kind of workout you may have in mind for yourself, you really would need someone more qualified in the area. You see, I'm not sure whether Samantha told you, but I'm employed primarily as a nutritionist and a physiotherapist. I do a few classes but that's with the over-sixties. Mostly stretching exercises, very light-weight. You could probably do those in your sleep.'

'Finished?' he enquired politely, when she had dried up. He waited for her absolute, undivided attention. 'Do you normally approach everything in such a negative manner? Spotting all the obstacles before you take one step forward? If so, then I feel very sorry for these clients of yours. Do they know what they're getting into? That you won't make them better but in fact will see every pitfall, point them out and then lead them to the nearest bridge so that they can jump off?'

'That's not fair!' Melissa's normally warm, sunny disposition abandoned her completely. This man was hateful. Cold, emotionless, forbidding, arrogant and *hateful*. She couldn't think of anything worse than helping him in any way, shape or form. Or even being exposed to him unnecessarily. The man should carry a health warning. She opened her mouth to tell him just that, but he spoke first.

'We seem to have got off on the wrong foot.' He leant forward to rest his elbows on his thighs and she distractedly took in the rippling of muscle under the thin shirt, the powerful arms lightly dusted with a sprinkling of dark hair. 'I'm not here to hire you for myself. I'm here to hire you for my daughter.'

Melissa's mouth fell open and she gaped. The man *had a daughter*? Yes, he looked virile. In fact, physically at least, he was every inch the alpha male, just the sort magazines had a habit of pointing out was the average fertile woman's subconscious dream man, the sort that sent fantasies of reproduction into overdrive.

Melissa tried to picture him as a father and failed.

'You look shocked,' Elliot pointed out politely. 'Am I stretching the bounds of your imagination here?'

'Yes,' Melissa squawked truthfully. 'You have a *daughter*? I'm sorry…it's just that you don't seem…

well…you don't strike me as the sort of man…not that there's a *sort*…of course not—'

Elliot interrupted. 'This is something of a long story. If you're interested in hearing about the job, then I suggest we meet at a more civilised time to discuss it. I *had* expected to have sorted this matter out tonight, but it's now nine-thirty and I assume you have to get home, so shall we say six tomorrow evening? In the bar downstairs?'

'Six tomorrow. Yes. Fine,' Melissa repeated, still struggling to take in the impossible fact that Elliot Jay was a father.

He stood up and stared down at her. 'And just in case you're inclined to gossip, don't. I abhor it. This will be a private arrangement between us and I won't want the details to be spread around this gym.'

'I don't gossip.' Her wide blue eyes met his and then she couldn't look away. She just kept staring until he nodded curtly at her and swung around, leaving her still gaping like a stranded goldfish.

'And make sure that you're here on time tomorrow. I'm a busy man.'

Really and truly, Melissa had had no intention of taking whatever job he had in mind. The financial carrot he had dangled in front of her had barely registered, even though it was true that money was tight. She had arrived in London six months previously, clutching her newly gained qualifications and with no real appreciation of the fact that prices in London were on a completely different scale from prices in the north. Everything, she had rapidly discovered, was more expensive, and the most expensive of all was the housing market.

Right now, Melissa rented a studio apartment in Shepherd's Bush, which had optimistically advertised itself as warm, cosy and perfect for the single professional non-smoker. In reality it was poky, basic and not perfect for anything that had a pulse. The bathroom and toilet facilities were shared, which was hideous, and the kitchen was so tiny that cooking anything more elaborate than pasta required juggling skills she didn't possess. Her salary at the gym covered the rent and left a bit over for living expenses, but her hard-saved cash was slowly expiring. However much she tried to rein in the spending, life was just expensive in London.

The financially lucrative side of the proposal should have struck a chord but it hadn't.

The mention of a daughter had struck the chord.

Curiosity, she reminded herself over and over during the course of the following day, killed the cat. So he had a daughter. Big deal. That didn't make him unique, it made him a statistic.

A very persistent statistic, she discovered. The image of his dark, cold face hovered at the edge of her mind, alternately sending chills down her spine and spiking her curiosity. Curious enough to find herself at the internet café during her lunch break, surfing the net for information about Elliot Jay.

There was a wealth of it.

Thirty-two years old, with an illustrious academic background, having boarded at Winchester College and then moved on to Oxford University, which he left with a first-class degree in law and economics. His rise to power was chartered succinctly, a little background preceding the onslaught of information on his current status as financial giant with a talent for reading market trends and betting audaciously on the outcome.

No mention, she noticed, eating a baguette and scanning down the pages and pages of information, most of which covered details of deals that didn't interest her, of any daughter. Or, for that matter, of any wife.

In fact, not much information about his personal background at all. She wondered whether he kept his wife and daughter locked away in a closet somewhere. Maybe the basement of his house, where they couldn't interfere in his life. He was, as he had said himself, *a very busy man*. Too busy for a family? They had probably come along at a time before his glittering career had taken shape and had since had to take a back seat to the deals and acquisitions. From what she read, the only thing the man seemed to do was work.

Or maybe, she thought, reluctantly switching off the computer, the daughter was a ruse to get her interested in whatever proposal he had in mind.

Melissa, despite her practical training, had a vibrant imagination. One wayward thought could spiral into a series of improbable scenarios which she savoured with childish enjoyment. Even she, though, couldn't see why someone like Elliot Jay might have concocted a daughter out of thin air for her benefit. Which meant the daughter must be real. Which spiked her curiosity even more. Which, in turn, meant that by a quarter to six she was waiting for Elliot Jay in the bar, nursing a glass of sparkling mineral water.

And she had even spent an unheard-of length of time in one of the plush ladies' rooms trying to do something with her appearance. Her hair was beyond control. Too blonde, too curly and too fond of doing its own thing, which usually involved staging an all-out rebellion against hair-clips and tie-backs. She had done her best with it, which meant tying it back as firmly as she could into something of a French plait. It was long enough to succumb to that attempt at restraint, but just not sleek enough to do so gracefully. As a result wispy tendrils floated around her face and it would have taken a bulk buy of hair grips to subdue them.

Her face, though, she had worked with. She had always thought that the advantage of having an ordinary face was that it could be made up to look less plain than it really was. And she had an ordinary face. There were no cheekbones you could cut with, no wide, full lips for a truly sensual look, no thatch of black eyelashes like those that always stared back at her in an unbelievably long manner from the pages of magazines advertising mascara. She had an oval face, blue eyes with no mysterious green flecks, a small, straight nose and a mouth that looked ready to smile at the slightest opportunity.

That about summed it up. She had applied some lip gloss and livened up her colour with some blusher. Her figure she had played down, just as she always had, ever since the age of thirteen when her curves and breasts had become an unwelcome focus of adolescent male attention. Her dress, just like the one she had worn the previous day, was functional and summery and twinned with a lightweight boxy jacket, and successfully managed to conceal most of her figure. At least the bits of it she didn't much like.

She sipped her water, feeling in control, and glanced down idly at the *Financial Times* resting on the small circular table in front of her. When she looked back up at the door, it was to see Elliot Jay framed in it, his sharp eyes glancing across the room and finding her.

Melissa felt her stomach go into brief, unpleasant free fall. If it was possible, he looked even more intimidating from a distance than he had from close up the night before. His body was long and elegant and muscular. His conventional grey suit should have disguised the fact but didn't. He looked like a sophisticated predator. From what she had read about him, he looked the way he was. A ruthless financier who had no time for the frivolous

side of life. Did he ever laugh? For that matter, did his
face ever crack into a smile?

He covered the distance between them while she was
still staring at him.

'You're on time. Good.' He sat down and glanced at
her.

'I usually *am* on time. You caught me off guard yesterday, as I explained.'

'You're drinking water. Is that to impress me or is it
in accordance with your diet? I expect as a nutritionist
you take your food very seriously.'

'I didn't think I had to impress you, Mr Jay.'

'Elliot.'

'Elliot. And I'm drinking water because getting
sloshed on wine in the bar of the health club I work in
doesn't seem appropriate.' Melissa could feel every nerve
in her body standing to attention.

'No, I don't suppose it does. Least of all if you're a
nutritionist by profession. Samantha gave me a bit of
background about you. Perhaps you'd like to fill me in
yourself?'

For one dizzy minute, she thought that he was asking
her about her private life, inviting her to launch into an
explanation of what she did aside from working at Vigo,
but then common sense kicked in. The man wanted to
put a deal to her and he needed to find out what qualifications she had and what her experience was.

'Don't you think you should tell me what the job is
that you have in mind for me first? Then, if it sounds
promising, I can go through my work experience with
you.'

Elliot sat forward, his body shifting only by a matter
of a few inches, but enough for Melissa's instincts to
shriek in alarm and cause her to pull back.

'Let's get one thing straight, Miss Lee; I ask the questions. You provide the information.'

'That sounds like a democratic process,' Melissa commented blandly and for just one second she caught astonishment in his eyes. Surprise that she had dared respond to something that didn't invite a response.

'I'm glad you agree,' he said coolly. 'Now I'm going to get something for myself to drink. Would you like another...water?'

'Oh, no. I find one glass is enough for me. Another one and it might just start tasting medicinal.' She waggled her glass at him and in return he nodded in a clipped fashion before stalking off to the bar. Noticeable how the bartender scurried over to him, she thought wryly. Must come with being an autocrat.

As soon as he sat back down she handed him her CV, which she had thought to bring only at the last minute. Elliot read it quickly, put it on the table between them and sat back in the chair, nursing a glass of white wine.

'Good A levels but no university degree. How come?'

Well, he *was* a *very busy man*. No time for any polite leads into the interrogation process.

'I decided to take a year out in America. The easiest way was down the au pair route and I enjoyed the work so much that I returned to England and put the degree on hold.'

'That would imply that getting a degree wasn't of any great importance in the first place.'

Melissa shrugged. 'I thought you were going to ask questions. You didn't tell me that you were going to put your own interpretation on the answers.'

Elliot felt another surge of frustration, like an itch in the middle of his back, which he just couldn't reach to scratch. 'It's part and parcel of getting to know you, which I believe is part of the point of an interview...'

'For a job which I may or may not accept.'

He resisted a sigh. 'Why did you decide to switch from nannying to physiotherapy?' His eyes roamed unconsciously down her body and came up against the immutable barrier of another flowered dress. This time the flowers were smaller and closer together. It reminded him of a quilt cover used by one of his girlfriends many years ago. He stopped his lazy, hooded inspection to listen to her telling him about the switch in her career path, explaining that she had always taken a keen interest in the practical workings of the body, that it had seemed a sensible thing to do in terms of a long-term career. The course had been up north and she had been able to live with her parents while she did it, so that the money accumulated from her nannying days could be saved.

'Thank goodness,' she was explaining now in what struck him as a very melodic voice for someone so drab. 'The cost of living in London is ridiculous. Have you any idea what sort of prices landlords are charging for rooms? No, I don't suppose you have. Well, a lot. Just in case you ever feel the need to know.'

Elliot relaxed. Money. Whoever said it wasn't the universal language? Never mind the hard-to-get, I-just-might-turn-your-offer-down approach she was taking. She needed the money, just as he had expected.

'Shocking,' he drawled. 'Samantha has a high opinion of you. Says you're reliable, you know what you're talking about and you're prepared to take on new challenges. She also says that you're very good with people.' *Forthright* might have been a better word, he thought.

Melissa's face dimpled into a smile. 'I like to think so, but it's very nice knowing that someone else agrees.'

The smile gave her face a radiance that now matched her voice and for a few seconds he was a little taken aback.

Like all facets of his life, women were neatly slotted
into a category. Not that he ran through them at a rate of
knots. He didn't. The lifestyle of a workaholic could not
accommodate the lifestyle of a playboy and there had
never been any question of making the choice. He dated
women as driven as himself. They had always been high-
ranking professionals and the conversation was always
invigorating. It was an eye-opener and damned useful to
see how the female population considered business problems, to understand the angle they came from.

And right now…

Elliot glanced down at his watch. He still had time. He
wouldn't be meeting Alison for another hour and a half,
a rare treat to meet her so early in the evening, and on a
weekday, when one or the other of them, more often than
not both, just wouldn't have been able to get away.

'Do you enjoy your job?' he asked suddenly, switching
his thoughts from his date.

'Of course I do.'

'What I have in mind would require your full attention,
at least from four in the afternoon onwards. You might
also be asked to report for duty on some mornings, probably around seven.'

'Report for duty.' She gave him a quizzical smile.

'That's about it essentially. Naturally, there would be
no need for you to carry on working here while in my
employ, as the salary would be for a full-time position,
but you might want to continue with some of your clients
during the day when you had free time. The weekends,
I'm afraid, might involve work but overall I don't think
the position would be for longer than three months.'

Sick of pussyfooting around, Melissa decided to take
the bull by the horns. 'I looked you up on the internet.
During my lunch break. I found lots of stuff about you
but not a word about your wife or daughter.'

'I don't have a wife.'

'Oh. Divorced?'

The question met with a cold look of disapproval and Melissa raised her shoulders apologetically before he could launch into an attack on her nosiness. 'OK. I can tell from the expression on your face that the question was out of bounds. Am I right? No personal curiosity?'

'You got it in one,' Elliot grated.

'Because you hold the monopoly on asking questions. Am I right there as well? No, don't bother to answer that one. Tell me about your daughter, about the job. Not,' she felt constrained to add, 'that there's any guarantee that I'll take it...'

'Even though you obviously need the money?' Elliot said silkily. He named the figure he had in mind and watched with great satisfaction as she did a double take. 'Thought so,' he said softly. 'Too good to pass up, wouldn't you say? Especially when you consider that the job would leave you more or less free to carry on with whatever regular clients you've managed to recruit at the gym...'

Melissa looked at him with dislike. 'Not everyone is driven by money.'

'True. But most can be persuaded into accepting it.' A cool, cynical smile curved his mouth.

'What's your daughter's name and why is there no mention of her in any of the articles I read about you on the internet? Is there something wrong with her?'

The humourless smile vanished, replaced by a frown. 'No, there's nothing wrong with her, at least not in the sense I think you mean.' He had finished his drink and stood up. 'I need another one of these. You? Still going to stick to the mineral water because it just wouldn't do to be seen drinking alcohol in the health club bar?'

The way he said it made it sound like a challenge. Too

big a challenge to resist, especially when it was coming from him. 'OK. I'll have a white wine too.'

'So,' he said, minutes later when he had resumed his seat, 'about my daughter. I'll start with the easy bit. Her name's Lucy and she's fourteen years old.'

'Fourteen!' Melissa tried to do some rapid maths in her head. He would have been a teenager when he'd become a father! A young, hopeful husband with life stretching out before him with its infinite promise. Except he wasn't divorced, which meant that he had never married the woman who had fallen pregnant with his child.

'I see you've worked out the sums,' Elliot drawled, sipping the wine and looking at her over the rim of his glass. He seemed to be the master of the unreadable expression. There he sat, presenting her with this extraordinary fact, and there wasn't a flicker of emotion on his face. No wonder she felt so hot and bothered around him, she told herself, she just wasn't used to this level of emotionless coldness.

'I was at university when I met Rebecca. She was over from Australia doing her Masters in psychology. I was an undergraduate doing my degree in law and economics.' He paused and looked at her assessingly. 'Talking about my private life isn't something I'm accustomed to doing, but there seems to be no choice at the moment.' He carefully placed the glass on the table and linked his fingers together on his lap.

'Everybody has a private life,' Melissa said in bewilderment. 'I don't suppose anyone is interested in yours any more than you're interested in theirs.'

'In case you hadn't noticed, I'm not just *anyone*.'

Melissa looked for arrogance behind the remark, but surprisingly there was none. He was stating a fact.

'I know you're important, but you're still a human being.'

'An intensely private one. I do my utmost to keep my personal profile low. I'm telling you this because…'

'You think that the minute you walk out of here, I might just run around the gym spreading the salacious news. Not to mention going to a few of the tabloids and trying to flog the story.'

For the first time he smiled. Reluctantly but appreciatively. A genuine smile that knocked her sideways for a few suffocating seconds because it changed the harsh contours of his face. She had a glimpse of the sexy man underneath the ruthless, cold business machine and it was like receiving an electric shock.

She dodged her confusion in a quick gulp of wine. 'I won't. Believe it or not, I am a professional and I don't blab. Not that I would blab even if I wasn't a professional. So you had a fling when you were still a kid and discovered that the fling had slightly more permanent consequences than you'd anticipated.'

'Not really, no.'

'But you just said…'

'Yes, I had a fling. She was twenty-seven to my eighteen. Lust met opportunity and…' He looked at her from under his lashes, expecting comprehension, and Melissa nodded, head inclined to one side.

Lust meeting opportunity was a situation she had personally never encountered. Friendship meeting curiosity, yes, she'd experienced two of those, both short-lived and amicable in their endings. Lust, on the other hand, was something of an alien concept. She glanced at that brooding, darkly handsome face and shivered.

'And…?'

CHAPTER TWO

'AND a relationship was born.' He shrugged.

Eyes wide, Melissa leant forward and looked at him with frowning concentration. 'You make it sound like a mathematical equation. Didn't it mean anything to you?'

Elliot clicked his tongue dismissively. 'This isn't about what that relationship meant to me. It's about dealing with the consequences of it.' When she looked at him like that, big blue eyes wide with interest, it was like being gazed at by a puppy. He suppressed his irritation and brought the subject unequivocally back to the matter in hand. 'The point is that what we had lasted six months or thereabouts. It was fun but it was never destined to last.'

'Who broke it off?'

This time he snapped and leaned towards her with an aggressive thrust of his jaw. 'It doesn't matter. Can you understand that? The details are irrelevant! The fact is that Rebecca returned to Australia with no forwarding address. I never knew she was pregnant. Until, that is, six months ago, when I was contacted by my lawyer and informed I had a daughter.'

Melissa's mouth opened in shock. 'What happened?'

'What happened was a road accident. Rebecca and her husband were apparently both dead by the time the ambulance got to the scene.'

'How awful.'

'Yes, I imagine it was,' Elliot conceded. 'The bald truth of the matter, however, is that Rebecca was an only child. Her only living relative close to her was her

23

mother, who lives in an old people's home in Melbourne and Brian...well, her husband had an assortment of relatives, none of whom he was particularly close to. He was English and hadn't actually returned to this country for nearly fourteen years.'

'And how did they...find out about...well, *you*?'

'I was named on the birth certificate, for a start. It was also lodged in their joint will that should anything happen to them, I was to be contacted.'

He was relaying a string of facts. His face, as Melissa stared at him, was unreadable. She felt an unexpected pang of sympathy for him. She felt an even bigger surge of compassion for his daughter, abruptly having to face the loss of her mother and stepfather as well as the disorientation of finding herself in another country, far from home and the familiar things she had grown up with.

With sudden impulse, she reached out to put her hand on his wrist and their eyes met. He didn't physically withdraw his hand, but he might just as well have because his eyes were cool and unwelcoming.

'There's no need to feel sorry for me. It's a situation that has to be dealt with, which is where you come in.'

Melissa removed her hand as though she had been stung.

'Lucy hasn't settled in very well over here.'

'Can you blame her?'

'Of course not. But that doesn't change the reality of the situation. She's at a school she claims to loathe, she takes refuge in her bedroom whenever she can and she eats. She's put on quite a bit of weight since she arrived on my doorstep five months ago and there's no sign of her breaking out of the pattern.'

'And what do you want me to do about it?' Melissa asked, bewildered. Couldn't he see that that was a problem he had to sort out himself?

'Put her on some kind of controlled diet, encourage her to do some exercise.'

'But…'

'Does the job appeal to you or not? It's as simple a question as that. If not, then I won't waste my time further.'

'It's not really about whether the job appeals or not,' Melissa felt obliged to explain, even though his expression wasn't encouraging. 'It's about whether I would be of any use…well, in a situation like that. It seems to be a very complex one and…'

'All situations, complex or not, have solutions. Cut away the waffle and the psychobabble and there is always a solution, and the easiest solutions are usually the most effective.'

'That might work in the world of business,' Melissa retorted, 'but it doesn't work when it comes to real life.'

'As I said, problems have solutions. Being naïve and emotional doesn't get anyone very far in coming up with the solutions. Now, are you prepared to take this job on?'

Was she? Was she prepared to have anything further to do with this man? He was as unfeeling as a block of ice and working for him would be a lesson in endurance, which was something that didn't feature highly on her list of *must do* experiences.

On the other hand, her imagination was stirred at the thought of his daughter.

She nodded silently.

'Right. Then let's get down to business.' He reached inside the pocket of his lightweight jacket and produced an envelope, from which he extracted a sheet of paper. 'It's a contract,' he said shortly, interpreting her bemused expression. 'It lays out all the terms of conditions of this placement. You just need to sign…there.' One long finger pointed to the bottom and he handed her a pen that was as classy as his clothes and his watch and his shoes and everything else about him.

'Is a contract really necessary?' Melissa asked dubiously. 'I mean, we can keep things informal…'

'We could. But we won't.'

She reluctantly took the pen, signed on the dotted line and wondered what she was signing herself up for.

'Good. I'll hang on to your CV so that I have all the details of your address and phone number, and a copy of this will be sent to you tomorrow. I've spoken to Samantha and she'll release you whenever you feel free to start. My preference is for next Monday. That way you'll have a couple of days to readjust your appointments because your day here will effectively end by three-thirty, in time to meet Lucy from school.'

'You want her to exercise *every day*?'

'That might work.' He hesitated, thinking about what he was going to say next, how he was going to phrase his intentions. 'I'm not talking about gruelling workouts…'

'Oh, I doubt I could oblige there anyway…' Melissa couldn't resist grinning. 'My workouts are strictly geared towards the less energetic…'

The grin was infectious. Not that Elliot was inclined to grin back. He did, however, find himself slightly put off his stride. 'Why would you choose to work at a health club if you don't like exercising?'

'Oh, I never said that I didn't *like* it. In small doses, exercise is good fun. But intense workouts don't do a great deal for me. And to answer your question, I came here to work because it offered an interesting clientele and the surroundings are terrific. Also, it was the first place to offer me a job.'

'Interesting clientele…'

'Yes. This place is popular with lots of sports people.

I get a fair amount of practice working with sporting injuries.' She paused and looked at him curiously. 'What do *you* do here?'

'Squash,' Elliot said abruptly. He suddenly realised that he had swerved off the subject. Time was moving on. He glanced down at his watch. 'Twice a week if I'm lucky. It's fast, it's furious and it's competitive.'

Three things that a man like this one would relish, she thought, particularly the competitive aspect of it. Swimming could be fast and furious but then it would lack that essential ingredient of pitting one's skills against someone else.

'Which is beside the point,' he said, snapping her out of her speculations. 'The point is that the job would involve slightly more than a simple diet sheet and some light sit-ups.' He sighed heavily, the first sign of any human emotion, and leant forward, elbows resting on his thighs. 'I would want you to motivate my daughter. I am not utterly insensitive. I understand she's going through a very difficult time but I am rarely around at civilised hours. I have an intensely demanding job.'

'What do you mean by *motivate*?'

'Take her jogging now and again in the park, maybe followed by something to eat afterwards. Introduce her to some of the shops. Naturally you will have a bank account opened for you and a credit card issued so that there will be no necessity to think about the money aspect of it.'

'But...'

'I'm coming to that. It all might eat into your private life, hence the substantial salary I'm offering. However, it will be of a limited time duration. I'm sure whatever boyfriend you might have in the background could adjust for a short while.' Actually, he hadn't really considered whether she had a boyfriend or not. Now he found himself wondering what sort of boy he would be, should she have one. She seemed spectacularly unimpressed by material things, so he imagined someone fairly run of the mill, a nice, unchallenging lad, the kind that mums and dads up and down the land would love to see their daughters bring home.

'It's not a question of a boyfriend...'

'No one around on the scene? That's good.'

'Which isn't to say that I don't have a social life,' Melissa informed him, feeling like someone trying to swim against a strong current.

'Which isn't to say that I have implied that,' Elliot said, gravely mimicking her turn of expression. 'All I am saying is that some flexibility might be required and I'm sure I can leave that in your hands. All you need do is to show up at my place next Monday at, let's say, four? Lucy should be back from school by then and if not Lenka can always let you in.'

'Lenka?'

'My Polish housekeeper. She's there every day.'

And that was it? End of discussion? She could see that he was getting ready to leave.

'And what about *you*?' she squeaked urgently, and was granted a puzzled look.

'What about me?'

'Are you in touch with Planet Earth? I mean, I know you're a bigwig in the City and you're probably used to snapping your fingers and having everyone jump to attention without asking any questions, but that's just not how it works in a situation like this!'

Elliot opened his mouth to speak. No one, but *no one* talked to him like this! Least of all someone he was about to employ and on a damned good salary besides! Although the remark about him snapping his fingers did carry a certain element of truth. He swallowed back his immediate impulse and looked at her coolly and politely.

'I can't just present myself to your daughter when she gets back from school. She won't have a clue what to do and neither will I.'

'Naturally I will forewarn her of your arrival.'

'By telling her what?'

'By telling her that you've been employed to help her work on an exercise and diet programme.' He shrugged. 'It seems pretty straightforward to me.'

'Well, it might seem straightforward to *you*, but it doesn't seem straightforward to *me*.' She stuck her chin out and braced herself to rush headlong into the full blast of his disapproval. 'And furthermore, there will be no question of my taking this job unless I get a little co-operation from you!'

'Feel free to explain,' Elliot said in a withering voice.

'You need to be there when I am introduced to your daughter! It's going to be an awkward moment and you might just want to get the arrangement off to a good start by smoothing things over from the beginning!'

'Smoothing things over...' He laughed mirthlessly. 'I think you've picked the wrong candidate for that particular job. In the past five months I can say with my hand on my heart that smoothing things over with Lucy is something I have abundantly failed to achieve. However, I'll make sure that I'm there to do the introductions.' He stood up. 'I'm afraid I really have to leave you now. Is there anything else you need to know?'

All the surface details were in place, but there was so much else Melissa felt she needed to know that she was stuck for words. She got to her feet and shook her head with a little laugh. 'Nothing that you'll probably feel inclined to tell me.'

'Meaning?' Elliot asked, turning away and heading for the door, which he proceeded to hold open for her.

'I suppose meaning how you feel about all of this, not just the practical issues involved. Meaning what your daughter is really like, as opposed to your description of her as an unhappy teenager who happened to find herself at your door one day. Meaning where you'd like things to end up, where you'd like to see your relationship with your daughter heading. It must be very hard for you, but you must have some thoughts about all of that stuff…'

'You're right,' Elliot said flatly, barely pausing in his stride towards the exit to spare her a brief look. 'There are no answers there that I feel inclined to tell you. I'll see you on Monday at four. Till then.' He nodded curtly in her direction and she watched as he disappeared from sight.

He'd vanished with a contract signed by her for a job which she was grappling to understand. On the surface, it bore all the hallmarks of a business arrangement, but scratch the surface and she knew that there was nothing businesslike about it at all. Whether he wanted to admit it or not, this arrangement was anchored in emotion. The emotions of an adolescent she didn't know and wasn't sure would even like *her*.

Why on earth would an unhappy, displaced teenager want to throw herself with delight into a diet and exercise routine with a perfect stranger? Someone employed by a man who was her father by blood only? Would she see it as a helpful gesture on the part of a newly found father trying to understand, or an insult from someone who couldn't be bothered to take time out to sort the situation?

The latter, she assumed, if Lucy was an ordinary mortal and not someone blessed with supernatural powers of insight. Elliot Jay was a study in coldness and if he intimidated *her*, then lord only knew what kind of effect he had on his daughter.

The thoughts ran round and round in her head for the remainder of the week and over the weekend, like little mice scurrying around in a cage. The worst of it was the fact that not only did she have to deal with a situation that was beginning to look like a disaster in the making, but also there was no one she could share the problem with.

Elliot had cautioned against gossip, which ruled out talking to all the people she knew at the gym, and she even felt treacherous thinking about asking an opinion from any of her friends she had left behind up north.

In the end she phoned her mum and after the usual pleasantries, which always included the key question about whether she was eating properly, she hesitatingly confided that she had managed to land a job outside working hours at the gym.

'Job? What kind of job?'

Melissa instantly regretted her foolhardy impulse to confide, least of all in her mother. Mothers, she belatedly thought, fussed, and her mother was the queen of fussers. How could she have forgotten all those anxious phone calls when she had been in America, checking to make sure that her baby was all right and hadn't been abducted by any stray perverts?

'Oh, as a nutritionist and exercise trainer,' Melissa said vaguely, plopping herself on the uncomfortable sofa that doubled up as a bed. She pictured her adorable mother, with her short, fluffy hair, frowning in concern. Imagination was definitely an inherited family trait. Thank goodness her father would be in later to spread some of his common sense and reason.

'Why would you need to do that outside normal working hours?'

'It's for a girl. A teenager. Her dad is a bit concerned about her eating habits. He's employed me to help out after school. Now and again.'

'Why on earth would he do that? Why not just get the child to join the gym?'

'Because...' Melissa tried to find a perfectly sensible answer to a perfectly sensible question... 'it's a question of transport,' she answered eventually. 'London isn't like home, Mum. There are tubes and trains and hundreds of buses...' That much was true at any rate, and she could almost hear her mother thinking that perhaps there was a little sense in that. The thought of teenagers and the underground system didn't go hand in hand in her mother's mind. Since she'd never been to London, her ideas of the transport system there were riddled with inaccuracies, only some of which Melissa had been able to put to rest.

'I can understand why a concerned father might not want his teenage girl to use public transport, I suppose.'

'And the salary's fantastic.' Which brought a new host of concerns. Why was this man paying her so much? She hoped there was no hidden agenda there! Melissa should know that men could be very underhand!

Melissa half listened, half thought about Elliot. His face was strangely recurring. In fact, she realised that she had been thinking of very little else for the past few days. She grinned to herself, listening to her mother, at the thought of how her mother would react should Melissa tell her that there was a man on her mind. She didn't think that Elliot and her parents would get along very well. They were a traditional, homely couple who enjoyed the simple things in life. He was...the opposite. She tried to imagine him as a homely type and had to stifle her laughter. He was about as homely as a charging rhino.

The phone call, even though she had said nothing much about the job, helped. Just talking to her mother helped. She just had to imagine her sensible, loving, supremely normal childhood to get everything else into perspective.

As a result, Melissa arrived at his apartment block on Monday at four precisely, still in an upbeat frame of mind.

Only as she stood outside, staring up at the white-fronted converted Georgian house, did her heart begin to fall.

She had thought to bring some books on diets and foods, a couple of easy-reading ones that a teenager might not find too offensive. She had been careful in choosing them, not wanting to look like someone who solved a body-odour problem in a colleague by giving them deodorant for a birthday present.

It had seemed an optimistic plan this morning. Now she felt horribly inexperienced to tackle what was hiding under the superficial problem. She took a deep breath and entered the building. There were no name-plates on the outside behind little plastic windows. She discovered the reason as soon as she walked inside. This was no ordinary converted house. Several houses had been knocked into one complete apartment block. Most of the ground floor consisted of an enormous porter's block and beyond that stretched gleaming flagstone tiles with sofas discreetly dispersed amongst large, abnormally healthy-looking plants.

There were two porters behind the shiny oak desk. One of them immediately and sharply asked whether he could help and Melissa tentatively approached, gave her name and asked for Mr Jay.

'Oh, yes. You must be Miss Lee. Mr Jay is expecting you. I'll just ring up.'

They both kept an eye on her while she looked around. Even the atmosphere in the place seemed different, smelled different. There was the smell of extreme wealth as opposed, she thought, to the vague smell of boiled cabbage that always greeted her whenever she walked into her block of flats. The exquisite flooring and the giant plants also helped with the impression. When she walked into the tiny hallway of her place, there wasn't a plant to be seen, never mind ones that looked as though they could swallow people whole, and the flooring was tired, cheap and stained round edges which had not seen any form of cleaning fluid for years.

'The lifts are through to the right,' the porter informed her, pointing. 'Straight up to the fourth floor.'

'Tell me,' Melissa said confidentially, 'how on earth do you manage to get your plants to look so healthy? I mean, are they *real*?'

It was an irresistible question for the plump porter, whose face had not cracked into a smile since the minute she had stepped through the door.

'Real,' he said in a triumphant voice. 'Chose them myself. The company that maintains the place wanted to have them provided by one of those plant firms but I persuaded them to let me have a go at kitting the place out. Bit of a plant fanatic, I am.' He leaned towards her. 'Just between you and me, I would love to move out to the country, get to see a bit of nature. Not much of that in London, I'm afraid.'

That made her think of her own home. Before she knew it she was chatting to him, telling him about the Yorkshire landscape, its rugged beauty, telling him about the orchids her father painstakingly cultivated.

'I haven't inherited his magic touch, though,' she finished sadly, thinking of her own efforts to brighten up her bedsit with one or two flowering plants. After their

initial burst of good health, the flowers had all dropped
off and all that remained were leaves. The leaves were
thriving but defeated the purpose since she had wanted
colour.

She left for the lift with the offer of a gardening book
on its way.

With her cheerful frame of mind back in place, she
headed up and was disgorged with a ping into a plushly
carpeted hall. Two large blue and white urns greeted her,
sandwiching a massive oval mirror, just right for checking her appearance, which, as usual, was not inspiring.

Not quite sure what to wear to win over an unhappy
adolescent, Melissa had chosen a pair of casual cream-
coloured trousers and a knitted cotton short-sleeved top
with broad stripes. Now, inspecting herself in the conveniently placed mirror, she realised that the top was a
tad too tight for her liking. Well, too tight given the size
of her chest, which really needed camouflaging if her
breasts weren't to stick out the way they were doing now,
making all sorts of statements. And the broad horizontal
stripes weren't too flattering either. Broad horizontal
stripes, she decided glumly, should only be worn by very
tall women who weighed under eight stone.

'Finished?' a voice enquired politely from somewhere
to her right and Melissa jumped. 'Not that I want to rush
you in any way, of course.' Elliot emerged fully from the
doorway and stood there, inspecting her with his arms
folded.

'I was about to knock on the door,' she said, her face
bright red with embarrassment. 'Well, one of them.'

'Lucy's not back from school as yet.' He stood aside
so that she could walk past him and a tingling feeling
feathered through her as she brushed past him.

After the impressive entrance hall, Melissa was expecting more of the same from Elliot's apartment. She

wasn't disappointed. This was truly an eye-opener into
how the other half lived. The flat was open plan and
stretched the entire length of the converted houses. There
was no carpeting in sight. Just gleaming wood liberally
scattered with richly coloured rugs. The sitting area was
casual, with long, low sofas picking up the reds of the
rugs and the kitchen was a marvel of avant-garde crea-
tivity. Towards the back, a short, curving staircase with
wrought-iron banisters led up to what she could plainly
see was an office. She could just about make out the
bookshelves, the desk and the compulsory computer. In
the little niche below the staircase was a small sitting
area with a plasma-screen TV.

And away to both sides corridors led to other rooms.
Bedrooms and bathrooms, she presumed.

When she finally swivelled back round to look at
Elliot, it was to find his blue eyes on her and something
very nearly like amusement on his face.

'Don't blame me for staring,' Melissa said with a grin.
'It's not every day that a working-class gal finds herself
in a place like this.'

'Approve, do you?'

He hadn't expected to feel as gratified as he was feeling now at her reaction. When, after all, had been the
last time someone had entered his apartment and had
been so obviously bowled over? God, he couldn't remember! Money was a huge insulator. He mixed in circles where splendid apartments and country retreats were
the norm. People didn't merely take holidays, they had
travelling experiences, and because luxury was so readily
available, curiosity and wonder were reactions of the
past.

'It's absolutely…well…magnificent.' Melissa giggled
nervously. 'Should I take my shoes off? What if I scuff
all this expensive flooring?'

'What if you do?' Elliot drawled. 'No, you can keep your shoes on. They're nice, flat, sensible shoes. Very wood-flooring friendly.'

'That's me. Sensible.' She glanced down at her foot-wear, suddenly not much liking the fact that they were practical. 'It doesn't work wearing high heels when you have to travel on the underground. Too uncomfortable. What happens down the corridors?'

'What do you mean?'

'I mean, what's on either side?'

'You really can stop hovering there by the door.' He pushed himself off and headed towards the kitchen. 'Bedrooms and bathrooms happen. Six of the former and three of the latter. Do you want something to drink while we wait for Lucy to get home? Tea? Coffee?'

'Coffee would be fine. Thank you.' Should she go and sit on one of the sofas, she wondered, or should she join him in the kitchen, where bar stools were perched under the curving counter? Bar stool. Less formal. Plus she wouldn't have to shout to him while he rustled about in the kitchen doing something clever with a machine that looked as though it would be at home on a spaceship.

She hadn't banked on being quite as mesmerised by the movement of his hands as she watched him fiddle with the machine. She cupped her chin in the palm of her hand and stared, only launching into conversation when he moved away from the machine to get some milk from the fridge, and then, typically, she heard herself rattling on in an inane manner about, of all things, the wretched coffee maker. Asking him how on earth he could possibly understand something that looked so alien, sounding like a brainless bimbo instead of the qualified professional that she was.

'Really,' she said, in a last-ditch attempt to rescue her-self from complete idiocy, 'what I mean is that I really don't understand why anyone would want to bother with something that just takes so much time to do so little.'

'It's an expensive gadget.' He handed her a royal-blue cup filled with some very frothy coffee and then leaned down, resting his elbows on the counter, which was a manoeuvre that brought his disconcertingly close to her. Melissa pulled back and made indistinct yummy noises while her heart began to thud like a drum inside her.

'Men like gadgets and rich men like expensive gadgets. Or so one of my exes thought when she decided to buy this for me as a birthday present. Makes good coffee, though.'

'What…an unusual present to buy your boyfriend,' Melissa mused aloud, her imagination now swerving madly to what sort of women he went out with. There had been no seedy pictures of him leaving clubs with a woman on his arm but now she thought that any woman who gave a man a sophisticated piece of kitchen gadgetry must be as sophisticated as he was. 'Maybe it was a hint that she wanted you to spend more time in the kitchen,' she said, voicing her thoughts. When there was no response, she glanced at him to find that he was watching her coolly. 'Or maybe,' she continued, remembering that she was there in an official capacity and not as some kind of chum free to express her thoughts on any and everything, 'her father owned a kitchen shop and there were a few going spare.' She smiled nervously and sipped some coffee. 'What time does Lucy usually get home?'

Elliot glanced at his watch and frowned. 'A little before four, I believe.'

'You believe?'

'I can't say that I'm generally around to meet her when she gets in from school,' he answered irritably. 'Lenka is normally here, although the child *is* fourteen years old, after all, and fully capable of letting herself into the apartment. That's nothing that a lot of teenagers don't do themselves.'

'I never did,' Melissa said. 'My mum was a great believer in a stable home environment. I would get the bus home from school and she was always there, waiting by the door. Probably a very old-fashioned concept these days. I can't really imagine what it must be like to still be a child and then have to get back to an empty house and start preparing some food for yourself...'

'Can't you?' He strolled over to the fridge, hunted out a plastic container of juice and poured himself a glass. He didn't return to the counter, but instead remained where he was, on the opposite side of the kitchen, half leaning against the imposing American-style fridge. 'I don't really think it takes an unusual amount of imagination to deal with the concept and, unlike you, I don't think accepting some responsibility at the age of fourteen is undesirable.' He didn't like the expression on her face. She had the slightly superior look of someone who thought that whatever they were hearing was really a lot of drivel. It grated. 'In fact,' he said flatly, 'I myself was quite accustomed to doing much the same myself. My parents lived in the Far East and from the age of fourteen I was quite used to spending at least some of the holidays and all of the half-terms in our London flat, often by myself. It never did *me* any harm.' He drank down the juice in one long gulp and dumped the empty glass directly into the sink.

'Didn't you get...lonely?' Melissa asked. She cradled the cup in her hands and stared absentmindedly at the remainder of the coffee, which was now quite tepid. In her head, she was imagining Elliot as a teenager, letting himself into a flat somewhere, laden down with school books and a rucksack full of dirty washing.

'Of course not!' Elliot dismissed scornfully. The conversation was now really beginning to get on his nerves. 'I gained self-reliance and believe me when I tell you that, to get anywhere in life, self-reliance is essential.'

She didn't say anything to that, but she was looking at him now, blonde hair escaping in tendrils around her face and big blue eyes full of disbelief. It took a supreme effort not to pursue the topic until he wiped that disbelief from her face, but then he reminded himself that her thoughts on matters unrelated to what she was going to be paid to do were of no relevance to him whatsoever.

'Yes. Of course.'

Mouthing platitudes, he thought with another huge surge of irritation. Just saying what she expected he wanted to hear because he was, after all, now her employer and a very generous one at that.

'Which brings us back to Lucy. Where the hell is she?'

'Sometimes there are after-school things going on.'

'Sometimes there are,' Elliot grated, 'but not today. I made it perfectly clear to her that she was to be back here promptly by four so that she could meet you.' He pulled out his cellphone, flicked through the directory and scowled at his watch while he waited for whoever he was calling to pick up. When it was picked up, there wasn't much Melissa could glean from the conversation. He barked out a few questions then listened, finally ringing off, only to make a couple more calls. These she could understand. One was to the school, the other to a private number. Both parties confirmed that Lucy had left school on time.

'Where is she?' Melissa asked. 'Did they say?'

'Where she should be,' Elliot said, 'is here. Where she is…' he prowled restlessly, frowning, into the sitting area and Melissa swivelled on the bar stool to follow him '…no one appears to know…'

CHAPTER THREE

IT WAS nearly forty minutes before Lenka arrived at the apartment, flustered and concerned. Melissa was sitting on a sofa and for a few minutes the girl had no awareness that Elliot wasn't alone. In that time, Melissa had the opportunity to watch their interaction.

Lenka, from what she could judge, was no older than eighteen or nineteen, a thin, brown-haired girl with an anxious face, now creased into further lines of worry as she spoke to Elliot in broken English.

And, judging from the poor girl's expression, she was as intimidated by her employer as everyone else on the face of the earth probably was. Melissa could understand why. The minute she walked through the door, Elliot had made no effort to put her at ease. He had towered over her like judge and jury rolled into one, and Melissa could see Lenka visibly flinch as a series of questions were fired out at her. There was nothing accusatory in any of the questions, but he was not a sympathetic inquisitor.

Did the man ever relax? she wondered. And behave like a normal human being?

At the end of five minutes, with her role of spectator becoming increasingly uncomfortable, Melissa pointedly cleared her throat and Lenka immediately swung round to look at her. The relief at seeing another female made her shoulders sag and then she promptly repeated every-thing she had just told Elliot, wringing her hands with such obvious dismay that Melissa stood up and walked over so that she could give the girl a comforting hug.

'Calm down,' she said, drawing Lenka to the sofa,

'nothing is your fault.' She glanced over her shoulder to see Elliot staring at them with a face still like thunder.

'Perhaps Lenka might like a cup of tea, or coffee?'

Elliot looked at her as though tempted to ask where she was proceeding with that remark. Melissa decided to make it perfectly clear.

'She's distraught,' she said firmly. 'I think a strong cup of tea with some sugar might be a good idea. Would you mind...?'

She realised what it must feel like to ask someone a question that was so utterly incomprehensible that you might as well be talking in another language, and for some reason she felt a sudden rush of heady power. For the first time she had come into contact with him, he was not in a position to assert his stamp of authority and to do precisely what he wanted to do. She was trying to calm down his hysterical housekeeper and, with a question placed so directly, he had no option but to do as she had requested.

He brought the tea over, sat down heavily on the chair facing them and watched as Melissa coaxed some calm into Lenka. It was all a protracted business and one that was bringing them no closer to sorting out the disappearance of his daughter, if disappearance was what it was.

After a few minutes, during which time his impatience went up a few more notches, he said curtly, 'It's now nearly six. Lenka, have you any idea at all where Lucy might be?'

He had to stop himself from obeying his instinct to act by telling the girl to pull herself together. As though reading his mind, Melissa looked across at him warningly.

'Any idea at all, Lenka?' Melissa translated the question into something less blatantly and impatiently aggressive.

Lenka, after fighting the temptation to resume her hysterics, dabbed her red-rimmed eyes with a handkerchief that had been produced seemingly from nowhere, and gave the question some thought.

Lucy, apparently, had no friends, or none that she had ever brought back with her to the apartment. She very rarely stayed at school for any extracurricular activities, apart from sports, which was on a Friday. But even taking that into account, no, she couldn't understand why Lucy would not be home.

'I do not know where she could go!' Lenka looked completely bewildered by the situation.

'What about…' Melissa looked hesitantly over at Elliot '…any boys, Lenka? Has Lucy ever mentioned a boy to you? It's important you tell the truth here—'

'Don't be ridiculous!' Elliot interrupted harshly. 'Boys? The girl is fourteen!'

'Old enough, according to you, to come back here and stay on her own, to develop some essential *self-reliance*. Well, if a girl is old enough to do that then she's old enough to have a boyfriend!' Old enough, she left unsaid, to seek an outlet for her own unhappiness by trying to find a bit of understanding in the arms of a boy. Fuelled by testosterone, a boy would be more than happy to get rid of a girl's unhappiness in the sack.

It wasn't a palatable thought, but if he wanted to be realistic about her non-appearance, then why spare him the details? Much as it made her sick to think of a child of fourteen being sexually active, Melissa knew that it happened.

Lenka, who had only just managed to follow the sharp conversation between the two of them, was shaking her head.

'No boys,' she said at last. 'She never mentioned one to me. No.'

'In which case,' Elliot rose to his feet and snatched the phone from its cradle, 'we get in touch with the police.'

Melissa didn't bother to tell him that a teenager missing for less than two hours was not going to have them rushing out 'Wanted' posters all over London and gearing up a team of fifty strong to go hunting.

She waited until he had replaced the receiver and then listened diplomatically to his colourful invective as he paced the room, cursing an inept police force, gesticulating to emphasise his complete disgust and challenging her to interrupt, to just *dare*.

Although she wasn't in the firing line for this overwhelming tirade, Lenka cowered further into the sofa as though wishing she could somehow push her way through the upholstery and emerge somewhere else, somewhere safer.

Melissa, on the other hand, felt oddly calm.

She waited until he had finished storming around the room like a caged animal and had flopped into the chair, his face dark with fury.

'I have an idea.'

Elliot looked at her and glowered. 'Why would you suggest that she might have got herself tangled up with some boy?'

'Because,' she sighed, 'it was an avenue that had to be explored. Do you have any experience at all of teenagers, Elliot? I mean, prior to Lucy?' This was the first time that unprompted she had called him by his name and just saying it made her stomach curl. She was horribly and acutely aware of the sheer force of his masculinity as he sat there, his blue eyes broodingly angry and focused on her face with such intensity that she could feel her face slowly suffuse with colour.

She almost forgot about Lenka, sniffing beside her on

the sofa, eyes downcast, hands compulsively twisting the sodden handkerchief.

'What does that have to do with anything?' Elliot growled.

'I take it that means no. Well, girls these days aren't quite the shrinking violets they were a few years ago...'

'Whoever said they were shrinking violets *then*?' His sexy mouth curved into a sudden knowing smile.

'A vulnerable, isolated young girl would be a very easy target for a boy or even, heaven forbid, a man. But I'm pretty sure Lucy would have mentioned something to Lenka.'

At the mention of her name, Lenka looked up and nodded vigorously.

'She say nothing to me about going out with a boy. She come home and go to her bedroom and do her homework.'

'I think we should check the cafés close by. She might just have gone into one of them and forgotten the time.'

Melissa stood up, itching to be out of the grand apartment and the gathering storm clouds. Whatever Lenka had said, there was still a chance that Lucy had become involved with someone, possibly someone undesirable, and heaven help her if she had. She glanced at Elliot's closed, angry face and shivered.

He turned to Lenka, who automatically cringed back into the chair, and informed her that she could leave.

'We'll handle the search,' he said, looking round at Melissa. 'There are enough cafés on Gloucester Road to keep us busy for hours. Dammit! This is just what I didn't need. Scouring the streets of London for a runaway child.'

'We don't know that she's run away,' Melissa said, as they hit the warm pavement outside.

'No, you're right. Like you said, she might just have

got herself tied up reading a really good book in the park somewhere.'

'I didn't think about the park. Maybe we should check there first.'

'And how do you suggest we do that?' He stopped and looked down at her. 'Maybe find ourselves a couple of loud-hailers and stroll around asking for one miscreant by the name of Lucy to come out of hiding and face the music?'

Melissa met his hard blue eyes steadily. She would love to have told him how dislikeable he was but common sense warned her to hold her tongue. Elliot was not a man to be criticised and she didn't want to find herself dismissed before she had even begun her job.

But he was right. Searching the park was out of the question. It was too big. But they did go there to have a quick look, on the slim off-chance that they might just get lucky and spot Lucy.

On a balmy early-June evening, it was crowded. Groups of people were sitting on the grass, office workers who had discarded their jackets and rolled up their sleeves. Some of the girls had come prepared for the weather and were lying back with their trousers pulled up as far as they possibly could be and bikini tops on, enjoying the warmth. The paths that wound around and through the park were full of people on bicycles and skateboards. There were even a few on horses, which looked bizarre to Melissa, who associated horse riding with country lanes.

It was only just June but already the summer was proving to be a hot one. Melissa found it uncomfortable. She was accustomed to cooler weather and up there in Yorkshire, even on hot days, there was still a breeze that blew across the open land and carried some relief from the stickiness that had built up in the city.

Elliot hadn't changed out of his suit, but he was no longer wearing a jacket and he, too, had rolled back the sleeves of his shirt, exposing his muscular arms dusted with fine, dark hair.

He moved with quick, purposeful strides through the park. He had told her that there was no point trying to scour every inch because it was impractical, but they could look around the area of park closest to the road, where she might have gone to laze around in the sunshine.

No one could have mistaken him for a tourist or an office worker detouring for some free relaxation on his way back home. No one could have confused him for anything but what he was, a man grimly searching for someone, inconvenienced and enraged by the fact that he was having to do it.

Not knowing who to look for, Melissa followed him from behind, watching as he strode a while, stopped, squinted slowly in a semicircle the area directly in front of him, then, finding nothing, moved on to do the same until finally he turned to her, his face hard with suppressed anger.

'This is pointless.' He pulled out his cellphone, dialled and waited for a couple of minutes before ending the call. 'No answer on the home phone, so she's either not back or not picking up.'

'What about her mobile phone?'

'Switched off. I suppose this now brings us to plan B. The cafés. And if that doesn't work, then I'll personally go to the police station and force them to start looking.'

They walked along in silence for a short while, away from the park, over the main road and then down towards Gloucester Road, Melissa barely glancing at the elegant, tall edifices on either side. Some were run-down, several fronted with scaffolding, but others were exquisitely maintained, glamorous dwellings in a glamorous post-code. They walked past them, Elliot still lost in his own thoughts.

'What sort of coffee-shop would you imagine a four-teen-year-old girl might frequent?' He finally broke the silence, although he carried on walking while he spoke, not looking at Melissa.

'Ones where they don't mind someone on their own lingering. You know what I mean.'

'If I knew, I wouldn't have asked.' He sighed heavily and raked his fingers through his hair, then he did turn to her with a crooked smile. 'Great start to your new job, wouldn't you agree? You should have been sitting down with my daughter, having a civilised chat in civilised sur-roundings, and instead you're tramping up and down the highways and byways of London searching for her.'

'I don't mind.' She smiled hesitantly.

'That's very generous-minded of you. Do you think we should believe that there isn't a boy involved, even though Lenka is adamant that there's been nothing along those lines going on?' He pulled her towards him to allow someone to get past and continued to watch her face in-tently. 'I doubt she and Lenka would have had the sort of relationship that encourages confidences.'

'There's no point thinking about that now.' Melissa didn't think it would help for him to know that she ech-oed his own suspicions. 'Let's search the places around here first.' She began moving away and he fell into step with her, although now the silence was broken. For the first time, something human peeped out from behind the steel exterior.

'I expect you think that I had a hand in this,' he said expressionlessly. 'That if I had thrown myself into the role of parenting, I wouldn't now have a daughter who thinks that she has to run away from an insupportable situation.'

'I expect it must have been difficult for you,' Melissa conceded. 'Having a daughter suddenly appear on your doorstep, and a teenager at that. Trying to fit it in with your hectic work schedule… On the other hand,' she continued, compelled to give the full breadth of her views now that she had been asked, so to speak, 'work is nothing compared to family. I mean, did you take *any* time off to get to know her?'

'Of course I did.' Some, he thought, deciding that he had no obligation to justify himself to a complete stranger. 'But teenagers are a fairly uncommunicative species…'

'So you gave up.'

'I gather that work, for you, is a little something that gets done to make way for the bigger issues of having family meals together and singing songs round a piano on winter evenings, but work, for me, is much more than that. It's the driving force that gives meaning to the very act of getting out of bed.'

'Is that why you never married? Never had a family?' Melissa was amazed that she had asked the question, but walking side by side meant that those fabulous, intimidating blue eyes were not on her face, making her squirm inside, scaring her away from the very thought of asking him a personal question. The problem was that asking personal questions was just part of her personality. It was why her clients liked her, why she had been so successful with her charges and with their parents when she had been nannying. She wasn't nosy, she was warmly and vitally interested, although she was surprised why she should be curious about a man for whom she had scant respect, even with his high-powered job, his vast wealth, or, she thought uncomfortably, his incredible looks.

There was something abstracted and only mildly interested in her voice. She wasn't trying to pump confidences out of him, trying to open him up and make him vulnerable, which was the ploy of some of the women he had dated in the past, the ones who thought that they could get past the 'No Entry' sign and somehow turn him into one of those sensitive New Men who were keen to bare their inner souls and were proud of crying.

Melissa was asking a question with no hidden strings attached, and for the first time in as long as he could remember, Elliot didn't automatically go into immediate shut-down.

'Got it in one,' he answered lazily. 'I was smart enough to realise that to have a family and kids would take time, and time was the one thing I didn't have at my disposal.'

'And you…never thought…what it might be like…?'

Elliot laughed, struck by her simplistic view of life. 'No, I really can't say that I ever have. You might think that a teenager is hard to inherit but I'm grateful that I didn't suddenly find myself the father of a toddler. I have no idea what I would have done in that situation.'

'Changed,' Melissa said simply. 'I don't think we need to look in restaurants. I doubt a teenager would be drawn to a restaurant if she wanted to go somewhere to think.'

On either side of the road were two restaurants. If he had wanted to unwind in his own company, he would have gone to either of them. But then, as she had said, what did he know about teenagers? The money angle would not have stopped Lucy from going into whichever damned establishment she chose. He might not have given her his time, but he had been generous with her allowance; overgenerous, some might have said.

'What do you mean *changed*? Changed into what?' Elliot suddenly demanded.

The conversation was punctuated by Elliot stopping so that he could look into some of the shops they walked past. The only way they could cover both sides of the road was by going down one side, turning back on themselves and covering the other, although he had given Melissa a brief description of what Lucy looked like. Approximately five feet seven inches, dark hair, blue eyes, slightly overweight. It could have fitted a thousand girls but she kept her eyes peeled to the other pavement anyway, just in case.

'Changed into someone who had to fit another person into their life, some other responsibility. If you had suddenly found yourself in charge of a toddler, then you wouldn't have had much choice. You might be selfish, but a toddler would have put you to shame.'

'Being selfish is completely different from enjoying what you do for a living.'

'Hmm. I suppose so. Sometimes.'

Well, that was as much a non-answer as he had ever heard, and it got just slightly under his skin, where it was like a burr, rubbing away through the ensuing silence as they continued the search.

It would shortly be getting dark. He tried the phone at the apartment again, and got no reply, then he tried her cellphone and got no joy there either.

It was maddening. Walking up and down like this, stopping in every window so that he could peer in and establish that she was nowhere to be found.

It was also, in a funny kind of way, enjoyable.

He realised that as a form of exercise went, he actually hadn't walked for a very long time. He played squash, he swam, occasionally he used the gym on the ground floor of the apartment block, but walking was something he had come to view as unnecessary and, besides, as with so many things, he simply didn't have the time.

There was more of a purpose to the people hurrying around them now. Some were heading back home, others were starting out for their night's entertainment.

He was about to take her to task for her inaccurate description of him when he stopped suddenly and peered through the window of a coffee-shop. It was busy with an eclectic mix of scruffy youths and smart-looking business people, all perched alongside one another at tables, some staring vacantly into space over their coffee-cups, others talking animatedly in groups.

'She's in there.'

Melissa reached out and held on to his arm. 'Are you sure? Where?'

'Towards the back, reading a book.' His voice was tight with anger.

'Maybe we should just wait a few minutes before we go rushing in.'

Elliot turned around and looked at her coldly. 'Why?'

'Maybe it would be a good idea to calm down a bit…'

'I'm perfectly calm, and let me remind you that you're not being paid to act as amateur psychiatrist. You work at a gym and you've been hired to help with my daughter.'

The human face was gone. The man she disliked was back in full force complete with that withering expression that could make a person feel as small as an ant. But he was right. She worked for him and her place was to do as he said. He might tolerate the occasional flare of rebelliousness, the odd one question too many, but he was an impatient man, accustomed to having his orders obeyed, and when her openness ceased to amuse he would have no qualms in putting her firmly back where she belonged. In her place. In a way, she was surprised that she had been allowed to ask him any personal questions at all, but half his mind would have been engaged in the hunt for his daughter.

'Fine,' Melissa said politely. 'I just thought…'

'Don't. Leave the thinking to me. If I wanted a sparring partner with thoughts and opinions, I would have employed a university lecturer. Got it?'

Elliot didn't give her time to answer, instead swinging round to walk through the glass doors, which had been wedged open to accommodate the fine weather. They had to skirt round the people seated outside and then weave their way through the tables, not one of which was empty. It was a popular café belonging to a chain that was nationwide. Melissa used to go to one very similar to the one right here, when she lived in Yorkshire. Every Saturday she would meet there with her friends because it had a great atmosphere and, although the drinks and coffees were overpriced, they were good and the staff never seemed fussed about moving you on.

Judging from the three mugs in front of her, all with dregs of caramel-coloured liquid at the bottom, this café sported the same easygoing philosophy. Lucy was absorbed in her book and looked as though she had been sitting in the same spot for hours.

In fact, she had no idea that anyone had approached her and Melissa wasn't that surprised. There were so many people in the place, queuing up for drinks, hovering around for a table while staff rushed about busily cleaning vacated surfaces, that she had obviously tuned out the noise factor.

It gave Melissa time to look at the girl in front of her. Long, straight dark hair was loosely tied back into a pony-tail and, although she was definitely plump, her hands were slender, as were her legs, which were tucked under the chair so that she could lean forward to read.

Surprisingly, Elliot hadn't dragged her to her feet so

that he could tear into her, and she was beginning to think
that he had maybe come to his senses and realised that
understanding was going to be a better way of dealing
with the situation than confrontation, when he said softly,

'You'll have an explanation for this, won't you?'

Lucy looked up, not seeing Melissa, just seeing the tall
dark man towering over her, and her face blanched.

She was pretty. The long dark hair framed an oval face
that had the same vivid blue eyes as her father, and the
same expressive mouth. The expression in those blue
eyes now went from fear to mulishness.

'I believe you were supposed to return home this afternoon by four? Expressly on my orders?'

'I forgot. Sorry.'

Elliot looked as though he could happily have strangled her, but instead he remained where he was, hands
in his pockets, and only the hardening of his jaw betraying his rage. Rage that he had spent hours involved in a
frantic search, rage that he had phoned the police station
and rage that at the end of all of that her carelessly
tossed-out *sorry* was the only thing she was offering by
way of an apology.

'*Sorry?* Is that all you have to say?'

Lucy shrugged. It was one of those teenage gestures
redolent of insolence and guaranteed to make an enraged
adult even more enraged. Melissa felt her lips twitch with
an inappropriate smile. For the most part she had been a
conformist adolescent, but she could still remember the
odd occasion when a gesture very much like the one
Lucy had just made was enough to make her parents
hopping mad. It was the biggest trump card for the teenager who wanted to be rude without saying a word.

And it was working beautifully.

'Right, miss,' Elliot said through gritted teeth. 'Home.'

'Home? I'd need an airplane to take me there.'

The silence that greeted this remark was shot through with tension, at which point Melissa decided to intervene. She smiled warmly, ignoring Elliot, and held out her hand.

'I'm Melissa.'

Lucy's eyes swept over her, dismissive and sullen. 'Oh, yeah. The keep-fit person he thinks will get rid of my fat.' She didn't take the outstretched hand, nor did she stand up, although the book had fallen shut. 'Bad enough being stuck with a daughter, never mind one who's so unsightly she can't be paraded in public.'

'This isn't the place to be having this conversation,' Elliot said tightly. 'Pick up your schoolbag. We're leaving.'

For a few seconds, Melissa thought that Lucy intended to do no such thing, but then she stuck the book in her rucksack and stood up, taller than Melissa by several inches in her school shoes.

Caught between Elliot, who was striding out of the coffee-shop with a face like thunder, and Lucy, who was dragging her steps behind him like someone on the way to meet a firing squad, Melissa finally opted for Lucy. She fell into step with her and began asking her a few questions about her school, the least provocative line of questioning she could come up with. Answers were either monosyllabic or non-existent, and after a few minutes she fell into an uneasy silence as she eyed the man in front of them.

'He was worried,' she finally said to Lucy, who turned to her for a few seconds before giving a short, bitter laugh.

'Worried? I don't think so. Not in the way you mean. He was annoyed because I was being inconvenient and he doesn't like anyone or anything to inconvenience him.'

That was the longest sentence she had spoken. Her voice was soft, with a pleasing Australian accent.

'People can sometimes get set in their ways,' Melissa offered placatingly. 'And the older they get, the more set they can become.'

She had meant it as an excuse, but Lucy caught on to the concept with spiteful delight. She gave a laugh that caught in her throat and nodded vigorously. 'An old man set in his ways.'

'Well, maybe not *that* old...'

'I don't know what my mum could ever have seen in him. I don't know why she ever went out with him in the first place. If she had never gone out with him...she must have been mad, or stupid or...or...' Unable to get hold of suitable vocabulary to register her emotions, Lucy fell back into silence and Melissa didn't consider it the right time to break it.

They walked on, staring ahead. Elliot obviously assumed that they would be obediently following in his wake because not once did he turn around to make sure that they were still there. He was as consumed in his thoughts as his daughter was.

As soon as they reached the block of apartments, Melissa said as cheerfully as she could under the circumstances that it might be best if she left.

'To try and sort things out...between yourselves...' she finished lamely, when her suggestion was met with deafening silence. Lucy's body language was telling her that she could go or she could stay, it wouldn't matter to her, but there was something of a plea in her eyes that made Melissa feel guilty. Then she wondered why she was feeling guilty when this particular drama had nothing to do with her.

Elliot was more forthcoming. He told her bluntly that she still had work to do, that he would appreciate her trying to put aside the hitch to proceedings and carry on as normal.

'Carry on as normal?' Melissa parroted incredulously.

'That's right. I can order some food in for us to eat.'

Neither he nor his daughter were looking at one another and Melissa was struck by the awkward feeling of being the piggy in the middle.

How had she ever got herself talked into this bizarre arrangement? She had no place being here and being an unwilling audience to words that she would be better off not hearing. She would intervene. She knew she would. And then she would become embroiled in their saga when she didn't want to be.

'I'll just stay to leave the stuff I brought with me...' she stammered, fishing into her capacious handbag. 'I can't stay for anything to eat because...because I have a date...'

'A date?' Elliot frowned. 'You told me you were unattached.'

'Oh, dear,' Lucy said with dripping sarcasm. 'What a nerve, having a private life when it doesn't suit him!'

'I'll get to you in a minute, Lucy.' Elliot swung round to look at her through narrowed eyes.

They had taken the lift up and he unlocked the apartment door, entering first with Lucy scuttling in behind him and Melissa trailing uncomfortably in the background with her pamphlets and book clutched in one hand.

'I'll just leave these things here...' she said, hovering by the door. If she could have managed it, she would have flung them on the nearest counter surface and raced out of the apartment as fast as her legs would take her.

'There's no need,' Lucy said, not looking at her, but staring at her father with hostility. 'I don't need anyone babysitting me!'

'If you're childish enough to think that running away sorts things out, then—'

'I was *not running away*!' Two patches of angry colour had appeared on her cheeks. She had dropped her ruck-sack on the ground and was glaring at her father with loathing, hands squarely placed on her hips. He, in turn, was looking at her coldly, a man on the brink of losing it completely. Melissa seriously considered sneaking out of the door and making a break for it, but, coward that she was, she remained rooted to the spot.

'No?'

'No! Where would I run to? I didn't feel like coming back here to sit and listen to someone give me a lecture about losing weight so I decided to stop off at a coffee-shop and read instead! So what? Big deal! Maybe you'll see that you can't force me to *do anything*!'

'I'm not forcing you to do anything, but while you're in this house—'

'Oh, please! I'm sick of that stupid argument. It's not my fault that I'm stuck here with you! Do you think…that…that…?' She turned away and flopped down on the sofa, biting back the tears of rage and frus-tration.

'I apologise for you having to witness this show of behaviour,' Elliot said, turning to Melissa with eyes like ice.

'Why apologise?' Lucy looked at Melissa stormily. 'In case you haven't found out yet, he doesn't apologise for anything! Ever! *I* should be apologising to you!' She looked at her father and Melissa could see her face so close to crumpling that her heart went out to her. 'Apol-ogising for ruining your cosy life with your work…and your meetings…and your *bloody, bloody* fiancée!'

CHAPTER FOUR

'YOU don't have to do any exercise if you don't want to, you know. I mean, I can't force you. On the other hand, I *am* being paid to at least try and encourage...' Melissa had already given up on anything like vigorous exercise. She had come to the apartment at four-thirty, been confronted by a teenager who would barely speak to her and she was getting very frustrated.

Lucy, probably under orders to be obliging, was making sure that she did exactly the opposite. Right now she was sitting on the sofa with a can of soda in one hand and the remote control in the other, while she flicked from one music channel on the television to another.

'What are the school lunches like?'

No answer.

'What do you have for breakfast?' She was realising that she could actually ask any number of dietary questions until the cows came home and she would get zero response. Lucy wasn't listening. With sudden inspiration, she realised that there was probably only one topic that might encourage her stubborn charge to talk, and so she tacked on, innocently, 'I expect that, since your father wants to encourage you to eat healthily, he sends you off with toast and scrambled egg? Or maybe a bowl of cereal and some fruit...?'

'He's not my father. Don't call him my father. My father was killed in a road accident six months ago.'

Bingo.

'Oh. OK.' Melissa closed the book on her lap, a teenager's guide to healthy eating which she had rummaged

59

up from the stock of reference books she kept in a suitcase under her bed. 'What do *you* call him, then?'

'I don't call him anything. In fact, I try not to talk to
him at all.'

'I can't hear you with that music in the background.
What did you say?'

Lucy switched off the television with an elaborate sigh
and turned to face Melissa. 'I *said* that I just don't talk
to him.'

'You must talk *sometimes*.'

'Why? He has nothing to say to me that I want to hear
and vice versa. Anyway, he's hardly ever here.'

'We could talk about this outside,' Melissa suggested
coaxingly. 'Go for a walk in the park…'

'Oh, yeah, I forgot. You're here to babysit me and
make sure I get rid of all this disgusting fat.' The bored
voice was back and Melissa sighed inwardly. It was going to be an uphill struggle every inch of the way, and
the unfortunate circumstances of their meeting weren't
going to make things easier. She hadn't a clue what had
been said between father and daughter the night before,
but she would have bet her last pound that it hadn't been
a pleasant confrontation. After the revelation about his
fiancée, she had managed to sneak away, leaving them
facing one another across the living room like adversaries
about to do battle with one another. And, as expected,
Elliot had been nowhere around when she had arrived
earlier. Nor had Lenka.

'OK, to be blunt, I am supposed to be doing a job,
although I'm beginning to wonder what it is considering
you seem just fine to me.' A tiny white lie never went
amiss, Melissa thought, crossing her fingers behind her
back. The truth was that Lucy was comfort eating, which
wasn't good, and the more the pounds rolled on the lower
her self-esteem would get, and the more her desire for

comfort food would increase. She was at the edge of a vicious circle.

'There's no need to lie. I know I've put on a lot of weight. Nearly two stone since I came over here, but…'

'And if your father thinks that I've been shirking my duties,' Melissa said with a straight face, 'he might just kill me. He can be a very scary man…'

'Tell me about it.' This was spoken with sincerity as Lucy stood up, stretched, looked at her garb, which was some baggy hipster jogging pants and a T-shirt with an obscure band plastered across the front. 'Well, I guess we *could* go out, but I'm not jogging or running or anything.'

'Oh, good. I hate that stuff.'

By the time they were in the park, Melissa felt that some progress was being made. This progress depended on her not mentioning anything about diets, healthy eating or the benefits of an active life, but instead asking questions about Elliot, allowing Lucy to give full vent to her dislike.

After fifteen minutes of strolling, they had covered most of Elliot's more noticeable faults, and Melissa couldn't disagree with any of the findings. He was cold, arrogant, insensitive and impatient of anyone who did not meet his standards.

'I expect that's what comes of devoting so much time to your work,' Melissa felt obliged to contribute, although it was a half-hearted attempt to be unbiased, because, when she thought of the expression on his face when he'd seen his daughter in that coffee-shop, she found herself agreeing with everything Lucy had said.

After half an hour, Lucy had opened up sufficiently to talk about school and what she hated there. This seemed to include everything from the school lunches to the schoolchildren.

But at least she was talking, even though the conversation was almost entirely negative.

'But he's going to send me away to boarding-school anyway.'

Lucy informed Melissa of this as they were heading back to the apartment. The leisurely stroll had at least extended to a brisk walk. Lucy hadn't noticed. She had been too wrapped up in her litany of complaints. Underneath every complaint was a comparison to what she had enjoyed in Australia, although she had not mentioned that part of her life at all. Melissa could feel it simmering unhappily under the surface and she knew better than to try and prompt any discussion of it. When Lucy was ready, she would discuss her past if she chose to.

'Don't be silly. Of course he won't!'

Lucy's reply was scathing. 'I overheard them. That awful woman said that it made sense, that there was no way he could pretend to play happy families, that he'd been landed with me and it would be best for everyone concerned if I boarded, that it would do me good.'

'That awful woman...?'

'His fiancée. Alison Thomas-Brown.' Lucy made a face. 'She's a witch.'

In the interests of being impartial and adult, Melissa scrabbled around to find something to say that was soothing. Of course Elliot wouldn't have become engaged to someone unpleasant enough to be called a witch, although to a displaced teenager that might well be the description that came to mind when her one slice of fragile security was being threatened. Lucy might not have found herself the cosy, welcoming father she had hoped for, but he was still her father, still her one certainty in her suddenly fractured life. In other words, underneath all the bluster and antipathy, he was still better than nothing.

They had reached the apartment block. The porters knew Lucy very well by now and Melissa's gardening book was waiting for her, courtesy of the porter with the interest in plants. They chatted for a while about plants, then about his daughters, who were both at university, and about his wife, who worked as a cleaner in one of the hospitals. Eventually Lucy cleared her throat and Melissa broke off their chat to smile at her.

'I know,' Melissa whispered sheepishly as they took the elevator up. 'I can't help it. I just find people so interesting; there's always something going on in their lives even though you'd never guess it to look at them.'

'There's nothing going on in my life,' Lucy said sadly. 'There used to be but now...'

'Would you like to go to a movie with me tomorrow?' Melissa asked, on the spur of the moment. 'I know it's a weekday but perhaps your father would let you just this once. There's a great Disney film showing...'

Without realising it, Melissa had hit on a shared love that lit up Lucy's face. The permanent sullenness vanished and the first true shy smile peeped out.

So Melissa was feeling rather successful on day two by the time they made it up to the apartment, where Elliot was waiting for them.

Neither of them was expecting him. Wasn't he the man who only had time for work? The man who found it nigh on impossible to tear himself away from the seductive allure of the office? What was he doing back at...Melissa surreptitiously looked at her watch...at six thirty-five? And in casual clothes, which implied that he had been back at the apartment even earlier?

He was sitting on the sprawling sofa, with a glass of white wine in one hand, and he had been reading the

Financial Times, which he lowered as soon as they walked in. On the table in front of him was his open laptop computer.

Warm, sticky and fairly sweaty after twenty minutes of brisk walking, Melissa was suddenly and acutely conscious of her appearance. She had dressed in leggings, trainers and a short-sleeved white T-shirt that was far more fitted than the usual baggy tops she normally favoured. Practical gear but now woefully unflattering as she stood here, being appraised by her elegant, dangerously sexy, good-looking employer.

'Where have you two been? Had a good time?'

Lucy flounced into the kitchen, opened the fridge, took out a block of cheese, then she caught Melissa's eye and put it back. 'What are you doing here?' she asked ungraciously. 'Did you come back to check and make sure that I hadn't run away again?'

Elliot's mouth thinned. 'I wanted to see how your first day with Melissa went. I'm not asking for anything too elaborate but a civil response might be nice.'

Lucy reddened. 'We went for a walk.'

'It's absolutely beautiful out there.' Melissa decided that a rescue operation was called for. How was it possible for tension levels to rise within such a short space of time? The minute Lucy had walked through the door and seen her father, a shutter had dropped over her eyes. And she had immediately reached for some comfort food. 'Makes you want to be outside.' She tentatively approached Elliot, ready to account for her time but guiltily aware that strolls in the sunshine weren't perhaps quite what he had had in mind when he had originally employed her. Aggressive sprinting, maybe. Followed by a dinner of carrot juice and wafer thins.

'You never said why you were home at this hour.' Lucy stood in front of him with her arms folded. 'Home early two days in a row! Isn't the company going to have some kind of nervous breakdown without you at the helm running it?'

Elliot's lips twitched. 'I think they just might be able to cope with my absences, although I can't promise anything if I decide to have another day home early. The paramedics might just have to be called in.'

Not knowing whether he was joking or not, Lucy remained frowning. 'Well, I've got homework to do,' she muttered eventually.

'What about some dinner first?' he asked. 'Lenka usually sees about Lucy's evening meal but she's got some kind of cold.' He turned to Melissa, who looked at him innocently.

'And I guess you've prepared something?' Melissa enquired.

Lucy, who had been heading towards her bedroom, paused and looked over her shoulder with a smirk, tempted to watch him wriggle out of that but eventually deciding that she just couldn't be bothered to show any interest.

'Does it look as though I have?' Elliot asked politely.

'Oh, yes, I forgot. Teenagers are fully capable of looking after themselves.' And yes, at the age of fourteen, Lucy probably could knock up something halfway respectable in the high-tech kitchen. But still... 'I really should be heading home now if there's nothing left for me to do...'

Elliot shoved the newspaper off his lap and extended his long legs on the coffee-table in front of him. Then he linked his fingers behind his head and leaned back to give her the full benefit of that look, that disconcerting, intrusive gaze that made her stomach twist into knots.

'The reason I came home early was that we could have a talk,' he informed her, 'before I go out.'

'It's too early to be making progress with...with Lucy's weight,' Melissa replied faintly. Of course she now had to stay, which meant that she would have to sit down instead of hovering, and that was something she was becoming adept at whenever she was in the man's presence. An idea struck her. 'I could cook something for her to eat,' she suggested, 'unless you'd rather question me here...?'

Elliot suppressed a sigh of pure annoyance. 'I wasn't planning on *questioning* you,' he said levelly. 'I thought we might have a chat, to find out your impressions.' He stood up in one swift, fluid movement, which had her taking a few awkward steps back. 'The cooking idea sounds good.'

It had. Until it occurred to Melissa that running around in his kitchen, making herself at home, would involve her being under the microscope even more than if she had just kept her mouth shut, answered his questions and then left.

Too late. He was heading towards the kitchen and she trailed along behind him.

'Lenka does the shopping,' he said, pulling open one of the cupboards and then staring inside as though the contents were as much a revelation to him as they would be to her. 'Feel free to use whatever you want.'

He pulled out a stool, sat down and proceeded to watch as she rustled in the salad compartment of the fridge, extracted ingredients for something very quick and very simple and then, after a couple of aborted attempts, found the utensils she needed.

She could feel him watching her. 'You could help,' she said at last. 'Chop this.' She handed him a knife, a board and an onion. 'You do know how to chop, don't you?'

'I think I could manage. Tell me how your afternoon

went. I came home because I thought that Lucy might just refuse to be compliant.' He was meticulously peeling off the outer skin. 'Why did you give me the onion?' he asked. 'It's damned fiddly.' He began chopping. 'And it's making my eyes water.'

'Surely you've cried before,' Melissa said, grinning, and he raised his eyebrows.

'Not that I can remember.'

'Because real men don't cry?'

'And quite a few don't chop onions either. What did the two of you talk about?'

'Stuff.' She had efficiently disposed of the mushrooms, the red pepper and the courgette. 'Teenage angst.' After a few seconds of thought, she went to stand where he was still struggling with the onion.

'Have you come to dry my eyes?' he drawled. 'Kiss my tears better?'

Melissa's mouth dropped slightly open and she blushed. Here was a woman not used to flirting, Elliot thought drily, and it was unfair to embarrass her, but it was still gratifying to see her go pink like that. He had never met a woman who blushed as easily as she did. She looked as though she literally couldn't find it in herself to speak.

'I wasn't being serious,' Elliot said gravely.

'I realise that!'

'I don't suppose very many of your clients flirt with you…'

'Most of my clients are of the female variety and no, they don't flirt. I really think that that sort of thing isn't appropriate, given our circumstances…'

'Our circumstances?'

Was he laughing at her? 'I work for you,' Melissa elaborated uncomfortably.

'True.' He sounded suitably in agreement but now, for

some reason, there was a devil inside him. This was a
devil that rarely made an appearance. In fact, he couldn't
think offhand when the last time was that he had found
such enjoyment in stringing out a situation, and he found
himself delighting in the delicate bloom of Melissa's
cheeks as she fought against her discomfiture.

'Oh, yes, of course you do. And I genuinely didn't
want to make you uncomfortable, although…' he paused,
pressed his thumbs against his eyes and then looked
straight at her '…flirting is only dangerous if it gets out
of hand.'

'Gets out of hand…?' Melissa repeated nervously.

'Of course. You're experienced enough to realise that,
I'm sure. Any flirting that leads beyond the bedroom door
is dangerous…'

'I wasn't suggesting…!' Melissa burst out, horrified.
Had he been thinking that she might take him seriously?
Think that he was making a pass at her? She thought of
him leading her to that dangerous place beyond the bedroom door, and her cheeks burnt.

'I realise that.' Elliot also realised that he had a fiancée,
one he was due to see in under an hour, and that amusing
himself at the expense of a shy, inexperienced young
woman was inexcusable. Efficient she might well be at
her job, but he had known enough women in his lifetime
to recognise one who was still green around the ears.
Moreover he never mixed business with pleasure.
'Onions chopped. Anything else?'

'No. What I'm cooking is a vegetable pasta dish. It's
very healthy, very nutritious and it's filling. I think the
main thing should be to get Lucy eating healthily and her
metabolism will do the rest. I've noticed that she has a
tendency to perhaps resort to junk food when she feels

under pressure. We all do it, but it's a habit that can be easily stopped.'

Elliot listened in silence as Melissa chattered with her back to him, busying herself with the process of frying ingredients in a pan. His first impression of her had been of someone small and shapeless. She wasn't. Or rather, she wasn't shapeless. Far from it. His eyes wandered lazily over her, taking in the curves that were so unfashionable nowadays. She half turned and reached up to fetch the pasta from the top cupboard. Her breasts, he thought, were surprisingly large for someone not particularly tall. Was that why she wore such unflattering clothes? Because she wanted to cover them up? Even her T-shirt was prudish, with its high round neckline, the sort of T-shirt that made damn sure that not one extra inch of skin was exposed than was absolutely necessary.

'You'll have to go into all this diet stuff with Lenka,' he said, more sharply than he had meant, because he hadn't cared for the road his imagination had decided to go down. Or the ache in his groin it had caused.

'Because you're not interested?' Melissa turned towards him and folded her arms. His sudden change of tone had her immediately on the defensive. Maybe he had clocked that she had actually rather enjoyed that light banter for a while, and this was his way of reminding her of her position. It wasn't as his conversational equal. She was there to impart information.

'Naturally I'm interested, but, as I've already said, I lack the time to put all your helpful culinary hints into practice.'

'Lucy's miserable over here. I gather she feels that she can't talk to you...'

'Of course she can talk to me!' he snapped.

'What about?'

'What do you mean, *what about*?'

'She's lonely and confused. I don't think she feels at home here.'

'It'll take time. What are your plans for tomorrow?'

Melissa guiltily wondered how going to a movie with his daughter could be construed as helpful exercise, which was what she was being paid for. 'I need to get to know Lucy before I can start preaching to her about what to eat and how to exercise. It's a little different from working in a gym.' She went to stand in front of him and leaned against the counter. At least with him sitting on the stool, she was more or less on eye level with him. 'When people come to a gym it's because they want to be there, and they want to be put through their paces. I don't suppose Lucy wants me around and she probably thinks that it's an insult that she's being made to exercise.'

'Why would she think that it's an insult?'

'Wouldn't you?' she asked, without bothering to beat about the bush. 'If someone signed you up to start lifting weights, what would you think?'

'I would be quite flattered that they cared enough to go through the trouble.'

'You're deliberately being obtuse.'

And she was getting all hot under the collar. 'I get the point,' he said eventually. 'But you still haven't told me your plans for tomorrow.'

'What are *yours*?' Melissa threw the question neatly back at him, catching him on the back foot. 'It's not good enough for you to shift your responsibilities onto my shoulders. You have to have some input as well!'

'Shift my responsibilities?'

Melissa chose to ignore the soft menace behind the question. 'I'm going to take Lucy to see a movie tomorrow if that's all right with you, and I think you ought to come along.'

'You're going to a movie?'

'I need to gain her confidence. And I think it might be a good idea if you came too.'

'You mean just drop everything I have on at the moment so that I can go to the cinema.'

Melissa drew in her breath and refused to feel like the naïve moron his tone of voice had implied.

'That's about the size of it.'

'Amazing,' he said, shaking his head the way someone did when confronted by a spectacularly thick child. 'Nothing's sunk in there, has it?'

'What do you mean?' Melissa turned away to go and switch off the hob.

'I can't just take time off work whenever I choose to go to the movies. That's not how business operates.'

'I think it would be nice for Lucy.' The man was from a different planet. Yes, sometimes he seemed human enough, but most of the time he was an alien.

The silence stretched on for so long that she was about to drop the subject completely when she saw him nod imperceptibly.

'OK. I'll come.'

'You'll come?' Melissa heard herself ask incredulously. 'But what about all that work that can't possibly be left? What about the world of business and how it operates?'

'Getting cold feet now that you've got what you wanted?' Elliot drawled silkily. He would have to cancel a few meetings, but what the hell? He and Lucy seemed to have reached a point of total communication melt-down. A movie, with Melissa there as a third party to help dilute the inevitable tension, was a good idea. And besides... He looked at Melissa through half-closed lids and held back the thought.

'Not at all! But if you come, you have to promise that

you won't moan about the work you're missing. There's nothing worse than someone constantly reminding you that they're doing you a favour.'

'Have you ever considered a career in the prison service?' He was beginning to enjoy the way she blushed at the slightest remark. Like now. Except this time she turned away and began filling a saucepan with water for the pasta. 'It was a piece of sarcasm, Melissa, not a personal insult.'

'I know that!'

'You'll have to toughen up in this city, you know.' He looked at her as she buried her thoughts in the pretence of being busy.

'Toughen up?' Melissa repeated vaguely.

'Not let other people affect you quite so much.'

'You don't *affect* me!'

'Because,' Elliot continued, overriding her denial with an expertise born from experience, 'London is full of predators and an innocent like you could end up getting badly hurt.'

Melissa wondered how the conversation had managed to come round to the mortifying place that it had. She wondered whether he had started thinking about her over-reaction to his passing, unthinking, flirtatious one-liner. Did he think that he was suddenly responsible for her because she happened to be working for him?

'Thank you for that. I think I can deal with predators.'

'Can you? Have you had much experience of them? In…Yorkshire?'

'Yes, I do happen to know that there are people out there who will take advantage of someone else, but I'm not the country hick you seem to think I am.'

If he had carried on the conversation, it wouldn't have been so bad—at least then she might have had the opportunity to win her case that she wasn't the complete simpleton he thought she was—but he didn't. He just looked at her steadily and speculatively for a few seconds, then asked her which cinema they intended to go to and what time the film started.

'I'll head home as soon as I've cooked this…'

'No need to rush. You can stay and share dinner with Lucy. I won't be around.' He glanced at his watch and stood up, stretching.

'Are you going anywhere nice?' Melissa asked politely.

'A very expensive restaurant in Sloane Square. Would you consider that nice?'

'I suppose it depends who you go with,' Melissa said immediately. 'I guess you're going with your fiancée, so I'm sure it'll be lovely, just as anywhere would be lovely when you're with someone you're in love with.'

'You're really going to have to do something about your naïveté if you're to survive in London,' Elliot commented wryly. He sauntered towards Lucy's bedroom and Melissa could hear him knocking on the door and, when it wasn't opened, saying goodbye to it.

Melissa was beginning to get the picture of what he thought about her. She was inexperienced and simple and when he wasn't laying down laws around her and treating her like something unfortunate he had happened to bump into, he was patronising her.

She was on the verge of telling him just what she thought of *him* when the doorbell rang and Elliot went to answer it without sparing a glance in her direction.

From where she was, wiping down the kitchen counter, she had a bird's-eye view of him as he pulled open the door, could see the slow smile tilt the corners of his mouth, softening the harshness of his face into an expression of devastating charm.

Melissa felt her heart skip a beat. Then she heard a husky laugh and he stepped back to let Alison in.

He was still smiling as he brought her over and introduced her. Alison Thomas-Brown, his fiancée, a barrister in chambers. Melissa had never felt as undersized, underdressed and under-prepared as she felt now. This woman took sophistication into another dimension. She was tall, wafer-thin, with straight black hair and dark eyes that radiated intelligence. Melissa had to look up at her and the hand that briefly shook hers was cool and beautifully manicured.

'Elliot told me about you,' she said politely. 'I do hope you make headway with Lucy. It's been rather dreadful for poor Elliot being stuck with a surly teenager he can't handle.' She turned to Elliot and smiled. 'Although everyone needs one unmanageable situation in their life at some point.'

'I fail to see why,' Elliot replied.

'Most people have more than just one unmanageable situation crop up in their life,' Melissa added truthfully. 'Actually, a lot of people have unmanageable situations crop up virtually on a daily basis!'

Alison laughed politely and Elliot disappeared, saying that he had to get his mobile phone from the bedroom.

Which left Melissa staring up at Alison and wondering what to say next. She was beautiful, she was intelligent, but warm she certainly wasn't.

'I dare say you've already noticed how absolutely impossible it is for Elliot to tailor his lifestyle around Lucy. It smells awfully good in here. Have you cooked?'

'I wouldn't say *impossible*...'

Alison had taken a few steps into the kitchen and was now lifting the lid of the saucepan and inspecting the simmering sauce. 'You clever little thing,' she said appreciatively. 'I can see that Lucy will absolutely thrive

in your company!' Her dark eyes hardened fractionally.
She glanced quickly in the direction of the bedrooms.
'Poor child. I feel for her, I really do, but I hope you'll
agree that we must all be practical about this. Lucy needs
people with her and Elliot and myself simply cannot fit
our hectic working lives around that bald fact. I've suggested to Elliot that perhaps a boarding-school might be
worth thinking about.'

'I don't think—'

'You're not paid to think,' Alison said flatly. 'You're
paid to try and get the child into shape so that she can
feel a bit more self-confident. Body image is a crucial
part of a young girl's sense of self-esteem.'

'Yes, that's true enough but—'

'Call me a fool, but in my profession hard facts speak
for themselves. I do suggest you try and warm Lucy to
the idea of boarding. I'm sure a talented girl like yourself
wouldn't find that an impossible feat?'

Melissa couldn't imagine anyone having the nerve to
call Alison Thomas-Brown a fool. They wouldn't dare.
She looked as though she might have ways of making
her critics suffer and some of them would hurt.

'It's not up to me to try and persuade Lucy to think
anything. I'm not an intermediary. Like you said, I'm just
here to do a job.'

Alison didn't answer. She had removed herself from
the saucepan of food. Just in case some of the sauce
spilled accidentally on her designer outfit, Melissa imagined. Now she looked at Melissa thoughtfully.

'But you'll be seeing a lot of Lucy,' Alison said in a
low, calm voice, the sort of voice that brooked no argument. 'And sooner or later Lucy will begin chatting. I've
tried to draw her out of her shell, but she's been hellishly
uncommunicative. You, on the other hand, are probably
far more on her level than I, and so will undoubtedly

have more success on that front... Elliot will take your cooperation for granted. He is, after all, your employer.'

Melissa, still wrestling with the implied insult that she was on the same wavelength as a fourteen-year-old child, took a few seconds to register the hint of a threat in the latter part of Alison's speech. Before she could open her mouth to protest, Alison continued in her mellifluous voice,

'And for your own protection, I suggest you be careful with Elliot. He can be a charismatic man. I don't think even he is aware of just how attractive that can be to a woman.' She laughed huskily and gave Melissa one of those girlish you-know-what-I-mean looks that was supposed to draw her into the little confidential circle.

'I haven't noticed,' Melissa said, pulling back and hoping that either Lucy or Elliot would emerge from wherever they had inconveniently hidden themselves.

'Oh. Well, maybe it's your tender age. I suppose you're into young lads, boys more your own age?'

Melissa was spared the ordeal of finding a suitable answer to this by the appearance of both Lucy and Elliot at the same time, coming from different directions. When you're looking for a bus, she thought...

She glanced at Elliot and yes, she could see that he might be considered charismatic.

What Alison had forgotten, even with that sharp brain of hers, was that charisma only worked when it was applied and Elliot had absolutely none to spare for an employee. And even if he had, Melissa thought, watching as he bent to murmur something into Alison's ear before turning to Lucy and exchanging their usual monosyllables, she would still be immune.

Good looks and money might work wonders with most women, but when everything else was missing, then, as far as Melissa was concerned, both were about as useful as a box of matches in a fire.

CHAPTER FIVE

THE movie was showing at a small cinema on the King's Road that looked as though it had been lifted out of another century. At first, Lucy was appalled at the size of it but after five minutes she had come round to saying that she supposed it was quite sweet.

'I've never been to a cinema that had a real bar in it,' she commented, scanning the room and sipping her diet soda. 'He's cute.'

'You need to come up to Yorkshire,' Melissa said, smiling; 'where I grew up, there's still the original cinema, and if you think this looks old-fashioned you need to see the one where we still go in my village. Maybe cute isn't quite the right word though…' She grinned. 'Maybe downright uncomfortable. There's still someone who comes round selling ice creams before the movie starts. She looks about a hundred.'

So far Melissa had managed to avoid telling Lucy that her father would be coming to the movies with them. She feared the inevitable outburst and, besides, she was fairly sure that Elliot wouldn't turn up and, however much Lucy professed to loathe him, she would still be disappointed if he didn't appear.

But Melissa's eyes kept skittering towards the door, and her nerves were on edge.

'What did my father say when you told him that we were going to be spending day three at the cinema?' Lucy asked with a little sneer in her voice. 'Did he hit the roof? Bet he did. He wouldn't be able to stand the thought of you not actually having got me going on a treadmill as

77

yet. Ha, ha. He probably thought that by now I would have shed bucket-loads of weight, and then I could become a happy, normal teenager and he could forget about me without a guilty conscience!'

'We'll have to get around to some dietary facts and exercise soon,' Melissa said evasively. Every three seconds, she glanced towards the door, expecting to see Elliot's tall, muscular frame outlined in the doorway, but there was still no sign of him. Perhaps he had mentioned it to Alison and she had decided to ban him from coming.

The little woman-to-woman chat Melissa had endured had stayed with her for the day. She wasn't normally the sort of person who dwelled on unhappy thoughts, but Alison's warnings had hit home. She had chewed over the suggestion-cum-order that she do as she was told and recommend the bliss of boarding with Lucy even if she didn't agree with the concept, and she had fretted over the insinuation that she was somehow inferior. Overriding both of those niggles was Alison's mortifying warning that she should make sure to have as little to do with Elliot as possible just in case she lost her senses and fell for his so-called charisma.

She hadn't even had the opportunity to defend herself! No wonder the woman was a barrister. Melissa felt heartily sorry for anyone confronted with a cross-examination by her. Even if they hadn't committed the crime, they would have been inclined to confess through fear.

Her eyes had gone blank as she replayed the conversation in her head. When they refocused she saw him, just as she had pictured, standing in the doorway, looking around, eyes sharp.

He had come straight from work. That much was obvious from the suit, although he was carrying his jacket slung over one shoulder. Their eyes met and something curled inside her stomach before she looked away hurriedly.

Must be his dashing charisma, she told herself sarcastically, positively exuding from lips that seldom smiled and eyes that could freeze blood.

Melissa had just enough time to interrupt what Lucy was saying and exclaim that her father had just arrived.

The surprise momentarily deprived Lucy of speech and her mouth was still half opened by the time her father had closed the space between them and taken a chair at their table.

'I take it Melissa didn't remember to tell you that I might be coming along this afternoon?' He looked at Lucy, eyebrows raised. 'Close your mouth—you'll catch flies.'

Lucy abruptly closed her mouth and Melissa could see her grappling to find a truly horrendous dig, but just seeing him there had done something to her vocal cords.

'I wasn't sure whether you would be able to make it,' Melissa said coolly, 'and I didn't think it would be fair to get Lucy's hopes raised only to be dashed if you failed to appear.'

'Get my hopes raised? I don't think so!' Lucy scoffed.

'Thank you, Lucy. That makes me feel truly welcome.'

'Well, what can you expect? You haven't been around for the past six months!'

'I'm around now.'

'Why?'

Elliot sighed wearily and glanced across to where Melissa was sitting nervously cradling her cappuccino. 'Although,' he continued, looking at her, 'I glanced at the board outside and there's nothing showing under fifteen.'

'Oh, please!' Lucy interrupted. 'I've been going to fifteen-certificate movies for over a year! I *do* happen to know about sex and bad language!' She flushed and scowled to cover her embarrassment.

'Actually,' Melissa said, rescuing her, 'we're going to see the Disney movie.'

Elliot looked at them. It was on the tip of his tongue to make the obvious remark, that taking valuable time off work was bad enough, but to take it off in order to watch a cartoon was unthinkable. Then it occurred to him that he didn't mind being here. He had had very little time for his daughter since she had moved in with him; in fact had avoided her whenever possible because he had no idea how to connect with her. Being here was good. He looked at the amused grin tugging the corner of Melissa's mouth and felt a dangerous kick of excitement which he kept to himself, surveying her blandly with hooded eyes.

'Don't tell me,' she said, 'you've suddenly remembered an appointment you have to keep.'

She and Lucy exchanged a quick look which Elliot didn't miss.

'Are you two ganging up on me?' he drawled.

'When was the last time you went to see a Disney movie?' Lucy shot at him, always ready to wage war, although her tone wasn't quite as belligerent as it usually was. 'I bet you've never seen one in your life before!'

'You're right. I haven't. So this should be a learning curve for me. On a number of counts.' He stood up. 'We've got fifteen minutes. Would anyone like anything to eat?'

Melissa was acutely conscious of him during the movie. Lucy had made sure to be the first in the row. Consequently Melissa had found herself stuck in the middle, clutching an enormous bag of salted popcorn into which Elliot's hand dipped at regular intervals, occasionally brushing against hers. Just as well she had seen this particular movie already because she wouldn't have taken much of it in.

She couldn't wait for it to be over. Whenever she tried to rest her arm on the armrest, she felt his and immediately withdrew. When she did manage to relax she would suddenly feel his arm brush hers, the warmth of his skin making her pulses race.

She blamed Alison. She had been fine before. Yes, she had known Elliot was sexy, but in a detached way. Now she kept thinking about that warning, to stay away from him.

It was a blessed relief when the whole experience was at an end and they were outside, back in the waning sunshine with lots of space to manoeuvre.

Lucy was abnormally subdued and it was only when they reached the apartment block that Melissa discovered why. It emerged as a statement but was laden with curiosity.

'I can't believe you've never been to see a Disney movie!'

'In my days there were no cinemas. We kids all had to make do with playing with our tin soldiers and making games for ourselves. No television, you know,' Elliot joked drily.

'Stop lying!'

'OK. I'm not that ancient. I just didn't go to movies as a kid. Nothing strange about that.'

Lucy was reluctant to take the bait, but in the end she couldn't help herself. Curiosity got the better of her. 'Your parents must have taken you to the cinema!'

'My parents lived abroad. They led hectic, cosmopolitan lives. Movies with their kid never featured. Now that I've discovered what I've been missing, I shall have to go out and buy the entire Disney collection.' He was joking and if Melissa wasn't mistaken there was just the dawning of something like a smile on Lucy's face, not that she was going to give in to any sign of warmth. And neither did Elliot expect it. He merely asked them whether they wanted to have a meal with him at the restaurant on the corner and shrugged when his daughter rejected the offer without a second's thought.

'In that case, it'll have to be just the two of us,' he said, turning to Melissa.

'I must get back home,' she said, colour rushing into her face, thinking back to the way her body had felt as though it were on fire every time his arm had unwittingly come into contact with hers during that wretched movie.

'Why?'

'I have things to do!'

'What things?' He took a couple of steps towards her and she wanted to flee.

'Things!'

'When are you going to start Lucy on an exercise programme?'

Melissa's wildly beating heart slowed to a more normal rate. Work. He wanted to go out and have a meal with her so that he could discuss work, most probably to point out that she should be doing what she was being paid to do and not having jolly little outings at his expense. Elliot was a man whose life was ruled by the acquisition of money and power. Naturally he would be concerned that he was in the process of tipping money down the drain.

'It's only been a couple of days…'

'Tell me about it over dinner.' He vanished towards Lucy's bedroom and reappeared minutes later. The jacket was still off but as he walked out into the sitting room he began undoing the buttons of his shirt, starting at the collar and working his way downwards.

Melissa looked at him with alarm. Where the buttons

were now undone, she could glimpse a slither of hard, muscular chest.

'What are you doing?' she stammered, gulping, and Elliot stopped directly in front of her and looked at her with amusement.

'What do you think I'm doing?' He really would have to stop this crazy desire to see her flustered, he thought. He noticed the way her eyes were glued to his face. What did she think they might encounter if they travelled south? He carried on removing his shirt, slowly releasing the cuffs from their cuff-links.

'I'm just going to have a quick shower before we go out,' he said lazily. 'Won't be ten minutes.'

'If you like I can meet you at the restaurant,' Melissa said, eyes still riveted to his face because now the shirt was off and she was just too conscious of the broad, firm expanse of his bronzed chest. He had a superb physique, not too overdeveloped but with fine-honed muscle giving his torso breathtaking definition.

'Don't be silly. In fact, why don't you have a shower yourself? There are two guest bathrooms; you can have your pick.'

Just the thought of stripping off under the same roof as him was enough to give her a mild attack of the vapours. She imagined herself naked under the running water, while on the other side of the sitting room he was the same, naked and...

She gathered herself. 'No, thank you. I'll just go and see what Lucy's up to. She...she's probably hungry, wondering what she might eat a bit later on...what better time to give her a short lecture on nutrition? Not that teenagers are in the least bothered by what they eat...' During the meandering ramble, she had managed to take a couple of steps backwards, which was good and bad. On the one hand, she was no longer breathing the scent of him in, like a drowning man gulping down his last lungfuls of fresh air. On the other hand, she now had a much more all-encompassing view of his semi-nudity, which her eyes insisted on taking in, against all commands from her brain.

He allowed her all the time in the world to finish talking then looked at her in silence for a few seconds. He felt charged. Why?

'Well, if you change your mind, Lucy will point you in the direction of the towels…' He turned away, whistling under his breath, and Melissa remained rooted to the spot until he had disappeared completely, then she collapsed onto the sofa in a heap. Her breathing was rapid and painful, like someone who had just finished a five-mile walk up a steep hill. Had he noticed? she wondered anxiously. More importantly, was this any way for a sensible working woman to behave?

She composed herself enough to go and pay a little visit to Lucy, who she eventually found after a trial-and-error exercise, in the bedroom at the very end of the apartment. Because the apartment ran the entire length of three huge converted Georgian houses, it was sprawling. She stuck her head into several bedrooms, a sitting room and two bathrooms, and finally knocked on the right door to find Lucy sprawled out on her bed with books scattered around her.

'I've decided to go on a diet,' Lucy said, rolling to her side and propping herself up on one elbow. 'Just look at how skinny I used to be.' She nodded to a picture framed on the dressing table of a girl sandwiched between an attractive woman and a fair-haired man wearing wire-rimmed spectacles.

'Your parents?' Melissa asked, picking up the photo and inspecting it.

'Well, one of them.' A long sigh punctuated this remark. 'It's awful to think that I never knew that Brian wasn't my real dad. I keep thinking back, wondering how they could have lied to me all those years.'

'I guess sometimes if you don't tell the truth at the right time, it just gets more and more difficult.'

'Where is he?'

'Having a shower. We're…actually, your father's asked me out to dinner. I think he wants to have a chat about the fact that I haven't got around to chaining you to a treadmill.'

They looked at each other and grinned. 'You were awfully thin,' Melissa said, returning the photo to the dressing table. 'Lucky old you. I used to long for a figure like that when I was your age.'

'Did you?' Lucy seemed pleased by the compliment.

'Short and big-breasted was never much of a fashion statement. There were so many clothes I just couldn't wear. Anyway, I'm glad to hear that you're going on a diet but we'll have to have a chat about that tomorrow. You have to lose weight sensibly or else you'll just end up putting it all back on the minute you start eating properly again.'

'I won't. I just have to cut out all the junk I've spent the last six months piling into my stomach.'

'We'll talk tomorrow, I promise. What are you going to eat tonight?'

'Salad, I suppose. Yuk. I can't stand tomatoes and please don't tell me that they're very good for you. Where is he taking you out to dinner? Somewhere cheap and cheerful, I expect,' she answered her own question in the same breath. 'I can't imagine he would waste much money on the help. Sorry, but it's true. He escorts the witch to all the expensive restaurants, but then again he is trying to impress her.'

Melissa couldn't imagine Elliot trying to impress any-

one, but she bit down the remark. Being referred to as
the help had stung, although it was essentially true. 'They
are engaged,' she pointed out reasonably. 'Naturally he's
going to want to take her out to smart places.'

'You mean she wouldn't dream of putting a foot anywhere that wasn't,' Lucy retorted. 'Just his type.'

'How can you tell what type of woman he likes?'
Melissa was drawn into the conversation against her will
and only came to her senses when her brain did a rethink
of the question. It was no business of hers what type of
woman the man went for and it was crazy to try and
elicit opinions from his teenage daughter, who had her
own enormous axe to grind with him anyway.

'Good question.'

Neither of them had heard Elliot coming. Maybe they
had been too involved in their own conversation and so
his deep, cool voice had Melissa spinning round to face
him. His hair was still slightly damp from the shower and
he had changed into a pair of cream trousers, loafers and
cream shirt that hung outside the waistband of his trousers. The colours of the clothes did something for him,
made him look darker and more exotic.

Lucy shrugged and returned to her mound of school
books, which she flicked through with sudden, frowning
concentration, little realising that that in itself was the
clearest signal she could have given that she was paying
absolutely no attention to what was in front of her. Elliot
passed his usual courteous remarks, which met with the
usual grunt of non-acknowledgement, and then he stood
back to let Melissa walk past him.

The brief thaw Melissa had noticed in Lucy after the
cinema had vanished and the frost was back in full force.
She tried to imagine three more months of atmosphere,
but instead of feeling dismayed she felt a certain level of

excitement. Her curiosity had been piqued, she decided, had lured her into the situation almost when her back was turned.

And, dislikeable though she found Elliot, really, he was the most stimulating man she had ever come into contact with. Maybe it was to do with the hum of energy that vibrated around him. Her eyes slid over him, taking in his arresting sexiness, and she felt a guilty stirring in her veins.

In an attempt to cover it up, she launched into an animated spiel about his apartment, asking a series of banal questions about the décor, how long he had lived there, whether he enjoyed living in London, didn't sometimes long to get away from the fast pace of city life.

Throughout this she managed to avoid direct eye contact, preferring to gaze ahead of her in the lift and breathing a little sigh of relief when they finally stepped outside into the evening air, which was still clinging to some remnants of warmth.

'And I guess you want to ask me about my plans for Lucy,' she continued, effortlessly filling any potential for a gap in the conversation.

'In due course,' Elliot murmured. He signalled for a taxi.

'Where are we going? I thought we were just going to pop into the Italian on the corner. The cheap and cheerful place,' she reminded him, with a question in her voice.

'There *are* other cheap and cheerful places around,' he said, opening the door of the cab to let her in and finishing his sentence when he was sitting inside, next to her. 'A French cheap and cheerful might make a change.'

'Are French restaurants ever cheap and cheerful?' There was an enforced intimacy in sitting in the back of the taxi with him that was disturbing. 'I'm not dressed for anything fancy,' she carried on, stammering.

'Won't…well, won't your fiancée mind you taking another woman out for a meal?'

He greeted this question with a slow, amused smile, and Melissa groaned inwardly to herself. Why did she behave like this whenever she was in his company? She was always the picture of cheerful, detached propriety with all the other male members of the gym, even the ones who occasionally made suggestive remarks to her.

'I mean,' Melissa qualified hurriedly, 'this is purely a business date but, you know, some women can be very jealous and I wouldn't want to…be responsible for any unpleasant situation arising between the two of you…' Her voice trailed off and she thought back to the warning Alison had given her the evening before.

'Alison isn't prone to fits of jealousy,' Elliot pointed out.

'You say that but…'

'But what…?' he asked softly, his voice wrapping around her in the hushed bubble of the cab.

'But women can be jealous…' she said feebly.

'That's not what you meant to say. I've noticed you do that when you're feeling nervous.'

'Do what?'

'This.' He reached forward and tucked some wildly straying blonde hair behind her ear. For a few seconds, shock at the unexpected gesture made her go completely still.

A crazy thought leapt into Elliot's head. How would she react if he did somewhat more than just flick a few strands of hair away from her face? How would she be if he touched her? Really touched her?

He laughed at himself a little incredulously.

'So? Going to tell me what you meant to say?' he continued teasingly.

'I think you might find that your fiancée is a little more

jealous than you think,' Melissa stuttered. She kept her hands firmly clutched on her lap to resist the urge to give in to the nervous gesture he had just commented upon.

'And you get that idea from…where?'

Melissa felt like a rabbit pinned in the headlights of a rapidly approaching car. The fact that the taxi was slowing down, stopping, in front of a chic little restaurant with tables and chairs set outside under umbrellas, was short relief, because as soon as they were shown to their seats he resumed the conversation.

'You were about to tell me why you've come to the conclusion that Alison is jealous or possessive.'

'I really don't like repeating conversations,' she squeaked in a last-ditch attempt to change the subject. He was having none of it. His blue eyes were hard and waiting.

'And I really don't like aspersions being cast on someone's character which are not backed up by some kind of evidence.'

'I wasn't casting any aspersions. I don't see anything wrong with two people who love each other being a little jealous and a little possessive!'

'You're stalling.' He ordered a bottle of wine, keeping one eye on her. 'Do I make you nervous? Stupid question. Of course I do. You act like a cat on a hot tin roof whenever I'm around, but I know that you're not normally like that. When you were recommended to me, the first thing Samantha said was how mature you were for your age, how you hardly ever became rattled by any of the clients, and some of them can be quite…forthcoming, I gather. So, tell me, what is it about me? Does it make you uncomfortable to work for me?'

Melissa nodded vigorously and waited for her vocal cords to return to working order.

'And with regards to your fiancée,' Melissa didn't

want to get involved in any conversations about why
Elliot made her nervous, so she opted for the truth about
Alison instead '…she told me that I should be encouraging Lucy to consider boarding-school, that it was the
best solution given the circumstances, and she also told
me that I should make sure…'

'Yes…?' He inclined towards her, absentmindedly taking a sip of the wine being held out for him to taste by
the waiter and nodding impatiently when asked whether
it could be poured.

'Make sure that I don't get any ideas,' Melissa finished
in a rush. 'That some women might find you attractive
and that it would be easy for me to become one of them.'

Elliot raised his glass to his lips and sipped, regarding
her over the rim with those penetrating blue eyes of his.

'And would it be?' he asked with interest.

Melissa downed a large mouthful of wine. Here she
was, floundering again. Was this more urbane conversation? He wasn't really interested, not at all. He only
wanted to know what she had to say about her plans for
Lucy, because his money was tied up there, but he certainly wasn't concerned by the thought that she might
end up being attracted to him. And why on earth should
he be? He just wasn't ready to get around to talking about
his daughter just yet, and this line of conversation probably appealed to his male ego.

She decided to stamp on any such far-fetched notion.
'No,' she said, shaking her head and smiling. 'Not at all.
I've always been able to draw a line between work and
play and, anyway, you're not my type at all.' The wine
was going down a treat. She suddenly felt very expansive
and very self-confident.

'You have a type?' Elliot was enjoying this. He really
hadn't noticed exactly how rigid his life was until now.
Despite her job, which must have entailed some structure,

she seemed by nature a highly unstructured individual and it was certainly a novel and amusing experience to see how she operated. In fact, it was doing his jaded soul a world of good.

'There's a fantastic choice of food,' she murmured, rereading the menu from the top down and realising that her glass had been refilled when she went to have just a tiny sip more.

Elliot grunted. He was intrigued to hear what this type of man was that she was attracted to. Discussing the choice of food on the menu was a tedious interruption. Her hair was doing it again, flopping over her cheek. She had tied it back into a pony-tail but now, without thinking or looking in his direction, she released it and he drew in his breath sharply as the mane of blonde curls scattered down around her shoulders. Suddenly she didn't seem quite so much like the amusing girl-next-door variety.

'Don't you think?' Melissa looked up at him, her wide blue eyes thrilled. 'I suppose you come to places like this all the time, but I don't. In fact, I haven't been to a single smart restaurant since I came down to London.'

Her hair must be a thousand shades of blonde, he thought, trying to pay attention to what she was saying. Some bits were incredibly fair, others were warmer, more like honey.

'Awful, isn't it?'

'I beg your pardon?'

'My hair. I could see you looking at it.' And no doubt comparing it to Alison's sleek black bob, she thought glumly. No points for guessing who had won the Hair Contest. 'Have you decided what you're going to have?'

'Oh. Oh, yes. And incidentally, your hair isn't awful. Far from it. And you were telling me about your type...'

'Well, I thought we'd finished that bit of conversation and moved on to something else. The food. And really, we ought to talk about Lucy. I feel very guilty that I haven't started anything dramatic as yet. I know that you're paying me and I promise you that I'll do a good job…'

'I'm sure you will. She seems to have taken to you already.' Reluctantly, Elliot dragged his mind back into focus. Luckily there was no need for him to concentrate too hard because after the best part of a bottle of wine, Melissa was doing most of the talking. He could eat his food and allow his eyes to drift lazily over her as she indulged in her lamb noisettes with a gusto he had never before seen in a woman, while she happily chatted about her lack of experience in fine dining, described her plans for Lucy, told him all about her past working as a nanny and laughing at various episodes that had taken place, and making him laugh as well.

'You're staring at me,' Melissa finally said as her plate was taken away, scraped clean. 'I suppose finishing every last morsel of food on your plate isn't really the done thing in an expensive restaurant, is it?' She looked momentarily sheepish at the thought. 'It was absolutely delicious, though. I don't get to do much cooking where I am. I've not much of a kitchen, actually.'

'I think it's very…rare but engaging to see a woman actually finish eating everything on her plate.'

Melissa suddenly didn't feel rare or engaging. She felt awkward and lumpish. 'And their figures show it,' she laughed, realising that she was now hardly a walking advert for moderation in one's eating habits, which would be what she would have to instil in Lucy presumably. At least she had resisted the dessert menu and had drunk her coffee decaffeinated and black. She thought of the long, slender Alison and felt a nasty twinge of jealousy.

'Do you have a problem with your figure?'

'Don't all women?' Melissa sidestepped the question.

The room was beginning to spin ever so slightly and when she stood up at the end of the meal she found she had to grip the back of her chair to steady herself.

Elliot was on his feet before she could sit back down, holding her by the waist. 'Sudden onset of flu, do you think,' he murmured softly into her ear, 'or a little too much wine?'

His breath was warm and gave her the most wonderful, squirmy sensation in her stomach.

'Ha, ha. I don't normally drink. I'm fine now. You can let me go. I promise I won't embarrass you by falling in a heap on the floor.'

'Very little embarrasses me and that certainly wouldn't.' His arms remained exactly where they were, supporting her, and together they walked towards the door, only stopping so that he could pay the bill. Even when he was writing out the slip, one arm stayed around her, his hand only inches away from the curve of her breast, and Melissa was horrified to realise that her body was responding to him, nipples tautening against her sensible cotton bra.

'Where are you taking me?' she asked drowsily. Her eyelids felt like two pieces of lead, and with a little sigh she slumped against him in the back of the taxi, which he must have summoned without her noticing. His deep, lazy drawl seemed to reach her from miles away.

'Where would you like to be taken?'

She felt his fingers curl into her hair and she closed her eyes and yawned. She wondered vaguely how a little bit of wine could have mellowed her so much that she felt absolutely wonderful lying against Elliot and feeling his hands in her hair.

'I'm taking you home,' he said softly, 'your home.'

'You don't know where I live.'

'I know everything.' He laughed under his breath. 'Including where you live.'

Melissa could feel her eyes getting heavier and heavier and the next time she opened them she was looking at the walls of the stairwell in her house travelling past her, even though she didn't appear to be moving. She realised that she was being carried up the stairs and she made a token effort to dislodge herself.

'Ah. You're up,' Elliot commented lightly.

'You'll damage your back carrying me.'

'I could take that as a slur on my virility,' Elliot murmured huskily.

Except, of course, he never would, she thought. Because he was as virile as they came. She could feel the muscles of his arms lifting her and the corded strength of his neck under her hands. Lord only knew when he had managed to get her keys from her—probably when they were in the taxi and he was thinking clearly while she slumbered in total abandonment against him.

He fiddled with the lock on her door without putting her down before kicking it open and then stepping inside.

'God,' he muttered incredulously, 'you live *here*?'

Melissa yawned and giggled. 'Wonderful, isn't it? I call it cosy and compact.'

'Where's your bed?'

'The thing with the cushions on it.'

He laid her down and then stood up and looked around him in disgust while Melissa watched his reactions through half-closed eyes. She felt crazily alive and suddenly very daring. The wine had gone to her head but had not tipped her over the edge, and although her head was still swimming a bit, her senses were on full alert.

'I'll leave you now,' he said, when his inspection of her tiny room was over. 'You need to get out of your clothes and get some sleep.'

The sidelight he had switched on was buzzing with its usual inefficiency. That was something that had always bugged her because she needed to switch on both table lamps whenever she wanted to actually see what she was doing, but right now the subdued lighting suited her just fine.

'Would you make me some coffee?' she heard herself ask, and after a moment's hesitation he nodded and disappeared into the kitchenette, where she could hear the clink of a mug being fetched from the cupboard and the hissing of the kettle as it gathered steam.

Her clothes felt tight and uncomfortable now that she was lying down.

On sudden, urgent impulse she began wriggling out of them, eager to get some cool air on her body. Every bit of her was on fire and a languorous feeling of utter wantonness swept through her as she heard him switch off the kitchen light.

CHAPTER SIX

MELISSA saw Elliot stop in shock. For a few seconds he looked as though his brain had received information which it was finding difficult to decipher, then it all clicked together and he approached her slowly.

One small part of her was desperately trying to reassert some reason, but it was fighting a losing battle against the greater part that was wildly turned on and fuelled by a desire she had never felt in her life before. That wicked part of her now made her stretch out, extending her body on the sofa bed and watching him as he finally came to stand in front of her, over her, the mug of coffee incongruously in his hand.

'What the hell are you doing?' he rasped.

'You said I needed to get undressed.' His voice was harsh but his eyes roamed over her and his scrutiny made her blood heat.

'You've had way too much to drink. It was my fault. I should have stopped you.'

'Why? You might be my employer but I'm a big girl and you're not my moral guardian.' She was speaking slowly, making sure that she didn't trip over her words.

With an indecipherable oath, Elliot dumped the coffee on the mantelpiece and began gathering her clothes from the floor. He seemed to have second thoughts and asked her roughly to point him in the direction of her pyjamas.

His normally superb cool was shattered. He was making a good attempt to gather it but she could tell from his jerky movements that he wasn't succeeding. It gave her a feeling of heady power.

When she failed to supply him with the information he had requested, he went to the chest of drawers, pulling each one open until he had located the one that contained the oversized T-shirts that she used as nightwear. He yanked out the first one that came to hand and seemed to inhale deeply before he turned round.

Elliot knew what he should do. He should just drop the T-shirt on top of her and bid her goodnight. She had been capable of removing her clothes so she shouldn't have any problem putting some on.

But when he looked…

He felt a rush of attraction that was so powerful it nearly rocked him on his feet. Her tangled blonde hair seemed unnaturally light against the dark cushion and her body was smooth as satin.

He perched on the side of the sofa bed. 'Come on. Sit up and I'll stick this on you, or else…'

'Or else what?' Melissa obediently sat up but she didn't take the T-shirt from him. Instead she propped herself up on her hands so that her breasts were thrust out at him, ripe, delectable fruit waiting to be picked.

Elliot groaned under his breath and went to put the shirt over her, his hand grazing her breasts as he did so.

The contact of his hand against her nipples was electrifying. Melissa let her head drop back and closed her eyes. She heard him mutter something forcefully under his breath, then she felt his mouth against hers, pushing her back, claiming her with white-hot, driving urgency.

He dropped the T-shirt. With frantic hands, Melissa began undoing the buttons of his shirt so that she could slide her hands against his chest and feel the hardness of his torso.

'Oh, God,' he muttered thickly, 'this is lunacy.' But already his hands had found her breast and he was cupping it, massaging it roughly, rubbing the tip of his thumb over her sensitised nipple.

'Yes, oh, yes!' Her own voice sounded oddly strangled. She pushed him down, arching up and releasing a long, shuddering sigh of satisfaction as his mouth covered her throbbing nipple, drawing it in, licking and sucking and teasing. Her body couldn't keep still. She moved sensuously against him and the roughness of his trousers sent shivers of excitement racing through her heated body.

When he had finished with one breast, he began his exquisite plundering of the other and then his hand was on her inner thigh, stroking its smoothness, edging higher. With a gasp, Melissa parted her legs, waiting for those clever, experienced fingers to touch her, in the grip of the most overwhelming roller-coaster ride of sensation she had ever experienced.

She moaned when he finally did touch her there, in her most intimate place, rhythmically rubbing while she writhed against his fingers, offering her breasts to his warm mouth and everything else to his expert exploration.

Like a flower that suddenly began to bloom, she was besieged by a feeling of newness, of her body opening up and becoming alive for the first time ever. She reached for him, seeking out the hardness she felt pressed like a rod of iron against her, but it was too late. The swollen bud he was rubbing was already soaring towards fulfilment and with a cry she reached the pinnacle of enjoyment, which seemed to last forever. She stiffened and pressed her hand to the back of his head, urging his mouth against her breast as wave after wave of pleasure rocked her.

All trace of wine had disappeared from her veins when she next opened her eyes to meet his staring down at her.

'I think it's time I left, don't you?' Elliot's voice was unsteady and he was already standing up, drawing away from her.

Suddenly the room felt icy cold to Melissa. Reality was piecing itself together slowly but surely and it wasn't pleasant. In fact, it was a nightmare. She hooked the throw around her and watched with growing mortification as he buttoned up his shirt, making sure not to glance at her at all.

What had happened to the wild, soaring recklessness that had consumed her? Where had it gone? Its rapid departure had left her with a picture she could scarcely bear to look at. An image of a foolish woman throwing herself at a man who was unavailable, a man for whom she worked, someone who had not once shown the slightest glimmer of attraction towards her. Her mind screeched to a halt before she could contemplate the awfulness of it in too much detail.

She struggled up to sit and curled herself protectively under the throw, pulling up her legs and propping her face on her knees.

'I'm sorry.' She made herself talk as loudly as possible. She also forced herself to look directly at him because this wasn't some casual one-night stand she could leave behind forever with a sigh of relief. This was someone she would be seeing again and again over the next few months.

'Save it,' Elliot said harshly. 'I should be the one apologising. You had too much to drink and I took advantage of you.'

Melissa didn't say anything. She tucked her hair behind her ears and then stopped when she remembered what he had said about noticing how she did that every time she was nervous. It seemed like a lifetime ago since he had uttered that statement. Her eyes left his and she stared miserably down at the ground, waiting while the silence gathered around her like treacle.

Eventually she heard the quiet click of the door being closed and when she looked up it was to find that Elliot had gone, leaving her alone to painfully consider the implications of what she had done.

And also her options.

They were simple. She could either stay and spend the next few weeks in a state of painful suspension with his presence reminding her daily of her own stupidity. Or she could go. She had never set eyes on him in the gym before and it was entirely likely that she never would again, especially now that she knew exactly when he tended to go there. That way there would be no uncomfortable confrontations and no chance for her own attraction to him to grow, not if he wasn't around. And Lucy...well, Lucy would probably be relieved in a way that she was again free to do what she wanted without being overseen by someone her father had seen fit to put in place.

Alison had warned her against falling for his considerable sex appeal. At the time she had laughed off the warning. It was to her shame that she had gone and done just the thing she had dismissed as ridiculous.

Sleep eventually claimed her before her thoughts could fully switch off and she slept fitfully, waking at the crack of dawn and experiencing a few seconds of blissful amnesia before the sickening memories of the night before descended with remorseless speed.

Some time in the night she had arrived at her decision, and before getting dressed she sat down and composed her bland letter of resignation.

Then she went to work at the health club, as usual.

If anyone noticed a change in her, no one commented, and by the end of the day she assumed that whatever was going through her head, it certainly wasn't showing on her face or in her demeanour.

She had no idea when he would be at the apartment, and as soon as her last client for the day had gone, instead of catching up on some paperwork, she went across to the manager's office, to which she was allowed free access as a member of staff. Fortunately Samantha wasn't there to ask any piercing questions, and her secretary was accustomed to Melissa coming in, having a look at files and updating them with information.

She didn't pay a scrap of notice when Melissa fished out Elliot's file and noted down his office address. Nor did she bat an eyelid when she told her that she would be leaving early to catch up with some paperwork.

Elliot's office was in the City. It only occurred to Melissa belatedly, when she was standing outside the imposing building, that there was a better than average chance that he wouldn't be in. Or if he was in, he would be in one of those high-powered meetings he seemed to enjoy so much.

I'll just have to wait, she decided. It wouldn't be nice, not when she was prepared with her letter in her bag, but she couldn't possibly wait for him at the apartment if it was one of his late nights. Lucy would be curious and then there was the strong possibility that she would overhear part of their conversation, which would be a disaster.

She took a deep breath and walked through the large revolving glass door, to find herself confronted with acres of marble. At this hour it was relatively quiet, but as offices went there was, she realised, next to no chance that she would be allowed up to his office to wait for him. And this was confirmed when the woman at the reception desk, having looked her up and down, informed her that no one was allowed in without an appointment.

The letter of resignation was burning a hole in her bag.

'I'm afraid I won't be leaving until I see Mr Jay,' Melissa said stubbornly.

'Mr Jay is an extremely busy man.' Her name badge proclaimed her to be Ms Cribbs and she certainly looked like a Ms Very Icy and was very determined not to allow any ordinary mortals access to one of her important directors.

'I'm sure he is,' Melissa said tartly, 'but...' she lowered her voice and allowed a few seconds of meaningful silence to stretch between them '...I think you'll find that he'll be very angry *indeed* if he learns that you've asked me to leave. *Very angry indeed.*'

Their eyes met and the woman hesitated for a second or two. 'I take it your visit is of a personal nature?' she enquired coldly.

'Of an *extremely personal nature*,' Melissa said, enunciating each word with deliberate slowness.

'Hold on a minute.' She didn't want to do it, but the thought of incurring Elliot's wrath was obviously too much. She picked up the phone, spoke for a few minutes in hushed tones, back half-turned to Melissa, and then replaced the receiver. 'Mr Jay is in a meeting but his secretary has given permission for you to wait for him in his offices. He's on the fourth floor. She'll be waiting for you by the lift. You do understand,' she continued stiffly, 'that in an organisation such as this, stray members of the public are not allowed to wander through the building unchecked.'

Tense though she was, Melissa nearly grinned at the thought that her unprepossessing attire might well have engendered the *stray members of the public* remark. Amongst these high-level business people in their dark suits and crisp white shirts, her light blue summer skirt and sandals stuck out like a sore thumb.

'I quite understand,' Melissa said solemnly. 'Fourth floor?'

'Mrs Watkins will be there.'

There was the general smell of money being made in these offices. There were two people in the lift Melissa took up. Neither spoke and nor did they look at each other. The woman was dressed in a sober grey suit, with high heels and the regulation white blouse, and the man was in a pinstripe suit. They stared ahead of them, both sporting identical little frowns, while Melissa stood between and slightly behind, a great vantage point from which to observe how the other half operated.

There was no time for Melissa to feel really nervous until the lift doors opened on to the fourth floor and there was the fabled Mrs Watkins, waiting for her. She, too, was in a suit but, because she was in her fifties, her clothing was not quite so imposing. She also had a friendly face that displayed no hint of curiosity. Though curious she must certainly be, Melissa thought. After all, who could this woman in the summer skirt be, there to see the great Elliot Jay on *a personal matter that couldn't wait*?

'I haven't been able to interrupt Mr Jay at his meeting,' she confided, ushering Melissa into an office within an office. 'But it's scheduled to finish in about half an hour. Perhaps you might like a cup of tea or coffee while you wait?'

'I'll just wait,' Melissa said, and contemplate my behaviour last night for the millionth time, she added silently to herself.

'I'll be out there if you need me.'

Once the other woman had gone, Melissa looked around her with interest. She was seeing another side to Elliot. This was the side that really showed how powerful he was. The carpeting was lush and his offices seemed to have been designed with a process of filtration in mind.

Outer office number one appeared to house a few crucial
secretaries, who had barely glanced up when she and Mrs
Watkins had passed through. Just off this outer office was
Mrs Watkins' own, small, private office, complete with
walnut desk, computer, phones and a flowering pot plant.
Through the outer office was the room in which Melissa
now sat. This was clearly a waiting area for clients, and
a very tasteful one at that. Of course, she thought, it
wouldn't do to allow any hint of his personality to in-
trude. The pictures on the walls were bland sketches of
London, the two small sofas were beige, to match the
carpet, and the squat coffee-table was of smooth, blonde
wood that bore not a single stain or mark. People sat here
to discuss matters of importance. The last thing they
needed would be any visual distractions.

And beyond this room, she assumed, was Elliot's own
office, to which the door was shut. Through two long
glass panels she could make out an enormous desk, the
obligatory computer, phones, a fax machine and files. In
her head, she perked it up with some plants, a dashing
faux leopard-skin rug and a comfortable reclining chair,
in matching leopard skin. It was an amusing game and it
managed to take her mind off things just long enough for
her to miss his arrival. One minute she was squinting
through the glass panels and mentally redecorating his
office, the next she had turned around and there he was,
framed in the doorway, staring at her.

How did he manage to do that? He was dressed in the
same sober charcoal grey suit as everyone else, but he
didn't look like a drone. He looked all man. Dark, powerful and unsmiling.

Having prepared herself for this meeting and rehearsed
in her head all the cool things she would say, Melissa
now felt sick with tension and overwhelmed with dis-
graceful memories. She could still feel his hands on her,

touching her at her own invitation, sending her senses flying in every direction while he played with the most intimate part of her body. She licked her lips, half stood up and then sat back down on the sofa.

'What are you doing here, Melissa?' He strode into the room and shut the door behind him. Instead of sitting down, though, he simply stood behind one of the sofas and leaned forward, propping himself up on his hands.

'I've come to deliver this to you.' Melissa rummaged in her bag, found the envelope and held it out shakily.

'What is it?'

'Read it.'

Elliot pushed himself up, opened the envelope and sat on the sofa facing her, reading her carefully worded letter of resignation slowly, then he placed it on the table between them and looked at her.

'Why do you feel that under the circumstances your position is untenable?'

'I haven't come here to take up your valuable time with long explanations,' Melissa told him quietly.

'Oh, I think I can decide how I want to use my valuable time, and right now I'm very interested in hearing your explanation. What happened last night was a mistake, I'll grant you that, but mistakes happen and there's no reason for this particular one to affect your contract of employment.'

'And I don't think that an apology is good enough.' She could feel her cheeks burning and she looked away, past him to the door he had shut. She just couldn't bring herself to meet those shuttered blue eyes. 'I behaved abominably.'

'You drank a little too much; it went to your head. These things happen. I should have had more control, while we're pointing fingers, and I think we both realise that.' He was grimly aware that he had never felt so out of control in his life before. In a life where parameters were firmly drawn and nothing ever got out of hand or found him floundering, his experience the night before had left a disturbing, sour taste in his mouth. He hadn't for a single second thought about Alison. In retrospect, that said it all about their relationship, gave him the message loud and clear that, however convenient their arrangement was and however much he liked her, marriage to Alison was out of the question. He would break it to her later. Right now, he had his own anger with himself to deal with.

'It still makes things very awkward for me,' Melissa said. 'I really don't see how we can continue having any sort of professional relationship.'

'Why? Because you think you might be tempted to fling yourself at me again?'

Melissa's mouth dropped open at the sheer nerve of the remark. Who the hell did he think he was? Universal sex god? Did he imagine that she had been secretly lusting after him and then she had thrown herself at him because she just couldn't resist any longer?

'Your silence is illuminating.'

Melissa snapped shut her mouth and glared at him. 'I'm just staggered that you could think that. I know that wine isn't much of an excuse but I can't hold my drink very well.'

'In other words, I could have been anyone?'

No, her mind screamed. 'Who knows?' she said, shrugging.

'In which case I suggest you make sure that you drink alcohol well away from the public at large or you might find yourself in a situation you hadn't quite bargained on.' Elliot's mouth tightened. He wasn't vain. He certainly didn't spend hours preening himself in front of a mirror, nor did he carry a comb in his back pocket for emergency situations when he might just need to spruce himself up. However, he did know that women singled him out. The implication that he was merely in the right place at the right time stuck in his throat.

'Let's be logical about this,' Elliot said grimly, leaning forward to rest his elbows on his knees. 'From what I see, you're doing a good job with Lucy. You're far more of a companion to her than Lenka has ever been, and you may well be the stepping stone to help her through this period. And, judging by the state of your bedsit, you clearly need the money, if only to save up so that you can afford something slightly more salubrious in due course.'

'That's not the point…'

'No, it's not the point, but these are things that are strongly in favour of you staying on for the duration. You say that you don't feel that you can maintain a normal working relationship with me after what happened…' He could see mortification stamped on her face like a brand, and he knew that it was a measure of her inexperience. To have derived pleasure from the circumstances in which she had found herself was a bitter pill she had to swallow and he could have kicked himself be-cause…because…

Because she deserved to have pleasure in the right cir-cumstances. With the right man, he told himself.

'I don't see the point of talking about it,' Melissa whis-pered, staring at the table now.

'Of course we have to talk about it,' Elliot snapped impatiently. 'There's no sense in beating yourself up for a crime you haven't committed. As we've already estab-lished, it was a mistake. I'm not your type of man any more than you are my type of woman.' Something nig-gled at the back of his mind and he ignored it. 'But some-times things happen. I promise you that when you leave this room, you leave this conversation, and what happened between us, behind. No more will be mentioned on the subject. You could say that it never happened.'

I could never say that, Melissa thought in dismay. Because it *did* happen and it will keep on happening in my head. What was wrong with her? Why couldn't she just laugh about it and then consign the episode to history?

'It's not the end of the world, Melissa,' Elliot interrupted her thoughts, his voice husky and incisive. 'Haven't you ever done anything that was…shall we say, regrettable?'

'What do you mean?'

'I mean, have you never indulged in a wild sexual experience just for the hell of it?'

'No!' Melissa was shocked. 'I'm sorry but I simply don't see the point of that and, anyway, casual sex is not good for one's health.'

'You don't think it has some benefits?' Elliot's mouth curved into a slow, sexy smile that sent shivers racing up and down her spine.

'Maybe for someone else but not for me.' She stood up and cleared her throat. 'OK. I'll stay on working for you because, as you point out, I think Lucy and I are beginning to forge a bond, which is good, and because I need the money. Or rather, the extra money would be very helpful, but you have to give me your word that none of this…what happened…is ever mentioned again.'

'I already have given you my word.'

For the time being at any rate, Elliot thought, watching her as she hovered there, anxiously wondering whether she had done the right thing. In due course, the subject of sex would be raised again because she roused his curiosity.

'You'll be gone by the time I get back tonight,' he

said, standing up and ushering her to the door. 'What are you planning to do with Lucy?' His mind was already zooming ahead to what he himself had to do later as Melissa spent a few minutes outlining her plans. She knew he was barely listening to a word she was saying. His expression was frowning, distracted.

Was he thinking about whatever meeting he had planned for later? Maybe he was going to be seeing Alison. That thought arrested her flow of conversation. 'I don't know how to say this…' she began and after a few seconds the sound of her prolonged silence finally regained his attention. He focused on her once again, although the frown was still there.

'Say what?'

'And I know we both made a pact never to drag this subject up again, but…'

Elliot tore his mind away from the uncomfortable evening that lay ahead. He hoped that Alison wouldn't kick up a fuss when he broke the news that it was all over between them. The fact that he would be unable to give any concrete reason why their relationship was at an end would not be helpful. Women liked reasons. Still, he didn't imagine that she would shed any tears. She was a high-powered barrister, insured against emotionalism. Sobbing would not be her scene. But the recriminations would be bad enough.

'Drag…drag what?' Elliot murmured, barely registering what she had said.

'When you see your fiancée, I would appreciate it if you didn't mention what happened between us… I know I'm encouraging you to be deceitful, but I really would appreciate it, at least while I'm working under your roof…'

'Fair enough,' Elliot said, thinking that really that little episode would be irrelevant anyway, considering his fiancée would be no more as of tonight. He watched as her shoulders sagged in relief.

Melissa was a study in ingenuity. Every emotion was written on her face. She had missed the toughening-up pill that most girls swallowed when they were teenagers, the one that made them adept at concealment, that turned them into women who could handle the occasional lapse and laugh it off in an adult, carefree manner, that turned them into the sort of women that he had always dated.

He looked at her speculatively. He had a meeting in ten minutes' time but suddenly his purely masculine curiosity got the better of him. He poked his head out of the office door and told his secretary that he would be running slightly late for his meeting.

'Oh, no,' Melissa said anxiously, 'I've already used up enough of your time. You have…important things to do…'

Elliot closed the door and signalled for her to sit back down. 'Nothing that won't wait for me.'

'Because you're…'

'So very, very important.' He gave her a crooked smile, coaxing a tentative one in return, and then moved to sit next to her on the sofa. He couldn't really work out what it was about this woman, but she intrigued him. In the space of only a few days, for a start, she had made him aware of shortcomings in his relationship with Alison that he had not consciously been aware of. Then again, thinking about it, how often did he and Alison meet, spend time together? Juggling evenings with their joint busy schedules was a tricky procedure, prone to cancellations, something which he had happily lived with and indeed accepted as perfectly normal. They had good sex, when they got around to it, but was it magnificent?

'Believe me, I understand your doubts about us continuing to work together.'

'Do you?' Melissa eyed him sceptically. This was not the kind of conversation she wanted to be having. She certainly didn't want him sitting so close to her. He was facing her and she was acutely, alarmingly aware of his proximity. Everything was so vibrantly, intensely *male* about him that simply breathing in the scent of him made her feel a bit faint. She made a few edgy movements and came up against the solid barrier of the sofa arm.

'I do.' He placed one hand soothingly over hers and Melissa felt as though she had suddenly received a massive electric charge. This is exactly what I'm talking about! she wanted to shriek. Last night was hideous enough, but worse still was that it had brought with it, along with all the expected feelings of mortification and abject embarrassment, an overriding awareness of him as a man, which was something she had done her level best to ignore since she had first set eyes on him. She awkwardly tried to slide her hand out from under his. To no avail.

'It's very important that you don't harbour any wariness where I am concerned. You have to be free to have an unconditional relationship with me, safe in the knowledge that you can tell me anything.' Elliot continued to rest his hand on hers.

Unconditional? Melissa considered that a poor choice of word.

'OK.'

Elliot frowned. 'So we understand each other?'

'I think so.' Actually, the only thing she was currently thinking was how much she wanted to escape the suffocating impact of his presence. She thought about telling him that she had changed her mind, had decided that she couldn't possibly work for him after all, but that would have been pathetic. She had painted herself into a corner

and now she would just have to sit through his kindly
lecture as best she could.

'There can be no room for you avoiding me.'

'I wouldn't do that,' Melissa lied, blushing. 'How
could I? I would have to deliver Lucy back to your apartment and I wouldn't duck behind the kitchen counter if
I heard your key in the door.' But she would have to
fight the temptation, she acceded to herself. With the way
her body behaved when she was around him, the option
of unglamorously squatting behind a counter to hide
would be almost irresistible. She thanked her lucky stars
that Elliot wasn't a mind-reader as well as everything
else. If he had been, he would have spotted in seconds
how powerfully he affected her.

That was something which he could never be allowed
to see. To have him aware of the fact would scupper any
chance of that perfectly normal, unconditional, feel-free-
to-talk-to-me boss-employee relationship he was recom-
mending.

'I'm relieved to hear it,' Elliot said drily, meeting her
eyes and holding her gaze. He removed his hand and
noted how hers speedily went to her lap, well out of
harm's way. 'I admit that I won't be making a habit of
coming home at six, but I will want weekly reports of
how you're doing with Lucy. A run-down of what you've
been up to.'

With the conversation back on a work footing, Melissa
allowed herself to relax. She nodded, eager to be gone.
For someone whose working life was so meticulously
ordered, Elliot's line of conversation always seemed to
contain an unsettling air of unpredictability. Was that part
of his compelling fascination?

'Of course,' Melissa agreed promptly.

'I think Fridays would be good for that, don't you
agree?'

'Yes, that would be fine.'

'I know it can be an awkward day. Most young women want to celebrate the end of the week by going out partying...' He dropped his eyes and sat back, leaving this tantalising carrot dangling in the air between them.

'If I know what time you'll want me to stay until, then I'll make sure that I'm available. But can you arrange your working hours to suit? I thought you found it difficult to take time off...'

'Up till now, I admit I haven't been around for Lucy,' Elliot said heavily. 'I've done all the things that needed to be done, made sure that she got into a good school, arranged for a personal shopper to kit her out in whatever clothes she wanted, bought her whatever she needed or asked for, but I failed to put in any time with her.' Alison hadn't helped. Had she felt threatened by the sudden appearance of his teenage daughter? He hadn't thought so at the time, but in retrospect it made sense. She had maintained a firm hand, never once questioning his lack of personal input, and, unaccustomed to having his actions curtailed in any way, Elliot had obligingly gone along for the ride.

Melissa thought that if he had come to that point of knowledge, then there might be a chance that they could alter the battle lines that were slowly but surely setting like concrete between Lucy and Elliot before it was too late. She smiled in appreciation of the prospect.

'I'll make sure that I'm back at the apartment by six every Friday,' Elliot continued. It was a suggestion that had come off the top of his head, but now it seemed like a really good idea. 'We can go out for a meal together, the three of us, and then you can spend a few minutes filling me in on what's been happening afterwards.'

'A meal?' Melissa frowned, not too sure how a quick

debriefing once a week had turned into dinner out and her whole evening spoken for.

'Unless you generally have plans for a Friday…? You never said…'

'I…' Suddenly it felt a little abnormal having to admit to Fridays spent in, doing nothing. She had not been in London long enough to make any solid friends, and those she did see she generally saw on a Saturday. 'I…I do sometimes go out on a Friday. Clubbing,' she added, for good measure. 'You know. But I could make sure that I'm available for the next couple of months.'

'*Clubbing?*'

Melissa mumbled something under her breath.

'You go *clubbing*?'

'It's what young people tend to do,' she said defensively. That much was true enough at any rate. Young people did do that. She just didn't happen to be one of them.

'As opposed to dinosaurs like myself?' Elliot grinned slowly and mesmerisingly. That warranted another mumble.

'I'm sure you go to *different* clubs,' Melissa stammered.

'Maybe. We'll have to compare notes one day.' Melissa's face was saying no, but her chest was heaving. He'd love to touch her again—the thought sprang from nowhere and was lost before he could hold it—to touch her slowly, bit by leisurely bit…to send her soaring, but next time without embarrassment and with the right man, yes…him.

CHAPTER SEVEN

ELLIOT stared at his computer screen and impatiently tapped his pen on the black leather pad on which his keyboard rested. He was not accustomed to this, to being at the mercy of feelings he could not identify. It was like an itch that needed scratching. And he had felt like this for the past six weeks.

In his highly focused life, Elliot had always been able to conduct his private life without it overlapping work. He enjoyed women but they never intruded into the intensely enjoyable and demanding area of deals and mergers and the tremendously invigorating and time-consuming business of making a fortune. In fact, it wasn't even about making a fortune. With several already at his disposal, Elliot had become used to working simply for the challenge of it. Women had always filled necessary slots but they just never crossed the threshold. He had always had the enviable ability to compartmentalise. He could have a very satisfying night of passion and leave his apartment the following morning with a clear head.

Not so now.

He sighed and pushed himself back from his desk, swivelling in his chair to stare out of the window at another perfect summer day. From several storeys up, his only view was of the sky, a crisp, vibrant blue. If he went to the window and looked down, he knew what he would see. The uninspiring sight of people striding along pavements, hailing taxis, going places.

On the spur of the moment Elliot buzzed through to

his secretary. It took a matter of fifteen minutes but at the end of it he felt immeasurably better.

All he had to do now was pay a little visit to Melissa at the gym and fill her in.

Melissa had no idea who was waiting outside her door until she finished her session with her physiotherapy client. Adam Beck worked at the gym too. He supervised people in serious training, had a number of high-profile clients whom he saw on a one-to-one basis, and additionally taught a number of high-impact classes. Melissa had been to just one of his sessions and almost collapsed under the pressure of it. She had afterwards laughingly told him that he was a sadist in disguise and from that moment on they had become friends, bonded by the fact that they worked in the same building, were the same age and were not at all attracted to one another. He had a girlfriend with whom he was deeply in love and was touchingly indulgent of her contented lack of interest in any form of exercise. He spoke about her all the time.

Now Adam was trying to arrange something for the three of them when Melissa pulled open the door and was confronted with Elliot, standing outside, jacket hooked over one shoulder, shirt carelessly rolled to the elbows.

Surprise made her mouth drop slightly open. It was one thing seeing Elliot at the apartment. She expected to see him there. Even when he wasn't due back and suddenly showed up, she was always on the alert, every sense tuned to the possibility that he might just walk through the door, that he might be there when she and Lucy returned from their workouts in the park. When, weeks ago, he had mentioned his plan to chat with her on a Friday about how things were progressing, she had hoped that that would be the one and only day on which she was forced to see him, but not so. Increasingly, he had taken to just showing up. It puzzled her because it didn't fit in with the workaholic image she had tagged on to him and, after the first few bouts of heavy sarcasm, even Lucy now seemed to take his unpredictable movements for granted.

Melissa couldn't do likewise. There was nothing about Elliot that she could take for granted. Every time he was in her presence, she could feel her body prickle with an awareness she did her best to keep concealed. She tried hard not to stare, but her eyes would sweep surreptitiously towards him, and however much she attempted to maintain the cool, detached demeanour of a woman simply doing her job, he could still drag a laugh from her, have her hanging on to his every word, smiling at that dry, witty way he had with words.

He was being the perfect employer. He had stuck rigidly to his promise that no more would be said about that fateful night, and had done his utmost to make her feel relaxed in his company.

It wasn't his fault that she just couldn't relax whenever he was around. Or that her memories of him touching her kept her awake at night and still sent her imagination into overdrive as she concocted ever more wildly detailed scenarios in which he didn't just touch with his fingers... No, that was her guilty secret.

Now Elliot was staring at Adam, his lips drawn into a tight line, and Melissa was forced to make introductions.

'We work together,' she explained, plunging into the awkward speech.

'So I see,' Elliot drawled. He made no effort to extend his hand in greeting. In fact, he did the opposite. He thrust it very firmly into his trouser pocket and proceeded to lean against the door-frame. Physically, he was not as beefy as Adam, but he was taller and there was a leashed aggressiveness about him that made him appear tougher and more dangerous.

'What are you doing here at this hour? Is everything all right with Lucy?' She turned to Adam briefly. 'I'll get back to you about Saturday the 31st, shall I?' She smiled, but her mind was occupied with the man lounging in front of her. Normally, after she'd pummelled Adam, they would chat for a few minutes. Neither now seemed inclined to do that and of course Elliot was entirely to blame. He could depress an atmosphere without having to say a thing and he was doing it now.

'Well?' Melissa said sharply, once Adam had sauntered off, leaving her on her own with Elliot. 'How can I help you?'

'Sorry, but was I interrupting?'

'I *do* see clients during the day,' Melissa reminded him shortly. 'That was part of the deal, if you recall. I carry on seeing my clients and then devote the late afternoons to Lucy.'

'Yes, of course I remember the details of our contract.' He raked his fingers through his hair and stared at her.

What had she been doing with that man?

It was crazy to be thinking like this. In fact, so alien was the emotion that it took him a little while to work out that what he was feeling was good, old-fashioned jealousy.

'I have a proposition and I want to put it to you without Lucy around. Could you break for lunch?'

'Yes, but I have another client at two and I'm teaching a class for my old dears at three.' No way would she let Elliot think that it was fine to just breeze in and interrupt her day on the assumption that her hours were at his disposal, terms of contract or no terms of contract. It was trying enough dealing with him outside hours without the stress of wondering whether he might just decide to start popping into the gym during the day as well.

'These old dears…would they be roughly my age?' Elliot asked, pushing himself away from the door-frame and heading down towards the café.

'Are you in your late sixties?'

'Is it only you who teaches those classes, or are they shared between everyone? I can't imagine that body-builder chap teaching stretching exercises to the over-fifties…'

Melissa picked up the mild disdain in Elliot's voice and it didn't surprise her. A man like Elliot would have little time for someone like Adam, someone who didn't pursue a demanding intellectual career.

'It takes an awful lot of dedication to do what Adam does,' she said defensively. 'It's physically very gruel-ling.'

'Is that why their brains tend to be so underdevel-oped?' Elliot enquired sarcastically. 'They devote so much time to making sure their biceps look just right that their brains wither away from lack of activity?'

Melissa held on to her temper with some difficulty. 'Not everyone needs to pour all their energy into making millions and running empires.'

'Not many can.'

They had reached the café, which at lunch-time was busy. It was a queuing system and sold the most mouth-wateringly delicious sandwiches and baguettes Melissa had ever tasted. For those who were feeling virtuous, there was also an array of salads, but it was a standing joke amongst the employees of the gym that most clients felt they had earned a few calories after working out. The baguettes were their biggest sellers.

Melissa grabbed a tray and tried to ignore the man next to her as she opted for a salad and bottled water. Not that he could criticise her if she chose to pile her plate with every form of carbohydrate on view. As far as Lucy was concerned, she was doing a good job. In the space of the past six-odd weeks, her excess weight was dropping off and her levels of confidence were rising accordingly. She had stopped moaning about school, had made a couple of friends and had even joined the netball team, which practised four days a week during the lunch-hour.

'You had a proposition to put to me,' Melissa said, as soon as they had found a table.

'I've decided that a holiday with Lucy might be a good idea. What do you think?'

'You want to go on holiday with your daughter? I think that's a brilliant suggestion.' She unscrewed her water, poured some into a glass and took a few sips. The salad stared uninvitingly up at her. 'Where were you planning on going?'

'I have a holiday house in the West Indies. It, too, suffers from lack of activity.'

'Would…would your fiancée be going as well?' Melissa asked casually. She had not set eyes on the other woman in weeks and it had not occurred to Melissa to ask after Alison. For a start, it was none of her business and she had been scrupulously wary of stepping anywhere near any subjects that could be construed as personal, and for another thing the thought of Alison only reminded her of that night when she had thrown inhibition to the wind and made a fool of herself, never once sparing a thought for the fact that the man she was flinging herself at was engaged. 'I'm not sure Lucy would relish the prospect of a holiday with Alison in tow,' Melissa added as neutrally as she could.

'She won't have to. Alison and I are no longer involved.'

About to dig into her salad, Melissa stopped, fork

poised, and stared at him. He'd uttered just seven words and she felt her heart skip a beat. 'You didn't say.'

'Was I supposed to?'

There was genuine surprise in his voice and Melissa rapidly worked out the reason for it. Elliot was not a man who accounted for himself. He had probably become so accustomed, in fact, to never accounting for himself that it would have taken a leap of indescribable proportions for him to have done so about this. Never mind that it was something that affected his daughter.

'You might have considered that Lucy would have wanted to know,' Melissa said quietly, and he frowned at her.

'Why on earth should it concern her?'

'She's part of your life. Everything you do concerns her.'

Elliot, at least, had the grace to flush, she noticed. It encouraged her to continue in the face of his uninviting silence. 'At the back of her mind she's been afraid of the prospect of being sent away to a boarding-school and she knows that Alison was very much in favour of that course of action.'

'Why didn't she mention something?' Elliot asked with a frown.

'I imagine because she thought that if she questioned Alison's absence it might bring the whole subject of boarding-school out in the open. She's only a child and, like a child, she decided that it was better to bury her head in the sand.'

'If you'd known about this, you should have said something about it. That was the whole point of our Friday meetings. So that you could fill me in on what had been happening.'

'I filled you in on...the essentials...'

'And I was supposed to guess the rest because I'm a mind-reader?'

Melissa looked at him stubbornly. At times like this, Elliot felt as though he had come up against a brick wall, and there had been many times like this over the past few weeks. Times when he had persuasively tried to lure her into discussing something other than work and superficialities, only to meet with the same silence followed by a swift change of topic. Every dead end only served to fire him up with a determination to break through the brick wall, to somehow find the way in.

'You're not eating,' he said. 'There was no need for you to take the salad just to impress me.' He watched her lazily as she immediately concentrated on enjoying the food in front of her.

'I didn't take a salad to impress you,' Melissa muttered, and he leant forward in an exaggerated parody of trying to catch what she was saying.

'Because you've worked wonders with Lucy.' He unhurriedly had another mouthful of his baguette. It was not his normal lunch-time fare but very good nevertheless. 'The thing is that you have completely different body shapes.'

Melissa gaped at him, taken aback by the sudden intimacy of his choice of words. Did he know what the effect was of what he'd said to her? Of his provocative personal remarks, which she had stolidly ignored whenever they had cropped up over the past few weeks? She had maintained a firm grip on the work front. Work and general chit-chat about impersonal things like what was happening in the news or the latest movie she had been to.

'Wouldn't you agree?' he pressed and Melissa succumbed with a shrug.

'People tend to,' she said. Elliot waited patiently as

she expounded on various body types and the efficacy of certain diets depending on shape and level of physical exercise. He politely allowed a few thoughtful seconds of silence to elapse.

'I mean,' he said, finishing his baguette and sitting back in the chair, 'Lucy is essentially tall and rangy. I suppose, having been blitzed with junk food, she's now getting back to her original shape.'

Melissa hung on to the slim life-jacket of relatively safe conversation being offered. She ignored the invitation to discuss herself. 'She's more settled now and, as I've said to you, it's because you're showing so much more interest in her. You ask her about her homework. She even told me that a few evenings ago you sat with her and did some physics homework.'

Melissa had done her best to restrain her hair. The curls were held in place with a no-nonsense tortoise-shell clip, but feathery bits still persisted in breaking free. Elliot found it highly distracting.

'I know it's wrong to say this and you must be very upset with your broken engagement, but Lucy will be pleased. I don't think she found your fiancée a very warm person. Perhaps it would have been different if she had been more at home here in England when she met her...' Curiosity was eating away at her and eventually she said, offhandedly, 'I thought you two were so suited to one another. What went wrong?'

'Nothing *went wrong*,' Elliot said briefly. 'Things went *adrift*. You must have been in a relationship that meandered?'

'Meandered?'

'Lost its way.' He restlessly glanced around them. 'As for being very upset...' He shrugged. 'These things happen. It's always disappointing when things don't work out the way you predict they will, but at the end of the day you move on.'

'What an uncomplicated way to live. It must be fantastic.' Melissa thought of how rooted she still was in the memory of their passionate encounter, a non-event for him that he had relegated to the past. Just as he had moved on from the disaster of a failed engagement. He was as cool and as composed as he always was. Not even a flickering change of expression marked any feelings stirring under the surface.

Elliot wasn't too sure whether he liked his life being described as uncomplicated. He had noticed over time that Melissa's criticisms were never overt. Instead her implications were quietly made and all the more forceful for it.

He met her wide gaze steadily and coolly. 'I would say so,' he drawled. 'Who wants unnecessary complications when simplicity will do?'

'You mean like the complication of emotion?'

'Call it what you will.' He raised one shoulder indolently. 'Let's take a hypothetical situation. Let's assume that I want you and you want me. How much easier would it be for us both to explore the interesting avenues that open up without the pointless complexities of analysing feelings?'

Melissa felt the warm rush of blood to her face and fought to keep her shock in check. Elliot played with words. He found it amusing to embarrass her and she could only suppose that it was because she was unsophisticated enough to be a novelty.

His brooding eyes gave nothing away. 'How can I assume that when we've established we're so obviously not each other's type?' Melissa laughed but her pulse was racing frantically and the directness of his gaze was causing her to squirm inside and visualise just what he was encouraging her to imagine. The fact that it was a hypothetical situation didn't make a scrap of difference. Nor did the fact that he was toying with her.

'Who's talking about type?' he pointed out. 'In this hypothetical situation, we're talking about sex, plain and simple.'

'Sex is never plain and simple.' Her cheeks were burning and her mind was scrambling to get a foothold on which she could steady her nerves. She was dangerously fascinated by the impossible scenario he was fabricating, even though she desperately wanted to dismiss it. She wasn't into playing these kinds of games, but…but…

'Never?' His vivid blue eyes swept over her speculatively and a shiver fluttered down her spine. 'That's where you're wrong. Or at least only partially right.' He allowed an infinitesimal pause before he carried on. 'Sex can be very simple but it should never be plain. But enough of that. Would you like some coffee before I get on with telling you the rest of my proposition?'

Melissa blinked and emerged from her dazed abstraction with a little start.

'Coffee?' he reminded her politely and she nodded, eager for him to be away from her even if it was only for a few minutes. She asked him for a latte, made some trite remark about it being a luxury she liked to enjoy once a day because it was so superior to the awful coffee she always managed to produce for herself, and then felt her body go limp as he headed off to the counter.

She couldn't allow him to get to her like this and she was angry with herself because this was the first time she had slipped up for a while. By the time she saw him coming back with a tray on which he balanced her latte and a black coffee for himself, her wayward nerves were firmly back where they should be.

She greeted him with a bright, interested smile and propped her chin in her hands.

'You were going to tell me about this proposition of yours to take Lucy on holiday. I understand if this means that you won't be needing me to complete the full term of my contract.' The thought of the job coming to an end left her chilled. She hastily reminded herself that it was a brilliant position and would leave her savings account bursting with good health. What more could she ask for?

'Not at all.' Elliot watched her over the rim of his cup as he sipped some of the coffee. He had seen more of this health bar in the space of two months than he had seen in the previous eighteen. He had also been less driven in his work over the past few weeks than he had been in fifteen years.

'In fact,' he said slowly, 'I think it might be an idea for your contract to be slightly more flexible than originally intended.'

'More flexible?' Melissa frowned and wondered where he was going with this particular remark.

'Do you have a passport?'

'A passport?'

'I can't stand it when you repeat what I say. How about just answering the question?'

'Yes, I have a passport. Why?' The light dawned. 'Ah. No. I really can't.'

'Why not?' He was prepared to spend a bit of time going through her objections, but in the end he was determined to break them all down.

'Because I have commitments here. You seem to forget that I still work for the gym. I can't just vanish for weeks on end at a moment's notice.' The thought of disappearing anywhere with Elliot in the vicinity filled Melissa with dread. It was bad enough having those

Friday meetings with him and they only lasted a matter of an hour or so.

'Employees have certain things called holiday quotas. Take yours,' Elliot demanded.

Melissa spluttered at the arrogant assertion. While she was busily working on an appropriate rejoinder, he stepped into the fulminating silence and carried on remorselessly.

'For a start, it's not a matter of weeks on end. It will only be for two weeks. And it's not at a moment's notice. In fact, you'll have three weeks' notice to give the gym, as I intend for this holiday to be taken during the summer holidays so that no school is missed by Lucy. But that's just the practicalities of the thing and those are the simplest elements to sort out. Consider this: it will be the first period of concentrated time that my daughter and I will have spent together. Yes, recently we've been communicating but it's been an uphill struggle and, were just the two of us to go abroad together, there's a very real possibility that all the good work that has been accomplished over the past few weeks will be reduced to nothing.

'In an ideal world,' Elliot continued, brushing aside any possible interruptions, 'Lucy and I would suddenly undergo an immense father-daughter bonding. Sadly, it's not an ideal world. More likely is that she will find herself cooped up with me and retreat quickly into her shell, from which she will nurture all the old resentments that have certainly not completely disappeared. She will feel obliged to converse and that obligation in itself will put immense pressure on her. I didn't know a damn thing about teenagers a year ago, but one thing I've discovered is that a teenager under pressure clams up, gets sullen and moody.'

'You wouldn't be stuck with each other all the time,'

Melissa pointed out. She didn't like the feeling that a net was closing in around her. 'You say your house is on an island. Well, there must be other people on this island, perhaps even people her own age. It's during the summer holidays. The whole world will be going abroad. Unless, of course, you've got your own island.'

'Which is accessible only by private jet. I use my Gulfstream.'

Melissa's mouth dropped open and she gaped. 'You don't, do you? Own an island? Have your own jet?'

'Would you find it more tempting if I did?'

Melissa considered the prospect of being trapped in paradise with a man to whom she was disastrously attracted, against every scrap of common sense in her head, with only his daughter as unwitting chaperon. She pictured a beach at night, deserted but for the two of them, unless she chose to confine herself to her bedroom with a book. She shuddered.

'No,' she said firmly.

'Good. Because I don't own an island and I don't possess a jet. I find that level of ostentation a little offensive, as a matter of fact.' He flashed her a complacent smile. 'So it'll be a normal plane to an island that is occupied by many other people. I'll get my secretary to book the tickets.'

'But—'

'No buts, Melissa. You're being offered a holiday abroad, in the sun, all expenses paid. You'll even be earning while you enjoy yourself. What could you possibly object to? Unless it's the fact that I'll be around…'

'No, of course that's not a consideration,' she mumbled faintly.

'Good. Then that's settled. You can break the news to Lucy when you see her this afternoon and maybe you two can go and do some shopping. That includes shopping for yourself,' he added. 'Put it on Lucy's credit card.'

'That's very kind but—'

'Why don't you just accept the offer, Melissa?' He stood up, waiting for her. 'You don't have to grind yourself into the ground, analysing the pros and cons. I've seen where you live. I'll bet my job that you don't have much of a holiday wardrobe to fall back on. Go out, buy some stuff for yourself. If you don't,' he leaned down to murmur in her ear, 'then I'll be forced to take yet more time off work so that I can drag you to Knightsbridge and assist you personally.'

Elliot knew the reaction his threat would evoke. She was, if nothing else, predictable in that regard.

He also knew that it would never have occurred to her in a million years that there weren't many other women who would have refused his offer to be equipped with an entire wardrobe for a holiday for which they weren't paying. And not many who would have seen his presence as a positive drawback.

He headed back to his office feeling remarkably light-spirited. It had been a while since he had taken a holiday. He hadn't been lying when he told Melissa that his house in the sun was suffering from a serious case of inactivity. He hadn't actually visited it for well over a year, although he had lent it out on several occasions, usually to friends with families. A housekeeper and her husband, who looked after the tropical gardens, were employed full-time to basically stop the cobwebs from staging a take-over.

He found himself wondering what her impression would be of the house. Favourable, he would imagine. Lucy would love it, of that there was no doubt. She might have taken her time to approve of him, but she certainly would approve of his holiday home. One out of two wasn't bad going, he thought wryly.

It would do him good to get away, he told himself.

And why deny it? He needed to get Melissa out of his system and there was only one way he could do that. By bedding her. He wanted her and he intended to have her because she was ruinous for his concentration.

She was wary of affairs, but she wanted him. He knew that and the thought was a constant turn-on. He felt like a randy teenager whenever he was around her. Of course, she was absolutely right when she said that they were not each other's type, but then hadn't he been truthful as well when he had told her that, in the face of lust, the question of types didn't come into the equation?

He was humming softly under his breath by the time he made it back to his office and set in motion arrangements for two weeks away from it all.

Which, when presented to Lucy several hours later, was an immediate drawback.

'But I don't want to go away,' she moaned, slinging her bag on the sofa and heading towards the fridge for a bottle of mineral water. 'Especially to some island in the middle of nowhere with a couple of adults.'

'Your father wants to use the opportunity to get to know you,' Melissa soothed, already writing off any thought of exercise for the day.

'He can get to know me here if he's all that interested.' The protests were the same but the tenor was different. Lucy was no longer fighting to the same extent. In the past month, she had begun confiding in Melissa, talking about her past, her childhood, her parents, and in some part reconciling events that had occurred with the circumstances as they were now. When Melissa had asked whether she could share some of her accounts with Elliot, she had shrugged indifferently but hadn't said no. Things had been progressing slowly and between Elliot and his daughter Melissa was a medium, aside from anything else, and that was the role she was to play on this holiday he had offered her.

'And it's only going to be for a fortnight,' Melissa encouraged. 'You can't possibly be missing out on that much in the space of two weeks.'

'I know, but...' Lucy hesitated. 'I'm just beginning to...you know...make friends and if I'm away...'

'They won't forget you.'

'They might. Besides, I don't know if I'm skinny enough for a bikini.'

'Well, I'm sure we can find you one of those old-fashioned swimsuits sculpted for older ladies,' Melissa said mock-seriously. She flopped down on the sofa and gave her a conspirational look. 'Your dad says I can take you shopping...'

'Well...I suppose it's only for two weeks, and there are some super things in the shops now...'

'Sure you can fit into any of them?' Melissa teased.

Lucy laughed and looked at her smugly. 'I guess I could squeeze into one or two things. The weight's been dropping off since I gave up the fried food and crisps and stuff. Course, I'm not as slim as I used to be. Funny, Australia seems like so long ago now. It's still all there, in my head, but every day little things take over. Is that wrong?'

They had had this conversation many times before. It had been traumatic losing her mother and stepfather, and then distressing having to move to England, to discover a parent she never knew she had. Now life seemed to be moving on, and that, too, was upsetting. Melissa always listened and tried not to give too much advice. As she saw it, Lucy had to come to grips with her changing destiny in her own time.

In a way, she suspected that it had felt more comfortable to Lucy to be swamped in misery, to feel isolated. Breaking out of that pattern and beginning the fragile process of settling down brought a whole new array of problems to grapple with.

She murmured all the right platitudes and continued listening as she prepared a light meal for Lucy to have later in the evening.

'Thank God you're coming on this jaunt with us,' Lucy eventually concluded. These daily cooking sessions were a valuable bonding routine, with Lucy chopping vegetables while Melissa did the actual cooking. Lenka's duties had been progressively refined and now all she did was the shopping during the day, and the cleaning of the apartment. By the time Lucy arrived back from school, she had already left.

'I'm sure if I weren't, you and your father would get along just fine.' She tasted her sauce and covered the pan with a lid, then helped herself to some mineral water.

'Yes, he would carry on working on his laptop and I would skulk around a pool pretending to be having a good time.'

'He's not an ogre and you know it.' Melissa grinned and leaned against the counter, glass in her hand. 'I mean, he's told me that I can go shopping for myself as well. Apparently he harbours the suspicion that my wardrobe might not be up to expensive tropical standards.'

Lucy was scathing. Who cared about keeping up with the Joneses? Who cared what was worn on holiday? Why did it matter if your clothes weren't expensive and designer?

Melissa heartily agreed. She'd checked her wardrobe and come to the conclusion that she could just get by on what she had.

And the last thing Melissa wanted to do was to draw

attention to herself while on this enforced holiday. She would do her best to fade into the background and make sure that she emerged only when Lucy was around, and even then she would not deviate from her safe role of assiduous chaperon, so to speak.

CHAPTER EIGHT

A HOUSE in the sun didn't go very far in describing the villa that was perched at the top of the incline, overlooking its own private cove.

Melissa, enervated after the long flight, gasped as she stepped out of the car and took it in. Thinking about it, she had spent the past few hours gasping in various stages of delight. She had marvelled at the first-class lounge, in which they could relax with drinks and snacks, away from the throng of people flooding the airport with pre-holiday hysteria. And felt in awe of the opulence of the first-class cabin on the plane, where the seats smoothly and miraculously transformed at the push of a button into fully extended beds in which you could sleep in a normal manner without having to contort your body into various unnatural positions. She had been almost overwhelmed at the heat that enclosed them the minute they stepped off the plane so that they could catch a much smaller island-hopper to the place where Elliot's house was. And now here she was, agog again at the sight of the villa that was spread before them in all its magnificent glory.

If Elliot hadn't already had the full measure of her lack of sophistication, Melissa thought, then he pretty much must have it by now.

To his credit, he had not been patronising. When she had rambled on at the airport about never even knowing that something called a first-class lounge existed, he had merely smiled and explained that businessmen found it quite a plus because it meant that they could carry on being dull workaholics in relative privacy. When she had insisted on pushing the various buttons on the armrest of her seat on the plane, he had not looked away in embarrassment, simply pulled out a stack of files which he proceeded to review, leaving her peacefully to experiment with her gadgets. He had shown not the slightest hint of condescension at her amazement with her miniature television, which popped up from the armrest of her seat and which showed a choice of movies and television programmes.

'I haven't done an awful lot of overseas travel,' she had confessed, by way of explaining her overdone reactions to everything. 'As you've probably guessed by now.'

He had been unusually patient and understanding, and of course Lucy and Mattie, Lucy's new school friend, recruited at the eleventh hour to join their little party at Lucy's pleading insistence, didn't really allow time for much else. They had been as excited as two kids on Christmas Eve and had dressed for the occasion in small skirts, even smaller tops and platform shoes. They had chattered endlessly, helped themselves to vast quantities of muffins and biscuits in the first-class lounge, most of which they left, and took pictures of one another in various posed attitudes, much to Melissa's amusement.

'So, what do you think of my little house?'

Melissa drew her eyes away to look at him. After hours of travel, he appeared unfairly bright-eyed and bushy-tailed. And something about him just seemed to *belong* in this setting, probably because he was olive-skinned and faintly exotic-looking. She, on the other hand, felt dishevelled and greasy. She hadn't managed any sleep on the plane, despite the cunning fold-down bed scenario, and, while she wasn't tired, she still felt as though she looked like someone who hadn't slept for the better part of a day and hadn't had much chance of freshening up either.

'It's not quite what I imagined,' Melissa confessed. Lucy and Mattie were busy walking around, pretending to be celebrities, while the driver, who was apparently half of the duo who lived in the house and looked after it when it was not being used, was bringing their luggage out of the car. It was now dusk, but still very warm and the air was fragrant with the smell of various unknown flowers. It seemed silent, even though it wasn't. Insect sounds were all around them, quite, quite different from anything Melissa had ever experienced before. She breathed in deeply and Elliot felt his mouth curve into a smile. He wondered how on earth she could survive in the rat race of London with so few hard edges. The entire day had, from all appearances, been a voyage of discovery for her and she had made no attempt to conceal the fact. Right now she was inhaling deeply, head flung back, eyes half-closed, her face a picture of wonder.

'What did you imagine?' he asked, watching her as she slowly focused on him and blushed.

'Smaller. Less…grand.' They began walked towards the door and the moment for conversing was lost in the helter-skelter scramble of Lucy and Mattie as they stormed inside, chatting to the housekeeper as though they had known her a lifetime, then wandering off to have a look around.

Melissa wondered how Elliot could fail to be impressed by what he was seeing. Yes, it was his house and he had undoubtedly visited it many times before, but surely he couldn't be immune to its charm?

They had walked into an open area. Pale, marbled tiles were relieved with various faded, silky rugs, Persian in pattern and very well matched to the rattan furniture. It was not an amazingly big house, but it was very cleverly

designed with lots of open spaces, so that the salty breeze
could waft through and the sound of the surf could be
heard as clearly as if you were sitting on the beach. The
colours of the furnishings were pale, shades of oatmeal
and cream and terracotta. Out through the sitting area, a
sprawling porch surrounded the entire back of the house.
It was to this that Lucy and Mattie had been attracted,
and Melissa followed behind them, breathing in the
uniquely tangy smell of the sea. The wooden porch was
absolutely enormous, big enough to hold sun loungers,
and down one end there was a long hammock stretched
from massive hooks. In the background, Melissa was
aware of Elliot talking to Lucy and Mattie, telling them
a bit about the layout of the land, pointing towards a
swimming pool that wasn't visible from where they were
standing. She went and leaned against the railing, looking
out towards gardens that were already shrouded in inky
darkness. She could make out the shapes of trees and
shrubbery and bushes and, to the right, the path that led
down the slope to the cove which Elliot had described to
them in the car on the way to the house.

Being here was unreal. It amazed her to think that a
matter of a few hours could take her out of England and
deposit her here, thousands of miles away, where everything was so vividly different. She was glad that she had
swallowed her pride and gone out and done the shopping,
which she had sworn blind she wasn't going to do, glad
that none of the dreary, much-used summer clothes she
had been wearing in England had followed her out here.
This was a place made for bright colours. She sighed and
had her eyes closed, trying to imagine what those dark
shapes would turn out to be in the morning when the sun
was out, when suddenly Elliot spoke from behind her,
causing her to jump.

'Glad you came?' He went to stand next to her, propping himself up on the railing just as she was.

Melissa reluctantly opened her eyes. 'I've got no idea why you spend all your time working when you've got this at your disposal,' she said. 'Lucy and Mattie seem to have fallen in love with the place. I've never seen Lucy so excited. Amazing to think that she didn't want to come at first.'

'Amazing to think what you've done for her.' He turned so that he was now perched against the wooden railing, looking down at her, arms folded.

Under normal circumstances, Melissa felt that she might just have begun her usual edging away, but the air was so soft and musky that she didn't feel nervous at all. 'Thank you,' she said.

'I'm glad that Lucy suggested inviting Mattie.'

Melissa laughed, relaxed. 'I know. A teenager's life is riddled with the potential for boredom even when there are a million things to do and see.'

'Unless, of course, there's a computer around.'

'How long have you had this place?'

'Years,' Elliot said. With light coming from just the two swinging overhead lanterns, Melissa's face was all shadows and half-shadows and the breeze was lifting her fine, curly hair and sending it into tousled disarray. 'Roughly five or so. Since then it's been used a handful of times and almost not at all in the past couple of years. The plight of a rich man's life. Enough money to buy whatever he wants but not enough time to enjoy his purchases.'

'Oh, poor old you.' Melissa laughed and sent him a wry look. 'It's a tough life, isn't it?'

'I'm glad you sympathise.' He grinned back at her. He would have liked to smooth those wayward curls from her face but instead rammed his hands into his pockets, where he could keep them safely under control.

'On the other hand it's your own fault if you spend every waking moment in an office.'

'Ah, back to what I know and like. Your pragmatic approach to life.'

'Simple approach,' Melissa corrected, 'and if I'm not mistaken you were the one to preach that piece of wisdom.' Her face warmed as she gazed up at him. 'You never said where Lucy and Mattie were. Is it safe for them to wander outside?'

'Absolutely safe,' he assured her. 'You're unlikely to find a safer place on the face of the earth. Anyway, they're not outside; they're in the kitchen. Merle is feeding them. Apparently, having eaten on the plane, they're still hungry.' He laughed softly without taking his eyes away from her flushed face. He felt as though every cell in his body was revving up, on full alert. 'Actually, I came to find out whether you wanted anything to eat. I suggest something light. There's fresh shrimp salad and bread.'

'Sounds tempting.' She sighed. 'Though it seems a shame to go in.' She pushed herself away with reluctance and gave Elliot a sheepish smile. 'Sorry. I'm not being very cool and casual about all this, am I? You must find it very amusing. Or annoying, of course.'

'Come on. Let us go and get something to eat,' he said roughly. 'It's best to try and go to sleep as early as possible, to give your body the rest it needs.' What the hell was he doing? Pandering to his curiosity? Filling his head with thoughts of seduction? This was a young woman, if not in age then certainly in experience. Yes, he found the novelty of that immensely appealing. Yes, he could think back about the way she had lain there, abandoned and eager to touch him, and his whole body would race in a surge of pure desire at the memory, but they were not in the same league. He was jaded and experienced. Just travelling with her had proved it, if nothing else had. Every new sight, every new experience had been a source of wonder to her.

'What's wrong?' Melissa asked worriedly. 'Am I getting on your nerves?' She almost added *already* but bit it back. They had a number of days in each other's company and she could see now how her excited reactions at every turn might have got under his skin a bit.

'Wrong? What could be wrong?' Elliot asked.

'You just seemed a bit tense, that's all.' She put her hand tentatively on his arm and Elliot felt his skin tighten. All his high-minded thoughts of bringing her to this paradise, seducing her because there was no other way of putting it, now seemed like the illusions of arrogance.

'Jet lag,' he said abruptly, nodding in the direction of the kitchen. 'Affects us all.'

Lucy and Mattie had already made themselves at home and were sitting at the large table in the kitchen, tucking into salad and bread while Merle talked to them about what they clearly had uppermost on their minds, namely what the town was like.

'We have dune buggies,' was the first thing Lucy said to Melissa, when she had swallowed a mouthful of food. 'Did you know? Mattie and I can actually drive into the town and shop around. By ourselves!'

Melissa had visions of two teenagers swerving around roads, but before she could open her mouth to voice a protest Elliot was telling her about the buggies, describing them, reassuring her that there was virtually no traffic at all. While he spoke, he filled her plate with salad and poured her some fruit juice.

The food was delicious. Melissa ate and listened to

Lucy describing the fortnight of high excitement she had
in store for herself and Mattie. Intermittently, she would
calm down and insert an appropriate statement about perhaps meeting Elliot and Melissa for lunch, which was her
token effort at the bonding that Melissa had stressed was
all-important. Mattie, by no means a shrinking violet,
took up the excited monologue whenever Lucy decided
to tuck into her food. They made an excellent duo and
Melissa shuddered at the thought of them joyfully invad-
ing a sleepy little town in the middle of the island. It took
her a while to realise that Elliot wasn't eating. He wasn't
even sitting at the table. He was perched against the
counter, watching them with a beer in his hand, while
behind him Merle cleared dishes, obviously content that
there were people in the place.

His reticence was all the more noticeable because he
had been warm and friendly for the entire journey over,
humouring her wide-eyed ingenuity. She wondered
whether perhaps he had just got sick of being the perfect
gentleman and was already bored at the thought of being
surrounded by two giggling teenagers and a woman who
didn't have the wit or sophistication to be at home amidst
all this luxury, or at least to even pretend to be.

She made sure not to remark on the rest of the villa
as he showed them to their bedrooms after they had finished eating. Their bags had already been laid out in the
respective rooms, and Melissa left it to the girls to express their delight with the big beds, the softly draped
mosquito nets, the blonde wooden flooring, the wicker
furniture and the magnificent overhead ceiling fan. She
herself kept quiet and did her best not to look impressed.

Her room was as big as the girls', although with only
one king-sized bed in it instead of two. It was decorated
with different colours as well, more greens and ivories.

'All the bedrooms lead out onto the porch we were

standing on earlier,' Elliot explained. 'It was designed that way so that anyone could benefit from stepping out of their bedroom directly outside.' He waited as she strolled over to the French doors and stepped right back outside onto the porch, though now from a different angle.

'Your luggage is all here ready to be unpacked, and there's bottled water by the bed so that you don't have to trek through the house in the middle of the night if you get thirsty.'

Melissa swung round to face him. 'And tomorrow?' she asked. 'What would you like me to do?'

'Whatever you want to do,' Elliot said irritably. 'This isn't a busman's holiday. You're here to enjoy yourself. You can go into town with the girls if you like or else you can relax in the cove with a book.' He raked his fingers through his hair, torn between wanting to leave and wanting to stay. Having always been firmly in control of the steering-wheel in his life, he suddenly felt as though he had lost his grip. For the past couple of weeks, he had been content to bide his time, having reached the decision that there was nothing wrong with seduction. He would not, he knew, be seducing an unwilling woman; that wasn't his style at all. Now he was asking himself whether seduction itself was desirable and the questions he posed himself made him feel unaccountably and frustratingly helpless.

He tried to match her even tone with a similar one of his own.

'Or alternatively, there are lots of beaches. You needn't content yourself with the one here. Ten minutes on the dune buggy and you'll find yourself on a coastal strip that belongs on a postcard.' She was reaching behind her, taking her hair out of its pony-tail so that it was displayed in all its unruly splendour. Elliot all but moaned. With great effort, he pushed himself away from the door-frame and curtly bade her goodnight, barely giving her sufficient time to answer.

Puzzled and depressed at Elliot's about-turn, Melissa went to bed and nevertheless slept soundly, awakening to find the sun trying hard to stream through the French doors. It was a losing battle. The curtains were thick and designed to block out light, even the iridescent light of the tropics.

When she pulled back the curtains the sky was cloud-free, and a high turquoise colour, and the gardens beyond the porch, which had enchanted her in darkness, were splendid in daylight. Every shade of green glinted in the light, and the flowers, neatly pruned back, were bigger and brighter and more extravagant than any she had ever seen.

Where was Elliot? She wondered whether she had imagined his coolness the night before. Was he regretting his impulse to ask her along? As buffer? With Mattie now on the scene, perhaps he realised that he hadn't needed her after all, but, having already bought her ticket, had been reluctant to cancel her seat and lose his money.

And to make matters worse, once Melissa had changed into some shorts and a halter-neck T-shirt, she emerged from her room, full of plans to make herself useful just in case he really was having second thoughts about his generosity in bringing her along, only to find that the house was empty. The girls and Mr Elliot, she was informed by Merle, had already headed off to the town to check it out, and would not be back until lunch-time.

Melissa had been left instructions to relax.

'Relax?' Melissa looked at the housekeeper, aghast. 'But I'm here to work! I have to…' She wondered what she really had to do. Certainly not accompany Lucy everywhere, making sure that no arguments broke out between her and her father, making sure that delicate situations were sidestepped. And with Mattie on the scene, their routine of exercise and walking was clearly not appropriate and even cooking healthy meals was a nonsense, considering Merle would be in charge of the food.

Which leaves me, she thought, slinking back into her room so that she could change into a swimsuit, an employee without a job.

She cringed again at the thought of Elliot brooding over the money he had spent on her ticket, not to mention the dent in his credit card, which he had generously offered to her and which she had stupidly used. Good heavens, she had been so wrapped up the day before, with her oohing and aahing, that she had failed to notice his reticence until it was staring her in the face! She had idiotically imagined that he was being the perfect gentleman because he was *putting up with her*! When in fact he had probably been groaning inwardly and kicking himself!

By the time Melissa made it down to the cove, she had convinced herself that, far from trying to be as useful as possible with Lucy, she should simply try as hard as she could to keep out of everyone's way. With a bit of luck, she could become virtually invisible. The gardens were huge. She was sure that there would be a number of trees behind which she could hide, and the cove would be useful as well. She doubted whether Lucy and Mattie would see the charms of an isolated bathing spot, when other, more crowded ones were easily within reach.

As for Elliot...

Melissa did her best not to think about him. She made herself enjoy the scenery, which wasn't hard, as it continued to be spectacular. The back of the house, with its expanse of shrubbery and open lawn, eventually came to an abrupt halt. A wall, criss-crossed with curling bright red and orange bougainvillaea, overlooked the sloping drop down to the cove. Further up, to the right, lay the path that wound its way down in a series of loops to the secluded bay. Melissa took this path, clutching her beach bag, in which she had a bottle of water, her suntan cream, a book, her towel and her sunglasses.

Merle had been vague on giving a definite time when the trio would be back.

'Lunch-time,' was what she had stuck to, and Melissa had realised that the single word could incorporate any time from twelve onwards. The pace of life over here did not appear to be dictated by watches. She decided that she would return to the house no later than eleven-thirty, an hour and a half from now. She would then be able to change into some dry clothes, adopt the appropriate attitude and try and work out how best she could last the fortnight without getting on Elliot's nerves too much.

The small bay was idyllic: a semicircle of pure white sand, as fine as castor sugar, and backed by shrubs, interspersed with palm trees, and the gentle incline of the hill on which the house sat. Looking up, it was impossible to see the house at all. It was set too far back into its gardens, and looking out there was just the sea, very calm and very blue.

Melissa neatly spread her towel on the sand, decided that reading would be a huge waste of time when it was just so much nicer to enjoy the beautiful views, and instead lathered herself in sun cream, protecting her face with her cap.

It would have been absolutely peaceful if her thoughts would leave her alone, but they continued raging inside her head as she tried to piece together what she could remember of Elliot's attitude from the minute they had met at the airport.

Had he been solicitous and indulgent of her obvious, gauche delight in everything or had he been quietly an-

noyed? He had certainly been cold when he had left her
bedroom the night before, but had he been cold before
then? And had she just not seen it because she had been
too wrapped up in the wonderful novelty of it all?

The sound of the water lapping against the sand was
like melodious background music. It was gentle and
soothing and, with jet lag beginning to kick in, it worked
its magic. The chaotic tangle of her thoughts and her
futile attempts to try and put them into order began to
fade away.

Melissa woke suddenly. Something had startled her out
of her sleep. She sat up, horrified that she had nodded
off in the first place, blinking into the bright light until
her vision adjusted to the sun.

'You need to be careful. Falling asleep on a beach in
the tropics isn't a very good idea.'

His voice came from behind her and with a muffled
cry of surprise she twisted round to see Elliot standing
above her with a huge canopy-style umbrella in one hand
and a cooler in the other.

Even more alarming was the fact that he was dressed
in swimming trunks and a thin cotton shirt that was un-
buttoned down the front.

Every pulse in her body roared into life and she hastily
stuck her sunglasses on, hoping that her bright colour
could be put down to overexposure to the sun and not to
the effect his body was having on her. Because it was a
beautiful body with long, muscular legs, a powerful torso
tapering to lean hips on which his trunks dipped and the
flat, taut stomach of someone naturally inclined to an
athletic physique.

'I'm sorry,' she stammered, standing up and dusting
sand off her. 'I didn't realise the time! I meant to be back
up at the house by eleven-thirty! Where are the girls?'

'Relax. They're at the Coral Reef Hotel.' He walked

over to her with the umbrella, which he began prodding into the sand at an angle, so that it was secure but resting on its side, providing some shade from the sun. Melissa watched him while he did this in mounting panic.

'What are you doing?' she asked and he stopped and looked at her with a wry smile.

'What does it look like I'm doing? I'm protecting us from the sun.'

'There's no need to bother about me. I'm just off to the house.' She stooped to gather up her belongings, aware that Elliot was still looking at her. In her swimsuit. It had seemed a modest enough bikini when she had tried it on in the shop, certainly a lot more modest than the ones Lucy had been urging her to buy, but now the frivolous black number felt indecent. She was aware of every inch of her exposed cleavage, not to mention the expanse of thigh generously on show, thanks to the minimally cut bottoms.

'You were sleeping,' Elliot pointed out, while she busily continued not looking at him and stuffing her things into her beach bag. 'Anyway, there's no point going up to the house. As I said, Lucy and Mattie aren't there.'

Melissa paused, hearing an implied criticism in his voice, but she really didn't know what her role should have been on this holiday. She was no longer needed by Lucy, who had a friend in tow.

'And I've brought us some lunch in the cooler.'

'That's very kind but really, there was no need to think of me. I'm fine being on my own. I mean, obviously I'll be around when the girls are here…'

Her voice dried up in the ensuing silence and Melissa licked her lips nervously. The breeze blew apart his shirt and she was given a glimpse of his chest, broad and well-toned. There seemed to be no way of avoiding his eyes without having to stare at his body, so she reluctantly looked at him.

'I could go to that hotel and find them,' she suggested feebly.

'So that you can do what?' He grinned crookedly at her. 'As luck would have it, they met a friend of a friend of a friend in the town and I should think your presence would go a long way to putting a dampener on their fun.'

'Oh.' Melissa sighed and wanted the ground to swallow her up. So now her charge was going to spend the holiday doing her own thing. Elliot would feel obliged to pay Melissa some scant attention, look after her because she would be on her own, while gnashing his teeth in irritation behind her back.

'There was no need for me to come along on this holiday, was there?' she asked quietly. 'I'm sorry. I should have dropped out the minute I knew that Lucy was bringing her friend along. My role originally was to be there as a buffer between you and your daughter, a third party to ease the way. I realise that I now don't have a role…'

In the middle of her speech, she was appalled to realise that he was walking off, fetching something from the bag he had brought down, which turned out to be a huge square beach mat that he proceeded to place under the umbrella. The matting on the underside was designed to lie flat on the sand but the top was soft towelling.

'Did you hear a word I just said?' Melissa asked, folding her arms.

'All of it. I just don't see the point of wallowing in self-pity. You're here and I suggest you stop feeling guilty and get down to enjoying yourself.' He took off his shirt and she reluctantly found herself staring at the flex of his muscles as he tossed it on the beach mat.

'I didn't realise I was wallowing in self-pity,' Melissa informed him stiffly. Now he had proceeded to lie down on the mat so that she had to move in front to see him. He had his hands folded beneath his head and his eyes were closed. 'I thought I was being open and honest and giving you a fair chance to tell me what a mistake you made in importing me over here.'

Vivid blue eyes met hers. 'Maybe it was a mistake.' She looked luscious. How he could have bypassed those curves when he first met her he had no idea because, when he looked at her now, that was all he could see. Her generous breasts, barely restrained by a top that was clearly meant for a less abundantly proportioned woman, her slender waist and softly rounded hips. Proper hips. No bones jutting out like those stick insects he had always dated. And a personality to match. Yes, it had been a mistake bringing her over. Brilliant idea at the time when he was nurturing thoughts of getting her into bed, but now he was retreating from that idea, definitely an error of judgement. He felt a stirring in his loins and sat up abruptly, shading his eyes from the glare.

'So you admit it, then,' Melissa said flatly. She turned away, her eyes stinging from hurt, and dropped everything she was holding. Without another word she headed towards the sea, away from him. She barely noticed the spectacular clarity of the water as she stepped into the shallows. The scenery just seemed to be swimming around her. With a choked sob, she waded out and then plunged in, lashing out without thought for safety, just needing to get as far away from Elliot as possible.

He hadn't been joking or teasing her when he had told her that her presence on the island was a mistake. He had been deadly serious and it was no consolation to know that only her prodding had elicited the truth.

She was aware of Elliot only when she felt his arms around her waist and immediately she began to thrash, first in the throes of her self-pity, then in anger. Anger at herself and at him. Out of her depth, though, she was no match for Elliot's powerful grip and eventually her flailing arms fell limp. They were both treading water and she was exhausted. She was aware of him pulling her back to shore and as soon as she could she stood and waded in, ignoring the arm still around her waist.

'I'm sorry,' was the first thing she said, when she was confident that she could actually string the words out without her voice cracking in the process. She pushed him away from her and didn't look in his direction as she walked tiredly up the beach, back to the wretched beach mat and the damned cooler he had brought from the house, stoically prepared to do his bit even though he hadn't wanted her around. It seemed he would grit his teeth and put up with her because he had no choice but to make the most of a bad mistake.

'It's an uncomfortable situation for you.' She took a deep breath and gritted her teeth so hard that her jaws ached. 'But obviously there's a way around this sorry business.' She gathered her things up and stared straight past him at some distant and unfocused point. She was aware of him looking at her, but she wasn't about to explore the concern and pity she would find there.

'There must be flights back to England. I can always get one.' Oh, God; eyes filling up. She gritted her teeth a little harder and took a deep, steadying breath.

'Look. I apologise. I shouldn't have said that.' Elliot raked his fingers through his hair and stared out at the sea for a few seconds before looking at her. 'Of course I won't let you go back to England…'

'*Won't let me?* In other words, I'm supposed to stay here, knowing that you don't want me around? Am I supposed to pretend that I've forgotten about that little detail while I get on with the business of enjoying my-self? Would that make you feel better? Because you are, after all, paying me to be here so I guess the most important thing I should do is make sure that you don't feel badly about letting slip what you really think!'

'Stop this!'

'Will you arrange for me to leave? Please? I can't possibly stay.'

'No.'

'Then I'll have to do it myself.'

She turned to walk away and he reached out and circled her wrist with his fingers, yanking her back towards him so that she stumbled and collided into his rock-hard chest.

'You don't understand,' Elliot muttered savagely, keeping her right where she was, pressed up against him, both their bodies perspiring in the heat. She felt hot and slippery and she was trembling.

'I understand very well. I may not be experienced but I'm not dense. You don't want me here because there's no need for me to be here and what you're stuck with is someone you now have to be responsible for when it would be so much easier if I just wasn't around!'

'Is that what you think?' Elliot ground out. 'That you're a spare part? Yes, it is a mistake you being here but your reasoning is way off target.'

Melissa could feel her heart hammering angrily in her chest and she guessed he could feel it to because her breasts were crushed against him.

'You complicate things being here,' he murmured huskily. 'It's a mistake because I look at you and I want to do things to you.'

'Do things to me? Things like what?' In that split fraction of a second, she knew exactly what, then his mouth covered hers and his hand moved from her wrist to the nape of her neck so that he could lock her against him, hold her tight while his tongue did its devastating work, eliciting a shuddering response as Melissa stopped being held against her will and remained where she was purely of her own accord...

CHAPTER NINE

IT TOOK a lot of will-power to pull away so that she could look at him. He still held her, his hands on her arms, and she was glad of that because without that support Melissa thought she might have keeled over.

'I can't apologise,' Elliot told her roughly. 'I meant every word I said. Having you here is having temptation paraded in front of me.'

Melissa's mouth was still burning from where he had kissed her. The meaning of his words took a little while to sink in, then she blinked and looked at him in confusion.

'But…I don't understand,' she whispered in utter bewilderment.

'I mean,' Elliot brushed some hair away from her face and then let his fingers remain there, trapped in the wild effervescence of her blonde curls, 'by being here, you put me in the position of having to take too many cold showers.' The long fingers curved against her cheek and his thumb stroked the soft, peachy skin. 'Ever since that night at your flat I've thought about this, about touching you and, believe me, my thoughts have not been innocently confined to merely kissing…'

'Look…' Melissa cleared her throat. This wasn't happening. Was it? 'This is crazy…I mean, I work for you…I can't believe what you're saying…you told me yourself that I wasn't your type!' She was aiming for control but her body was letting her down badly. It was on fire and her breasts ached and throbbed.

'I thought I had a type. I was wrong.' He took one

step towards her and then proceeded to run his fingers along her spine, sending shivers of excitement racing through her body. 'If you really feel that you want to leave the island, then tell me now,' he said unsteadily, 'and I'll arrange it. But if you stay, I can't guarantee that I'm going to be able to keep my hands off you.'

Heady, reckless abandon filled Melissa's head like incense, blurring common sense and reason.

'Maybe I don't want to leave,' she sighed.

'Just *maybe*?'

'I don't want to leave.' She reached up and coiled her hands around his neck, pulling his head down to hers, closing her eyes as she initiated her own kiss and melting when his mouth softened against hers and his tongue found her probing tongue.

He had said that he had thought about her. She finally admitted to herself now that she had done nothing but think about him. She had been living in a state of heightened awareness, her body tuned in to the thought of when he might be around, when he might suddenly appear in the apartment. Fridays, the one day when she knew that she would see him, had become the highlight of her week. She had managed to keep her feelings under lock and key, had managed to focus on her job, but that was in England. Here…here there was no job to focus on, no lines of demarcation that she could fall back on, no sensible returning to her flat in the evenings and going to her normal job in the day, all those hours during which her head had plenty of time to subdue her feelings.

'Good,' Elliot said thickly. He pulled back but only so that he could lead her to their patch of shelter under the umbrella, then he was kissing her again, deeply and lingeringly, enjoying the way she squirmed and purred under him.

'What about the girls…?' Melissa asked breathlessly.

'Won't be back for a couple of hours.'

'And Merle? What if she decides to come down here…to get you…?'

'She won't.' Elliot grinned at her. 'Relax. There's just you and me and the beach and the sea.' He nibbled her ear and then kissed the side of her face, tugging her head back so that he could carry on kissing the delicate column of her neck. With his hand, he slowly peeled down the strap of her bikini, just one side, the side he could reach.

Melissa moaned. Part of her couldn't believe that this was happening. The other part wanted it so badly that she was shaking with desire. The slow scrape of the Lycra against her skin, as the bikini top was peeled off, was unbearably exciting and she trembled when finally her breast was freed from its constraint.

'God, you're beautiful,' Elliot murmured unsteadily. Her breast had the fullness of a ripe fruit and it was twice as tantalising. Her large pink nipple was swollen and the peak was taut and stiffened. He looked, drinking in the bountiful feast before him and then he could no longer resist. He grazed the sensitised peak with his tongue and felt her wriggle under him and arch up, proffering herself for more of what he had begun. Elliot smoothly positioned himself so that he was kneeling over her and rapidly relieved her of the remainder of her top, straightening up so that he could just take in the sight spread before him.

Last time he had seen her, sprawled naked on that makeshift bed in her flat, he had been stunned by the scale of her sexuality, so well camouflaged by her workaday clothes. But even then he had been under severe constraint. He himself had still been in a relationship and she had been under the influence of alcohol.

This time, he could enjoy her body. They were coming together in full knowledge of what they were doing. He intended to savour every last piece of her, very, very slowly.

Her full breasts pouted back at him. With one easy movement, he curved his hands around them and massaged them, pushing them up and rubbing the pads of his thumbs against the nipples. Had he ever felt this insistent throb of excitement in his life before? He couldn't think. She had extended her arms wide to either side of her and her head was thrown back, eyes shut, nostrils slightly flared as she breathed in jerkily.

He released a silent groan and bent so that he could lick and suckle at the rosy circles beckoning him. Tasting her was like tasting honey for the first time. While he gave his lavish attention to one nipple with his mouth, he played with the other with his fingers, rubbing the hard nub and loving the way she responded with shuddering enjoyment to his touch.

He had big hands and, even for him, her breasts were more than a handful.

Melissa tugged him up, but when she tried to touch him, he stopped her hand firmly.

'I don't think I have the will-power to make this last if you touch me there,' he muttered. 'And that's a first for me.'

Melissa smiled at him, eyes slanted teasingly, and instead ran her hand from his broad shoulders down to his waist. Then she slipped her finger under the waistband of his trunks and slid it along his skin, eliciting from him a groan of pure pleasure.

It was thrilling to know that she could make him feel just exactly how he made her feel, hot and out of control. She could read it in the fiery depths of his eyes when he looked at her like that, hungry and in need.

'Let me,' she coaxed huskily, and he breathed in deeply as she grasped his hard member with her hand, feeling its rigidity through the damp fabric of his swimming trunks. She began to caress and he squeezed her hand, stopping her.

'What are you trying to do, woman?' he rasped, putting himself well out of reach so that he could kiss the sexy smile off her lips.

'You just make me feel so good,' Melissa confessed huskily.

'Glad to hear it.' His voice was smugly pleased. He felt like a ten-year-old kid told that he was top of the class. 'What have I done that's made you feel so good?' he encouraged, moving lower and looking back at her through his lashes, catching the delighted glint in her blue eyes as they gazed back slumberously at him. 'Is it this, do you think?' He dipped his head so that he could once again circle her nipple with his mouth, suck on it, drawing it in and then flicking his tongue over the tightened bud, over and over until her breathing was coming in little gasps.

'Or is it this, perhaps?' He broke off to run his hand along her thigh. He parted her legs and then settled his palm over her mound, leaving it still for a few seconds before rhythmically moving it against her while he resumed his relentless assault on her breasts.

Besieged at every angle by all these conflicting physical sensations, Melissa lay back and simply enjoyed. She had never felt so wonderfully free in all her life. She was giving her body to him and the act seemed to liberate her from every hang-up she had ever had. A sigh of pleasure escaped her parted lips when he trailed his tongue over her stomach, down to her belly button, then he was skilfully removing her bikini bottoms, allowing her to wriggle out of them, so that he could continue downwards, taking his time to savour every inch of her and then breathing in the sweet smell of her femininity. She was, he discovered, a true blonde. He blew on the fair, soft, downy hair and then slipped his tongue into the crease. Lord, how he wanted to spend time tasting her. He had to exert every ounce of will not to let his body dictate a faster tempo.

Melissa moaned as his tongue explored her most intimate place. An explosion of pleasure started somewhere deep inside her and carried on growing as he slid his tongue along the throbbing bud. When she thought she could bear the exquisite soar upwards no longer, she was aware of him feeling the same, discarding his trunks, and then he thrust into her and began moving swiftly and firmly.

They came as one and for a moment time seemed to stand still as every fibre of her being roared into satisfied completion.

Their bodies were both slick from the heat and from their lovemaking as he rolled off her to the side, only to turn so that he could face her.

'I can't believe we made love on a beach,' Melissa said with a tentative smile. Now that the passion had ebbed, she wondered what happened next. So he had made love with her. Did that mean, she wondered with a sudden attack of nerves, that he would consider his appetite and his curiosity both satisfied? He set her mind at rest by gently capturing her face in his hand.

'Life is full of first experiences,' he murmured.

Melissa felt as if she was flying high up somewhere, on cloud nine. She wanted to share every one of those first experiences with this man lying next to her. It wasn't just about lust. It was all about the way he made her feel, the way he made her laugh, the way he made her think and see things from a different angle.

Later that evening, when the household had gone to sleep, Elliot offered her the chance of another first experience, swimming by the light of the moon and making love when the beach was cool, maybe taking along a bottle of champagne for company.

Over the next few days, Melissa tried to be as normal as possible when Lucy and Mattie were around, making a point of taking time out to wander into the town with them and visit the delights of the hotel to which they seemed to be drawn like magnets. On several of those occasions, Elliot remained back at the house, catching up with work on his laptop. She found that, however much she enjoyed spending time with the girls, visiting the beaches and seeing the sights, what few there were to see, she was always biding time until she returned to the house and to him, and he was always waiting for her.

And he was relaxed. He took them all out to dinner on a couple of occasions and even entered into the spirit of teasing the girls about their reasons for liking the hotel so much.

'It makes a change,' Lucy said airily. 'We're teenagers. Why would we want to be cooped up with two adults all day long?' This as the first blissful week was drawing to a close. They were in the hotel restaurant, a magnificent room with walls covered in colourful local paintings and batiks. Through the wide glass doors at one end, one of the hotel swimming pools was brightly illuminated with night lights and surrounded by gardens and palm trees.

'Because we're riveting people?' Elliot remarked drily, and they all laughed. He looked refreshed and utterly at ease. Every time Melissa found her eyes sliding towards him, she would make a concerted effort to look away, just in case the girls noticed anything. But it was very difficult. She wanted to touch him all the time. When they did touch, it was as if she was going up in flames, so powerfully did her body react to his.

'Maybe to each other,' Lucy pointed out, tucking into

her starter of shrimp with garlic sauce. Neither of them was looking at either Elliot or Melissa so they both missed the amused look that flashed between them. 'I mean,' she continued, surfacing after her first mouthful, 'you probably find it very interesting to talk about world affairs, but we don't.'

'And it wouldn't have anything to do with the fact that there are a number of teenage boys here, maybe at a loose end because they, too, don't want to be stuck all day with dreary adults?' Melissa grinned at them and didn't miss the sheepish exchange of glances.

'And girls,' Mattie pointed out, just in case the wrong idea was relayed. Four days into the holiday, Elliot had seen fit to give a small and very vague speech to them both on the need to conduct themselves in a respectable fashion. Listening from the sidelines, where she was curled up with a book, Melissa very nearly burst out laughing. She found herself having to translate everything he said into teenage-friendly language.

As far as bonding with his daughter went, the holiday was proving to be a huge success, even with Mattie in tow, which left relatively little one-on-one time as a result. Lack of stress, the lulling warmth of the weather, just being in the same place where time wasn't measured in the ticking of clocks, were all combining to soften the hard, driving edge that was so much a part of Elliot's personality.

But when it came to her relationship with Elliot...

It was something that Melissa thought about when she was alone and something which she avoided mentioning when they were together, because it was an unspoken question, the answer to which she already knew.

They were enjoying a holiday romance. Nothing more and nothing less.

He had told her all about what had gone on in his mind

during those long weeks when he had been formal and polite and scrupulously well-behaved towards her. He'd confessed in the heat of passion that under the surface she had been driving him crazy. He had even told her about his abandoned plan to bring her to his villa and seduce her. That had sent a delicious shiver of yearning through her and she had no doubt that he had been telling the truth.

It was all sweet music to her ears. How on earth could such a powerful and sexually exciting man see anything in *her*? She was neither as brainy as his ex-girlfriend, nor as skinny. When he told her that skinny and brainy didn't necessarily add up to sexy, she felt as though someone had given her a very unexpected gift.

But it was still a holiday romance. For him. He wanted her and he enjoyed her but beyond that no word was ever said. It was a thrilling present that led to no future and Melissa closed her mind off to the consequences of that because by now she was in love with Elliot. No holiday romance for her. She had found her soul mate, someone she wanted to share every piece of herself with, someone she wanted to spend the rest of her life with.

When did that all start? Melissa asked herself the question over and over, trying to pinpoint the window in time when respect for his cleverness but dislike for his arrogance had seamlessly merged into love for him as a whole. Yes, he could be arrogant, but he could also be gentle. Yes, he was supremely clever, but he never made her feel like a fool. Yes, she knew that she was a distraction for him, a break from the women he normally went out with, but when they made love she stopped feeling like a fill-in because he was such a generous lover.

And now the holiday was whizzing past and they had only a couple of days left to enjoy the island and each other. The days had begun to merge and the nights, when the girls had finally gone to sleep, had been theirs for the taking. The first experience of making love on a beach under the silver light of the moon had become three, although the champagne had only featured on one of those nights. When they happened to have the cove to themselves in the day, they swam and made love and swam and made love again. He told her that she did things to him and she treasured each of those remarks, keeping them to herself like a miser hoarded his gold, taking it out to inspect it when no one else was around.

Surely, she thought now as they finished their light supper in the kitchen and she retired to the sofa with her book while the teenagers washed the dishes, she meant *something* to him? Something more than just a fling? True, he had never said so, but Melissa, staring down sightlessly at the words in front of her, told herself that no man could be that solicitous without it meaning *something*.

'Penny for them.'

Melissa looked up from the book she hadn't been reading to see the object of her thoughts staring down at her. He was wearing a pair of longish khaki shorts and a faded tan-coloured T-shirt that made him look even more rugged and masculine. The sun had turned his skin even darker, far darker than she could ever get, although she, too, had noticed that her skin had become a golden colour and her hair was now blonder and even more uncontrollable. She had developed a habit of plaiting it, and it was plaited now, although enough of it had managed to wriggle free just in case neatness might be achieved.

He tugged the plait playfully and sat down heavily next to her. They never knowingly occupied the same space when the girls were in the house and she automatically edged away a bit.

'Oh, I was just thinking how well this holiday's gone,' Melissa told him brightly. 'The girls are having a wonderful time and you...well, you seem different over here...more relaxed...'

'It's a holiday,' Elliot pointed out wryly. 'People usually *are* more relaxed on holiday, and I have to admit, it's been a long time since I went on one. In fact,' he leaned back and tilted his head over the back of the sofa, his expression ruminative, 'it's been years since I took two weeks off in a stretch.'

'Maybe now that you've done it once, you'll need to do it again.' If it had been that long since he had taken a proper holiday, then he surely hadn't been anywhere with Alison, and he *had been engaged to her, for goodness' sake*! He may not have said anything about love or commitment, but surely that meant something? The fact that she had been the one with whom he had seen fit to spend a concerted amount of time?

And after that first day, when he had told her that her being here was a mistake, before he had explained his reasons for saying so, they had got along swimmingly. He was witty and sharp and fascinating and he had told her on more than one occasion that she was appealing. Appealing, she argued to herself, wasn't dynamite to her ears, but it was a start. She was in love with him and there was enough love inside her to make things work. Surely.

There was no denying that he wanted her. He made that perfectly clear when he touched her and sometimes when she caught his slanted looks they were hot with hunger.

Thinking about it made her shiver inside, and her pulses quicken. It was all she could do not to reach across and pull him towards her.

'Maybe,' Elliot answered the question she had forgotten she had asked, so wrapped up had she been in her thoughts. 'The girls want to go to a disco the hotel is having later this evening.'

'Later?' Melissa looked at her watch. 'It's eight-thirty now. How much later?'

'Apparently things don't get going until ten.' He shot her a lazy, seductive smile. 'Ten until one.'

This was the killer look in which he specialised. The long, speculative, veiled stare that could make her body burn. He had a way of looking at her, just as he was doing now, that made her feel as though he were actually touching her. She knew exactly what he was asking and her heart began to race. Yes! She lowered her eyes, hiding the burst of love that threatened to show.

'Would you need to stay there with them, do you think? Make sure they don't get up to anything?'

'I know the hotel,' Elliot drawled. 'There will be security everywhere, making sure that nothing gets out of hand. Don't forget, this is primarily a very expensive tourist resort. They can't afford to be associated with any wild parties or drunken teenagers, and I must say, those two have behaved themselves while they've been over here. No, I think I can return home and leave later to pick them up.'

'You're going to stay up until one in the morning?' Melissa asked with feigned innocence.

'I was hoping someone would manage to keep me up.' He briefly stroked her wrist with one finger and heat pelted through her like a burst of fire.

Her head suddenly cleared of all her muddled thoughts and she realised that with only two days of the holiday left to go, she was being given a chance to give him an unforgettable night, a magical few hours.

'Oh, right. Would that person be me by any chance?' There was a time when Melissa would never have thought that she could play these teasing word games with any man, but Elliot had changed that, just as he had changed everything about her.

'I don't see anyone else around here who could possibly fit the bill, do you?' He smiled slowly at her.

'No, no one else,' she murmured. Fleetingly, she wondered how she had managed to reach this stage, the point of being utterly vulnerable and in love with a man who saw her as fitting the bill right here and right now, but for how much longer? A man who gave magnificent pleasure, and not all of it physical.

Then she thought of a world without this man and it was like sudden darkness falling.

She would wait for him to return. While she helped the girls decide what to wear, she wondered what she would wear herself later.

Innocence seemed like a long time ago, she thought as she watched Lucy and Mattie parade a succession of outfits in front of her. They were on an excited high, chattering about who would be there, whether any other people not staying at the hotel would make an appearance. It took roughly forty-five minutes for them to agree on what they would wear, which seemed to be outfit number one in both cases, and then a further hour to get ready. The sun had turned Lucy's skin a wonderful shade of brown and she positively glowed. It was hard to remember the insecure, defensive teenager she had been a couple of months ago.

By the time Elliot had dropped them off and returned, Melissa was waiting for him in his bedroom wearing the most tempting outfit she could think of. Absolutely nothing.

They had never actually had the house entirely to themselves since they arrived. During the day, if the girls weren't around, then Merle was, or else her husband, who was the handyman and gardener. Or they were out themselves, at a beach with Lucy and Mattie, or having lunch in one of the excellent restaurants on the island. They made love on the beach and at night when the house was perfectly quiet, if not completely empty. Greeting him with nothing on was a first and the appreciation in his eyes filled her with a glorious, soaring sense of satisfaction.

'You take my breath away,' he said thickly, coming into the room and kicking the door shut behind him.

Instead of lights or the lamps on the dressing table, Melissa had lit fragrant candles, and the French doors leading out to the porch were open, so that the night breeze billowed the voile curtains.

She had left her hair loose, wild though it was, and the mayhem of corkscrew curls framed her face and trailed halfway down her back.

Elliot doubted he had ever seen anyone so beautiful in his entire life. Underneath those clothes, she was every man's dream. How could she not be? He moved towards her, slowly unbuttoning his shirt, never taking his eyes off her glorious nakedness. Her breasts were shadowy, succulent shapes in the candlelight. His hands itched to feel them, to feel her move sinuously against him in heated response. He tossed his shirt onto the ground and stopped to remove the remainder of his clothing, half smiling as her eyes were drawn downwards to his impressively erect manhood.

'Oh, no,' Melissa murmured, when he reached to pull her towards him. 'Not yet.'

She trailed wet, hot kisses along his chest, circling his flat brown nipples with her tongue. She had to force herself not to circle his sheath with her hand, so that she could feel it pulse between her fingers. She would get there soon enough.

Elliot breathed in sharply as he watched her blonde head descend the length of his body and he uttered a groan when finally her mouth covered his throbbing member. He coiled his fingers into her hair and flung his head back with a deep grunt of pleasure as she moved erotically, keeping up a rhythm that had him fighting for control. His eyes were closed as he fought not to bring proceedings to a premature conclusion, but his mind provided the powerful image of her down there, her breasts gently bobbing as she moved, her large nipples jutting out because he knew that she would be as turned on as he was. When she began licking his aching shaft, he could bear it no longer, and in one easy movement he tugged her up and then dragged her over to the bed.

'You witch,' he groaned.

Melissa laughed throatily. If she were a witch, her first spell would be to turn his lust into love, his desire into need.

'Lie flat,' he commanded. 'Don't move a muscle.'

'What are you going to do?'

'Nothing you won't enjoy…to the hilt.' He opened the drawer of the table by his bed and, to her surprise, brought out some red ribbons she had worn in her hair when she had first arrived.

'I wondered where those had disappeared to.' The breath caught in her throat as her mind grappled with the possibility that she meant more to him than he had verbalised, enough for him to hang on to the ribbons she had used for her hair.

Elliot didn't answer. With a glinting grin, he loosely tied her hands on either side to the bedposts. She could shrug off the silky fabric if she chose, but she had no intention of doing that. Instead she curled her fingers round the vertical wrought-iron posts. She was his willing captive, and when he began to explore her body she could only lie back and writhe in ecstasy.

Her nipples were hard, waiting for his touch, and she moaned deeply as he circled first one, then the other, with his mouth, sucking hard until it seemed as though a current of electricity had connected straight from her breasts to her melting core.

He loved her breasts. He had told her that repeatedly, had told her that their size and weight turned him on, as did her big, rosy nipples that darkened when she was aroused, which was always when she was with him.

Just knowing that turned her on even more now and he drove her mad by spending so much time there, sucking and licking and teasing the tight peaks with his fingers, rubbing them until she wanted to scream in frustrated pleasure.

With her hands out of the way, there was no guiding him as he savoured her. Instead, he pleasured her at his own leisurely pace, kissing every inch of each breast, licking below where the sensitive skin of the underside met her ribcage. It was exquisitely arousing.

'Enjoying yourself?' she dimly heard him ask, with a satisfied laugh in his voice, but she was too heated to formulate a reply.

He was straddling her, but as he moved lower, he spread her legs to either side of him.

The scent of her was wonderful, unique. As was the glorious, impassioned immediacy of her response as he delved into that most private part of her with his tongue. Her body arched up to meet his mouth and he plundered the innermost depths of her femininity, savouring the smell and the taste of her. When he felt her coming too close to her peak, he stopped, taking time to gently lick her warm thighs while she begged for more, then he would recommence his exquisite torture.

The only time he drew away was to apply protection, which he had used every time apart from that first day, when they had made love on the beach.

Melissa's body seemed held in excited suspension for those few seconds, as she waited for him to fill her, waited for the feel of him against her. He had become familiar to her even though each time they made love it was more earth-shattering than the last.

He entered her in one forceful thrust that brought a moan of satisfaction to her lips, then he began to move. He had come to know her so well, in the space of a scant two weeks; he knew how to move until her breathing became jerky and she whimpered for him to take her to that final place.

With no one in the house but the two of them, with all the privacy at their disposal, neither of them was hampered by a need for relative silence. She was aware of him huskily groaning, saying things to her that made her fevered pulses race as his movements became faster. Her final shuddering orgasm made her cry out and she freed her hands from their loose ties to clasp her arms around him, raking her fingers along his skin.

'God, woman, what do you do to me?' he asked, when their energies were finally spent and he had rolled over to the side. He propped himself up on one elbow and looked down at her. Tenderly, she thought, or was she mistaken? Was it just the ebbing of passion that softened his features?

'What would you like me to do to you?' Melissa murmured softly.

'Anything and everything,' he replied softly. 'We've two more days. A lot can be achieved in that time, although,' he added ruefully, 'the restrictions of making love on the beach are now very apparent.' He burrowed his face into her neck. It was a very tender gesture, but she didn't fail to notice that, as far as he was concerned, the time scale for them ran to the end of the holiday. There was no mention of anything after that and she knew that she couldn't press him. For all the passion of their lovemaking and the easy freedom of their days, there were certain things he kept under tight control. His emotions were one of them. He wouldn't appreciate her opening up the floor for debate on the topic of whether they had a future, just as he never discussed why his relationship with Alison had come to an end. She was his temporary and very willing plaything.

Elliot's *two days* statute of limitation left her feeling cold, but then to back out now was unthinkable, not that she wanted to.

She would, she decided, just have to be optimistic. Hadn't he told her that he had spent weeks thinking of her? When they hadn't even slept together?

Well, she thought to herself now, when they were back in England, he would think of her all the more, remember the times they had shared. He wouldn't want to break off their fragile, newly born relationship. Surely…

And she wouldn't put pressure on him. She loved him. Her love would be their glue. She caressed his head, thinking her thoughts and seeing rosy pictures in front of her, even though there was still that malicious little voice in her head telling her that she was being a fool.

'You're right,' she murmured, even though it hurt, 'a lot can be achieved in two days…'

Which went by with the speed of a bullet shooting through open space.

The villa and the sun and the carefree days seemed to fade into a blurred water-colour wash the further they were from the island, on their way back to London. Even

Lucy and Mattie, both unnaturally sober, slept most of the journey home.

Melissa tried not to let the yawning pull of reality affect her. She watched Elliot doze and dozed off and on herself, but her sleep was light and fitful. In one breath, she remembered what they had done together and told herself that he cared about her, even if he didn't necessarily show it. Maybe words of love and affection didn't come easily to a man as proud and controlled as him. In the other breath, she succumbed to the full force of facts. He had made love passionately and completely, but he had promised nothing, not even a relationship lasting a single day once they had stepped foot on British soil.

She would have to sway him, she decided, and the thought kept her cheerful all the way through Customs, and out into the crowded arrivals area.

Later Melissa wondered how long it might have kept her going if they hadn't cleared the crowds and spotted Alison standing to one side, immaculate in a pale blue suit, waiting for them, waiting for Elliot to arrive back home...

CHAPTER TEN

This was the time of day that Melissa was getting accustomed to enjoying most. It was six in the evening. Her parents would be downstairs, bustling in the kitchen, and she could sit up in her bedroom without interruption. She could allow her thoughts to wander freely over that disastrous final day with Elliot.

It was five weeks ago but it felt like only a few hours. She could see clearly in her mind's eye Alison standing there at the tail end of the waiting crowds, impeccably decked out, face smiling as she moved forward to greet Elliot. In that one instant, every resolution Melissa had made and all the hopes she had nurtured in her idiocy, to somehow get him to love her, just a little, just a fraction of how much she had grown to love him, had disappeared in a puff of smoke.

If Elliot had been surprised to see his ex standing there, he hadn't shown it. After a few seconds of checking out the new arrival, Lucy and Mattie had disappeared, with Lucy straight back to her old, sullen self, announcing that they would meet them in half an hour's time, leaving it clear from the belligerence of her tone that she dearly hoped that Alison would have left by then.

Alison ignored her completely, just as she had paid scant attention to Melissa. Good breeding forced her to be polite, but after that initial icy smile all her attention had been for Elliot.

Melissa sighed softly and stared out of the bay window of her bedroom. She was sitting on the broad, cushioned seat that could also double as a trunk, and had done when she was a child, a storage place for all her toys. The view, as always, was inspiring. In her better moments, she took some consolation from the fact that nature just kept going, that her problems were small and transitory, really. Most of the time, though, she was overwhelmed by a huge sense of loss and a feeling that, if she had just listened to that voice that preached caution, she might not have found herself where she was now.

She might not have tried to insert herself between Alison and Elliot, horribly nervous but still reckless enough to try and fight for the man she had grown to love. She had hoped that her presence would remind him that Alison was in the past, whatever her reasons for turning up unexpectedly, that *she* was the present, the woman he had taken to his bed, laughed with, gone sightseeing with.

It had been a mistake. She hadn't banked on meeting the shuttered indifference of his response. She still shivered now when she thought about it, the way he had glanced down at her, his face cool and expressionless. It had felt like being punched and, though she had kept her smile wide and bright, her stomach had coiled into a small, hard, painful knot.

Alison, it transpired, had found out from his secretary what time he was going to be flying in, and she had arranged her day around the event.

Right to the last, Melissa had clung desperately to the hope that Alison's presence was all to do with business; maybe something urgent had come up and she needed to see him.

It was only when he had gone in search of the non-appearing teenagers that the full force of her stupidity was rammed home to her. Left alone with Alison, she had got the whole story from the horse's mouth.

Alison had explained that she and Elliot had never bro-

ken up in a voice that could cut glass. It was the voice
Melissa imagined she used when reducing someone
standing in the dock to size. She had simply got a temporary transfer to New York.

'I must be crazy to forgive him,' she had said. 'I know
he's probably slept with you, but he's a man and men do
what they do. You were available, I wasn't. And before
I left for the Big Apple, it was an unspoken assumption
that we could take time out if need be.'

'So you were no longer an item,' Melissa had pointed
out, still fighting.

'Of course we were. We're made for one another. I'm
afraid I did warn you against getting too close to Elliot.
He's a very charismatic man and clearly one who took
full advantage of an easy lay.'

Coming from that coolly sophisticated figure, the
words were even more shockingly vulgar and Melissa
had recoiled as though she had been physically struck.

The fight had drained out of her. She had wondered
why Elliot had never been disposed to discuss Alison.
Now she realised she knew. There had been no big break-
up, no showdown, no anguished acknowledgements that
he had become engaged to the wrong woman. Instead,
Alison had been transferred abroad temporarily and while
the cat was away, the mouse, put simply, had decided to
play. She knew now that all the things he had said about
spending weeks thinking about her, had been lies. He had
just used the ammunition at his disposal. He had thought
that he probably wouldn't have been able to get her into
bed with a simple invitation, so he had persuaded her
with golden words that had foolishly ended up turning
her head. He had charmed her and she had fallen for it
hook, line and sinker.

The scenery outside the bedroom window blurred. She
could feel tears threatening and she swallowed them

down. Actually, the crying was getting much better. At first, when she had arrived on the doorstep of her parents' house, she had been unable to stop crying. It helped that they had left her in relative peace, had been content to accept the surface explanation she had offered them, that she had fallen in love with someone and it just hadn't worked out. She had left out the details of their affair, of Alison, of her hasty departure from the airport, running away with her tail between her legs before Elliot had returned with Lucy and Mattie. She hadn't looked back. She had gone straight to her flat, cleared out her things and headed up to Yorkshire. A few days later, she had e-mailed her resignation to the health club and e-mailed Lucy with a vague excuse for her sudden disappearance, telling her that she had had to go back home for personal reasons but that she would be in touch as soon as she possibly could.

And as for Elliot…he still burned a hole in her heart. His image was with her every moment. She dreamt of him and woke up to continue thinking of him.

But time would heal that. There was no sign of it yet, but she was recovering. Three days ago she had begun scanning the newspapers for jobs.

She dragged her gaze away from the lilac, rolling views and glanced at the clock on the wall. In fifteen minutes, her parents would call her down for tea. They ate early and always bang on time. It was both frustrating and endearing.

She lapsed back into her thoughts and the next time she glanced at the clock, forty minutes had rolled by. Surprised, Melissa reluctantly abandoned the comfort of her bedroom and began heading downstairs. Maybe her little chats had worked, she thought with weary amusement. She had told her parents on several occasions that eating a high tea early in the evening was bad for them, because they invariably snacked later on before they went to bed. It had fallen on deaf ears, but maybe they had listened to reason after all and come to the conclusion that too many carbohydrates followed by inertia was a recipe for blocked arteries.

She met her mother halfway down the stairs.

'What's the matter?' Melissa asked sharply, forgetting her problems at the sight of her mother's flustered face. Her mother rarely got flustered. 'What's wrong? Is it Dad?' Her voice had risen with each syllable.

'You're wearing that old pair of jeans again,' was her mother's response. 'Why don't you go and change your T-shirt? Put something a little prettier on?'

'What?'

'And your hair's a mess.'

'My hair's *always* a mess!' Melissa shot back, taken aback at this line of conversation. 'And why would I need to get into a pretty T-shirt anyway?'

'Because you have a visitor.'

'Oh, Mum, you didn't.' Melissa had steadfastly ignored the teasing suggestions that had been popping up over recent days that maybe meeting a nice Yorkshire lad would be a good idea, to take her mind off things. Her mother had even gone so far as to mention a friend of a friend of a friend who had a son… The rest she had left tantalisingly hanging in the air and Melissa had chosen to ignore it. Now she felt a flutter of irritation and alarm run through her. 'Tell me you haven't arranged a date for me with whatsisname, because if you have I'm going back upstairs to my bedroom and locking the door.'

'I've put him in the ''good'' room,' her mother contented herself with saying, which made him sound as though he were a new stick of furniture, and Melissa groaned silently to herself. 'He's having a nice little chat with Dad.'

Melissa dragged her steps, following her mother down the stairs, past the little kitchen and the sitting room, and finally she became aware of low voices. 'I'm not going out with anyone, Mum,' she warned, just in case her mother was nurturing thoughts of fairy-tale romances. 'I'll talk to him because he's here and that's it. Understood?'

'There's no need to take that tone with me, young lady.'

She pushed open the door, which had been ajar, and, still frowning at her mother, Melissa took several seconds before she realised who the visitor was. This was the visitor who was too good for the sitting room, the visitor who had interrupted the punctuality of their tea time. And her heart stopped.

After five weeks, there he was, as cool as a cucumber, sitting down on the flowered chair and looking as though he belonged. Melissa turned away, ready to take flight but was firmly propelled back into the room by her beaming and obviously excited mother.

'Now, darling, your father and I have some errands to do so we'll leave you here with your young man.'

'He's not *my young man*,' she hissed virulently, watching in dismay as her father stood up and shook hands with Elliot.

Good lord, Elliot was even more fabulous in the flesh than she remembered. With impeccable manners, he stood up as well and came across to her mother to deposit a kiss on one receptive cheek.

Then her parents were going, leaving, deserting her. She heard the front door slam shut and the silence wrapped itself around her like a vice.

'What are you doing here?' Her voice was icy cold and filled with loathing.

'What do you think? That I was just passing by so I thought I'd drop in? I came to see you.'

'Well, I don't want to see you! I want you to leave! Right now!' She had backed away from the threat of him and was pressed against the wall, trembling, not daring to look at him in case that old familiar weakness set in again. But she could feel all the masculine energy emanating from him in waves and pooling around her. Behind her back she clenched her open palms into fists, until her fingernails bit into her skin.

The weather had cooled as summer turned into autumn and he was wearing a pair of faded jeans and a sweatshirt. Out of the corner of her eye, she could see his leather jacket on the upright chair at the side, beaten brown leather.

'I'm not leaving, Melissa.'

'My parents shouldn't have let you in! How did you find me?'

'You told me roughly where they lived. I made a few calls. For God's sake, woman, why don't you go and sit down and stop standing there as though you're in mortal terror of me?'

Melissa scuttled over to the sofa and collapsed onto it, drawing her feet up and tucking them under her. Her heart was beating like a sledgehammer in her chest. She was aware of him sitting down on the sofa at the other end and she could feel the hesitancy in his silence. She had no idea why he had come but she had her suspicions, and if he thought that he could revive any kind of sexual relationship between them then he was in for a shock.

'Lucy misses you,' he said eventually, at which point Melissa finally looked at him, noticing for the first time that his face seemed drawn and there were lines of tiredness etched by his eyes.

He hadn't come for her, she thought numbly. There

she went again, imagination running riot and in all the wrong directions, reading messages that weren't there. He had come because of his daughter. Her emotions went into deep freeze as this slice of bitter reality presented itself to her. She made herself look at him squarely in the eyes.

'I'm sorry. How is she?'

'Subdued since you left.' He raked his fingers through his hair and rubbed his eyes with his thumbs. 'She blames me, of course.'

'And of course we can't have *that*, can we?' Melissa asked with cutting sarcasm. Anger gave her strength. 'I mean, *heaven forbid* that the great and wonderful Elliot Jay should ever be blamed for anything!'

His mouth tightened and she could sense him holding himself back. Why? Because, she thought with vicious clarity, he knew that he was on the back foot. Even *he* must be aware of how she had felt at the airport five weeks ago, when he had looked at her as if she were a stranger instead of someone he had shared the most intimate moments with!

He wanted to retaliate, probably give her another of his famous speeches on living for the moment or whatever, but he couldn't because he was here to ask a favour of her.

'I'm not going back. I'm sorry Lucy misses me. I miss her, too, but I'm here now and here is where I'm going to stay.'

'Why?' He slanted her a look of burning intensity, his blue eyes settling on her face until she felt her insides begin to squirm. More than anything else, she hated herself for that, for reacting to him even when she knew him for what he was.

'Because I've realised that I'm not cut out for life in the big city. I'm a small-town girl and a small town is where I belong.' She thought of the excitement and buzz of London, and then of the Yorkshire lad waiting round the corner and maybe getting a job twenty minutes away, returning home in the evening for tea with her parents until she found someone and settled down. Except, after Elliot, she wasn't sure there ever would be that someone. Who could ever survive the comparisons?

'I'm sorry.'

'Don't. Just don't. I don't want you feeling sorry for me. In fact, I don't want you here at all. I'm not going back so that I can be used to smooth things over with your daughter. You'll just have to enlist the help of your fiancée for that.'

'I don't feel sorry for you,' Elliot said brusquely. He stood up and began pacing the room. 'And there's no fiancée.'

'Oh, right. Does Alison know that?'

Elliot paused in his restless pacing to look at her narrowly. 'Alison has known that for several months.'

'Really? Pull the other one.'

'Meaning?'

Melissa inhaled deeply and decided to let him have it or be damned. 'Meaning that you led me to believe that you and Alison had broken up. OK, you didn't seem keen to go into the details and I only discovered why later. Because, according to Alison, there had *been* no break-up. She had been transferred temporarily to New York, but basically she was coming back. That was why she came to the airport. To meet you. I thought…'

'Carry on,' Elliot said expressionlessly. 'I'm interested to see where this is going.'

'I don't know what I thought…' Melissa muttered.

'You thought that, after what we shared, I should have said something at the airport. Should have at the very least put my arms around you, staked my priorities?'

Put like that, it sounded pathetic, so she remained silently miserable. She couldn't even react when he moved
across to the sofa and sat down, closer to her this time.

'I should have,' he said in a low voice, and Melissa
reluctantly looked at his strong, handsome face, for once
vulnerable and hesitant. She absolutely refused to allow
hope to find a way into her heart. She had been used and
that was all there was to it. And here he was, using a
few smooth words so that he could use her again. No
chance.

'Why?' she threw at him bitterly. 'Why should you
have? When you already knew where your priorities lay?'

'With Alison? If you really believe that I'm the type
of man who has a casual fling with a woman for no better
reason than his fiancée happens to be out of town, then
tell me now and I'll walk away from this house and it'll
be the last time you see me.'

He stood up when Melissa stubbornly maintained her
silence. It was only as he reached the door that she looked
at him and allowed herself to contemplate the reality of
him disappearing out of her life forever. No, she had
already lived through that. But for him to vanish on this
ugly note…how could she ever live with herself again?
At least, she thought, she would speak her mind the best
she could, and now that he had refuted her assumptions,
did she really believe him to be an out-and-out two-
timing bastard? The answer was no. He'd just indulged
in, what was for him, a disposable relationship. The fact
that she had wanted more was her fault, not his.

'I was only repeating what she told me at the airport,'
Melissa said. 'And it made sense,' she continued, as he
paused by the door to hear her out, 'when you could
barely meet my eyes.'

'You haven't answered me. Do you believe me to be
the type of man who uses women?'

'Yes,' Melissa said honestly, 'but not two at the same time.' If he didn't like that answer, then he could leave. It was the truth. But if he left…her eyes glazed over with tears and she looked down hastily. She wasn't aware of him until he was kneeling in front of her, pulling out a handkerchief, which she accepted while informing him in a shaky voice that she wasn't crying.

'Why didn't you?' she asked, stumbling over her words and hating herself for even asking the question. 'Why didn't you see how rejected you made me feel when you just stood there, ignoring me? After those wonderful two weeks we'd spent together?'

'I'm sorry,' Elliot whispered, shoving her over so that he could sit right next to her and pull her against him. 'I suppose I was…'

'Was *what*?' Melissa whispered harshly.

'Afraid.'

Melissa pulled back to look at him uncertainly. 'Afraid of what?' she asked in a voice that indicated *pull the other one*.

'There I was. I'd just had the two greatest weeks of my life, and suddenly I'm confronted by a clash of realities. There was no question of Alison being a part of my life, but she did represent everything I had ever known in all my relationships. Order, predictability, restraint. And then there was you, impulsive, joyous, unpredictable. For a moment I wondered where the hell I belonged.'

The two greatest weeks of his life. Melissa focused on that little phrase and, while she marvelled at it, hope slipped in unnoticed and lodged somewhere in her heart.

Belatedly she remembered that this was the man who had kept well away from her for the past five weeks and had only shown up because his daughter missed her and he was having to cop the blame for it. She winced at the feel of his hard chest and tugged back so that she could resume some necessary distance.

'And there's no need to tell me what choice you made. What a shame you've had to find yourself here now, because Lucy's forced your hand.'

'No one forces my hand,' Elliot said softly. He reached to wipe dry the damp trail of a tear with his thumb and Melissa jerked back. 'Yes, I haven't seen you for five weeks and they have been the worst five weeks of my life.'

He waited for that to sink in, but Melissa stared back at him with mutinous disbelief. He really couldn't blame her, but God he wanted to hold that soft, frowning face between his hands and kiss it until the sun rose again and her wonderful smile emerged.

'I had to think,' he said flatly. 'Something had happened to me and I found that I couldn't deal with it.'

'Right.' *Lucy had reinstated war zones and he no longer had a useful buffer to oil his path.*

'For the first time ever I found myself standing on quicksand and that's why I had to come here. I thought I could rein things back to normality, told myself that if you walked out of my life then perhaps it was for the best because I could resume the life I had always known. I was wrong. I discovered that, actually, I couldn't live without you and I didn't want to.'

'But…you don't mean that… Alison said…'

'Alison lied. I broke off that relationship the day after I went to your flat. Another memorable evening.' He gave her a crooked smile and she flushed. 'On the back of that, she accepted a transfer abroad that, it transpired, didn't work out. She showed up at the airport because she wanted me back and she wanted to make sure that you knew. I haven't seen her since that day. Another man would have rushed to you, but I have never been one…'

He sighed deeply and expressively and Melissa risked stroking his face gently. He caught her hand in his and kissed her open palm. 'I find that I don't want to spend another day without you,' he said hoarsely. 'I love you. I don't know when it started and I'm not sure how it slipped in, but I do. Madly, deeply and for all eternity.'

There was a wonderful singing in her ears. 'You love me?' she asked. 'Me? You? Love?'

'And I know what you're going to say.'

'You do?' This came as something of a shock since *she* didn't know what she was going to say!

'And I agree. Nothing less than marriage will do. So...will you marry me?'

'Marry you?'

Taken aback by the quietness of her response, Elliot was gripped by a ferocious sense of urgency. 'Marry me,' he confirmed roughly. 'And there'll be no long engagement either. I want you with me as soon as possible. If I had my way,' he grated forcefully, 'it would be tonight, but I don't suppose the local registrar's office will still be open. And anyway,' he added for good measure, 'I know your parents would like something a little bigger and a little more church-oriented.'

'They *said that*?'

'They did,' Elliot told her smugly. 'After I told them how much I loved their daughter and asked your father for your hand in marriage. I also told them what a great husband I would make.'

Melissa laughed. She felt as though she was flying, really soaring, and there were no doubts and no inner voices waiting to clip her wings.

'Well, then, considering I absolutely adore you, too, I guess a church wedding is what it will have to be.'

'And in the meantime,' Elliot took a small box from his pocket and withdrew a ring from it, 'just to make sure that the world knows you're mine...' He slipped it onto her finger. It was a perfect fit.

'It's beautiful—' more tears threatened '—not that the world would think anything but that I'm a woman in love forever, with or without a ring...'

THE TAKEOVER BID

by

Leigh Michaels

Leigh Michaels wrote her first book when she was fourteen and thought she knew everything. Now she's a good bit older and wise enough to realise that she'll never know everything. She has written more than seventy-five romances, teaches writing in person and online, and enjoys long walks, miniatures, and watching wild deer and turkey from her living room.

E-mail: leigh@leighmichaels.com

CHAPTER ONE

THE wind was strong, even for April, and the walls and roof of the metal building creaked a mild protest with every gust. Melanie knew perfectly well that it was not nearly as cold outside as it sounded. Still, she thought, the whine of the wind was enough to make Santa Claus shiver. As if in echo, the lop-eared dog at her feet whimpered in his sleep.

She heard the bang of the door between the shop and the office. Melanie turned away from the computer screen and glanced up at the big old-fashioned clock on the office wall as one of the workmen came in, wiping his hands on an already-greasy rag. The dog raised his head inquisitively and then, seeing the workman, put it back down on his front paws.

Melanie pushed her chair back. "I didn't know you were still here, Robbie."

"I stayed to put another coat of wax on Mr. Stover's Buick," he said. "It just didn't look quite shiny enough."

Melanie smiled. "I appreciate that you take care of the cars we work on as if you own them yourself. And he'll appreciate it when he picks it up tomorrow."

He shrugged. "We want the customer to be happy. When he's paying as much as Mr. Stover did to restore a '70 Buick, an extra coat of wax is nothing. Want to come and see it?"

She'd seen the car that afternoon. She'd seen it every day for the last month, as a matter of fact, watching

5

every step of the restoration. But the gleam in Robbie's eyes and the note of pride in his voice told her it would be cruel not to go and admire his work.

She followed him back to the shop, the dog trailing behind. Robbie tossed the rag into a pile and picked up what looked like an equally-greasy one from a nearby bin.

"I'm never sure whether you guys are taking grease off your fingers or putting it on," Melanie said. Then she looked past him at the car sitting in the nearest bay of the shop, its baby blue paint and snowy white convertible top gleaming quietly under the harsh work lights. Souvenir of another age, it looked as long as an ocean liner by modern standards. "It's a beauty."

"Yeah." Robbie's voice was almost reverent. He brushed the back of his hand across the fender. "Quite a little different from when you found her sitting out in the back of the yard."

Melanie didn't have to think hard to remember what the Buick had looked like. "Buried under a pile of rusty fenders, with a mouse condo in the back seat and an engine that hadn't seen oil in twenty years—yes, it's a little different now."

"She runs like a dream. Want me to start her up?"

He'd love to have the excuse, Melanie knew. "Let's wait till morning and you can move it into the showroom so Mr. Stover will get the full effect."

The dog wheeled toward the door leading into the office, then bristled, growled, and started to bark.

Robbie frowned. "It's a little late for customers, and the door should be locked anyway."

"That'll be Jackson. He's got a key. Knock it off, Scruff." The dog stopped barking, but a soft growl lingered deep in his throat. Melanie pushed the door open and called, "I'm out in the shop."

A young man came out of her office, his camel-hair topcoat swinging open to reveal a black tuxedo. His white-blond hair was styled with such perfection that Melanie wondered how it was possible the wind hadn't ruffled it. Had he stopped to comb it the moment he came in, or was it actually sprayed into place?

He sounded almost grumpy. "I was beginning to think you'd forgotten and gone home."

"Oh, I couldn't forget your once-a-month visit any more than you would," Melanie said dryly.

Jackson's gaze fell on Robbie. "I'm not interrupting anything, am I?"

The tone of his voice obviously wasn't lost on Robbie, for his face turned red. "Want me to stay, Melanie?"

"No, Angie will be waiting for you." He went out, and Melanie said gently, "As a matter of fact, Jackson, you are interrupting. I was inspecting our latest project. Robbie just finished working on it." She walked slowly around the car, noting the finish on the chrome trim and the way light reflected from the paint. Robbie had been right about the effect of that last coat of wax. She'd have to remember to compliment him in the morning.

Jackson looked at the Buick. "Why anyone would pay good money for that…"

"That's the customer's choice, and don't expect me to believe that it bothers you to spend your share. You look very fine tonight, Jackson. And on a Thursday, too… Is it just dinner tonight, or the theater?"

Jackson raised his eyebrows in a well-practiced gesture. "It's never *just dinner* when you go to the Century Club."

Melanie wondered sometimes whether Jackson light-

ened his hair or darkened his eyebrows; the combination
was so improbable that she was sure it had to be one or
the other. "Of course. Well, you can't expect me to
know, since I've never been there."

"If you're hinting for an invitation, Mel—"

"Heavens, no. I wouldn't know what to do."

Jackson laughed. "Well, that's no doubt true. I'd love
to stay and chat, but Jennifer's waiting for me to pick
her up."

He hadn't needed to clarify that the no-doubt elegant
Jennifer wasn't waiting outside in his car, because he'd
never brought her to the shop. Melanie wondered sometimes if he'd ever told his most-recent girlfriend where
he got his money.

"So if you've got my check ready—"

"It's in my desk." She led the way, turning off the
shop lights as she went.

Jackson eyed the figures on the check. "Not much
this month. How do you live on this kind of money?"

"I don't," Melanie pointed out. "That's your share
of the profits of the partnership for the month. But in
addition to my share, I also draw a salary for working
here."

"That's not fair."

"Exactly what isn't fair about it? If we hired a manager, we'd pay him and then split what was left. I'm the
manager, so I get paid. If you don't like the bottom line,
you can start working for the business too."

"I do work for the business. I tell people about it all
the time."

"And in the last year, one of them actually turned up
to take a look. Of course, he didn't buy anything."

"That's not my fault. I tried."

"Well, maybe if you tried harder, you'd notice the results in your check. See you next month, Jackson."

Melanie locked the door behind him, shut down her computer, and called the dog, who was still standing pugnaciously by the entrance as if expecting Jackson to come back. "You won't have to defend me from him again for another thirty days, Scruff. Come on, let's go home."

She paused beside the back door and looked thought-fully at the board where at least twenty tagged car keys were hanging from pegs. "What should we drive to-night, Scruff? It's too windy for a convertible, even with the top up. Do you feel like riding in a Corvette that's older than I am, or a Thunderbird that's only slightly younger?"

The Thunderbird was closer to the door, so that de-cided it. She grabbed the key and went out into the wind, still thinking about Jackson. He must have been in a hurry to get to Jennifer tonight, for he hadn't started in on Melanie as he usually did about wanting her to buy his share of the business.

Not that she wouldn't like to buy him out. In fact, she'd do it the very minute she found a spare half-million dollars lying around. Or whenever Jackson de-cided to be more reasonable about his price.

In Melanie's opinion, it was a toss-up which would happen first.

By the time Melanie arrived at the shop the next morn-ing, Robbie had already moved the Buick. He hadn't put it into the showroom as she'd planned, however, but right outside the front door. He'd put the top down and parked the car at a rakish angle so the chrome caught the bright sunlight.

He was buffing the hood when she parked the Thunderbird nearby and strolled over. The dog hopped out of the car and began to make his usual morning rounds of the parking lot.

"Aren't you afraid it'll get a speck of dust on the windshield out here?" Melanie teased.

"I figured it would be good publicity." Robbie jerked a thumb toward the highway which ran along the front of the lot. "Traffic's been slowing down to take a look."

"I don't doubt it." She shaded her eyes with her hand and watched a pickup truck pull into the lot. "It's too bad we can't leave it here all week, but here comes Mr. Stover now."

She'd learned, in a couple of years in the classic car business, when to keep her mouth shut. So when Mr. Stover got out of the truck, she called, "Good morning," and then didn't say another word until he'd had a chance to look his fill.

That took a while—which was another thing that Melanie had learned from experience.

If it did nothing else, she'd found, being in the business of selling exotic, collectible, and antique cars taught patience. Patience with prospective buyers who wanted a specific model and color and wouldn't settle for anything else no matter how long it took to find. Patience with sellers who couldn't make up their minds whether to part with their treasures. Patience with the slow and painstaking pace of restoration work.

Of course, it was much more fun to be patient while Mr. Stover got his first look at a fully-restored, shiny-as-new Buick. If he wanted to stare at his new toy for an hour, Melanie would stand there quietly, leaning on a green Chevy, joining in his appreciation of a job well done, and waiting for him to break the silence.

From the corner of her eye, she saw a car pull off the highway and into the lot, and the shape of it rang bells in her brain. A Baritsa? She'd only ever seen one before, in person—but once noticed, the rakish lines and sporty silhouette were hard to forget.

She turned her head to look more closely at the car. It was a Baritsa, all right—a brand-new one, glossy black and showroom-shiny. Not at all the sort of thing that their regular clientele drove.

Maybe Jackson had taken her seriously. If he'd gone to the Century Club last night and started talking up classic cars to people who could afford fleets of them…

Don't get your hopes up. More likely it's someone looking for directions.

The Baritsa nosed in between the Chevy she was leaning on and a 1950s Packard with a "sold" sticker on the windshield. But the engine continued to purr.

Beyond the tinted window of the Baritsa Melanie could see only the shape of the driver's head and shoulders. A man, obviously. Probably tall, judging by the distance from the steering wheel up to the shadow that must be his chin. His hand was raised, as if he was holding a cell phone to his ear. But that was all she could tell.

Mr. Stover called her name, and Melanie jerked upright, wondering how long he'd been standing there in front of her while she gawked at the Baritsa. "Sorry," she said. "I didn't quite hear what you said."

"It's like a dream, you know." There was a catch in his voice. "I've always regretted selling my Buick, because it was the first car I ever owned. To get one just like it, and have it turn out so beautiful…" He smiled and reached into his pocket to pull out a checkbook. "I guess you're going to want some money, though— right?"

"Let's go inside to deal with the dirty work," Melanie suggested. She couldn't help looking back toward the Baritsa as she pushed herself away from the Chevy's fender.

Mr. Stover had obviously seen the Baritsa too. "I wonder what that guy wants. It looks sort of odd, him just sitting there like that."

"Maybe the Buick caught his eye and he wants to buy it from you."

"He can try," Mr. Stover said, and grinned.

Melanie ushered him into her office, handed him the car's papers, and went back to the showroom to get him a cup of coffee while he looked over the invoice.

The coffee machine was just finishing its cycle. She waited till it was done, poured two cups, and gathered up sugar and cream. The outside door opened, and she felt a flicker of excitement as she looked up. It was perfectly silly, of course, to get all breathless over a prospective customer, no matter what kind of car he drove. Still—a Baritsa…

But the man who came in was Jackson.

She could hardly believe her eyes. Jackson, dropping in on a Friday when he'd picked up his monthly check just the night before? Stopping by in daylight, when someone might actually see him there?

And since when did Jackson drive a Baritsa?

He probably borrowed it from Jennifer, she thought. *I wonder what she'd think about him using it to go slumming.*

"Mel," he said. "I need to talk to you."

"Not right now, Jackson. Customers first, you know—and I have one in my office waiting to write a check. A big check."

"It won't take long. I just need to tell you I've come for—"

She shook her head and walked past him, closing the office door firmly behind her.

Fifteen minutes later, she weighted Mr. Stover's check to her desk with a chunk of Missouri limestone and walked him through the showroom to the parking lot, watching with satisfaction as the Buick pulled out into traffic. The Baritsa was still there, she noted, but Jackson was nowhere to be seen.

As she went back inside, a muffled commotion from the shop drew her attention, and she walked across to open the door. "What's going on out here? Is somebody hurt?"

"Not yet." Robbie sounded grim.

"Then what's all the ruckus?" Melanie folded her arms across her chest and surveyed the group. Robbie, two of her other workmen, and Jackson had formed a sort of huddle in the empty bay where the Buick had sat till this morning. So this was where Jackson had gone.

Odd, she thought. He never went into the shop unless he had to, and then he'd hover by the door, obviously anxious not to touch anything—as if he was phobic about grease.

Robbie glared at Jackson. "He's trying to steal a bunch of tools."

"Steal!" Jackson sputtered. "That's slander! They were my father's tools, and now they're mine. I'm just taking what's mine."

Melanie stepped forward. "Wait a minute. Why do you even want them?"

"Good question," one of the workmen muttered. "He wouldn't know what to do with them, that's for sure."

"And in any case," Melanie went on, "they weren't

your father's personal property, they belong to the business. Which you own half of anyway, so why you're making a fuss about tools—''

The shop door opened behind her and she turned to face the newcomer. ''I'll be right with—'' Her standard smile of greeting froze on her face.

The man in the doorway was tall and broad-shouldered, with midnight-black hair and eyes that looked almost silver when he pulled off his sunglasses. His features were too craggy to be considered handsome—he'd be no competition for Jackson in a Greek-god contest. And yet there was something compelling about his face, something that wouldn't let her look away. Where Jackson was conventionally good-looking, this man was interesting. And in thirty years, when Jackson's good looks were long gone, this man would still be worth looking at…

Whoa, she told herself. She swallowed hard and started over. ''I'll be right with you.''

''I'll wait.'' His voice matched his eyes, smooth and polished as sterling silver. ''I'm in no hurry.''

''I'm sorry,'' Melanie said with genuine regret, ''but our insurance company doesn't allow customers to be in the shop area because of the potential for injuries. If you'll step back into the showroom for a moment—''

''I'm not a customer.''

Pieces clicked together in Melanie's mind. It wasn't Jackson who'd been driving the Baritsa, as she'd assumed. It was this man who had been behind the wheel.

Just my luck that he's not a customer.

His gaze had slid past her to the group of men. ''I'm looking for Mel Stafford.''

Melanie took a step forward. ''You found her.''

He looked startled. *''Her?''* He stared at Melanie,

That was another thing she'd gotten used to, Melanie reflected. People didn't expect a woman to be selling collectible cars. Keeping the books, maybe—but not running the business.

At least she'd thought she was used to that reaction— and there was certainly no reason to be irritated because this man had made the standard assumption. If he thought it would make a difference when it came to a deal, he'd find out soon enough that he was wrong.

But he's not a customer, Melanie reminded herself. *So what is he?* "What can I do for you, Mr.—?"

He didn't answer. His gaze was roaming over the building as if taking inventory of the eight bays, from the almost-finished Model T Ford right behind the group of workmen to the shell of a Mustang in the farthest corner.

"Jackson," he said, "I thought you told me this business deals in classic cars."

So maybe she hadn't been altogether wrong after all. Maybe Jackson had actually taken seriously what she'd said about promoting the business. Not that he seemed to have been very selective about who he talked to.

Jackson looked out from behind Robbie's shoulder. "Well, it does. Sort of."

"It's not what I'd call the Lamborghini capital of the world."

"I never said—"

"In fact, it looks more like a junkyard."

Melanie took a step toward the man with the silver eyes. "Excuse me for interrupting, but if you've only come here to insult our products, then you may as well stop wasting everyone's time and go away."

She heard Robbie gasp, and she had to admit that she was almost as surprised as he obviously was. She'd certainly never thrown out a customer before. Or a non-customer, for that matter.

The man didn't seem to hear her. "Mel Stafford," he said genially. "I believe you're the manager."

"Yes, I am. And I'm asking you—no, I'm *telling* you—that it's time to go."

"But I'm not going anywhere," he said. "I'm your new boss."

Wyatt had expected the news might come as a bit of a shock, because the moment he'd caught sight of Jackson—or more to the point, the instant Jackson had caught sight of him—he'd realized that Jackson hadn't yet shared the news with the employees. If he had, he wouldn't have ducked behind the nearest set of broad shoulders.

He's probably trying to pretend none of this is happening.

But Wyatt hadn't anticipated that his announcement would hit with the same concussion as a grenade. The three guys in grease-smeared coveralls looked as if he'd hit each of them right in the chin with a spade. Jackson turned an even more sickly shade of green and rubbed his index finger along the bridge of his nose. *Trying to hide behind his hand,* Wyatt thought.

And then the manager—what kind of a woman called herself *Mel,* for heaven's sake?—started to clap her hands together as if he were in the middle ring of a circus and had just pulled off an especially entertaining trick.

No, not at all the kind of reaction he'd anticipated.

She finally stopped applauding. "Nice try. As practical jokes go, that isn't a bad one. I don't quite know why Jackson would bother to set us up, but we've all certainly gotten his money's worth from the stunt. Now if you'll let us go back to work—''

Wyatt moved a little closer. "This is no practical joke, Mel.''

Her eyes were green, he noted. At least the part of them that wasn't shooting sparks at him looked green. A green-eyed redhead—now there was a dangerous combination.

"That's *Ms. Stafford* to you, Bub.''

"All right, Ms. Stafford. If this is a practical joke, why is my good buddy Jackson standing over there looking the color of mashed peas, instead of laughing?''

She wheeled around to stare at Jackson, and Wyatt watched with satisfaction as reality hit her. "What the hell have you done?'' she breathed.

Jackson seemed to shrivel.

Interesting phenomenon, Wyatt thought. *That's the first change we'll be making, because I can't have a manager who thinks she can order the boss around.*

He watched emotions chase each other across her face. Incredulity was followed by horror, which gave way to a sort of resigned shock. She blinked and finally noticed the gaggle of workmen who were watching, mouths agape.

"Robbie, get your crew to work,'' she said crisply. "Mr. Barnett will be expecting his Model T to be finished this week. Gentlemen, if you'll step into my office, the three of us will discuss this.''

"Mel, I—'' Jackson was almost whimpering.

Wyatt took pity on him. "There's no need for Jackson to be involved. He and I arranged the matter of ownership between ourselves last night. So it's only you and I who need to take up the details—Ms. Stafford.''

Jackson appeared too pathetically grateful even to

speak. He slithered past the workmen and out the side door before Mel Stafford could even react. Then she glared at Wyatt as intently as a vulture who'd been robbed of her prey. "You'll regret letting him go," she announced.

"We'll see." Wyatt stood aside to let her lead the way.

As he followed her across the shop and into the showroom, he noticed the crisp button-down Oxford tucked neatly into the waistband of her trim, well-worn jeans. And he wondered if the decided wiggle to her hips was an offshoot of being mad or if it was just a natural part of her walk. Not that he would have time to find out, for Ms. Stafford wasn't going to be around for long.

She led the way to the one small office which opened off the showroom and sat down firmly behind the cluttered desk. Wyatt decided not to squabble over who had a better right to the boss's chair. She was still the manager, after all. For the moment.

From under the desk a shaggy head protruded, and a long nose sniffed noisily at Wyatt's ankles. It looked like a mop with ears.

"Down, Scruff," Mel Stafford said firmly, and the mop retreated.

Wyatt lounged into the seat across from her, planted his elbows on the wooden arms of the chair, tented his fingers under his chin, and waited.

She moved a chunk of stone out of the way. "I gather, from what you said out there, that you think you've bought Jackson out."

I think I've bought him out? You wish I was only thinking, lady. But he had nothing to lose but a little time. Let her talk. Let her fool herself, if she wanted. *Let her think she's in charge.*

Of course, it was none of her business how the change of ownership had happened. "In a manner of speaking," he said.

She nodded. "Do you know him well?"

What was with the sudden chattiness? He might as well warn her that a feeble effort at charm wasn't going to get her anywhere. Not after the fireworks she'd already displayed. But why make it easy on her? It might be amusing to watch her attempt to beguile. "A few months, I suppose."

"I see. How much did you pay him?"

Wyatt lifted his eyebrows. "I don't see why that would be any of your business, Ms. Stafford."

"Oh, I assure you it isn't just idle curiosity—though I must admit to feeling some. The last time he mentioned a figure to me, he wanted half a million dollars."

"That's very interesting. You sound as if you think your…um…car business isn't worth that much."

She smiled.

Wyatt could smell danger. She looked as if she was having a good time. This was not going quite as he'd planned.

"No, I don't," she said. "In fact, I think that price is pretty steep—for his half."

Half? The bonehead had never bothered to mention that he only owned half of the business. *And that surprises you, Reynolds?*

Or was it Mel Stafford who was pulling a con, trying to convince Wyatt to give up and go away?

He must have looked suspicious, but she drew herself up squarely. "I have all the paperwork to prove that Jackson's a half owner."

Now he was really leery. "Right. It's here somewhere. And I'm sure you'll be happy to dig it out and show it to me someday—when you have enough time. Probably around the turn of the next century. Come on, Ms. Stafford, stop trying to run a bluff on me.''

''I assure you, it's no bluff. Jackson's father was a small-town mechanic. How he ended up owning half a junkyard, I'm not quite sure—''

Wyatt didn't think his expression had changed an iota, but she paused and looked at him thoughtfully.

''Oh, yes,'' she admitted, ''your assessment was quite right. It does resemble a junkyard, because it used to be one. It's only in the last couple of years that it's taken on a new role.''

''And become some kind of gold mine.''

She frowned. ''More like opals, I'd say. We shovel tons and tons of debris to find one small jewel.''

The woman sounded absolutely serious. But she couldn't be for real. Could she?

''At any rate,'' she went on, ''Jackson's father ran the junkyard for years, stripping and selling parts now and then, but mostly just piling up more and more odd bits of vehicles. Where he got them all, I have no idea. When he died a couple of years ago and Jackson inherited, he wasn't too wild about the idea of being a junk man, so he immediately started talking about selling out.''

''For half a million dollars.''

''That was the price he named, yes. Of course, nobody's been crazy enough to actually pay him that much.'' Her eyes were very wide, very innocent, very green. ''Until now.''

And for your information, lady, nobody's been that crazy yet. But if she hoped a fishing expedition was going to get her the information she wanted, she'd have to improve the caliber of the bait, because Wyatt wasn't biting. "So if Jackson's dear old dad only owned half, who had the rest?"

"My father," she said. "Who left his share to me."

Wyatt knew he should have seen it coming. He should have known from the very beginning that getting involved with Jackson was like playing chicken with a diesel locomotive—somebody was bound to get hurt. He just hadn't thought far enough ahead to realize it could be him who ended up pasted to the rails.

She looked up dreamily at the ceiling. "So now that you know the whole story, I'm sure you'll want to hunt up Jackson and bail out of your agreement. Remember? I did tell you that you'd regret letting him leave this morning."

"I'm not going to hunt him down." His voice felt as flat as it sounded.

"But—" He saw consternation flare in her eyes. "But since he didn't exactly tell you the whole story—"

"No, he didn't," Wyatt said grimly.

"Then that's fraud."

"Probably so."

"And that means the deal's off. If you didn't understand what you were buying, then he can't hold you to the agreement."

"Unfortunately," Wyatt said, "it wasn't that sort of agreement. So the bottom line, Ms. Stafford, is that you've got yourself a new partner."

For the first time since he'd walked into the office, he felt the stir of satisfaction—because Mel Stafford's face looked even greener than Jackson's had.

CHAPTER TWO

PARTNER?

For a few seconds, Melanie was afraid she'd forgotten how to breathe—because when she tried it was like inhaling icicles. *Take it slowly,* she told herself. *A little bit of air at a time.*

The entire situation was perfectly clear—at least to her—and the appropriate response was obvious. But apparently the man sitting across the desk from her didn't see it the same way, or he wouldn't have blithely announced that he was going to be her new partner.

How on earth, she wondered, could anyone have actually agreed to buy a business without realizing that he was purchasing only half of it? Without checking things like a balance sheet or a profit-and-loss statement?

And even if for some incredible reason the deal had gotten that far, then why hadn't he gone storming out of the office to find Jackson and get his money back the instant he'd found out that he'd been taken for a ride?

Melanie had been absolutely certain of her ground. As soon as the Baritsa man had announced that he was the new boss, she'd known exactly what had happened. What *must* have happened.

So all she had to do, she'd thought, was to straighten out this flaw in his thinking. Once she had corrected his mistaken impression that he'd bought the entire business, the rest would take care of itself.

Or, rather, he would take care of it. Exactly how he chose to clear up the mess was none of her business. If he chose to settle matters with Jackson by beating him to a pulp, that would be too bad for Jackson, of course. But if Jackson was idiot enough to mislead a prospective buyer, he deserved whatever he got. It wasn't up to Melanie to interfere.

But now it seemed that the prospective buyer wasn't even going to try to straighten out the mess.

It wasn't that sort of agreement, he'd said. *You've got a new partner.*

Which made no sense at all. Why would he sit still for being taken like that?

Of course, it was becoming increasingly clear to Melanie that Jackson hadn't been the only fool involved in the deal. Agreeing to buy a business without even knowing for sure what kind of merchandise it carried, without looking over the stock, without checking out the bottom line to be certain the seller was telling the truth—

"That's the sort of thing my father would have done," she muttered.

"Pardon me?"

"Nothing." But at last a little light had dawned in Melanie's head.

Nobody would make a deal like that, blindly and without investigation, if he thought there was a chance he was being cheated. But the only kind of person who wouldn't have a healthy dose of skepticism over an offer of that sort was one who thought he was getting a sure thing. Or maybe one who'd been doing a little double-dealing of his own.

If he had believed he was the one doing the cheating, he wouldn't have been on guard against Jackson.

She doubted the Baritsa man would put it quite that clearly, of course. But it was the only thing she could think of which accounted for everything—including his unwillingness to go after Jackson now. *It wasn't that sort of agreement…*

"Do you have a name?" she asked abruptly.

"Oh, you can just keep calling me Bub. *Bub and Mel's Used Cars*—it has a certain ring to it."

Maybe he was delusional, Melanie thought wildly, and none of it had happened at all. "I don't suppose you have proof of this transaction."

His eyebrows lifted inquisitively, and Melanie couldn't help noticing that they had a natural aristocratic arch that was very unlike the practiced curve of Jackson's brows. "After watching your former partner ooze out of here on a wave of guilt that would fill a swimming pool, you still think you need proof that his share of the business changed hands last night?"

She couldn't argue with his point. How could she have forgotten for an instant the pathetic way that Jackson had crept out of the shop, refusing even to look at her?

No, there was no question the two men had agreed to some kind of a deal. The question was what she was going to be able to do about it.

Play along, she told herself. *Don't agree to anything. Just get him out of here and then you can call a lawyer and find out where you stand.*

He pushed himself up from his chair and started to look around the office. "You have a very interesting philosophy of decorating, Ms. Stafford. Why take down expired calendars when you can just hang this year's at the end of the row? Of course, eventually you'll run out of wall space. May I call you Mel, now that we're partners?"

"No," she said, a little more sharply than she intended. "I mean, I prefer to use my full name. It's Melanie."

"Interesting."

She was puzzled. "My name? I'm glad you think so, but—"

"I mean the idea that Jackson would ignore your wishes about your name as well as the business. At least I assume you don't approve of him selling his half."

"Perceptive, aren't you?"

"The question is why. I can think of several possibilities."

The phone rang. She put a hand on it and looked up at him. "Hold it right there till I finish with this call. I don't want to miss a word of your logic."

The caller was a regular customer, looking for a part for a car he was restoring. She put the phone down and reached for the intercom. "Robbie, when Fred has time, ask him to pull the driver's side door off the blue Mustang that's sitting out by the back fence. Bill Myers wants to pick it up this afternoon."

Robbie's voice came back, tinny and distant. "Sure thing."

She released the intercom button. "Now—you were saying?"

"Do you know every piece you have in inventory by heart?"

"Of course not. There's a whole corner of the junk-yard we've hardly gotten into yet. But don't let me distract you from figuring out why I don't want Jackson to sell."

He held up a hand and began to tick off points on his fingertips. "You like having him around and wanted him to keep his share so you'd see him regularly."

"Don't make me laugh."

"Really? Then if you weren't gung-ho about having Jackson as a partner, what's so bad about him selling out?"

Melanie opened her mouth and closed it again. He had something there, she realized. Jackson had been a liability as a partner, a constant drag on the business. His unwillingness to reinvest any of his share of the profits had slowed the growth of Classical Cars, preventing Melanie from taking advantage of opportunities on more occasions than she could count. But since she couldn't do anything about Jackson's attitude, she'd concentrated on the things that she could control.

Now that he was gone, however...things were certainly going to be different.

"Another possibility," he went on, "is that you wanted to buy his half yourself."

"Not especially."

"But the two of you must have talked about it, because you had a figure in mind."

"Lucky you," Melanie said dryly, "to get there first and beat me out."

"I could be persuaded to sell, you know."

"I just bet you could—Bub."

"Wyatt Reynolds," he said, almost absently. "In fact, I'd like to sell."

"No fooling. And I'm sure all you want out of the deal is a teeny-weeny little bit more than you paid."

"I am a businessman, Melanie."

"If you say so—though if you regularly go around buying things sight unseen, I have my doubts about your judgment. Of course," she conceded, "even a few thousand would be a tidy little profit, considering you've owned it for just about twelve hours. I wonder what the interest rate would add up to on that investment."

"Would you care to talk about a price?"

Melanie looked him over thoughtfully. "Only if you'd be willing to buy my half at the price you're asking for yours."

"No, thanks."

"That's what I thought." Something was nagging at the back of Melanie's mind. "Reynolds— Do you mean as in the Reynolds family?"

"That was my father's name, yes," he said dryly.

"You know perfectly well I'm talking about the Reynolds family that started off with a mill on the banks of the Missouri River, selling flour to pioneers heading west in covered wagons, and ended up with a wheat empire that stretched all the way across Kansas."

"You know your local history."

"Seriously? You're part of that family tree?"

"A twig," he admitted.

"A good-size twig if you can afford to go around buying things without paying any attention to what you're getting. So what's the problem? You thought you'd bought the whole business last night. Why not finish the job and buy my half now?"

"You seriously want to sell it?"

Melanie started to nod, and then paused. Did she want to sell out?

It wasn't as if it had been her childhood dream to be in the old-car business. It had just happened, almost accidentally. She'd taken the lemon that life had handed her and tried not to dwell on the fact that she'd never liked the taste of lemonade.

But now that the possibility of getting out of the business was actually dangling over her head, she was hesitating, and she didn't know why.

It wasn't because she loved her job—though she had

to admit she didn't hate it anymore, either. At first, she had had to square her shoulders and grit her teeth every morning, and push herself with physical labor through the day so she'd be tired enough to sleep at night. But as the months and then the years went by, a weed-infested old junkyard had morphed into a moderately-successful broker of classic cars. And somewhere along the line, Melanie must have changed, too, or she'd be leaping at the bait Wyatt Reynolds was dangling.

Was she hesitating because she'd gotten to like the challenges of being in business? Or because selling would be like saying a final farewell to her father...? No, she wouldn't think about that.

More likely, she thought, it was because habit and inertia suggested that staying in a job she'd grown used to was less risky than venturing out into the world to chase a wild dream. But if the price was good enough...

"How much are you offering?" she countered.

"I'm not."

Melanie was annoyed that she'd let herself consider the possibility, even briefly. There was nothing to be gained by yearning over aspirations which were long gone. "Then what's the point in having this conversation?" She glanced at the old-fashioned clock mounted high on the wall. "I have work to do, Wyatt. I'll see you in a month."

He frowned. "A month?"

"To settle up," she said impatiently. "Jackson and I have—had—a pretty straightforward agreement. Once a month, I pay the bills and write the employees' checks. Then I take whatever's left and split it, half to each owner. Since he just picked up his check last night, the next one's not due for thirty days."

Wyatt was looking at her as if she'd snatched his brand-new wad of bubble gum.

"I see he also didn't tell you that he'd already collected this month's dividend." Melanie shook her head, feigning sadness. "You really don't know Jackson as well as you thought, do you?" The phone rang again and she reached for it. "When you leave, close the door behind you, please."

It was past noon when Melanie came out of her office, looking for coffee and an aspirin. She had to squeeze past the jutting tail-fin of a red Cadillac, and she wondered how on earth Robbie had managed to maneuver the car into a showroom that was approximately six inches wider than the car itself was. She was mildly relieved that she hadn't been there to watch.

The coffeepot was gone. The machine was still there, but the carafe to hold the brewed coffee had disappeared.

She growled and headed for the shop to raid the first-aid kit and the soda machine. But when she opened the door between showroom and shop, the mingled scents of engine exhaust, motor oil, and pepperoni almost knocked her over.

Three bays down, Robbie's guys had spread pizza boxes across the hood of an old Nash and pulled up stools, ladders, and odd parts to serve as chairs. Robbie's guys—and Wyatt. He was sitting atop a barrel which had once held clean rags, pouring coffee from the missing carafe.

"What are you doing out here?" Melanie demanded.

"Having lunch," Wyatt said. "We'd have invited you, but you said you didn't want to be disturbed."

"You know perfectly well I'm not asking about the pizza. Why are you still here?"

"I'm getting acquainted with the employees. Finding out about the business. Waiting for your lawyer to call back and tell you that you can't throw me out or void Jackson's deal."

"How did you—" She stopped herself, but it took a mighty effort.

"So you did try," Wyatt said.

Melanie decided not to dignify that with a comment. "I said I'd see you next month."

"That may have been the agreement you had with Jackson, but I don't happen to be the silent partner type."

"I'm getting the picture."

Robbie cleared his throat. "Time to get back to work, guys."

"Oh, don't let me interrupt the male bonding process." Melanie opened the wall-mounted first-aid kit and tore open a packet of aspirin. "If you can spare a cup of coffee, though…"

Wyatt filled a paper cup and handed it to her.

Melanie stared doubtfully at the cup. "You're sure this is coffee? It looks like ink." She took a tentative sip and winced.

"If that's all you're having for lunch, no wonder you're so hard to deal with."

"I am not hard to deal—"

"Let's talk about it in private." Wyatt picked up one of the cardboard rounds from a pizza box and chose three slices from the various leftovers.

One of the guys whispered to another, "A buck says he talks her around."

Robbie glared at him. "No betting on the premises, Karl."

Melanie led the way back to the office. Scruff sat up

in his basket and begged, and Wyatt pulled a scrap of ground beef off the pizza and tossed it to him. He set the makeshift plate on her blotter and perched on the corner of the desk.

Melanie walked around behind it and claimed her chair. She'd better, she figured, or he'd have his name engraved in the back before sundown. "I'm amazed you're still here. Surely you have other interests which require your attention."

"Not today. Now that you've had some time to think about it, Melanie…"

"What's to think about? It appears I'm stuck with you." She sat down. "You're right about the attorney, by the way. He read me a lecture about not getting a partnership contract drawn up a long time ago, but since Jackson and I have never agreed to any specifics about how to split up the business, he's perfectly free to sell his half to the first chump who comes along. Sorry—I meant, he's free to sell it to anybody he chooses."

"Thank you for telling me that."

"Why?" Melanie asked dryly. "Because it saved you the trouble of paying your own lawyer?"

"You could have strung me along."

"Would it have done me any good to try?" She picked a piece of pepperoni off the pizza and munched it absently.

"None at all. But your being honest makes things a little easier. Look, Melanie, this is the way it shapes up. You don't want me as a partner, but you can't afford to buy me out."

"That's about the size of it. And you don't want *me* as a partner—"

"And I don't want to buy you out. Which leaves both of us in a pickle."

She fiddled with a strand of cheese. "Are you summarizing for the fun of wallowing in pain, or do you have a plan for what we can do about it?"

Wyatt looked down at her, his eyes almost hooded. "We look for another buyer—and sell the whole thing."

"Easier to say than to do. Have you got any idea how long Jackson's been trying to sell out? Besides, I never told you I wanted to sell."

"Not in so many words, no," he agreed. "And of course I can't force you to. But the alternative is that you keep your share and I look for a buyer for my half."

Melanie shrugged. "Go ahead. I don't see that I'd be any worse off."

"Are you certain of that? You just pointed out yourself that without a signed agreement on how to handle a breakup, there's nothing preventing me from selling it to the first—how did you put it? Oh, yes—the first chump who comes along."

Melanie shook her head. "Nobody's going to buy it unless they're interested in old cars. Well, it's true you did, but even you have to admit you're not the average guy running around acquiring businesses."

"I wondered if you'd think of that. Your next partner might actually be the hands-on type."

"And even more trouble to have around than you are? That's hard to believe." He was right, however, and Melanie knew it. She'd thought Jackson was the world's worst partner because he hadn't been involved in the business. Now she was feeling nostalgic for the good old days. "Anyway, your chump will need to have half a million dollars to spend, too. The combination cuts the field down quite remarkably, I'd say."

"I never told you what I paid for my share. And I never said what I'd sell it for."

Melanie bit her lip.

"If I don't find a buyer soon," Wyatt went on, "I might even cut my losses entirely and give my share to the state prison system."

She couldn't stop herself. *"What?"*

He shrugged. "It's a natural. Some of those guys are already experienced at stripping cars down for parts. Of course they'd have to get used to the idea of buying the cars first, but I feel sure that you—as their partner—could persuade them to adjust."

She shivered. Which was silly, of course—he was only goading her to make his point.

At least, she hoped that was all he was doing.

Suddenly the room seemed stifling. She pushed back her chair, and Scruffy sat up in his basket and whined softly, the way he always did when he needed to go out. *Good old Scruff comes through again.* "I'm going to go walk the dog," she said.

"Great," Wyatt said genially. "You think about it and let me know. I'll be right here, getting up to speed on the business end of things. Which file drawer do you keep your records in?"

The bottom line was better than Wyatt had expected, though of course it was nothing which would excite a tycoon. And the cash flow was respectable, though there were times when the checkbook reflected a bank balance so low it would have kept Rip van Winkle awake at night.

He wondered if Melanie tossed and turned sometimes, worried about the business. He was dead certain Jackson hadn't.

The books were neat and clear and precise. Every part she'd ever sold—to a walk-in customer or at auction on the Internet—was documented. Every car that she had handled had its own code and its own file. Every piece which had been added to it and every hour's work were annotated, and with a glance Wyatt could tell precisely how much each job had cost and how much it had brought in. She didn't make a lot on any given car, but as far as he could see, she'd had only a couple that had been unprofitable. And they'd been early on—she learned from her mistakes.

But she hadn't been stretching the truth when she'd said she couldn't afford to buy him out. The wonder was that she'd managed to keep going, and keep growing the business, even with Jackson pulling his share of the profits out month after month.

Wyatt found himself puzzling not over the books, but the bookkeeper. The records she kept looked like a labor of love. They were meticulous, painstakingly complete. Yet when he'd asked if she wanted to sell, Wyatt had thought for a minute that she was going to leap at the chance.

He slapped the ledger closed. It was none of his concern whether she wanted to sell or not. And it was even more certain that he didn't care why.

He figured there were only three things she could do: Be sensible enough to throw in with him and sell the whole thing. Or be halfway sensible and not get in his way while he sold his share. Or lose her mind entirely and try to sabotage the sale.

It would be interesting to see which way she jumped.

He put the books away, glanced at his Rolex, and went out to the showroom to get another cup of coffee. Where had Melanie disappeared to, anyway? Was she walking the dog all the way to Oklahoma?

He inched his way around the end of the Cadillac and

stopped dead. A woman was standing near the door to the parking lot, her back turned to the room as if she was uncertain whether to stay or leave. She was young, she was very blond, and she was dressed in the tightest black leather pants he'd ever seen.

We need a buzzer on that door, he thought.

The woman's head was tipped to one side as she surveyed the bulletin board between the entrance and the office. It was full of photos of twenty, thirty, and forty-year-old cars, tacked up almost at random, and she was looking at the board as if she didn't believe what she was seeing.

She glanced over her shoulder and said, "It's about time someone showed up."

Lucky me. "I beg your pardon, but I didn't hear you come in."

She turned around then, her eyes wide as she soaked in the sight of him. "Do you work here?" She sounded astonished.

Wyatt stifled a sigh. "Not exactly. But I'll try to help."

She smiled and tossed her long hair. "I was looking for Melanie Stafford—but believe me, you'll do nicely instead. I'm Erika Winchester." She held out her hand.

"Wyatt Reynolds. Melanie will be back soon. She's just out walking her mop. I mean, her dog."

"I see." Erika's eyes narrowed. "*The* Wyatt Reynolds?"

A movement outside the front window caught Wyatt's eye. "Here comes Melanie now. That's a piece of luck." *Especially for me.*

The door burst open and Melanie came in on a swirl of wind. Her hair had come down out of its bun and was curling exuberantly around her shoulders. Her cheeks were pink, as was the tip of her nose, and her eyes were bright. She bent to release the dog's leash. "I hope you're not going to tell me that the black Mercedes out front is now a part of the inventory, because—" She stood up, caught sight of the woman, and broke off. "Erika?" She sounded almost as if the name had been forced out of her.

With obvious reluctance, Erika took her gaze off Wyatt. "Hello, Melanie. It's been a long time."

"A while, yes. What brings you all the way out here?"

Erika wrinkled her nose. "Now that you mention it, you *are* rather in the sticks, aren't you? I had no idea there were still little twisty highways like this one anywhere near Kansas City."

"Oh, we have all sorts of hidden treasures on this side of town."

Erika's gaze drifted back to the bulletin board, and then slid on to the Cadillac. "Whatever happened to all of your plans? The alumni office told me you were in the used-car business, but I didn't realize they meant such *very* used cars."

The rest of Melanie's face went as pink as her wind-reddened cheeks. Wyatt couldn't help seeing it. Unfortunately, he noted, Erika hadn't missed it either. Her eyes widened just a little.

And they say women are the gentle sex. "It's more like recycling," Wyatt said gravely. "You see—"

Melanie wheeled around to face him. "Thanks, Wyatt. But I don't think we need an explanation right now."

I was only trying to help, he wanted to say. But it was fine with him if she didn't want a hand. She was probably right anyway. *Reynolds, you have got to stop letting your Don Quixote impulses get the best of you.*

"So what can I do for you, Erika? Obviously you're not shopping for a car, if you're driving that black Mercedes."

Erika laughed. "No, of course not. Actually I'm not at all sure..." She started over with determination in her tone. "I'm working with the girls in the sorority house this year. Their project is raising money for the victims of domestic violence, and they've set up a charity auction for next week."

"So you're asking for donations?"

"Yes. Merchandise, services, vacation packages—of course, I thought of you and I knew if there was any way you could help, you would. It is your old sorority too, after all, even if you were only there for a couple of years." She turned back to Wyatt. "Tell me, is Melanie still a grind like she was in college? Always with her nose in the books. Biology and chemistry and..." She shivered. "Of course the rest of us all appreciated her, because she singlehandedly pulled up the house grade point average."

Interesting, Wyatt thought.

Erika looked around again, and put a hand out tentatively to brush the fender of the Cadillac as if wondering whether it could be real. "Honestly, it feels like a time warp in here."

"Thank you," Melanie said gently. "That's what we try to do—make every car look and drive as well as when it was brand-new."

Erika looked puzzled, then she shook her head and smiled. "Right. Anyway, that's why we're asking for donations. Though I'm not quite sure if you have anything... Well, perhaps you'll think of an idea."

The mop, who'd been sniffing the Cadillac's tires, stiffened and growled.

"Sit," Wyatt ordered him.

To his surprise, the dog sat.

"Well, I can't exactly donate a car without consulting my partner," Melanie said. "Let us talk about it and I'll get back to you. If you leave a number when I can reach you, Erika—"

Erika turned to stare at Wyatt. "Partner? You're a partner in this operation? You've actually got money in it?" She smiled. "No wonder you said you didn't exactly work here. I'm sorry. I'm sure it's not what it looks like, since you're involved, Wyatt."

Wyatt said, "I'm sure we could do something, partner—since it's for such a good cause."

Melanie glared at him. "And what do you have in mind—*partner?*"

"How about the Model T the guys are working on?"

Melanie gasped. "That's sold. You can't just give it away."

"How about giving it away for an evening?"

"If a musty old rattletrap is the best you can do—" Erika turned up her nose.

"I mean the use of a genuine antique car, restored to perfection, for an evening. If not the Model T, then perhaps this Cadillac." He patted the fender.

"Are you out of your mind?" Melanie's voice was low and almost hoarse. "Loaning out a car? I don't even let people test-drive these things without someone riding along. You can't take the chance of putting this car into the hands of a hot-rodder. It'll do a hundred and thirty on a straightaway—"

Wyatt cut across her. "A *chauffeured* antique car for an evening. And we'll throw in…let's say…dinner at Felicity's."

Melanie was sputtering. Between the red hair and the

sparks she was putting off, she looked like a firecracker that was about to explode.

"We'll get back to you with the details, Erika," Wyatt said. "But in the meantime—you can count on us for dinner for two at Felicity's, with chauffeur service."

Erika smiled at him. "Make it a really nice car," she murmured, "and I'll bid on the package myself."

She drifted out, and a couple of minutes later the Mercedes spun gravel in the parking lot.

Wyatt leaned against the Cadillac's fender, folded his arms across his chest, and waited.

"Well, it's obvious those leather pants of hers got to you," Melanie said.

"What? Oh, come on. It's a good cause."

"Maybe. But dinner at Felicity's? I thought you were going to look over the books. Surely you realize there is no money anywhere in the budget for dinner at Felicity's."

"I'll toss it in as my contribution to the cause."

"But why?"

"Just think of the attention it'll get when one of our cars pulls up in front of Felicity's. It'll cause quite a buzz. In fact, we should make a point of regularly getting the cars off the lot and out where they can be seen."

"I do," Melanie said. "I drive a different one every day."

"Where?" he asked shrewdly. "Back and forth to work? To the grocery store and the dry cleaner's?"

He'd got her, and it was clear that she knew it. "Not the dry cleaner's," she admitted, "because if a piece of clothing isn't washable, I don't buy it. Fine—it's your idea, you take care of it. Just think hard about which car you choose. Since Erika doesn't seem to be enthusiastic

about vintage Cadillacs, you might try one of the
Corvettes. Be careful, though—the transmissions can be
tricky on those if you're not used to a stick shift.''

"Oh, I'm not going to be driving it.''

"I beg your pardon? I thought you understood I'm
not about to loan—''

"Since you're so sensitive about who gets behind the
wheel of your cars, and I'm the one who's providing
dinner—''

He saw the instant she realized she'd been conned.
"Oh, no.''

"Then it's only fair that you be the chauffeur,'' Wyatt
said gently. "As you said yourself, we're partners.
Right?''

CHAPTER THREE

HE'D boxed her in very neatly, Melanie had to admit. Though in a way she'd almost done it to herself, without much effort at all on Wyatt's part.

She'd had no intention of making a donation to Erika's cause, because she simply couldn't afford it. At least, she couldn't afford to give on the scale that Erika would find acceptable—and if Melanie offered anything less, Erika would probably have turned up her aristocratic little nose, refused, and then said something even more condescending than the remarks she'd already made. Melanie was still gritting her teeth over that crack about selling extremely-used cars.

Still, even if it had meant listening to Erika oozing false sympathy over Melanie's terrible financial condition, she should have just told the truth instead of dodging the question. Erika's fake pity would have lasted five minutes at the top end, and then she'd have stopped wasting her time with Melanie and moved on to the next potential donor.

But instead Melanie had made an excuse, and it was going to cost her dearly. *I have to consult my partner…*

She should have realized that acting as if Wyatt had a say in the matter would make him believe that he really did. Even so, she was still in shock at how he'd taken the idea and run with it—and then dragged her in, despite herself.

Chauffeuring someone around for a night on the town…what fun *that* was going to be. Especially if it

turned out to be Erika Winchester. Melanie wasn't going
to whine about it, though, because that would only encourage him.

"You know," she said thoughtfully, "this could be a
very interesting dilemma. If I'm driving, a Corvette
won't be big enough because it only holds two passen-
gers. However, Erika will want it to be just the two of
you. So that means the Corvette would be perfect after
all, except that you don't want to drive it, so we're back
to needing a seat for the chauffeur…. I've got it. I'll
teach you how to handle it, and then you and Erika can
have a cozy—"

Wyatt shook his head. "I'm not sure I want to take
driving lessons from someone who knows exactly how
fast that Cadillac will go on a straightaway."

"Actually," Melanie said thoughtfully, "I don't
know. Not firsthand."

"That's a relief. Who actually tried it out? Robbie, or
one of the other guys?"

"I mean that I don't know precisely how fast it'll go,
because I'm only guessing. The speedometer was buried
and the car was still accelerating when I saw the curve
coming and let off the gas."

"I hope you're going to tell me this was on a track
and not a regular road."

"If it will make you feel better, I can tell you anything
you want to hear."

Wyatt rolled his eyes.

"For heaven's sake, of course it was on a track. You
don't think I'm idiot enough to drive that fast on a public
highway, do you?"

"I don't think I should answer that," Wyatt murmured. "Anyway, let's worry about all the details when
the time comes. Erika may not be the top bidder."

"You can hope. I suspect she'll not only win, but she'll want to spend part of the evening parked in a lovers' lane. Come to think of it, maybe the Corvette isn't such a good idea after all."

"Bucket seats," Wyatt mused. "Gearshift. I see what you mean."

"Definitely the Cadillac has more potential as a love nest. In the meantime, I have work to do." She eyed the narrow space between the car and the wall. Wyatt was occupying a good deal of it, and she would have to squeeze past him to get to the office. It would be easier to go around the car and climb through the back seat— except that would mean figuring out how to get the door open wide enough to get in. How had Robbie gotten out, anyway, with the car's convertible top up?

"If you're going to be hanging around here all the time," she added dryly, "I can find something better for you to do than polish that fender with the seat of your trousers."

He pushed himself away from the car. "I was just thinking about making a promotional tour."

"Good idea." She tried to stand aside to let him pass, but there was nowhere to go. As he slid by her, she felt the brush of his tweed jacket against her breasts. He paused, and Melanie had to restrain herself from climbing onto the hood of the Cadillac to get away.

How utterly foolish that impulse was, she told herself, because there had been nothing sensual about the contact. It certainly wasn't as if the man was incapable of controlling his impulses if he got too close to her. In fact, he'd probably laugh at the very idea of being overwhelmed by Melanie's sex appeal—especially with the image of Erika's black leather pants fresh in his mind.

Furthermore, Melanie wasn't attracted to him any more than he was to her.

But when the door closed behind him, she didn't go into the office. Instead, she opened the shop door and told Robbie to get the Titanic-size Cadillac out of the showroom immediately and bring in a car which would actually fit, with room left to walk around.

She told herself she was only doing it to show the merchandise in a better light and make it easier for the customers to get a good look.

It had nothing to do with Wyatt. Nothing at all.

Closing time passed, and Melanie locked the door. But an hour later she was still standing at the narrow counter which held the coffee machine, clearing up the last of the day's orders.

It had been busy all afternoon. Bill Myers had come as promised to pick up the replacement door for his Mustang, but instead of going home to work on the car, he'd planted himself beside her desk to chat for half an hour. The owner of the Model T which was nearing completion back in the shop had come to her to complain that the new upholstery wasn't quite the color he'd had in mind, and Melanie had had to talk him out of doing the interior in flame orange. And back in the shop, Karl had cut himself on the edge of a rusty fender and had to have three stitches and a tetanus shot.

Only during her walk with Scruffy had Melanie had a chance to think at all, and then her mind had been going in circles because of Wyatt's plan to sell the whole business.

She'd never given the possibility much thought before. As long as Jackson's share was drawing no nibbles, there had been no point in even thinking of selling her own. But Wyatt's conviction was contagious. If he was right, and they really could sell out…

The farther she'd walked, the more colorful her dreams had become. If the price was high enough, she wouldn't have to get another job. She could go back to school and follow through on the plans she'd made so long ago—the plans she'd had to put on the shelf when her father died. If only the price was high enough…

Then she'd come back to the shop. She had stood at the edge of the highway just outside the fence and looked at the makeshift metal building with its peeling paint and awkward lean-to additions. She'd looked at the row of cars out front, in various stages of restoration and repair. She'd looked beyond them to the still-weedy back half of the lot. And the grandiose dreams had burst like an overinflated bubble.

It was easy to dream when she wasn't looking directly at the facts. But once she was back on the lot, facing reality, it was impossible to fool herself. She didn't even have to dig out the ledgers; she knew the numbers almost by heart.

While the business was profitable, it wasn't such a stunning success that it could command top dollar from a buyer. Besides, she asked herself bluntly, who was going to want it?

It wasn't the sort of business anyone would buy as an investment, because there were easier ways to make a buck. Restoring old cars required large doses of labor, individual attention, and devotion to detail—not exactly the road map to high profits. So what were the odds of finding someone who not only had the money to finance the purchase but was fascinated with old cars as well?

Then there was the question of what Wyatt would consider to be a good price. Melanie was sure he'd want

more than he'd paid—if he could get it. But how much
was that? And even before he'd looked at the books,
he'd as much as said that he wouldn't hesitate to cut his
losses if he had to. What kind of penalty would he be
willing to pay to get out of a bad situation?

It was an important question because the price he got
would determine her cut as well. But if the payoff wasn't
enough to fund her dream…

Then she would simply be trading this job for a different one. And if that was the case, she might as well
stay right where she was. She knew she could make this
work, because she'd done it for several years. And at
least here she was her own boss.

She pulled a strip of tape off the roll and was slapping
it onto a box when a key clicked in the door. Scruffy
growled, but as Wyatt came in the dog gave one sharp
yelp of greeting and bounced across the showroom toward him.

Melanie looked over the top of the little green roadster
which had taken the Cadillac's place. "You again? I
don't remember giving you a key."

"You didn't, Jackson did. Or perhaps I should say I
insisted on getting it from him. Surely you wouldn't prefer that I'd have let him keep it so he could collect those
tools at midnight when there's no one to stop him."

Melanie frowned. How had Wyatt known about the
tools? She was certain he hadn't come into the shop that
morning until after Jackson had made his stand. "Robbie
must have told you about that."

"No reason he shouldn't tell me. They're half mine
now. What are you doing?"

"Boxing up the radio from a 1964 Thunderbird to
ship to California."

"California? How did the customer know you had it?"

"Have you ever heard of advertising, Wyatt?" She relented. "There's a bulletin board on the Internet for car restorers. People post what they want, or list what they've got for sale."

"Isn't that the kind of thing you could use yourself?"

"Not anytime soon. And considering what they're paying for this, I can't afford to hang on to it on the chance of needing it sometime in the future."

"What about the car it came out of?"

"Not restorable. It looks as if it hit a tree head-on, bounced off, and rolled. The radio's about the only thing that still works."

Wyatt pulled a stool from under the narrow counter and perched on it. "What do you do with the leftovers? If nothing but the radio works—"

"There's a place that buys scrap steel to recycle. Not that we make anything on it, but at least we get rid of the clutter that way. Hold this." She thrust the radio at him and padded the bottom of the box with foam.

"I walked around the lot this afternoon. There must be three acres full of cars and pieces out there, just sitting in the open to be rained on."

"It's more like five acres. What do you expect, anyway?" She felt a little irritable. "It would take a building the size of a football field to put it all under a roof. Probably several of them."

"What's the matter with you? I was only saying that—"

"Look, Wyatt, if you're going to spend your time around here, you need to get realistic, all right? It would cost the earth to protect every single part from snow and rust and rodents."

"I know," he said quietly. "I wasn't questioning your management."

Melanie bit her lip. It wasn't like her to be jumpy like this, and judgmental. "Sorry. I shouldn't have snapped at you. I'd like to have it all sorted and neatly arranged, but it would cost way too much to be practical. The shelving alone…" She set the radio into the box and added padding around the sides. "Anyway, what are you doing here? I thought you'd disappeared for the day."

"No, you thought you'd driven me off with that threat to put me to work. I could ask you the same question, you know. What are *you* doing here? Do you work all the time?"

"The phone rings all day, and customers want attention. So this is the only time I can concentrate on orders like this."

"Hire somebody."

"With what? The payroll's stretched as far as it will go. Unless you want the title of shipping clerk."

"I'd rather be in charge of sales."

"You have to earn that one. Get a few deals under your belt and then—"

"I don't mean selling cars. I mean selling the business."

Melanie folded in the top flaps of the box. "Hand me the tape dispenser, will you?" She didn't look at him. "Do you really think someone will buy it?"

"I don't see why not. There's bound to be interest."

"No, I mean sell it for enough money to…" She stopped, suddenly unwilling to admit how important the answer might be to her.

The silence drew out. "What is it you want to do, Melanie?"

She bit her lip. "Nothing."

"Literally nothing? Oh, no. I don't believe that you want to retire and sit in a rocking chair. Not at your age."

Melanie didn't answer. She hadn't shared her dream with anyone for so long—hadn't even let herself think about it—that now it felt just short of silly even to hope that it was still possible. Wyatt would probably laugh at the idea, and Melanie wouldn't blame him. Erika had certainly been amused by the fact that Melanie had ended up selling cars—and she'd known a lot more about Melanie's long-ago plans than Wyatt did.

"No," she said finally, "I don't want to be a couch potato. But I don't want to have to take another job I don't like, either."

"Another one?" Wyatt said softly.

She wished she hadn't let that slip. And yet, what difference did it make? If he believed she was passionate about this job, then he'd gotten the idea from someone besides her.

"How did you get stuck here, Melanie?"

"I thought I told you." The tape shrieked as she pulled a strip off the dispenser. "My father died, and someone had to take over."

"You didn't have any brothers who liked to tinker with engines?"

"No—there was just my mother and me. She died last year." She took a long breath and let it out. "So what's the plan for selling? I assume you have one?"

"We clean the place up while we're looking for a buyer."

She sighed. He wasn't saying anything she didn't already know. The entire yard looked tired and neglected—not exactly the way to a buyer's heart. But there were always a half-dozen places to spend each penny, and painting the trim on the building was well down the list.

"And beef up the business," Wyatt went on, "which means promoting."

"Wait a minute. If you have some big advertising campaign in mind—"

"As a matter of fact, I do—but not the kind that costs money. Erika gave me the idea."

"That would probably disappoint her," Melanie said under her breath.

"What do you mean?"

"Just that she'd rather have you thinking about her than about advertising."

Wyatt looked faintly interested. "You know, that's the second time you've warned me about Erika."

"And the last. A word to the wise, you know."

"Was she the kind who stole boyfriends in college?"

"Not from me."

Wyatt nodded thoughtfully.

Thanks for the tactful silence. But he might as well have come right out and said that Melanie couldn't possibly attract the kind of man Erika would be interested in. From the look on his face, it was absolutely clear to Melanie what he was thinking.

With a thump, she set the box atop the stack she'd already finished. She'd like to park it on his head.

"The charity auction idea caught my attention," Wyatt said. "Loaning a car for the evening is low-cost, and it potentially carries a big return."

"Or it might turn out to be a zero."

"Yes," he admitted. "But if nothing comes of it, we're only out a little time. So I was thinking, why stop there? If we get the cars out where they can be seen by the right people, we'll probably sell a few cars—but more importantly, we may also catch the attention of someone who wants the whole shooting match.''

Melanie shrugged. ''We don't have anything to lose by trying it, I guess. A tank of gas will go a long way.''

''And while we're doing that sort of promotion, we can be whipping this place into shape. Do we have to drop those boxes off somewhere?''

''No, the courier will pick them up tomorrow when he makes his regular deliveries.''

''Good. Because I think we should begin right now.''

''You mean tonight?''

''There's a new club opening up on the north side, and this week is their grand opening.''

Melanie stifled a yawn. ''Have a good time. There's a board full of keys by the back door. They're tagged so you know which car is—''

''Remember? I don't drive antiques.''

''Then you have a problem, because I didn't sign on to be your chauffeur.''

''How about being my companion? It's very dull going to a club alone.''

''Poor baby.'' She told herself it was silly to feel butterflies. The invitation had been issued only because she was convenient and handy, and it was about as far from being a date as she could imagine.

But of course the fluttering in her tummy definitely wasn't anticipation. It might be irritation. Aggravation. Maybe dread. But it certainly wasn't anything pleasant.

''I'd probably go to sleep during the first number,'' she muttered.

''Not at The Canteen Club. I hear it's the hottest place in town right now. Nostalgia's big, you know, and it's got some kind of big-band theme. Besides, you can start giving me driving lessons on the way.''

"I thought you'd given up the idea of a Corvette for your date with Erika."

"We need a backup plan, just in case we sell the Cadillac by then. I need you, Melanie."

The butterflies fluttered more strongly.

Wyatt said earnestly, "Because if anybody asks questions about the car, I wouldn't be able to answer them."

Well, that's a relief. I'd hate to think it was some personal need. "Oh, if that's the job you've assigned me," she said dryly, "I've got a better idea. I'll give you Robbie's phone number and you can take him instead."

Melanie hadn't seen him smile before—not a real smile—and she wasn't prepared. Wyatt's eyes crinkled just a little at the corners, and their silvery gleam warmed till it was like melted steel. There was a dimple at the corner of his mouth that made her want to reach out and touch it to be certain it was real. The overall effect was like focusing a bank of footlights on an ice cube, and almost instantly she found herself feeling a little warm and soft around the edges.

"I'm not dressed to go out," she said. But it was a feeble protest and she knew it.

"It's a casual club."

"What about the dog?"

"What do you usually do with him when you run errands? He can guard the car. Who knows, maybe we'll kick off a new fashion and people will want not only a classic car but a mop to match. We may even start a run on the animal pound. Come on, it'll be fun."

Melanie wasn't so sure of that, but she was dead certain he wasn't going to give up, so she whistled for Scruffy and went to get her jacket.

She looked carefully over the board full of keys and

offered Wyatt the one she finally selected. "Red Corvette, black interior. We haven't restored it yet, but it looks pretty good compared to most cars when we first start on them."

Wyatt shook his head and said solemnly that he felt he should observe for a while before he got behind the wheel of such a valuable piece of equipment.

Melanie shook her head in confusion. "I thought you didn't trust my driving because I raced the Cadillac."

He stopped halfway out the door. "You were *racing?* Not just running it on a track?"

"What's the point of driving that fast if you're not competing?"

"Hand over the key, Melanie."

"Wait a minute. What kind of a club did you say this is?"

"Nostalgia. Big band era."

"And it's called The Canteen Club? You mean like a world war soldiers' canteen?" She hung the key back on the board. "Then the Corvette would be anachronistic—what on earth was I thinking? We'll drive a 1940 Ford. A two-door with a flat-head V-8 engine."

Wyatt took a long breath.

"Relax, Wyatt. I didn't wreck the Caddy at a hundred and thirty, and I'm not going to tank the Ford either."

"That's a relief. I hadn't even thought to ask whether that little episode was the reason you had to rebuild the Cadillac."

"And the Ford won't do anything near that speed, anyway." She led the way across the yard. "Probably not over a hundred, in fact. Let's find out."

In the moonlight, she couldn't tell for certain whether Wyatt actually turned pale, but she felt a little better.

It was late enough that the freeway traffic was light,

but the Ford—chugging along precisely at the speed limit—got plenty of attention from the few other drivers on the road. A couple of them honked and waved, and a carload of teenage boys whistled.

Melanie waved back. "Maybe we should just drive around till midnight," she said hopefully. "More people will see the car that way than if it's parked in a lot somewhere."

"But you have to keep the audience in mind. Better one serious buyer than an entire busload of kids with no money."

"I suppose you're right. Wyatt... What about my guys?"

"You mean Robbie and the crew?"

"Yeah. What if they don't like the new owner? Or what if he lays them off?"

"If he's smart, he'll keep them."

"But what if he doesn't? Robbie's got a wife and a baby who's not a year old yet."

"Melanie, if you start putting conditions on a sale—"

"I know. Nobody wants to be told how to run their own business, and if they're paying for it, it's theirs." She sighed. "But I don't want my guys to be worried. There's no point in upsetting them about their jobs if nothing's likely to come of it."

"Now that's a defeatist attitude. You're assuming that no one will want to buy the business."

"That's not what I'm saying at all. You bought it, after all. I just want to wait to tell them till we know something definite."

Wyatt was frowning a little. "All right," he said finally. "If you feel that strongly about it, we don't have to tell them it's for sale till we know more. Here's the turn. The nightclub is that warehouse up ahead."

The building he pointed out didn't look like a night-club to Melanie. The building was big and mostly dark, though a couple of spotlights played back and forth across the facade, flickering on a sign which read The Canteen Club. The street was almost empty.

"I see there's no shortage of places to park," she muttered.

"The valet stand is right in front."

"Great. The parking valet will get a good look, but nobody else will. I told you we should stay on the free-way."

Wyatt smiled a little. "Are you always this grumpy late at night?"

"I'm fine. But now that you mention it, it *is* past Scruffy's bedtime."

"Then I'll definitely have to make it up to Scruffy." As soon as the car stopped, Wyatt got out and beckoned to the valet, who'd started around to Melanie's side of the car. She didn't hear their low-voiced conversation, but she couldn't miss the smooth movement of a couple of pieces of paper from Wyatt's hand to the valet's. Then the young man came around the car, opened Melanie's door, helped her out, and slid reverently behind the wheel. As she watched, the car backed up a few yards and turned slightly, and the engine died.

She took a step forward. "What happened?"

"He turned it off, Melanie."

"But that's a no-parking zone."

"Not tonight." Wyatt took her arm. "And everybody who comes in and out will see it sitting there."

Melanie hung back. "Are you sure you don't want to paint a sign on the windshield?"

"*'Buy me at Bub and Mel's Used Cars'?* How perfectly crass."

"But what good will it do for people to see it if they don't know it's for sale?"

"The valet will take care of that. Trust me."

"How much did you pay him?"

"Enough," Wyatt murmured. "Now let's go have some fun and let the car work for a change."

CHAPTER FOUR

IT WASN'T the first time Melanie had encountered a door-man wearing a military-looking uniform, but she was startled to be greeted by a snappy salute—and when Wyatt returned it, she felt her eyes widen in surprise.

"Automatic reaction," he said, and tucked her hand into the bend of his arm. "I spent some time in military school when I was a kid."

She said sweetly, "I see. Was that where you acquired this tendency to order people around, or did you already have it before you went?"

"Actually," Wyatt said. "I got sent off to school because I'd pulled so many stunts no place else would take me."

He sounded perfectly serious, but there was a twinkle in his eyes. Melanie just wasn't sure whether it was because he was pulling her leg or fondly remembering his past.

There was a line of patrons in the lobby, waiting to be seated. Melanie peered around the large woman standing in front of them to get a first look at the decor. She couldn't see much except the maître d'. He wore a general's stars, and he was acting the part as well. Rather than seating people himself, he summoned assistants who were dressed in army green uniforms and matching caps, and barked out table numbers.

The system was efficient, Melanie had to admit—the line was moving along smoothly. They had nearly reached the general when a man came in from the street and strode past the waiting crowd to the maître d's stand, ignoring grumbles from the patrons he had bypassed. His suit was cut with wide, padded shoulders and broad lapels, and he hadn't bothered to remove his snappy fedora when he came inside.

"George, there's a car parked out front," he said.

The general's air of authority slipped as if he'd just been addressed by the commander in chief. "Yes, sir. I'll have it towed immediately. And I'll find out which parking valet slipped up and fire him."

Melanie's fingers tightened on Wyatt's sleeve. "I told you we should have stayed on the freeway," she whispered. "Now you've cost that poor guy his job."

He patted her hand and drew her out of the line and toward the general.

The woman in front of them sniffed disdainfully as they passed. "Some people have no manners," she said loudly.

"So true, ma'am," Wyatt told her. "I've often despaired about that fact myself... Hello, Brad. Is the car a problem?"

The man in the fedora swung around. "Reynolds— good to see you. You mean that's *your* car out there stealing attention from my club? I thought you only drove Baritsas."

"That's true," Wyatt said. "Let me introduce you to the driver."

Great, Wyatt. Shift the blame onto me.

"Melanie, this is Brad Edwards. Brad—"

Melanie didn't wait for him to finish. She pulled the Ford's key from her jeans pocket and dangled it under his nose. "Mr. Edwards, I'll move the car right away. Please don't fire the parking valet. It wasn't his fault—"

"No, no," Brad Edwards said. "It's your car? Is it real?"

"—that Wyatt talked him into letting us park in..."

Wyatt's elbow bumped her rib cage, hard.

Melanie paused, distracted. "Did you ask if it was real? Of course it's—"

"Not some kind of faked-up replica?"

She bristled just a little. "No, it's the genuine article."

"And I bet she's got the paperwork to prove it," Wyatt said. "Why, Brad? Are you trying to buy it?"

"If the price is right," Brad said, "I might think about it. George, these people will be at my table." He swung around toward the main room without looking to see whether they were following.

"Better hold off on calling for a tow truck, George," Wyatt murmured. "The boss wouldn't like it if you hauled his car away." He tugged Melanie toward the door.

"Do you often have arm spasms like that?" Melanie muttered. "I'm going to have bruises where you hit me."

"*Nudged* you. Come on."

She couldn't help stopping in the entrance to take a closer look, however. The room looked like a cross between a ballroom and a YMCA. Along one side was a long counter which seemed to be part soda fountain, part bar. Opposite it was a huge stage, where a singer in blue taffeta was belting out a love song, backed by a big band that sounded heavy on the brass. Tables, nearly all of them full, surrounded the dance floor where a man in seaman's white was dancing with a woman in a sparkly pink gown.

"I am definitely underdressed," Melanie muttered.

Brad Edwards led the way to the last empty table near the bandstand, directly off the dance floor.

Wyatt followed her gaze to the dancers. "If you're talking about the admiral and his date, I'd bet they're part of the hired help."

Brad held Melanie's chair and grinned. "I don't usually admit it, but you're right, Reynolds. Their job is to provide a little encouragement to the regular folks to dance."

Melanie watched as the admiral and his partner executed a complicated spin. "*Very* little encouragement," she said. "If that's the expertise level you expect of your guests, I'll be sitting it out."

"While you're talking about a car," Wyatt reminded gently.

"How much do you want for it?" Brad asked.

Melanie drew a breath to tell him.

Wyatt stepped on her foot. "Let her think about it, Brad. Can she call you tomorrow, or do you want to call her?"

Melanie was exasperated. "Wyatt, I—"

"Sweetheart." His voice was like a caress. "You know how much that car means to you."

Yeah, she thought. *It represents a nice chunk of change—if we can shake hands on a deal before you mess it up.*

But before she could argue the point, Brad Edwards was pushing his chair back. He handed her a business card. "You can call me at this number tomorrow. And feel free to use the table the rest of the evening—I'll be circulating and greeting guests." He waved a uniformed waiter over and said, "Get these people what they want, Private."

The waiter pulled an order pad and pencil from his sock.

Melanie blinked in surprise.

He grinned. "It looks odd, I know, but it's the boss's orders—putting anything in the pockets ruins the lines of the uniform, and aprons just don't fit the image. What can I bring you?"

"I really don't— Oh, a white wine spritzer."

Wyatt ordered a scotch and soda.

Melanie held her tongue until the waiter was safely away from the table. "Thanks for killing the best opportunity I'll ever have to sell that car. Do you have any idea how long it's been sitting on the lot?"

"Since 1940?"

"I thought you wanted to promote the business."

"Melanie, you may know cars, but you don't know Brad Edwards. The longer he's denied something the more he wants it."

"Oh." She had to give him the point, because he obviously knew Brad better than she did.

"Besides, once he's had a chance to think over the idea, you may be able to sell him a package," Wyatt went on. "Maybe half a dozen cars. He could use them to ferry people around—provide a shuttle service for visitors who flew into town and don't have a car, or people who've had one too many drinks and need to be taken home."

"Nobody would put a drunk into an antique car. It would be too hard to clean the upholstery if he got sick, and too expensive to replace it."

"A vintage Jeep," Wyatt murmured. "No top, no windows. The passenger could just lean over the side."

"And they'd need to, because there's also no suspension and no springs. Have you ever ridden in one of those things?''

''I'd rather spend another year at military school.''

Melanie wasn't listening. ''What he really needs is a staff car.''

The private returned with their drinks.

Wyatt raised his glass and swirled his scotch and soda. ''Cheers. What do you mean, a staff car?''

''The kind that generals used, with a glassed-off compartment for the driver—separate from the back seat so the officers could discuss strategy without the driver hearing. Some of them were pretty plush.''

''Do you have one?''

''No—but I can start looking. Of course, a lot of them are in museums. Now that we've accomplished what we came for—''

''You mean by getting Brad interested? Why settle for one potential buyer when you could have several? Maybe you'll end up with a bidding war.''

She was watching the entrance. ''The place seems to be full, and I haven't seen anyone leaving.''

''We'll have to stay till the evening winds down and people start going home, to give them a chance to see the car. Let's order dinner. I promised the mop I'd make it worth his while to wait for us, so if I walk out without a doggie bag, he'll probably bite me.''

Melanie hadn't felt hungry until that moment, but she realized abruptly that she was famished. ''Scruffy growls now and then, but he's too well-trained to bite anyone.''

''I'll take your word for it.'' He waved the waiter over and asked for menus.

Melanie took one look and said, ''I have no idea what to order. There are no prices.''

"The general principle is that you order whatever you want to eat."

"And damn the expense? That's nice if you can afford it, but some of us are on a budget. And since I didn't get to the bank today to cash my paycheck—"

"Melanie, I'll buy your dinner. Have a T-bone steak and make the mop happy—that way he'll have two bones to chew on."

"I'll pay you back." She put the menu down, and he ordered for her.

"Let's dance," Wyatt said.

"I don't think so."

"Because you're not as good as the admiral?"

Because I don't want to forget that this isn't a date.

"Look at it this way," Wyatt said. "With the spot-lights glaring off that white uniform, it's impossible to see what anybody else is doing on the dance floor. Polka, fox-trot, waltz, twist—it wouldn't make any difference what you did, because nobody would notice."

"I'll have to take your word for that, since the only one of those I can do is waltz. And I'm lousy at that."

"Come on. Give it a try." He pushed his chair back.

Reluctantly, Melanie stood up.

From the corner of her eye, she saw a young blond woman in a strapless red cocktail dress jump up from a nearby table and flounce toward them in as direct a path as was possible between the close-set tables. She side-stepped Melanie without a glance, raised her hand, and slapped Wyatt across the cheek.

To Melanie, the crack of the young woman's palm against his face cut across music and conversation alike, and she was surprised when the room didn't settle into a stunned silence. But apart from a few people at nearby tables, no one seemed to have noticed.

She stole a glance up at Wyatt, expecting him to show embarrassment, maybe even shame. But his face was perfectly calm. To Melanie's astonishment, he didn't even look surprised.

She doubted that he was accustomed to being slugged in public. But obviously he knew the blonde, so perhaps he'd anticipated that she might react violently when she saw him with another woman—no matter how innocent the occasion.

That must be it. He wasn't surprised, because he'd known how the blonde was likely to respond. And he wasn't embarrassed or shameful, because he'd done nothing wrong.

I wonder what she'd have done if this had really been a date.

He guided Melanie onto the dance floor. Figuring there had already been enough of a scene that a simple dance couldn't possibly make it worse, she didn't resist. She took a minute to catch the rhythm of the music, and then she said as casually as she could, "Your wife, I presume?"

"Good lord, no." He sounded as if she'd knocked the breath out of him.

"Fiancée?"

"You're joking, right?"

"Not at all. *Former* fiancée?"

"Not even close. I thought you would recognize her."

Melanie ran through her mental catalog of friends, acquaintances, and celebrities. To the best of her recollection, the blonde didn't fit into any of those categories. "Should I have?"

Wyatt frowned. "I'd have thought so. That's Jennifer."

"Jennifer...." She was lost. "Jennifer.... You mean, Jackson's Jennifer?"

"That's the one. I wondered if she'd calmed down yet. Apparently not. You've been keeping a secret, Melanie."

Me? she thought in astonishment. *What about you?*

He swirled her around the floor and smiled down at her. "Lousy dancer, indeed. You're actually very good at waltzing."

By closing time, Wyatt was beginning to wish he'd put money into Brad Edwards's idea, because not only did The Canteen Club pack in the customers but it kept them there. Finally, however, the inevitable exodus began, and Wyatt said, "Are you ready to go?"

Melanie's eyes lighted up. "I've been ready for hours. I mean—" She hesitated and bit her lip. "Well, it's not like we were intending to have fun."

"It's all right," Wyatt said dryly. "Next time I'll try to find a form of entertainment that's more to your taste."

"Next time? If you're planning to make a habit of this, I'm not sure I can keep up." She tried, without much success, to stifle a yawn.

The air outside was crisp and cold, but despite a brisk wind, the Ford was surrounded by admirers. Inside, the mop quivered with indignation each time someone violated his personal space by touching the car. Wyatt opened the car door carefully so the dog couldn't get out, but Scruffy didn't even try. Instead he sniffed, whined, and retreated into the back seat.

"I told you he was well-trained," Melanie said. "He won't get out unless he's called."

"Care to bet? I expect it's the doggie bag he's feeling loyal to, not the rules."

"I don't bet," Melanie said.

The crowd began drifting away, except for a few diehards. Melanie answered questions and passed out business cards, but he thought she was starting to droop.

Finally Wyatt intervened. "Time to go. I'll drive."

"I thought you didn't drive antiques." But she was yawning, so the words weren't quite distinct.

By the time they got back to the yard, Melanie's eyes were closed and Scruffy had curled up in the back seat with his paws on the doggie bag.

Wyatt hated to wake her, but there was no alternative. "Melanie, do you want me to drop you somewhere?"

She said something indistinct.

"You're too nearly asleep to drive. I'll take you home if you can tell me how to get there."

She didn't answer.

He could hardly take her home when he didn't know where she lived. Maybe, he thought, the blast of chilly air when he got out of the car would wake her up enough to knock some sense into her. He pulled off the highway into the lot, parked the Ford, and opened the door. Cold wind swirled in.

Melanie's eyes snapped open and she sat up, shaking her head as if to clear it. "Thank you for dinner and everything. It wasn't a bad evening after all."

"I'm glad you enjoyed it," he said wryly. "I'll take you on home if you like. Just tell me where."

"No—I'll need a car in the morning anyway." She slid across the seat till she was behind the wheel and put the car into gear.

"I'll see you later, then," Wyatt said.

As the Ford pulled away, he crossed the lot to where

he'd left his car and flicked the remote to unlock the doors.

It wasn't a bad evening after all.

Well, he supposed there were worse verdicts. As far as that was concerned, if he were pressed, Wyatt would have to say much the same thing himself—the evening had turned out to be more pleasant than he'd expected. Melanie Stafford might be in the running to be named most disastrously honest woman of the year, but at least there wasn't a dull moment when she was around. On the other hand, she'd remained perfectly calm when Jennifer had made her grandstand gesture—which was more than he would have expected of most of the women he knew.

And on the dance floor, she'd been limber, yielding, graceful, seeming to anticipate his every move. *She dances like a lover...*

He caught himself just a little too late to bar from his mind the image of Melanie's lithe body wrapped around him—but not on a dance floor.

What was the matter with him? He'd known her less than twenty-four hours, and for two-thirds of that time he'd been ready to hire a hot-air balloon for the sheer pleasure of ascending to ten thousand feet and dumping her over the side. But for the other third of the day...

Go home, Reynolds. Maybe you'll wake up in the morning and discover it was all a nightmare.

He tried to start his car's engine, but nothing happened except a rapid clicking—the characteristic sound of a dead battery giving its feeble last effort. The trickle which it had put forth to unlock the doors seemed to be the last bit of strength it had possessed.

All that concern about whether she could get herself

home, he thought, *but she's safely tucked in and here you sit—stranded.*

He had raised the hood and was tinkering with the battery cables when the Ford drew up beside him and the driver's side window lowered. "That's always the problem with new cars," Melanie said sympathetically. "You're never prepared for it when something goes wrong."

Melanie didn't know what made her turn around two blocks from the yard and go back. She told herself it was a foolish impulse, that Wyatt would be long gone. Yet something was telling her to check, and she knew if she didn't follow her instincts, she wouldn't be able to sleep no matter how tired she was.

And sure enough, the car was still sitting there, with Wyatt leaning over the engine. She paused for a moment to admire the view of him from behind before letting the Ford creep up beside him so she could make a smart remark.

Wyatt didn't seem amused. "It's just the battery."

"Did you check the cables?"

"That's the first thing I looked at. There's no need for you to stick around."

"Hey, don't get grouchy with me. Just because you don't know what you're doing—"

"I'm not grouchy, and I do know what I'm doing."

"Guys are always grouchy when a woman comes along to rescue them."

"You don't have to rescue me. I'll call the motor club for a jump start."

"That's exactly what I mean. It's the middle of the night. You'll get the answering service, and it could be an hour before they wake somebody up and get them out here. And then, unless you drive around enough to recharge the battery, it'll likely be dead again in the morning. Let's run a drop cord out and put the charger on it, and you can take your choice of cars to get home.''

"I don't want to leave my car sitting out here with the hood open. If somebody doesn't steal the engine, they'll at least take the drop cord and the battery charger.''

"Well, I'm not helping you push it around the back of the building. So just let it sit till morning, and go grab another car.''

"I have a funny feeling about driving an antique vehicle across Kansas City at this hour of the night with nothing to prove that I actually own half of it.''

"Why?'' Melanie asked shrewdly. "Was it stealing a car that got you the stretch at military school? Never mind. I'll write you a note if it'll make you feel better.''

"All right, you want the truth? I don't feel like struggling with another unfamiliar car at this hour.''

"Fine. You drove the Ford here, you can drive it home.''

"Then you'd have to wake up the mop and get into a cold car yourself.''

"It wouldn't be the first time.''

"I could drop you off,'' Wyatt offered.

"I told you already—I need a car in the morning and I hate waiting around for a ride. Get in, and I'll take you home.''

He didn't move. "I live south of downtown, Melanie.'' There was a note of warning in his voice.

South of downtown Kansas City. That meant half an hour's drive each way, at least. *Me and my big mouth.* Melanie sighed. A deal was a deal. "I said I'd take you, so I'll take you.''

"I'll call a cab."

"That will take just about as long as the motor club—
if they find the place at all. You can't just sit here in the
cold in the meantime."

"I'll go inside."

"Look, keep arguing and it'll be dawn before you get
anything done."

In the back seat, Scruffy lifted his nose off the doggie
bag and whined softly.

"The mop wants to go home, Melanie."

"So do I. All right, you can crash at my place till
morning."

Wyatt's eyebrows lifted. "Are you sure I won't be a
nuisance?"

She smiled. "You want the truth? You'll be a lot less
of a nuisance there than if I have to drive you home. In
the morning, the guys can tow the Baritsa in and work
it over."

He didn't even flinch at the idea of turning Robbie
and his crew loose on a new Baritsa. He must be starting
to adjust, Melanie thought, and felt a tinge of regret—it
wasn't going to be nearly as much fun to tease him now.

Wyatt walked around the Ford and got in. "Your guys
work on Saturdays?"

"Half a day, at least. That's when the hobbyists come
in for their parts."

Her bungalow was only a couple of miles away. As
she pulled into the driveway, Scruffy sat up in the back
seat and sighed as if in relief.

In the fading moonlight, the bungalow looked a little
forlorn. There hadn't been time yet, or a pleasant enough
day, for her to clean up winter's leftovers. Leaves had
blown up against the foundation and tangled in the
shrubs near the front door, and stubble from last au-

tumn's chrysanthemums lined the flower beds by the driveway. Though Melanie noticed the debris every time she came home, tonight it seemed more untidy than usual. But perhaps that was only because of the long shadows.

"I didn't expect you to have a house," Wyatt said.

"I debated whether to sell it, after Mother died. It's a lot of upkeep—the flowers, especially. And now that there's just me, it's a bit big. But it's hard to find an apartment that will take the pets."

"You've got more than just the mop?"

"My mother had a couple of cats." She unlocked the front door, and two Siamese looked up from the seat of a deeply-cushioned chair. One yawned, the other closed his big blue eyes and snuggled deeper into the upholstery.

"There's an extra bedroom," she said. "Just let me run up and put sheets on—"

"Don't be ridiculous. Go to bed, Melanie. I'll just crash on the couch."

"You'll probably have cats all over you, and a dog crunching a bone at your feet."

"At least I won't feel lonely."

She started up the stairs. It felt odd, not being alone in her house. In the year since her mother died, she hadn't had an overnight guest.

Of course, she thought, it would have felt even more odd if he'd been coming upstairs with her...odd, and awkward.

It was sensitive of him to realize that and sidestep the problem. Unless it wasn't her feelings he was watching out for, but his own safety.

Sure, she mocked herself. *He probably thinks you're trying to lure him upstairs to your bedroom!*

* * *

The morning was so gray and gloomy that the cats didn't bother to wake up when Wyatt let the mop out into the fenced backyard. He found the makings for a pot of coffee, waited for it to brew, let the mop back in, drank a cup, but still there was no hint of movement from the second floor. It was almost nine, and Melanie had apparently not stirred.

Finally he got a second mug from the cabinet, filled it, and climbed the stairs.

It was utterly stupid, he told himself, to feel like a burglar. Just because he was exploring an unfamiliar house, one he hadn't been invited to roam through, it didn't mean he was doing anything wrong. She might be sick up there. Helpless.

There were half a dozen doors opening off the small hallway at the top of the stairs, and all of them were closed. Wyatt knocked on the first one, waited, and opened it a crack to discover a linen closet. Then he realized that the mop had followed him upstairs and was waiting expectantly at the far side of the hall, beside a door that looked just like all the others.

Wyatt was just reaching out to tap a knuckle against the wood when the dog reared up and nudged the doorknob with his nose. The door swung open as Wyatt touched it. The dog romped in, and Wyatt heard a muffled, wordless groan from the bed.

All he could see was a long, formless figure buried under the blankets. The curtains were closed and the room was dim except for a night-light in the shape of a seashell, low on the wall beside the bed. "Melanie?"

The cats had been asleep downstairs when he'd poured the coffee, but they must have joined the procession while he'd been knocking on the linen closet—

trying in vain to wake the sheets and towels. One of the Siamese hissed and darted under his raised foot; the other zoomed across the room, ruffling up a rug.

Wyatt tried to keep from stepping on the cat's tail, caught his toe on the rug, and started a forward flip that was abruptly interrupted when his elbows hit the edge of the bed. The coffee mug stayed firmly gripped in his hand, but the contents soared in an airborne puddle, hovered, and descended.

Melanie shot up from the blankets.

His eyes were quickly adjusting to the dim light, so he could see coffee dripping from her hair, beading on her eyelashes, and forming an irregular pattern like spattered brown paint across the front of her white pajamas. She took a deep breath.

Now you're in for it, Reynolds. The coffee might not have been hot enough to burn, but I bet her tongue will leave blisters.

"Thanks," she said. Her voice was still sleep-roughened. It was very low, very raspy, very sexy. "You've given me exactly what I wanted this morning, Wyatt—coffee and a hot shower. How efficient of you to combine them."

CHAPTER FIVE

HE STARTED to apologize—or perhaps, Melanie thought, he was trying to explain. She used the corner of the sheet to wipe her eyes. "This should be quite some story, and I'll be happy to listen to it—as soon as I'm not dripping coffee. I'd especially like to know how you ended up without a drop on you while I must look like I'm entered in a wet T-shirt contest."

His gaze dropped to her coffee-spattered pajama jacket, and he shook his head. "Not wet. Just damp." He sounded almost disappointed.

"Then next time you'll have to remember to use a larger mug." Her voice grew a little sharper. "If you don't mind getting out of my bed, Wyatt—"

"Oh. Sure. I'll be downstairs."

The pressure of his elbows as he pushed himself up off the bed rocked the mattress a little. It was utterly silly, Melanie told herself, to feel just a tiny bit seasick at the sensation.

As soon as he was gone, she climbed out of the soggy bed. She stripped off the sheets, intending to start the washing machine before she left for work. But when she came back from her shower and for the first time noticed the clock on her bedside table, the bundle of sheets was forgotten.

How could she have slept so long? She never over-slept—not even when she'd been up late, not even when the morning was gloomy enough that it looked as if dawn hadn't yet broken.

She thundered down the stairs and into the kitchen. "What's the matter with you? Why didn't you tell me what time it is?"

"That's what I was attempting to do when the cats got in the way," Wyatt said. "What did you think I was up to? Trying to seduce you with breakfast in bed?"

That's one in the eye for you, Stafford, Melanie thought. *Seduction would be the last thing on his mind.*

"I figured, considering the rate you drink coffee at work, you'd be less likely to kill the messenger if I was carrying caffeine. But things went a little wrong." He handed her a mug. "Be careful with this one, it's fresh— and hotter."

The liquid in the mug was steaming. "Do I need to remind you that I'm not the one who spilled the last cup?"

"Maybe we should just start over." Wyatt's voice was mild. "Good morning, Melanie. I hope you slept well."

"Just fine," she muttered. "Come on, let's go."

"I thought you said the shop's only open a half day on Saturday."

"Yes, but we aim for it to be the *first* half of the day." She swallowed her coffee and set the mug aside.

They weren't simply late. They were so late, compared to Melanie's normal starting time, that the shop crew should have been at work long since. But she had forgotten about the Baritsa, parked smack in the middle of the lot where Robbie and the guys couldn't have helped noticing it and wondering why it was there.

The Baritsa was the first thing that caught her eye when she turned off the highway, but the second thing she saw was a row of faces pressed to the glass overlooking the parking lot.

By the time she parked the car, the faces had disappeared from the window, and when they walked into the showroom Robbie was pouring himself a cup of coffee, one of his guys was straightening up the pictures on the bulletin board—an occupation she'd never known to attract his interest before—and the third man was fiddling with the hood ornament of the little green roadster. None of them looked at Melanie and Wyatt.

"How considerate of you, Melanie," Wyatt murmured in her ear. "Since you didn't want the employees to be worried about their jobs, you gave them something else to think about."

"I don't need any trouble from you," she growled.

"Man, that's some bark you've got." He pulled back in obviously-feigned apprehension. "Did the mop teach you how to do that, or did you teach him?"

Scruffy had apparently figured out that he'd acquired a new name, for he perked up, sat up on his haunches, laid a paw on Wyatt's ankle, and stared up adoringly at him.

"Hey," Wyatt told the dog. "Since when did I say I wanted you worshiping at my feet?"

"That's what you get for giving him steak bones in the middle of the night," Melanie gibed.

Wyatt grinned. She saw the silver shimmer of his eyes and winced, knowing that she'd put her foot in her mouth—but good.

"You're right, sweetheart," he said softly. "You *don't* need any trouble from me. You can create plenty all by yourself."

She sneaked a look around at her employees. All three of them were staring at her, their jaws lax as they took in the implications of Wyatt being anywhere near her dog in the middle of the night.

Of course they drew the obvious conclusion, she thought irritably. *They're guys. What did you expect?*

She tried to keep her voice casual. "Wyatt's car wouldn't start last night, so he camped out on my couch. Now he's anxious to get home."

"I wouldn't be so sure about that," the guy at the bulletin board said under his breath.

Melanie ignored him. "I know you're short-handed because it's Saturday, Robbie, but can you spring one of the guys to charge the battery and check the car over? There was no obvious reason for it to be dead."

The guy standing beside the roadster grinned and gave Wyatt a thumbs-up signal.

Melanie pretended not to have seen it and stalked past him into her office. The mail was already on her desk. She turned the computer on and began to flip through the envelopes.

Wyatt followed her.

"Leave the door open," she ordered. "The last thing I need is a crew out there wondering what's going on in here."

"Nothing they'd want to watch. We need to do a dry-run of the charity package before we give your friend Erika the details."

"Sorority sister," Melanie corrected. "She was never my friend."

"Whatever. Anyway, we can check out the arrangements with the restaurant and show off a car again all at the same time. Is tonight all right with you?"

"No. I'm not doing a repeat of last night."

"Of course not. Felicity's is an entirely different—"

"I mean I already have plans for the evening."

"We could do lunch instead."

"I'll be here through the lunch hour, working." She

slit open an envelope and extracted a check. "Besides, don't you have anything better to do? Like patching things up with Jennifer?"

"I wondered how long it would take you to ask about that."

"Who's asking? I'm only commenting that it appeared some fence-mending might be in order—unless she comes from some country I've never heard of, where a slap across the face is a form of greeting."

Wyatt snapped his fingers. "That must be it. I've always thought Jennifer didn't seem to inhabit the same planet as the rest of us."

Which of course told Melanie precisely nothing. *What did you expect—that he'd pour out his heart? Maybe even ask your advice?*

"Well, if she's an alien that makes her just about a perfect match for Jackson." She shot a look at him, but Wyatt looked only mildly interested, as if the whole subject had nothing to do with him.

Melanie turned her chair around to the computer to check if any parts orders had come in overnight. "I'm surprised you're not out watching your precious Baritsa, just to be sure the guys aren't injuring it."

"I have infinite trust in Robbie's crew. Be careful, Melanie—you're beginning to sound as if you don't want me around."

"Brilliant deduction, Sherlock."

"Last night," he murmured, "you wanted me to stay."

"Well, last night, you—" She looked up at a tap on the open door. "Never mind. What is it, Robbie?"

"I've looked at the Baritsa, sir. If you'd like to come out, I'll show you what I found."

"That sounds ominous," Wyatt said. But he slid off

the corner of the desk and followed Robbie across the showroom.

Melanie printed out a couple of orders and took them out to the shop. "Fred, when you get a chance, pull these parts and leave them on the workbench by the back door—I need them in time for Monday's shipment."

When she got back to the office, Wyatt was in her chair, using the phone. She considered sitting down across from him to finish the mail, and decided not to bother. "Bath time, Scruff," she said.

The dog leaped out of his basket and was waiting at the shop door when Melanie got there. He was almost vibrating with eagerness. "You know what day it is, don't you, pal?" She cleared out the deep utility sink which stood in a far corner of the shop and started to fill it with warm, sudsy water.

Before it was full, Wyatt had followed her. He studied Scruffy, who was sitting up on a tall stool, impatiently waiting for the sink to fill. "You're absolutely certain this is a dog? I've never seen one who didn't run the other direction at the mere mention of a bath."

"But then you don't know Scruff very well. The doggie bag may have seemed an easy route to his heart, but really he's far deeper than that." She turned the water off.

Scruffy stepped carefully into the sink.

"Good boy," Melanie told him. "Not even a splash—unlike some people I know, who can give an entirely new meaning to the simple phrase, 'Join me in a cup of coffee.' What's the verdict on the car?"

"Robbie says it's a faulty alternator. They're recharging the battery now."

"What good is that going to do?" She reached for a bottle of pet shampoo from the shelf above the sink. "If the alternator isn't working, it'll just drain the power again as soon as you start the engine.''

"Robbie thinks if I'm careful I can drive it to the dealership." He perched on the stool that Scruffy had just vacated.

"What if it croaks in the middle of a traffic lane? Have we considered the advantages of calling a tow truck instead?''

Wyatt didn't miss a beat. "What a good idea, Melanie. If I have it hauled in, I can stay here and help you for the rest of the day."

"On second thought, it would leave a terrible impression—a broken-down, brand-new Baritsa being dragged down the highway by a wrecker. Definitely you should drive it."

"I thought that's what you'd say. You'll be happy to know Fred has volunteered to follow me in case Robbie's wrong and it dies on the way.''

"That's a shame. I mean, what a good idea. We wouldn't want you to be stranded.''

Wyatt grinned. "Since we're not going to Felicity's tonight—''

"You may do whatever you like," Melanie pointed out. "I merely said I was already busy."

"It occurs to me that I'm the one who's come up with all the promotional plans so far. If you don't like my ideas, what do you want to do instead?''

"How about going to a drive-in movie?''

"I didn't know there were any still operating. Besides, it's a little early—and chilly—for them to be running.''

Melanie shrugged. "That's the extent of my ideas." She squeezed suds out of Scruffy's coat and pulled the drain plug. Then she adjusted the spray nozzle and began rinsing him from head to tail. Scruffy stretched his neck out blissfully.

"Does the mop have a date tonight?"

Melanie nodded. "He's going visiting." She turned the water off and reached for a towel. "All right, Scruff. No rolling in the dirt until I give you permission."

The dog gave a short yelp. Wyatt moved off the stool and Scruffy leaped down and gave himself a good head-to-tail shake.

Wyatt looked concerned. "You're not going to dry him off any more than that? I'd hate to see the mop come down with a head cold."

"You catch cold from a virus, Wyatt, not from the outside temperature. Besides, if I'd blow-dry his coat, he'd end up resembling a powder puff."

"I can't see it would be any worse than looking like a mop. At least he'd be warm."

The back door opened and Fred came in with a head-light and a cable which he set carefully on the work-bench. "There are the pieces you needed, Melanie. Are you ready to go, Mr. Reynolds? Robbie says your battery's got about as much of a charge as he can give it."

"Have a good time," Melanie murmured. "Oh, and Wyatt? Don't call me for a ride."

Wyatt did call, however, to let her know that he'd arrived safely at the repair shop. Very soberly and with almost no irony in her voice, Melanie thanked him for his thoughtfulness, and he laughed and said he'd see her on Monday. "I was afraid of that," she muttered, but he'd already hung up.

She put the phone down and shook her head in puzzlement. Was it actually only two days since he'd first turned up? It seemed barely possible. The man was like a migraine—annoying, unpredictable, and—once started—impossible to ignore.

A tall brunette who'd come in while Melanie was on the phone said, "What's the deal, Melanie? It's not like you to go around muttering to yourself."

It is now that Wyatt's hanging around, Melanie thought. "Hi, Angie. Robbie's out in the lot somewhere."

"I saw him. We're going to the zoo as soon as he's finished, so I decided to come on in and change Luke's diaper while I waited. Mind if I use the hood of the car?" She set the baby carrier down beside the roadster.

"I'm sure it's seen worse in its day."

Angie laid a changing pad on the car, unstrapped the baby from the carrier, and lifted him out. He gurgled and waved his arms and tried to escape by rolling over, and she pinned him with one hand while she unfastened his romper with the other. "Can you hand me a diaper?" she asked. "I forgot to allow for the slope of the hood."

Melanie dug in Angie's bag and then took hold of Luke's little hands while Angie worked. "Hey, there, big boy. Why haven't you come in lately to flirt with me?"

Luke grinned and babbled.

"He's grown so much, Angie."

"Nineteen pounds," Angie said. "And he's starting to walk around things—hanging on, of course. One of these days he's going to take off and run, and there will be no keeping up with him." She fastened the last snap and Melanie picked the baby up and snuggled him close.

But Luke wasn't in the mood to snuggle. He leaned out of her arms, trying to reach the hood ornament on the roadster.

"Boys and their toys," Angie said ruefully. "I had

no idea the obsession with cars started before their first birthday. No, Luke, Melanie doesn't want your fingerprints all over that shiny new wax job.''

"Go for it, Luke. Show me how well you can walk." Melanie set the baby down. He grinned, planted both chubby hands against the polished surface of the car door and began to work his way around on unsteady feet.

Angie leaned against the fender. "So was that the new guy in your life?"

Melanie was momentarily at a loss.

"The one who was on the phone when I came in," Angie explained. "Robbie told me—"

"About Wyatt owning half the place now? That makes him the new guy in all our lives."

"No, Robbie didn't mention that part."

"He didn't? Then what was he talking about?"

"The fact that the two of you came in together this morning."

Melanie groaned. "I thought guys never talked about that kind of stuff."

"Well, it does have to be pretty juicy before they get interested. Of course, I don't believe everything Robbie told me. Just because what's-his-name—Wyatt, did you say?—left his car here overnight and you came in very late and you made it such a point to talk about him sleeping on the couch that only an idiot would have bought the story—"

"Is that what Robbie told you? I'll..." Melanie couldn't think of any payback that was quite horrible enough. "I'll make him polish every last inch of rust off that Dodge that's sitting behind the building."

Angie laughed. "The one that doesn't even have an engine? Ooh, that'll scare him into silence all right. So what really happened? Dish it out, Melanie—it's just us girls now. If you tell me this guy didn't get within twenty feet of your bed, I'll take your word for it.''

Melanie opened her mouth and closed it again. She could say that Wyatt hadn't been anywhere close to her bed, but that would be lying. However, if she told the literal truth, nobody would believe it.

And if she even started to explain why they'd gone to the club together last night, she'd have to admit the business was for sale. So much for not wanting to cause her employees premature concern about their jobs.

No, the whole thing was just too complicated to explain—and what had happened in her bedroom this morning was nobody's business anyway. ''I didn't sleep with him, if that's what you're asking.''

Angie grinned. ''Well, Robbie did say you looked as if you hadn't had a wink of sleep.''

''You have a dirty mind, Angie. There's nothing going on. Honest.''

The door opened, and Melanie, relieved at the interruption, turned to greet the newcomer. With any luck it would be a last-minute customer and by the time she was finished Robbie would have swept his wife and son off to the zoo.

But instead the man who came in was wearing the uniform of Kansas City's best-known department store, and he was carrying an enormous bundle that barely fit through the door.

''I didn't know Tyler-Royale had started shipping car parts,'' Angie murmured. There was an undercurrent of amusement in her voice. ''So this must be a morning-after gift.''

''Probably some kind of token thank-you for putting him up last night. And putting up with him.''

''Pretty big to be a mere token.''

The deliveryman looked from one woman to the other. "Which of you is Ms. Stafford?"

Melanie took a half step forward.

"Will you sign for this package, please?"

Angie was right; it didn't look like a token. The package was too square to be flowers. And it was too huge to be a box of chocolates—unless for some unfathomable reason he'd had the store pack it in a cloud of foam.

Melanie's instincts told her it was too large to be anything but trouble.

She signed her name in an uncharacteristic scrawl and the deliveryman handed her the bundle and went away.

The package was heavier than she'd expected, considering how bulky it was. It was soft, too—there was no box under the silvery-blue wrapping paper, just some squishy, formless object. An enormous teddy bear, perhaps, curled up in a fetal position?

She gritted her teeth and tore off the wrappings.

"Is that a sleeping bag?" Angie asked in disbelief.

Whatever it was, it was white, quilted and puffy. Melanie shook it out, and several smaller packages which had been folded inside fell out. "It's a down comforter."

"Nice." Angie stooped to pick up one of the fallen packages. "Egyptian cotton pillowcases, and sheets to match."

Of course, Melanie thought. He'd practically destroyed her bed this morning, so he was making up for it. It was rather sweet of him, actually, to realize that the coffee stains might never come out of her sheets. Wyatt might be problematic to deal with sometimes, but he was certainly a gentleman...

"Oh, look." Angie swooped. "There's a card, too."

Foreboding flooded over Melanie. "Give me that!" she demanded.

But it was too late. The card was not in an envelope, and it had fallen face-up. Only a saint could have picked it up off the showroom floor without reading it, and no one who knew Angie would ever mistake her for Francis of Assisi. Her eyes went wide, and she handed the card over without a word.

To make up for spilling coffee in your bed, Wyatt had written.

Melanie wanted to shriek. She'd actually given him the benefit of the doubt for a minute, calling him a gentleman. What a fool she'd been! *I'll tear the sheets into strips, braid them into a rope, and use it to hang him.*

"There's nothing going on," Angie murmured. "Right."

Dusk was falling as Melanie parked the ten-year-old Chevy at the far corner of the hospital lot and opened the bag which contained Scruffy's equipment. In his excitement, the dog bounced over the seat and practically into her lap. "Enough," she ordered. "You have to calm down before you can go in."

He stood still, but he was still quivering with exhilaration as she fitted the green harness-vest over his shoulders and buckled it around his front legs. Once it was on, however, he calmed.

She fastened his leash to the ring on the back of the vest and walked across the lot and in the main door.

In the lobby, a stout woman spotted them and did a double take. "Well, I never!" she said loudly. "The very idea of bringing a dog into a hospital!" She put out her foot as if to push Scruffy aside.

Melanie shortened the leash and held her breath. If

Scruffy so much as growled inside the hospital—not that she'd blame him, because the woman had almost kicked him—he'd be out in a flash and he'd never be allowed to come back.

Instead, he held his head high and trotted in a dignified silence straight toward the elevator.

"Some people have no idea what's appropriate," the woman sniffed.

"Quite right," Melanie said over her shoulder, and pushed the elevator button. "And you're one of them," she finished under her breath.

On the sixth floor, she turned down the neon-striped hallway and stopped at the nurses' station to sign in. "Hello, Melanie," said a nurse in a red-plaid lab coat. "The dinner trays just went back down to the kitchen, and the kids are waiting for you in the schoolroom."

"They're not waiting for me, Janice. It's my pal here that they're anxious to see." Melanie lengthened Scruffy's leash a little, and he tugged eagerly.

She paused at the door of the schoolroom, as she always had to in order to adjust her thoughts. No matter what the hospital called it, the room was scarcely the kind to be found in any ordinary elementary school. It was brightly painted, with the alphabet displayed on one wall and a bulletin board full of drawings on another. There were small tables and bookshelves and drawing easels. But there were also wheelchairs and oxygen hookups, and the toys were mostly the sort that could be run through a sterilizer in order to protect the patients from infection.

Each week when she and Scruffy came there was a different mix of kids, as they came and went for their treatments. Today there were some familiar faces—Madison was back again, working a puzzle on the floor with an IV pole standing beside her. Jimmy was still there, though he looked better than he had last week; today he was sitting up by himself, not propped with pillows. And Andrea was there as well; her hair was starting to grow back, Melanie noted. There were also three children she hadn't seen before.

Scruffy stood quietly at the door, looking around the room. Then he pulled gently until Melanie followed him over to a small, wan-faced boy in a wheelchair, one of the newcomers. The dog sat on the rug in front of the chair and politely offered a paw.

"This is Scruffy," Melanie said. "He's come to visit."

The boy reached out a tentative finger to touch the dog. "Why is he wearing that jacket?"

"It's like a uniform," Melanie explained. "It helps him remember to use his best manners, and it helps everyone else remember to touch him gently."

"Does he like coming to the hospital?" The child looked sideways up at her. "I don't."

Melanie's heart twisted. "He likes to help sick people feel better, and sometimes just petting him does that."

"How?" The boy's tone was scornful.

"Want to try it?" Melanie looked around for an aide. "Will you hand me Scruffy's bench, please?"

"Is that his name?" the boy asked. "Scruffy? It doesn't sound very nice."

"Well, he wasn't very nice-looking when he first came to live with me, so it seemed to fit him." Melanie set the small carpeted platform next to the wheelchair. Scruffy jumped up on it, turned round, and lay down, his nose tucked between his paws. The bench put his back at exactly the right height for a child who was sitting in a chair, in order to pet him with the least possible exertion. The boy's hand fell almost automatically onto Scruffy's coat, and his fingers trembled as he began to stroke the soft fur.

Melanie backed off, still holding the leash and closely watching the child and the dog, but giving them as much privacy as possible.

"Amazing," the aide said under her breath. "That dog always goes straight to the sickest one in the room. It's like he can smell them." She moved off to help Madison reposition her IV pole.

Slowly, Scruffy moved around the room, setting his own pace as he visited each child for a few minutes and then moved on to the next.

Midway through the evening, as Scruffy was playing a very gentle tug-of-war with Jimmy, the nurse came into the playroom. "Ten minute warning, everybody," she said. "As soon as Dr. Scruffy finishes his rounds, it'll be time for snacks and bed."

For the first time, the schoolroom sounded almost normal, as the kids groaned and complained. Only the little boy in the wheelchair didn't seem to hear; he was sitting up a little straighter and still watching Scruffy, and suddenly the dog stopped pulling on the rope toy, nuzzled Jimmy gently, and came back to climb up on the bench beside the wheelchair. The child sighed, laid a hand on Scruffy's coat, and closed his eyes.

The nurse came across the room. "We ordered ice cream for you too, Scruff."

The dog's eyes brightened and his tail wagged, but he didn't move away from the child.

"You spoil him, Janice."

The nurse laughed. "Look who's talking. Thanks for coming, Melanie. It's always easier to get them to sleep after Scruffy's been here. I'd have expected it to be the other way around, but he doesn't rev them up, he relaxes them. Same time next week?''

Melanie didn't answer. ''Janice, is Andrea all right?''

''She's doing fine. She's just here for a last round of chemo. Why?''

Melanie shrugged. ''I don't know. Just a silly feeling, I guess.''

Janice pulled an electronic thermometer out of the pocket of her lab coat and crossed the room. Less than ten seconds later, she put the thermometer back, ruffled the stubble of hair on Andrea's head, and came back to Melanie. ''How did you know she was running a degree high? You're incredible.''

Melanie shrugged. ''You'd have caught it when you put her to bed.''

''Yes, but you've given us an extra half hour's start on whatever infection she's picked up. Scruffy's not the only one who has an instinct for dealing with sick kids. In fact, I'm pretty well convinced he learned it from you.'' Janice's eyes were full of compassion. ''You have a gift, Melanie, and you know it's a crime not to use it.''

The words echoed through Melanie's head as she drove home, and as she brushed Scruffy's coat where the uniform-vest had matted it, and as she made up her bed with brand-new Egyptian cotton.

She'd told herself for three years that she'd come to terms with giving up her dream. But in fact, it hadn't taken much to bring it back to life. Wyatt's suggestion that they sell the business, salted with Erika's snippy assumption that Melanie was dealing in cars because she couldn't do anything else, and topped off tonight with Janice's insight...

You have a gift, and you know it's a crime not to use it.

The question was, what was she going to do about it?

CHAPTER SIX

Sunday dawned bright and beautiful, the most spring-like day so far. When Wyatt pulled up in Melanie's driveway, he wasn't surprised to see her on her knees in a flower bed with a heap of winter debris beside her.

As he got out of the car, she sat back on her heels and watched him. At least, she seemed to be watching him, but it was hard to tell where she was looking because of the oversize sunglasses she was wearing. Between the glasses, the wide-brimmed hat which shielded her face, and the gauntlet-like gloves she wore, she looked smaller and much more fragile than the dynamo who had taken him on head to head when he'd first walked into the shop.

"It's not Monday," she said, and turned back to the flower bed. "You said you'd see me on Monday."

"I said I'd see you at the shop on Monday," he corrected.

"Don't you have anything better to do than hang around annoying me?"

Her words were tart, but the tone wasn't. Wyatt thought she sounded tired. "As a matter of fact," he said, "yes."

"Oh."

"You thought I didn't work?"

"I was starting to wonder if the flour mills ran entirely by remote control."

"I never had anything to do with the flour mills. I told you I was a twig on that family tree, if you remember."

"You'll pardon me for getting mixed up. So what brought you here today?"

"I couldn't stay away." He let a teasing note creep into his voice, but he was very nearly telling the truth. He'd awakened this morning thinking of yesterday's unfinished conversation about what they could do to promote the business. If her best effort was the suggestion that they go to a drive-in movie, for heaven's sake—

Melanie gave a little snort of disbelief.

"Actually, I tried to call, but you didn't answer your phone." He squatted down beside the flower bed and watched the rhythmic, almost mechanical movement of her hands. He could see green spikes poking through the freshly turned dirt. "What are you planting?"

"Nothing. I'm just clearing off last year's dead growth so the perennials don't have to compete with it as they come out of hibernation. Haven't you ever seen a crocus before?"

"I think I saw some once in a pot at the florist's shop."

"Where you were no doubt buying roses."

"What's wrong with roses?"

"Nothing, if you're looking for short-term perfection followed by immediate decay. Personally, I prefer flowers that last. I see you got your car fixed."

"Runs like a charm. Did you call Brad Edwards yesterday about the Ford?"

"I tried, but I only got his voice mail. I left a message."

"How much did you tell him you wanted for the car?"

"I didn't—I just asked him to call me. Whether he will or not is another question. I wish you would have let me cut a deal right then, when he was in the mood."

"He'll call."

"I hope you're right." She sneezed and made a face. "It's supposed to be too early for pollen. At this rate, it's going to be a horrible year for people with allergies." She shifted her position a couple of feet and began weeding again.

"Maybe the mop gave you a cold."

"People don't catch diseases from dogs any more than they do from getting chilled. Not if the dogs are clean."

"That explains you giving the mop a bath yesterday."

Her hands stilled for a moment.

He wondered why it was such a big deal. "Fred told me what you do on Saturday nights."

"Fred talks a lot."

"Why try to keep it a secret?"

"I don't. But some people think it's silly, and others think it's downright disgusting. The ones who approve think I'm some kind of a saint, and that's just as crazy."

Because it makes you even more uncomfortable than the ones who disapprove, Wyatt thought. *That explains it.* "So you don't say much about it."

"Not any more."

He pushed a pile of debris out of her way. "How did you get the idea of taking the dog to visit kids in the hospital in the first place? And how did you train him?"

"I didn't train him. Whenever I took him for a walk in the park, he'd seek out the sick kids. It took me a while to figure out what he was doing. Even after I was sure, it wasn't easy to convince the hospital, though I'd been volunteering there myself for quite a while. But once he proved himself—"

Wyatt looked over at the dog, who was sunning himself on the lawn and watching a squirrel in a nearby tree as if debating whether the excitement of the chase would be worth the effort of getting up. *Okay, he's a smart mop, but he's still a mop.*

"Where'd you get this extraordinary animal?"

Melanie shrugged. "He just wandered into the parking lot one Saturday to drink out of a puddle. No collar, no tags—he was a skeleton with hair. If you think he looks like a mop now, you should have seen him then, because he looked like he'd been used to scrub out a grease pit."

"So you took him home."

"I fully intended to clean him up and drop him off at the animal shelter when it opened again on Monday. Of course, that was two years ago and I haven't gotten around to calling them yet."

Wyatt grinned. "It sounds as if sick people aren't the only kind he can sniff out. You know, Melanie, this is a great story. Maybe we could get some publicity. Scruffy the junkyard dog developing this incredible talent—"

"You are not going to turn those kids into a publicity stunt." Her voice was firm.

"Sorry. I guess I didn't think about that part. I'm just trying my best to get some attention here, and so far you're not helping much. How about throwing a reunion?"

"What do you mean?"

"All the photos on that bulletin board in the showroom are of cars you've restored, right? I don't even have to ask if you still have the owners' addresses. I think we should invite them all to a reunion. Get all the cars back together."

"I'm sure they'll have a great time catching up on old times," Melanie said dryly. "Comparing odometers, gossiping about their owners, bragging about all the places they've been—"

"Drawing far more attention as a group than any one of them would individually."

"It sounds like it might be fun, but we don't have room. Did you count those pictures? There are more than fifty cars."

"We could clean out that back corner of the lot, which needs doing anyway. Or we could rent a big building somewhere, park all the cars inside, and charge admission to walk through and look at them."

"The owners would want a cut. If the cars are the big attraction—"

"They wouldn't expect anything if the ticket price goes to charity—like to your sick kids. Does that still count as turning them into a publicity stunt?"

"Probably. I don't know, Wyatt. I've been thinking about it, and I believe you're looking in the wrong place."

Wyatt shifted into a sitting position, reached for a paper bag she'd set off to the side, and began stuffing dead leaves into it. "I'm listening."

"You know people who have the money to buy it—but let's face it, not many of them are interested. Showing off at the clubs and restaurants may sell a car now and then, but it's not likely to get the attention of someone who wants the whole business."

"Unless Brad's starting up a whole string of theme nightclubs—"

"In the best-case scenario—which is a pretty wild dream—we might sell him half a dozen cars. It still wouldn't be like selling the whole operation."

"You're saying we need to hook up with a major collector."

Melanie shook her head. "No. You don't know car collectors, but I do. They're choosy. These people will hold out for years in order to get just the car they want rather than buying one that's almost like it. And the ones who can afford more than one classic car are still pretty particular about what they buy. They may want only Corvettes, or only cars from before the Depression, or only convertibles—but whatever their specialty is, they stick to it.''

''They take it so very seriously?''

''You'd better believe it. Some of them collect more than one kind of car, of course, and a few don't have any obvious theme. They buy whatever strikes their fancy—but even then, they're selective. Not everything appeals to them.''

''You're saying they don't buy old cars just because they're old.''

''Exactly. None of them want to end up with an odd assortment.''

''Which is what we've got.''

She nodded. ''That's why I think a collector isn't going to be seriously interested, because there's only so much bartering and trading they'll bother with. We need someone who knows cars, but who is more interested in buying and selling than in keeping them all. Someone who wants to keep the business running.''

''Unless we advertise it, I don't see how you're going to find this magical person who has money and business sense *and* likes old cars.''

Her shoulders drooped. ''I suppose you're right.''

Wyatt let the silence draw out. ''I know you're worried about the guys, Melanie, but they're going to find out sooner or later. It would be better to tell them up front than to let them get a nasty shock via the grapevine.''

She nodded again—but this time it was more automatic reaction than agreement, he thought.

"You know," he said, "instead of being scared out of their wits, they might appreciate the warning so they can get prepared."

"You may be right about that. But it wasn't the guys I was thinking about just now. The minute we advertise that the business is for sale, the restoration trade will drop like a rock. Nobody's going to bring in a car for months and months of work if they don't know who they'll be dealing with by the time it's done."

She had a point, he admitted. "If you've got an alternative to suggest—"

"And even worse, if we list it and then it doesn't sell, we'll have taken the hit for nothing. Wyatt, am I fooling myself to think anybody will even be interested?"

I sincerely hope not. "Someone will buy it, Melanie."

She looked up from the flower bed. "Of course you're right. I'd almost forgotten that you wanted it—at least for a while."

I wouldn't go quite that far.

"So someone else surely will too. Funny—it's only been a few days. How could it have slipped my mind that you bought it?" She took a deep breath. "I'm afraid I don't have any great plans to offer, but maybe this reunion idea of yours isn't so bad after all. People who are interested in cars all hang out together, and there's a good chance one of them will know someone who's interested in making a business of it."

"If you start asking around," he warned, "the word will get back to your guys pretty quickly."

She sighed. "Okay. I'll tell them tomorrow." She loosened the dirt around a pale green spike. "I'm really sorry that it didn't work out, Wyatt. I mean, that the business didn't turn out to be what you expected when you made the deal with Jackson.''

"It's my own fault for not looking further ahead.''

"Well—yes, it is. But I'm sure that's no comfort to you.''

She'd hit that nail squarely on the head, he thought. It wasn't any comfort at all.

By midday Monday, Melanie was not only sneezing regularly but her head was stuffy and her throat was sore. "So much for your diagnostic capabilities, Scruffy," she told the dog, who was sitting at her feet as she swallowed an aspirin from the first-aid kit. "Why didn't you tell me yesterday I was coming down with an old-fashioned head cold and not just spring allergies?''

Scruffy gave one short bark, as if protesting the slur on his reputation.

Melanie took a second aspirin and made a mental note to restock the bottle.

Robbie eyed her with concern. "Maybe you should go home," he suggested warily.

"I can't. I have too much to do, and I'm waiting for a call." Not that she was holding her breath or keeping one hand on the phone; if Brad Edwards had been really interested, she thought, he'd have returned her call before now. It had been forty-eight hours since she'd left a message for him.

I was right, she thought. *He had a passing fancy for the car, and now it's passed.* And of course his fickle interest—and Wyatt's interference—had cost her any hope for a nice little profit. Why had she let him stop her, anyway? She should have kept right on talking. At least she could have given it her best shot—and if it had worked there would be one less car on the lot and some extra cash in the till.

An hour later, with her head pounding despite the aspirin and her throat feeling raw—and still no telephone call—Melanie gave up.

She drove the Ford home. Then she made herself a cup of herbal tea, put on her favorite pair of flannel pajamas, drew the curtains in the living room, and settled down on the couch to watch an old movie. With any luck, it would be dull enough to put her to sleep. Scruffy was a warm, firm bolster under her knees, the cats behaved like a heating pad in her lap, and she sank into the couch cushions with a sigh of relief.

Her nose twitched. There was a half-familiar spicy scent on the pillow. Wyatt's aftershave, she concluded. She wondered, as she drifted off, what he would say if she accused him of marking territory....

She didn't know how much later it was when she woke, and in the first instant of consciousness she wasn't sure what had roused her. Then Scruffy, still lying under her bent knees, bristled and gave a low, almost hoarse growl, and she realized that what she'd heard was the click of the front door opening.

The room was dusky, but with the curtains closed she couldn't tell what time it was. Was it late enough that a burglar, prospecting for a target, would see the darkened house and assume it was empty? She was gone so much of the time— Surely she couldn't be so unlucky as to actually be at home on the one occasion when a burglar chose to pay a call. Maybe if she lay very still...

Scruffy wriggled free and bounded across the room toward the door as it slowly swung open. One of the hinges creaked a little.

The streetlights were on outside—she must have slept

for hours—and Melanie could see a figure silhouetted against the glow. A man, definitely. He was tall, broad-shouldered, and carrying something that looked like grocery bags.

She sank back with a sigh of relief. Burglars were usually burdened with packages when they left a house, not when they arrived. And besides, she recognized the shape.

Scruffy started to wag his tail and dance around the intruder, begging.

"Have you no pride, Scruff?" Melanie asked. "No dignity? Wyatt isn't always going to have a steak bone for you." She sat up straighter. "It's nice of you to stop by, but would you care to explain how you got in? Can you pick locks, along with all your other talents?"

"That would be a handy skill," Wyatt said. "I'll put it on my list of things to learn. But as a matter of fact, Robbie told me you always keep a spare key in your desk in case of emergencies."

"I don't like the sound of that," Melanie said. "What's going on at the shop that makes this an emergency?"

"Nothing. It's all under control. But I figured a mission of mercy would be better received if you didn't have to wake up, drag yourself out of bed, and come downstairs to answer the bell."

She couldn't exactly argue with that. "Well, it still wasn't too bright of you just to appropriate the key."

"I didn't steal it," Wyatt pointed out. "Robbie dug it out for me."

"It certainly didn't take you long to figure out how to get around him. But that's not what I meant. I was talking about you just walking in without even a knock. You're lucky I didn't hear you just a little earlier, or—"

"Or what? You'd have set the dog on me?" He looked down at Scruffy, who was sitting up on his haunches with one paw on Wyatt's knee, his eyes wistful. "I'm terrified."

"I'd have been standing beside the door with the rolling pin, and you'd be on the carpet right now with a very large bump on your head."

"Judging by what Robbie said about how you were feeling, you wouldn't have the strength."

"Don't underestimate me, Wyatt. I only have a cold."

"So if you're completely able-bodied, why are you sitting here in the dark? Turn on a light, will you? I'm afraid I'll trip over something and drop your care package. Or even if I manage to get it across the room safely, you might mistake the flowerpot for the soup carton and eat the tulips."

Melanie hesitated just an instant, then shrugged and reached up to turn on a lamp beside the couch. It wasn't like seeing her in pajamas was going to be any kind of a turn-on for him. Her man-styled outfit had been a long way from exotic lingerie to begin with, and it had been washed so many times that the flannel was faded almost to white. Besides, he'd seen her in pajamas before. "You brought me soup? I can't remember the last time anyone did that."

He nodded. "Chicken noodle—of course." He came across the room and set two bags down on the trunk which served as a coffee table.

Melanie watched as he unpacked the contents. There was a foam carton which smelled heavenly, a small loaf of crusty French bread, a box of chocolates, and a large pot of tulips, bursting with buds which were open just enough to reveal yellow petals tipped with red.

I prefer flowers that last, she'd said. He'd actually remembered.

He handed her a spoon and popped the lid off the soup carton. "Dig in."

"How did you know I was sick, anyway? From Robbie, obviously—but how? And why?"

"He called me." Wyatt sat down on the other end of the couch.

"To tell you I was sick? That's ridiculous." She took a deep breath of the steaming broth and felt nourished simply by the rich aroma. She hadn't realized she was hungry.

"No. He called me because he had a question and didn't want to bother you."

"A question about what?" Melanie asked warily.

"The price of the Ford. Don't worry, it's handled."

She paused with her spoon halfway to her mouth. "Brad Edwards called back? Damn, I knew I shouldn't have come home."

"Don't worry about it. I talked to him, and we cut a deal. All the paperwork's signed—I left it on your desk."

"You sold him the Ford?"

Wyatt nodded. "He wanted it right away, but I told him we couldn't deliver it until tomorrow. That's the other reason I stopped by—so you wouldn't take off with it. Eat your soup while it's hot."

"Wyatt, I don't remember telling you how much I wanted for the Ford."

"You didn't," he said cheerfully. "And you didn't tell Robbie either. That's why he called me—to see if I knew."

Melanie dropped the spoon into the container and pushed it aside. All of a sudden, she'd lost her appetite.

"I pulled the file, saw what you had paid for parts, checked the log on how much labor went into it, compared the markup on a couple of other cars you've sold lately, and took a guess about what it was worth." He sounded very proud of himself.

Melanie's head was throbbing again. The pieces were starting to fit together, but she didn't like the picture they formed.

Brad Edwards had been in no hurry at all to call her back, even to begin discussing a price. Yet when he suddenly found himself dealing with Wyatt instead, he'd been in a rush not only to finish the paperwork but to get possession of his new toy. She wouldn't be surprised if he'd been eager to get his hands on the car before Melanie even found out about the deal.

That led her to an obvious—and ominous—conclusion. Brad Edwards was a businessman. For him to agree to a price so quickly, he must have felt he was getting a deal he couldn't refuse. Which meant that Wyatt must have offered him the bargain of the century. "What kind of idiotic price did you quote him, Wyatt?"

"How odd that you should call it an idiotic price," Wyatt mused.

Melanie gritted her teeth. "Why is it odd?"

"Because that's just about the same phrase Robbie used."

"I don't suppose it occurred to you to consult him until after you'd already cut the deal?" It wasn't really a question. *Men,* she fumed. *Why do they always assume they know everything?*

If he had sold that car at a giveaway level…. She *would* set Scruffy on him, Melanie decided. Not that the dog would exactly tear him limb from limb—that wasn't

Scruffy's style—but in the long run, she supposed, being licked to death would be just as effective a punishment.

Wyatt was still talking.

Melanie pulled herself back from planning his imminent demise and, using every ounce of self-control she possessed, listened to how he'd arrived at an asking price for the Ford, and what Brad had said.

Then she forced herself to swallow hard, despite the rawness in her throat, and finally she managed to speak. Her voice felt hoarse and strained. "You got ten thousand dollars more than I would have dared to ask for."

"Funny," Wyatt murmured. "That's exactly what Robbie told me you'd say."

He had brought enough soup to feed the cavalry, so the least she could do in the way of making amends was to offer to share it and the French bread, and to add a glass of wine from the bottle in her refrigerator to toast Wyatt's success in his first deal.

Melanie was almost giddy over the news. The asking price she'd had in mind for the Ford would have produced a nice profit, but Wyatt's deal was phenomenal. An extra ten thousand dollars right now would not only ease the cash flow situation but would make the business look better to prospective buyers. "When we start showing the books, that will be a very nice entry to point out."

Wyatt swirled his wine and sipped. "So you're saying I didn't do badly for a rookie, eh?"

She held up her glass in salute. "You're a natural. Are you positive you don't want to buy me out and run the business yourself?"

"Absolutely I'm sure. What are you going to do with the extra ten grand?"

She frowned. "I wasn't planning on doing anything particular with it. Well, maybe give the guys a bonus—they're the ones who did all the work."

He grinned. "And you're saying I didn't?"

"Well, you get your half of the profits to start with, so—oh, stop pulling my chain."

"I didn't start it—you did, when you suggested I might want to buy your half of the business after all."

She didn't think it would be prudent to tell him that she hadn't exactly been joking.

"They must have taken the news pretty well," Wyatt said. "It seemed pretty calm when I was there."

"The news? Oh, yes. About selling." She plucked at her napkin and didn't look at him. "I didn't tell them. Fred was late this morning, so I decided to wait till I could tell them all together. Then we got busy, and then I felt ill—and I forgot."

"You *forgot?*"

She felt miserable. "I'll do it tomorrow."

He didn't say anything for a long time. "Nobody's forcing you to sell, Melanie."

"No—I want to. Really I do."

"It doesn't sound like it sometimes." Wyatt reached for the almost-empty soup carton. "If you're finished with this, I'll clear up the debris before I go."

She nodded, and told herself it was silly to feel let down that he was leaving. He'd been very generous as it was, bringing her supper and chocolate and flowers as well as the best news she'd heard all week. Of course he wanted to get home, get on with his life...

It was the first time she realized she didn't know much of anything about his life, and before she could stop herself, the question was out. "Is someone waiting for you?"

He paused in the doorway. "Like a girlfriend, you mean?"

"I'm sorry. That sounded as if I was prying. It's none of my business."

He walked on into the kitchen, and she heard the cabinet door open and the soup carton drop into the garbage can before he came back into the living room. "Not even a dog, I'm afraid. Sorry to disappoint you."

At her feet, Scruffy gave a little sigh.

Melanie forced herself to smile. "Well, he sounds relieved that there's no one to displace him."

To her surprise, Wyatt came back to the couch and sat down, at an angle where he was almost facing her. Scruffy pushed a rope-tug toy into Wyatt's hand. "I think it's time you tell me what you want, Melanie. Sometimes you sound eager to get away from the cars, and sometimes it seems as if you don't want to sell at all."

She bit her lip. "I suppose you're right, in a way. If I knew we could get a really good price—"

"Why? What's so important about the money? What do you want to do with it? Train more companion dogs for the kids in the hospital?"

She shook her head. "No." She took a deep breath and for the first time in three years gave voice to the dream which had been silent since the day her father died. "I want to *really* help them. I want to be a doctor."

A doctor. Wyatt supposed he should have seen that one coming. Hadn't she said something yesterday about having been a volunteer at the hospital even before she'd discovered Scruffy's talents? And Erika had made some derogatory remark about Melanie grinding away at science courses when she was in college...

She obviously realized that he'd been taken by surprise, and she drew back defensively. "I know it sounds silly. What makes me think I could do it, after so long? I never really got a good start in the first place—I was only halfway through college when my father died and I had to quit. Now that I'm older, it would all be so much harder. I'd almost have to start over, and it would take years. And lots and lots of money."

"There are scholarships. Loan programs."

She shook her head. "Only brilliant students get scholarships—and they're usually not people who have been running car dealerships for a couple of years, they're the ones who have already done major research. As for loans—do you have any idea how much it would actually cost? It's not just the tuition for college and medical school, it's all the living expenses along the way. I'd be so far in debt by the time I finished I'd never work my way out."

"Unless someone comes along who wants this business badly enough to pay very well for it," Wyatt said slowly.

"That's about the size of it."

As if it hadn't been enough of a challenge to simply get a decent price out of the business, Wyatt thought, now it was a matter of finding a fortune. He might as well try to push the Ford to New York City with his nose.

"If I can't get a good price, then I'd be better off not to sell at all," Melanie went on. "As my own boss, I can keep my schedule flexible enough so I can volunteer at the hospital. At least that way I can be involved with the kids, and I feel that I'm doing some good, even if it isn't as much as I'd like." She took a deep breath. "I know I need to be sensible."

He knew it, too. He knew what an enormous challenge she'd set forth, and how very difficult it would be to make it all work. And yet, as he looked at her sitting there, tiny and defiant in her faded flannel, he couldn't bring himself to agree. He heard himself say, "We'll figure something out."

She gave a heavy, hopeless-sounding sigh. "Right."

He reached out and turned her face toward his. "I said, we'll figure something out, Melanie."

Her eyes were emerald pools, full of loss and pain and longing, and he couldn't stop himself from leaning toward her. He tipped her chin up and noticed the little flutter of her pulse at the base of her throat, where the neckline of her pajamas plunged invitingly into shadow.

"You shouldn't get too close," she said almost hoarsely.

He brushed the pad of his thumb across her lower lip. "Why? Because you don't want me to?"

"Don't be silly," she said, but her voice trembled a little. "Don't you know anything about viruses? I'm contagious."

Reluctantly, he pulled back.

But she was wrong, Wyatt thought. She was a whole lot more than just contagious. This woman was life-threatening.

CHAPTER SEVEN

MELANIE could have slapped herself. *You shouldn't get too close—I'm contagious.* Oh, that was smooth…. She might as well have just come straight out and said that if only she didn't have this nasty cold, she'd want to be kissed.

Not that she actually *did* want to be kissed, of course. What was the matter with her, anyway? Normally she didn't have any trouble saying what she meant. Or— more to the point just now—not saying what she didn't mean. But if Wyatt was of a mind to take her literally… What if he brushed aside the idea of catching her cold and kissed her anyway?

Then you get kissed, she told herself. *Why are you making such a big deal out of it?*

It certainly wasn't as if she had never been kissed before. Compared to Erika's record, Melanie's experience would look like a guppy mounted next to a marlin. But still, she was hardly a novice. She knew her way around a good-night kiss, and she'd handled her share of lovers'-lane kisses, too. She'd dated a lot in high school, a bit less frequently in college as she'd settled down to her studies, and not much at all since she'd taken over the business. But kissing was like riding a bike, she thought. It was something that you didn't ever forget how to do, even if the skills grew a little rusty.

"Oh, the hell with it," Wyatt said under his breath, and his mouth came down on hers in a soft demand.

But there was a fallacy in relying on previous expe-

rience, Melanie quickly realized. None of it applied—
because this wasn't a good-night kiss. It wasn't even a
lovers' lane kiss. It was a sonata in seduction.

That was the last coherent thought to drift through her
head for quite a while, until she became aware that
Scruffy, sitting at her feet with his rubber ring in his
mouth, had started to whine, softly at first but with increasing volume and decreasing patience.

Wyatt obviously heard it, too, for he took one last
nibble at her lower lip and drew back. "I may have to
revise my opinion of the mop." He sounded a little
breathless. "It's beginning to look as if he's the only
one here who has any sense at all."

Wyatt had left in such a hurry, after that aborted kiss,
that they hadn't talked any more about the Ford. But
there was probably nothing to discuss, Melanie told herself as she drove to work the next morning. He had said
he'd left the paperwork on her desk, so he'd no doubt
also jotted down the address where Brad Edwards
wanted the Ford delivered. One of the guys could follow
her across town in order to give her a ride back. She
could even call a cab. There was no need for Wyatt to
be involved at all.

And it would be just as well if he wasn't, she thought
when she walked into the shop to say good morning,
because the first thing she saw was four very interested
faces turning instantly in her direction.

Fred almost cracked his head on the hood of the car
he was working on as he dragged himself out of the
engine to take a good look at her. It didn't take much
skill to deduce that Robbie and his guys had all known
where Wyatt was headed last night when he left the shop
with her spare key...

Which he hadn't returned, she belatedly realized. He must have automatically dropped it in his pocket as soon as he'd unlocked the door. She'd have to make a point of asking for it back—though she'd be careful to do it when they didn't have an audience.

"Good morning, everybody," she said briskly. "Mr. Barnett is planning to pick up his Model T tomorrow. Will there be any problem with having it ready to deliver?"

Robbie shook his head. "Just a little fine-tuning left to do, and a whole lot of cleanup."

"Good. Then the next one on the delivery list is Angela Dawson's Cobra. Have all the parts come in?"

"Pretty much," Robbie said. "We're still missing a few small things."

"Get me a list, will you, so I can check on them? After the Cobra I think we'll tackle that Pontiac, so we may as well pull it into the empty bay and take a look."

Fred nodded. "Want me to try to start it up?"

"For heaven's sake, no. Sorry, but you'll have to push it. Karl, as soon as it's inside, take a good look at it and then check out the far row in the yard. I think there are a couple more Pontiacs back there but I'm not sure what year they are or what shape they're in. Give Robbie an idea of what pieces we'll be able to pull off them and what we'll need to look for somewhere else."

"You got it," Karl said.

"Can you spring someone for an hour this morning, Robbie? I'm going to take the Ford over to Mr. Edwards and I'll need a ride back."

Robbie looked startled. "Wyatt said he'd come in to do that."

Melanie tried to keep her voice casual. "Well, he must have been planning ahead in case I was still off sick today. But since I'm here and feeling just fine, there's no need to wait for him.''

''Yes, ma'am,'' Robbie said. ''Fred's tied up with the Cobra, but Karl can take off.''

That's interesting, Melanie thought. She'd been working with Robbie for the better part of three years. Wyatt had showed up just three days ago. *But he calls Wyatt by his first name, and addresses me as ma'am.*

That reminded her of her promise to Wyatt. It was time to live up to her responsibility as the boss and tell her employees what was going on. ''Guys, I need to talk to you for a minute about some serious stuff. We're going to be a little unsettled for a while, here, because Wyatt and I are going to put the business up for sale. I wanted you to hear it from me rather than—''

Fred gasped. ''The whole thing?''

''The whole thing.'' She looked from one shocked face to the next. This was exactly what she'd been afraid would happen—that her guys would be worried and fearful long before there was any reason for them to be concerned about the stability of their jobs. She tried to soften the blow. ''Please don't panic. Nothing's going to change immediately. We haven't had an offer and we don't even have a buyer in mind at the moment. All the arrangements will take a little time, and there will be plenty of warning before there's any change.''

''So what do we do?'' Karl asked.

''We carry on just like normal.'' She smiled. ''Please—for my sake. If any of you quit on me now, I'll go jump off the top of the Liberty Memorial.''

''Is all this a secret?'' Robbie asked. It was obviously part question and part caution, because he was looking at Fred as if he expected the man would rush straight out and announce the news.

Melanie was grateful for both the warning and the opportunity to head off trouble before it began. "Not exactly secret, but I'd like to keep it to ourselves as long as we can. Any change of ownership will make customers uncomfortable for a while, but if we can keep it quiet until there's a new owner ready to take over, there won't be much disruption."

"But—" Fred began.

Melanie cut across the interruption. "If they hear the news before there's a firm deal, there could be serious fallout. It might mean—for instance—that Angela Dawson would decide to take her Cobra somewhere else to finish the restoration. And then you wouldn't be able to flirt with her when she comes in to check on it, Fred."

Fred grinned sheepishly and shuffled his feet. "Okay, not a word."

The shop door opened behind Melanie and a man called, "Hey, is anybody working around this place today?"

Melanie recognized the voice. Bill Myers, no doubt shopping for another piece for his classic Mustang. Which meant, if they had it, that she'd have to take one of the men out of the shop to go strip the part…

"If you have any questions about this, guys," she said quietly, "don't stew about it. Come and talk to me. Bill, what can we do for you today? What does the Mustang need now?"

"Not a thing." He beamed. "But now that it's almost finished, my friend who's been helping me wants a car of his own to work on. It seems I got him hooked on the whole idea."

She hadn't seen the other man standing behind Bill until then, but she recognized him from previous trips. "Hi, Joe."

"So I brought him down," Bill went on. "I told him—this is the only place to go, and Melanie's the only one to deal with."

Melanie was taken aback. That was an element of the deal which she hadn't even considered before—the fact that some of her customers might feel a loyalty to her personally rather than to the business as an entity. She'd never thought of herself as an icon of the classic cars business.... But then, Bill Myers was one of a kind.

She stepped from the shop into the showroom and pulled the door closed behind her. "What are you looking for, Joe?"

"I don't quite know," he said. "What have you got?"

Melanie wanted to groan. Bill Myers and his long-winded chats were bad enough, but if she ended up killing the entire morning showing his friend every car on the lot...

A customer is a customer, she reminded herself.

"Why don't you start by wandering around out in the yard, just to see what appeals to you?" she suggested. "Then once you have a model in mind, we can get down to business and see what kind of a deal we can make."

Joe nodded. "That sounds like fun. Coming, Bill?"

"No, no. You go ahead, I'm going to talk to Melanie."

Groaning wouldn't be relief enough, Melanie decided, but a good healthy scream might help. "Maybe you should go along with him, Bill. A second opinion is always a good idea, and with all of your experience, you can help Joe choose a car that he—"

"Oh, I wouldn't want to influence him. Just because I think the Mustang's the best car ever built doesn't mean that's what he'll want. You go look around, Joe. I'll just be in Melanie's office."

He followed her, almost stepping on her heels. She could hardly keep him out, especially since the only place to sit in the showroom was the single tall stool by the packing counter. *We need to add a waiting area,* she thought, and then remembered that it wasn't going to be her problem—or her decision to make—for much longer.

"I hope you don't mind if I work while you talk," Melanie said. "I've got an awfully lot to do this morning."

"You go right ahead," Bill said. He pulled the chair up close to the end of the desk. "I just like to watch you."

Melanie thought philosophically that his preference for watching people work might well explain why Bill's Mustang still wasn't done. He'd been working on it when she'd come to work at the junkyard. In fact, to the best of her recollection, he'd been her first customer—and he'd had to patiently explain to her what the part that he needed looked like, and where to find it.

Bill leaned forward as if to study her desk. "What's the big project today?"

Melanie looked thoughtfully at him. "Actually, you could give me a hand with this one, Bill. We're trying to get all the old cars we've worked on back together. If you'd help pass the word—"

"Sure thing. I'll tell the guys down at the car club. Or better yet, we've got a meeting this Saturday night—you could come and talk to them yourself. They'd love to have you as a speaker, and if you liked the meeting, you might even want to join. I could pick you up—"

"I'm sorry, Bill, but I've made plans for Saturday evening." She turned away from him to the computer screen and pulled up the database so she could start noting addresses and phone numbers. At least she'd have a list ready whenever Wyatt figured out what kind of a reunion he had in mind.

It was a couple of minutes before she noticed that Bill had gone silent.

She looked up, watching in fascination as he swallowed hard and his Adam's apple bobbed up and down.

"It's true, then," Bill said finally. "What I heard."

Melanie was lost for a moment, unable to figure out what he meant. Surely he couldn't have heard about the plan to sell. But what other rumor might be circulating...

"This new fellow in the business. I hear he's partners with you in more than just cars." His voice was low, as if he were talking about something X-rated.

Well, you didn't expect the guys to keep a good story to themselves, did you? An overnight stay on the weekend, a key borrowed last night so he could pop in to see her... She'd better put a stop to that tale, if it wasn't already too late. "No, Bill," she said firmly. "It's just the cars. What you heard is a juicy bit of speculation, that's all."

Bill's face brightened. "Then he's not the reason you're busy on Saturday night?"

Melanie was feeling wary, but she told the truth. "No, he's not. But I have already made plans. I always—"

Bill jumped up. "Then it's not too late."

By the time Melanie could turn her chair, he was beside her, his arm around her shoulders in an awkward bear hug.

She put both hands up, and she tried to find the right words to fend him off. "Bill, I don't think you understand."

He hadn't stopped talking. "I didn't realize until he

came along, and then I thought I'd lost my chance and you'd never—''

From the doorway, Wyatt's voice, low and firm, cut across Bill's babble. ''Is this man bothering you, sweetheart?''

Sweetheart? What in heaven's name had inspired him to say that?

Not as much as you're bothering me at the moment, Melanie wanted to say. Of all the ways to make a bad situation worse...

Bill was staring at her, his brown eyes wide and reproachful. All of a sudden, she realized what he'd reminded her of, the other day when he'd stopped in and sat beside her desk all afternoon. He'd looked exactly like Scruffy did whenever she scraped a chicken bone into the garbage instead of awarding it to him.

''Excuse me a minute,'' she said to Bill, and edged past him to the office door. ''Wyatt, would you step outside with me, please?''

''Certainly, my dear.''

Melanie gritted her teeth till they were outside the building. ''Look, knock off the *my dears* and the *sweethearts,* all right? I'm perfectly capable of taking care of myself, and the last thing I need is you interfering and making things worse.''

''I could have asked him if you were up to your old tricks of seducing the customers,'' Wyatt said mildly. ''That would have been making things worse. All I did was to clarify that he'd better keep his hands off.''

She dug her fists into her hips. ''And what makes that any of your business?''

''Do you want him climbing all over you?''

She sighed. ''Of course not.''

''So what's the problem? I'm just letting Casanova in

there think that he's been out-romanced by a better man. What's your solution, Einstein? To lose a longtime customer by telling him that you'd rather date a crash-test dummy than go out with him?''

Melanie opened her mouth to argue, and then shut it again. *He may have a point,* said a little voice in the back of her brain. Why smash Bill's ego entirely? Why not let him hang on to the dream that she might have chosen him if it wasn't for Wyatt happening into her life?

And what happens when he realizes you're not dating Wyatt?

She'd deal with that when the time came, she concluded. By then, Bill's obsession might well have passed—just as Scruffy eventually forgot the chicken bones. Or the business could have sold and she wouldn't be coming into contact with him anymore.

"How did you know he's a long-term customer?'' she asked suspiciously.

"You were so absorbed with your pal that you didn't see me go by the office door on my way to the shop.''

"I wasn't absorbed with Bill,'' she objected. "I was working on your reunion, I'll have you know.''

"Good. You can show me later what you've got done. At any rate, while I was asking Robbie to keep one eye on the showroom for a while, I got the low-down on your admirer, too.'' He checked his wristwatch. "Come on. I told Brad we'd deliver the car this morning, and if we don't get started, it won't be morning anymore.''

The Canteen Club looked a great deal different in daylight than it had on the night they'd shown off the Ford by the front entrance. It looked, Melanie thought, exactly like a soldiers' club of the period probably had looked on the morning after a busy night. There were dirty glasses everywhere, napkins crumpled and tossed, tables pushed askew. The only thing missing seemed to be the smell of stale cigarette smoke which she thought would probably have hung heavily over the club of days gone by.

A busboy who was clearing tables in a corner of the main room jumped at the chance to leave his work for a moment. Melanie didn't blame him—the task looked overwhelming.

He went to find Brad while they waited near the entrance, and a few minutes later Brad came bustling out, rubbing his hands. "I thought you'd never get here. Let's go look it over."

Brad went over the Ford in detail from the front bumper to the back. If he hadn't been wearing yet another vintage suit, Melanie thought he'd probably have climbed underneath to inspect it.

Melanie held back a bit. "I thought you said this was a done deal," she whispered to Wyatt.

"It is. He's just admiring his own brilliance in buying it."

Eventually Brad turned around to face them. "It's exactly right," he said simply. "I can't wait to see what my regular customers have to say about this. I already told one of them, and of course he thinks I paid too much money. He said a—what did you call the engine?"

"A flat-head V-8," Wyatt said glibly.

Melanie was surprised he'd remembered.

"Yeah. He said it wasn't all that rare," Brad said.

"Your friend sounds like a man who knows his cars," Wyatt said.

Probably better than you do, Melanie thought unsympathetically. But she had to admire how he'd changed the subject around without saying a word about the Ford.

"Oh, he does," Brad said. "He wanted to know all about you, and the business. Said he'd like to talk to anybody who could turn old cars into that kind of money. I'll give you his name if you like. Come on into my office, and I'll write the check."

Wyatt's face showed only mild interest, but Melanie knew him well enough now to recognize the silvery sparkle in his eyes. He was more than interested in Brad's friend; he was excited.

She had already known, of course, that Wyatt wanted out of the business, but his reaction made it painfully clear how eager he was to strike a deal.

The knowledge left Melanie feeling dismayed, which surprised her for a moment. Surely she should be happy that he didn't want to let this drag out any more than she did. But when she thought a little longer, her unease made sense. If he was so zealous to sell, he was likely to pressure her to accept any offer that came along, even if she didn't like the terms. And then what was she going to do?

Worry about that when the time comes, she told herself. She thanked Brad and tucked the cashier's check into her back pocket.

Wyatt waited until they were outside. "So what do you think?"

Melanie ran a gentle hand across the chrome on the Ford's hood and said a silent goodbye. "Seriously? I believe you have all the makings of a used-car salesman. You're picking up the lingo very quickly, and the way you ducked out of answering that question about whether the Ford is truly rare or only collectible was worthy of the best—"

"Idiot. I was talking about the potential buyer."

"What potential buyer? I only heard Brad talking about a friend who thinks he knows a lot about cars. Maybe he does, maybe he doesn't. I don't think you should get your hopes up too quickly."

"It's worth giving him a call, though." Wyatt held the door of his car and Melanie slid in. "If he would be interested—"

"You go right ahead." She settled into the seat, which hugged her close. "This is a bit of a change from the Ford. By the way, while you're pulling out keys—you still have the spare for my house."

Wyatt patted his pocket absentmindedly. "Sorry. I must have left it in my other jacket. I'll bring it by sometime." He started the car. "Let's have lunch."

"What about work?"

"You'll be much more efficient after you have a good meal. You're getting over a cold so you need extra nourishment. And this *is* work. Take your pick of the three—I don't care which reason you choose."

Melanie dismissed the first two. "What do you mean, this is work?"

"We haven't made the arrangements yet with Felicity's, and Erika's auction is this week. Besides, we need to talk about the reunion, which you obviously can't concentrate on while Bill's hanging out beside your desk."

Melanie shot a sideways look at him. "But you assured me this morning that you'd stopped Bill in his tracks with that fancy maneuver of yours," she murmured.

"Well, I didn't give you a guarantee. The trouble is, nobody can predict what a guy might do when he's crazy enough to think he's in love."

"Right. I'm so glad you clarified that Bill is only ob-sessed with the idea of being in love and not actually smitten with the emotion itself. However, as long as we're on the subject of fancy maneuvers and what guys might do—"

"Yes?" Wyatt sounded curious. "What do you think he might have in mind?"

"I'm not talking about him. I mean you."

"But I don't fall in the same category."

"It never occurred to me that you might," Melanie said crisply. "The point I'm trying to make is that there will be no repetition of that kiss last night."

Wyatt didn't even hesitate. "Okay."

Melanie had taken a breath to force home the argu-ment, to convince him that people who worked together shouldn't get involved in any way that was remotely romantic, to explain why it would be utterly stupid for them to continue down the path they had tiptoed onto last night. But Wyatt's brisk, no-nonsense agreement felt like something had blocked her throat and wouldn't let her exhale.

No, she thought. It felt more like a spear to her chest.

Which was perfectly ridiculous, because she'd wanted him to agree with her. Just not so quickly and so easily.

It seemed forever before she could manage to speak at all, and then it took effort to keep her voice from cracking. "Good. I'm glad that's understood."

"I couldn't agree more, so you can rest easy," Wyatt assured her. "I hate repeating myself. The next time I kiss you, it will be completely different."

The valet stepped into the car to park it, but as he pulled away from the curb and Wyatt took Melanie's arm, she obviously started having second thoughts. She paused on the sidewalk and said, ''I'm not exactly dressed for Felicity's.''

''You're fine. Once your feet are under the table, nobody will notice that you're wearing jeans.'' And that was a good thing, too, Wyatt thought, because otherwise every man in the place would be eyeing the trim silhouette of Melanie's backside…though since his own interest was partly caused by the contrast between last night's baggy pajamas and today's formfitting jeans, perhaps not every male in the restaurant would be quite as fascinated.

The maître d' showed them to Wyatt's favorite table. He glanced at the wine list while Melanie looked around the dining room. ''This is amazing,'' she said. ''It looks just the same as the last time I was here.''

''How long has that been?''

''Ten years. It was prom night, right before I graduated from high school, and my date brought me here before we went to the dance.''

''You remember it that clearly?'' He pointed to an entry on the wine list and the hovering waiter nodded and trotted off.

''It was our last date,'' Melanie said.

''It must have been a messy breakup.''

She frowned. ''Why do you say that?''

''Because you sound sad. If it's still bothering you after all this time, then it must have been pretty bad.''

''No, it's not that at all. It didn't shatter my heart that he never called me again. But you see, on the way home that night, his car died.'' She looked up at him over the top of her menu. ''I have no idea what to order. What do you recommend?''

''I'm having the salmon, but I've never run across anything here that isn't good.'' He laid the menu aside. ''What did the car dying have to do with him never calling you again? Unless—no, don't tell me. The car died very conveniently, in a remote spot, stranding you, and you slapped him when he made a pass.''

Melanie laughed.

A man at the next table stopped talking to look over at her. Wyatt wasn't surprised; she sounded like a musically-gurgling brook. It was, he thought, the first time he'd heard her really laugh.

''No, Wyatt. Remember what I told you about how guys react when a woman rescues them? That date was how I know. I had to fiddle with the engine a bit before I figured it out, but I fixed it for him.''

''The only thing that amazes me is that you were surprised he didn't ever call you again.'' Wyatt shook his head. ''Melanie, honey....''

She shrugged. ''It made perfect sense to me. I knew I'd never wear that frilly pink dress again, because it had so many ruffles and layers that it made me look like a wedding cake. So it didn't matter if I got dirt or grease on it. But his tux was rented, and if he damaged it he'd have to pay.''

The waiter brought the wine, and Wyatt sampled it and nodded approval. ''I thought you said you weren't much on cars till you got stuck with the junkyard.''

''I wasn't, really. But…'' She hesitated.

For a moment Wyatt thought she was going to tell him something important, and he almost held his breath. Which of course was a stupid reaction, because no matter what she confided, it could hardly be crucially important to him. She was a short-term, accidental business partner, that was all.

Then she smiled—a bright, meaningless smile—and said, ''Well, people pick things up here and there. Who knows where we learn it all? I think I'll have the salmon too."

He gave the order to the waiter and sat back, toying with his wineglass and telling himself that he was nuts to be curious about why she'd avoided answering. "Where did you pick up enough experience even to stick your head under the hood? From your dad? If he owned a junkyard—" But somehow, even though he'd come up with the explanation himself, it wasn't good enough to satisfy him. It was too simple, and too obvious.

"He didn't get involved with the yard till later. But he used to work on cars a bit at home."

That made more sense. "So fiddling with cars was a way to spend time with your father."

"I suppose so. What about you?"

Obviously she'd said just as much as she intended to. "My father didn't work on cars," Wyatt said. "He worked on paper. Lots and lots of paper. I don't think I ever saw him without a stack of—"

He felt the pressure of a hand coming to rest on his shoulder, and he turned his head to see a set of scarlet fingernails brushing the gray tweed of his jacket. Why, he wondered, did so many women think men would be attracted to claws that looked like those of a recently fed vulture?

"It's good to see you again, Wyatt," a low feminine voice purred. "Where have you been hiding out lately?"

He reached up to remove her hand so he could politely stand. Her fingers tightened on his and he had to tug to free himself. "Hello, Erika. Melanie and I were just talking about you."

"Were you?" she murmured. "How interesting. And what a lucky chance to run into you. I was going to call you this afternoon." Her gaze flicked across the table to

Melanie. "Actually, I've been meaning to drop in and finalize your offer for the charity auction—but I haven't had any reason to go that far out in the boondocks lately. You are planning to come, aren't you, and see for yourself how your package sells?"

"Of course," Wyatt said. "We'll be there." And then he pretended that he didn't see Melanie's green eyes shooting sparks at him across the table.

CHAPTER EIGHT

MELANIE held on to her temper—but only barely—until Erika oozed away from the table a few minutes later with a final coquettish smile for Wyatt. Then the waiter came with their food, and so she had to bite her tongue a little longer yet. But finally they were left to themselves.

She ignored her salmon to focus on Wyatt. "And exactly why do you think I'll agree to have anything to do with this auction of hers?"

"Because part of this package for her charity is your gift."

"A very small part. Anyway, I'm not talking about the package—obviously I have a certain level of commitment there. I mean the auction itself."

"You heard Erika—she wants us to make the presentation to the winner. Your lunch is getting cold."

"I heard her more clearly than you did, obviously, because it was apparent to me that she'd much rather have you do it alone. Besides, why on earth would I want to go and watch while she bids for the package and then cozens you into going to dinner with her?"

"Why on earth *wouldn't* you want to go?" Wyatt asked crisply. "I expect you'd find it fun to watch your old pal try to make a fool out of me."

He had a good point, Melanie thought. Why wasn't she looking forward to a good time? It should be very amusing to watch the dance as Erika schemed and Wyatt... But what exactly was it that Wyatt was plan-

127

ning to do? It didn't sound as if he was eager to cooperate. "I doubt she'd try to make you look foolish."

"Not intentionally, perhaps."

"Anyway, I'd think you'd find it flattering that she
wants so badly to get to know you. You're not actually
thinking of playing hard to get, are you? Because that
would only make her more determined."

Wyatt looked thoughtful. "Thanks for the tip."

"Well, I'm not guaranteeing how she'll react.
Remember I've barely seen the woman for several
years."

"That's why you should go—just to see how it all
plays out." He picked up his fork. "I can't make up my
mind which car we should take. The obvious choice is
the one that's going to be part of the prize. But it would
also be a chance to show off a different one."

"*You* can take whichever one you want."

"Now you're just being stubborn, Melanie. Unless, of
course, it makes you nervous even to think about Erika
going after me."

"Don't be ridiculous."

"Then you'll be going."

"I didn't agree to do anything of the—" Melanie
stopped, noting the speculative way he was watching
her.

*Unless it makes you nervous even to think about Erika
going after me…. The next time I kiss you…*

It was perfectly ridiculous for Wyatt to think that she
had any personal feelings about Erika's pursuit of him.
It was every bit as ridiculous, in fact, as it had been for
Bill Myers to think she would fall into his arms the
moment he declared himself. But that was the problem
with men, Melanie thought. They couldn't conceive of
a woman not noticing them, and they thought if she re-

acted at all to something they did, it must be because she was jealous.

And as for what Wyatt had said about kissing her— there wasn't going to be a next time, of course. But obviously the less fuss she made about it all, the better. Making a big deal of it would only encourage him to think it was important to her.

So she'd go to the silly auction, and she'd enjoy the show Erika put on. However, she wasn't about to surrender without a final shot. "I just hope I can get the grease spots cleaned out of that old frilly pink prom dress," she murmured, "because it's the only thing I own that's suitable for the occasion."

Wyatt didn't miss a beat. "Don't bother about the grease spots," he said gravely. "Wear it just the way it is. That way, if something goes wrong with the car on the way, you'll already be suited up to work on it."

When the Baritsa pulled into the parking lot at the yard, Melanie opened the door and looked back at Wyatt, who hadn't shut off the engine. "You're not coming in? What if Bill's still camped in my office?"

"If you want me there, Melanie, of course I'll come in to defend you."

"Never mind. Does anyone ever get the last word in a discussion with you?" She managed it this time by closing the door before he could answer.

She glanced at the big schoolhouse clock on the showroom wall and sighed. What she'd envisioned as a simple trip across town to deliver a car had turned into a half-day operation. And though they'd made a little progress over lunch in planning the reunion and deciding which car to drive to Erika's fancy auction, the heart of her day was gone and she hadn't even checked to see if there were orders needing to be packed and shipped.

She was startled to see Angie in the showroom. "What are you doing here? Not that you're unwelcome, but—"

"I brought Robbie a sandwich, and he asked me to hold the fort till you got back so he could work on the Model T."

Guilt washed over Melanie. "I should have been here."

"Why? For heaven's sake, how long has it been since you went out for lunch? Nothing happened around here anyway except that someone came in wanting to sell an old Chevy, and he's going to stop back later this afternoon. So you didn't miss a thing, and I've had fun. Talking to an adult now and then instead of to a one-year-old is refreshing."

"I should put you on the payroll," Melanie said. "You're paying a sitter—"

"Nonsense. Luke fell asleep, so I put him down on the floor in your office for a nap. Why didn't Wyatt come in?"

"I'm sure you'll get a chance to meet him. We're planning a sort of reunion and picnic for all the customers who have—"

Angie shook her head. "I met him yesterday. I dropped in to give Robbie the checkbook, and Wyatt happened to be here."

That's just great, Melanie thought. Was there anyone in the entire Kansas City metropolitan area who hadn't been present yesterday to see Wyatt pick up the extra key to her house?

Angie shot a sly look at Melanie. "So are you feeling better today?"

"I'm still stuffy, but the worst is over. Wyatt brought some chicken soup, and that helped."

"I'll bet it did," Angie murmured. "Along with other things... How was lunch? You and Wyatt must have been having fun, for you to forget the time."

Melanie said cautiously, "We had a lot to talk about."

"A reunion, a picnic...selling the business." Angie was obviously trying to keep her voice light, but the humorous note was gone.

"Robbie told you, then. Don't worry, Angie." Even as she said it, Melanie knew how preposterous the reassurance sounded. How could Angie not worry whether her husband's job would be secure under a new owner? "I'm sorry—that sounded sappy. I just meant we'll do the best we can to get a good deal for everybody."

"I know you'll try, Melanie." But Angie didn't sound quite convinced.

The trouble was, Melanie wasn't so certain either. They could try, but no matter what a buyer agreed to do, there was no guarantee he'd keep his promises once the deal was done.

From the office came a whimper, and as Angie jumped to get her son, Melanie looked over her shoulder at the baby. On a blanket next to her desk Luke had awakened and pushed himself up on his hands and knees. But then he'd stopped, as if he didn't know where he was going or what he should do next.

He looked, Melanie thought, just about as confused as she herself felt.

Melanie was only starting to get dressed when the doorbell rang. She glanced out her bedroom window and saw the Baritsa where Wyatt had parked it at the curb, so it wouldn't block the drive where she'd left the gleaming red Cadillac convertible.

She pulled up the sash of her bedroom window and leaned out. "Use your key," she called.

There was no response, but a moment later she heard the click of the front door opening, Scruffy's short, welcoming bark, and the murmur of Wyatt's voice.

She opened her bedroom door. "Make yourself a drink or something while you wait."

"Would you like me to bring you one?"

Not coffee, that's for sure. "No, thanks, I'll be down in just a few minutes."

"Does that mean you're still trying to decide what to wear?"

She eyed the dress which was lying across her bed. How did he know she was having second thoughts? Or did he just believe that no woman could ever make up her mind? Not that Melanie had that particular problem tonight—there was only one choice, and the sooner she quit agonizing and put it on, the sooner the evening would be over.

She slid the dress over her head and settled it around her hips, then eyed herself in the mirror. It would have to do. The dress wasn't new, and though it was too classic a cut to have gone out of style, she had no doubt that Erika would recognize it for exactly what it was. But there had been no time or money for shopping, even if she'd had any desire to impress. Which she didn't.

Wyatt hadn't gotten himself a drink; he was sitting on the couch playing tug-of-war with Scruffy. He let go of the pull toy and stood up as Melanie came down the stairs. There was an appreciative gleam in his silvery eyes, but all he said was, "And here I had my heart set on the frilly pink number."

"I decided it didn't go with the red car."

"Well, this one does—and nicely." He backed off a step to survey her cocktail dress. "I'll have to watch out not to lose you against the black upholstery, though."

Even in a bathing suit, she'd never felt quite so exposed as she did in the short-sleeved, low-necked little black dress. That was odd, Melanie thought. Though it had been a long time since she wore it, she didn't remember feeling quite that way before.

"I think you can tell the difference between leather and silk," she said crisply and held out a hand, palm up. "I'd like my house key back, please. And don't tell me you don't know where it is, because you had it just a couple of minutes ago."

"Cunning woman." He dug the small brass key out of his pocket and dropped it in her hand. "You planned that, didn't you? No wonder you weren't ready when I got here."

"No, I was running late because I got held up at the shop this afternoon by a guy who wants to sell us a rusted-out old Chevy for about a million dollars."

"Is it a rare rusted-out old Chevy?"

"No such luck. He's just delusional. Some people think anything old must be worth a fortune. Actually, he was supposed to come back to talk to me a couple of days ago, but instead he popped in tonight right at closing time."

"I was surprised you weren't already waiting for me."

"Oh, sure—I'm so eager to go tonight I just couldn't wait to come home and get ready." She reached into the hall closet for a wrap.

"I know," Wyatt said dryly. "But I was tied up at the last minute too—talking to Brad Edwards's friend."

Melanie's hand stilled on a lightweight black shawl. "The guy who said he wanted to find out how to turn old cars into cash?"

"The very same one."

She pulled the shawl out of the closet, and Wyatt draped it around her shoulders. "Does it sound like he's interested in the business?"

"We'll see. I'm meeting with him tomorrow. It's going to be chilly tonight, Melanie. This scarf thing doesn't feel very warm."

"It will do. Besides, it's the only black wrap I've got, and I can't wear a beige raincoat with this dress."

"Why not, if it keeps you comfortable? In that thing, you'll get chilled and make your cold worse."

"I told you, Wyatt. Getting cold doesn't cause—"

"Yeah, and you also told me I'd catch it if I kissed you. Which I didn't."

"Maybe you just have a very strong resistance," Melanie said.

He looked thoughtful, but he didn't answer.

She congratulated herself for having once been successful at shutting him up. "Come on, Scruff."

"You're taking the dog to a charity auction?"

"Not inside. He can guard the car."

She offered Wyatt the keys, but he declined the honor and settled into the passenger seat of the Cadillac. The convertible top was up, but by the time they reached the auction site at one of Kansas City's finest hotels, Melanie was having chills. She just wasn't certain whether it was the cool air, the evening ahead of them, or the news which Wyatt had dropped which was causing her discomfort.

If Brad Edwards's friend was indeed interested in buying the business...

They'd have a better idea tomorrow, Wyatt had said. She'd try not to think about it in the meantime.

The auction was being held in the elegant grand ballroom, and the event was as elaborate as the location. There were baskets of fresh flowers and miles of ribbon draped and knotted in intricate designs from the stage and balconies overlooking the dance floor. Ice carvings highlighted the long row of tables which overflowed with finger food, and white-coated waiters were circulating with trays of champagne glasses.

Melanie looked from the display to the slickly-printed program that a sorority girl wearing a formal gown had handed her as they came in. "I sure hope all the decorations and food and drink have been donated," she muttered, "or there won't be much left for the victims of domestic violence after the expenses are covered. It's a nice way to throw a party, though—all you have to do is say it's for charity, and you can have just as good a time as the charity can afford."

Though the room was already half full of people when they arrived, Erika had obviously been keeping an eye out for Wyatt. Before the chill had gone off Melanie's champagne glass, Erika had crossed the room to greet them, flinging her arms around Wyatt's neck and planting a kiss on his cheek. "How wonderful that you came yourself!"

Melanie sipped her champagne. "This is quite a party, Erika."

"It's been *so* much work." Erika's gaze flicked over Melanie's dress.

She was probably assessing how much it had cost and how long she'd owned it, Melanie thought irritably.

"But every bit of the work is necessary," Erika went

on. "One must give people a good time, or they wouldn't show up to bid."

"I'm surprised you haven't included a dance band and a full stage show. How much do you expect to net for the charity after you've paid for all this?"

Erika's eyes narrowed. "It's impossible to say until after the bids are all in."

"Of course," Melanie agreed. "It would be." She ran an eye over the program again. On the last page, halfway down the list, was their package. It looked pretty small compared to some of the others, she thought. There were trips to Las Vegas and vacations on the Mediterranean, weeks at golf resorts, retreats to spas, and cruises in the Caribbean.

"Are you choosing what you're going to bid on?" Wyatt asked.

"I don't have much time for things like this."

"Or money, either," Erika said, not quite under her breath. "The last page is all local things. Maybe you should bid on a weekend package at one of the casinos, Melanie. Who knows? You might be able to buy it cheap and strike it lucky while you were there."

Every muscle in Melanie's body tensed, and she had to force herself to relax. "Thanks, anyway, Erika," she said levelly.

Erika gave her a slow smile and moved away to greet a group of newcomers.

"What was that all about?" Wyatt asked.

Melanie didn't look at him. "Just Erika being her usual catty self. I have a thing against gambling and she knows it." Her champagne had gone warm, and as a waiter passed by, she set the half-full glass on his tray. "Isn't that Jennifer over there? Jackson's Jennifer?"

Wyatt looked over his shoulder. "In the flesh," he said calmly.

Tonight, however, the blonde didn't seem inclined to seek Wyatt out. Perhaps, Melanie mused, Jennifer thought she'd made all the comment she needed to last weekend when she'd slapped him at The Canteen Club. "You seem to be making some progress on that front," she said. "At least she doesn't seem to have an itchy palm tonight."

The auctioneer called the crowd to attention just then, but she didn't think Wyatt would have answered anyway.

She paid attention to the bidding only in order to have something to do, until their package came up and they were called up on stage to read the description and to give the certificates to the winning bidder. "I'll read, you award," Wyatt said under his breath as he helped her up the steps onto the stage.

"Forget it," Melanie muttered back. "You're just trying to chicken out because Erika might buy you after all." She smiled pleasantly at the auctioneer and snatched the description card out of his hand before Wyatt could reach for it.

The stage lights were so bright that Melanie wondered how the auctioneer could possibly see who was bidding. "Dinner for two at Felicity's," she read, "with chauffeur service provided by Classical Cars, in a fully-restored red 1960 Cadillac convertible—that's the one with the big tail fins, folks—it's parked out front."

The auctioneer started the bidding, and Melanie stepped back from the podium to stand beside Wyatt. "Besides," she said, "after that very public hug of greeting, what more could she possibly do when she wins? Even Erika has some limits."

Wyatt looked as if he doubted it.

But between the bright lights and the speed of the action, Melanie couldn't keep track of the bidding, though she thought she caught fleeting glimpses of Erika with a hand in the air. When the hammer came down, Melanie was startled at the final price level, and even more surprised when it was a septuagenarian man with more stomach than hair who stepped onto the stage to claim his prize.

"Congratulations," she managed. "Is this for you, or did you buy it for someone else?"

"Someone like Erika?" Wyatt asked under his breath. "You never give up, do you, Melanie?"

The buyer laughed. "At that price, I'd have to be nuts to give it away. No, it's for me—and the wife." He waved vaguely at the crowd and then stuck out his hand. "I'm Phillip."

The next presenters were already coming up the steps to the stage, and Wyatt took Melanie's arm to guide her across the width of the stage to the ramp leading back down to the ballroom floor.

At the base of the ramp, Phillip stopped them to ask a question about the restaurant, and while Wyatt answered, Melanie looked around the room. Her eyes were taking a while to readjust, after the bright stage lights.

She was startled when a man standing next to her spoke. "So you're hanging out with the big shots now, Melanie. I thought you weren't interested in this sort of thing."

"Jackson?" She blinked up at him. "I didn't see you standing there."

"Yeah, if you'd seen me you probably wouldn't have come this direction."

Not true, she thought, because she wouldn't go out of

her way to avoid Jackson—though she had to admit she wouldn't seek him out, either. And she didn't feel any obligation to comment about her reasons for being there, or for donating the package. Jackson certainly hadn't troubled himself to keep her in the loop when he'd sold out, and now that he no longer owned half of the business, she didn't owe him any explanations.

She was a little curious, though, about how paranoid Jackson sounded. Of course, in her brief and infrequent encounters with him, Jackson had often sounded like the king of self-pity. This was really nothing new.

"What are you bidding on tonight?" she asked lightly. "The Caribbean, or Europe? Now that you're free of all obligations—"

"Oh, I'm free all right," Jackson said flatly. "Very, very free. I'm single and broke—you can't get much freer than that." He turned on his heel and pushed between a purple-haired matron and a young man wearing seven earrings.

Wyatt shook Phillip's hand again, then reached for Melanie's arm to guide her toward the back of the room where the crowd was thinner.

Melanie frowned a little as she trailed after him, squeezing through the crush around the stage. She was trying to remember whether, when she'd spotted Jennifer earlier this evening, Jackson had been anywhere around. She didn't think so—but she hadn't been looking for him. At any rate, it could have been just a momentary absence; people often were separated in a crowd as dense as this.

But now that she stopped to reflect on it, she realized that he hadn't been close by at The Canteen Club, either. Jennifer had jumped up from a table where she'd been sitting with a group of people. Melanie hadn't paid much

attention to the woman's companions, because she'd
been too startled by the suddenness of Jennifer's attack.
But surely if Jackson had been part of the group, he'd
have caught Melanie's attention. Or even if she'd seen
him only out of the corner of her eye, her subconscious
would have recognized him, and then she wouldn't have
been so surprised to hear that the blonde who had
slapped Wyatt was Jackson's Jennifer. But she had been
astonished—which indicated that he hadn't been at The
Canteen Club—or at least not at Jennifer's table.

Single and broke—you can't get much freer than that,
Jackson had said. It sounded very much as if Jennifer
had given Jackson his walking papers....

It's not your business, Melanie, she told herself. *And
it's certainly not your problem.*

She paused and looked up at Wyatt. "Can we go
home now?" she asked. "Or do you want to hang
around a while longer and ask Erika why she didn't buy
you after all?"

Melanie didn't intend to ask Wyatt in. It was late; she
was worn down from her cold and from a series of long
days and late nights; and she was longing to get out of
panty hose and into pajamas.

Scruffy had other ideas. The instant Melanie opened
the Cadillac's door, the dog leaped out—but instead of
running to the front door, he took off toward the Baritsa.
Melanie yelled at him, but Scruffy ignored her and began
pawing at the door.

"What were you saying about the mop being so well-
behaved that he wouldn't get out of a car until he was
told to?" Wyatt said.

"You don't have a squirrel hidden in there, do you?
Or a steak bone? Scruff, knock it off—if you scratch the

paint, I'll deduct the cost of fixing it from your dog food allowance.''

''It's quite entertaining to listen to you trying to reason with a mop,'' Wyatt said. ''But I'd rather deal with this directly.'' He strode over to the car, grabbed the dog around the middle, and hauled him bodily to the house.

Scruffy didn't seem to object, for he twisted 'round in Wyatt's arms and tried to lick his face.

Wyatt paused on the porch. ''I hope you don't mind unlocking the door. If I hadn't had to give my key back, I'd be a gentleman and do it for you.''

''A gentleman wouldn't have had to be asked to return the key,'' Melanie pointed out. ''In fact, a gentleman wouldn't have had it in the first place. Just dump him in the kitchen. I don't know what's gotten into him.''

Wyatt carried Scruffy through the living room. ''Do you mind if I wash my hands? I don't want to go home smelling like the mop.''

She sighed. ''Go ahead. I suppose you're hoping for some coffee, too.'' She saw a red light blinking on her answering machine and pushed the button.

It was Janice, the nurse on the children's floor. Scruffy perked up at the sound of her voice, and Wyatt soaped his hands at the kitchen sink while he listened.

Melanie played the message through. ''Sorry about the coffee,'' she said. ''Come on, Scruff. We've got work to do.''

Wyatt turned off the faucet and reached for a towel. ''You're going out at this hour of the night to an inner-city hospital to take a dog to visit a sick kid?''

Melanie glared at him. ''Yes. Do you have a problem with that? Because it's really none of your—''

''You're planning to drive across town, alone, in the

middle of the night, in a car that's more than forty years old?''

"Let me remind you, Wyatt, that I'm not the one who was stranded over the weekend, and it wasn't a forty-year-old car that broke down.''

"Shush," he said. "Let's go."

She was still having trouble finding her voice when Wyatt's car pulled into the almost-empty parking lot at the hospital and she began to buckle Scruffy into his harness.

"Can I help?" Wyatt asked.

"You already have. Thanks." She smoothed Scruffy's coat and murmured to the dog, "Did you know Janice had called? Is that why you didn't want to go into the house?"

Wyatt rolled his eyes. "Let's just start calling him Scruffy the psychic wonder mop.''

The hospital was never quiet, but the hallways were dim and the noises were more hushed than usual. The schoolroom was empty and dark; at this hour all the children were in their beds. At the nurses' station Janice looked up from a chart. "I'm so glad you came," she said. "Matthew's not doing well tonight, and his parents can't get here for another few hours.''

"Why not?" Wyatt asked.

"They live in a godforsaken little town in Kansas. There are hospitals closer to them, but none that would be as good for Matthew. But they have other kids, and obligations. And he was doing better, so they went home for a few days.''

"But they're on the way?"

Janice nodded. "It's a long drive, and Matthew needs something to hang on to in the meantime. He doesn't want the nurses, because we're always poking at him.

But when I asked if there was anything which would make him feel more comfortable—'' Her voice quivered just a little. "I'm sorry I broke up your date, though."

"It wasn't a date," Melanie said. "Which room?"

"I'll take you down."

There were so many machines around the bed—so many tubes and wires and cables—that Melanie hesitated on the threshold. Then the child in the bed turned his head and saw them, and said, "Scruffy." His voice was barely as loud as a breath.

It was the child Scruffy had gone to first on last Saturday's visit, Melanie saw—the new little boy in the wheelchair, the one who had been so scornful of the notion that petting a dog could make a sick person feel better.

Janice put Scruffy's special bench down beside the bed. The dog trotted across the room, hopping onto the bench and then up on the seat of a chair. Then he stepped carefully over the railing and onto the bed. He worked each paw cautiously down between wires and tubes, clearing out a little spot on the blanket just barely big enough to curl up in. He lay down and wiggled his nose under Matthew's hand, moving slowly but steadily until the boy's palm rested atop the dog's head.

Matthew's fingers twitched, stroking the soft coat. His eyes closed, and his strained little face relaxed.

Melanie moved a chair closer and sat down, holding the leash with a light touch. "There's no need for you to stay," she told Wyatt. "We'll be here awhile."

"How long?"

"Scruffy will stay as long as Matthew needs him."

"And that means you will, too."

She nodded. "No matter how well trained or compassionate he is, Scruffy's still a dog—so he can't be left alone with a child.''

"If I hadn't seen it," Wyatt said, "I'd never have believed it.''

"Is this just a little more than you'd have expected from him?" she asked with a tinge of irony. "Scruffy the psychic wonder mop—''

"It's more than I would have expected from anybody.''

There was a strange note in his voice... Melanie looked up suddenly, and saw something like awe in his eyes. No one—not even the nurses who had fought to let her bring Scruffy into the hospital, not even Janice with her talk about Melanie's gift—had ever truly understood how important this was to her. Not till now.

Her heart twisted painfully, and settled into a new rhythm, a new reality. For now she knew what had been happening to her over the past few days.

Wyatt had frustrated her, but he had also fascinated. He'd infuriated her, but he was the only one who understood. He'd shaken up her settled little world—but he'd also comforted her.

And she admitted what she'd done. She had fallen in love with him.

CHAPTER NINE

SHE'D fallen in love—and that had changed everything.

It all made sense to Melanie now. The strange up-and-down feelings of the past few days. The way she'd felt annoyed every time Wyatt had showed up, but let down whenever he left. The weird sensation of being almost seasick the day that he and the cup of coffee had landed on top of her in her bed. The warmth she'd felt when he'd come to her house bringing soup when she'd felt sick. To say nothing of the way she'd reacted when he kissed her.

He'd even been right about Erika and the reasons why Melanie had warned him about the woman. She'd convinced herself that she would have warned any man about Erika—and she probably would have, because Erika was a menace. But if it had been any other man, it wouldn't have been as important to Melanie whether he believed her. She'd been so sensitive not because it was Erika—but because it was Wyatt.

This new knowledge even explained the odd hesitation she'd felt when he'd first started talking about selling the business. She'd found herself holding back—not quite willing to say that she wanted to get away from Classical Cars. The reaction had surprised her, because she would have expected that she'd greet with enthusiasm any opportunity to leave a business she hadn't wanted in the first place.

She'd rationalized it all out at the time, telling herself it was because of money. If the business didn't bring enough cash, then she couldn't pursue her dream of going to medical school, and she'd have to take another dead-end job, perhaps one with less autonomy and less flexibility. She'd almost convinced herself that it would be better to stay where she was.

But in fact, it wasn't the money which had been the true mental hangup, and it hadn't been autonomy and flexibility which were the attractions of staying in her current job. It hadn't been the business which she'd been thinking of at all. It had been Wyatt.

Even on that very first day, she had realized that selling the business would mean not ever seeing him again. In fact, she remembered thinking at the time that never running into Wyatt Reynolds again would be a major improvement in her life. But she hadn't believed it down deep, where it really counted.

In some secret corner of her brain she had realized that she wanted to know him better. She wanted him to stick around long enough for her to find out whether he was the man for her. Or maybe she had already known it....

But that was impossible, she told herself. She didn't believe in love at first sight. Interest, yes. Attraction, no question. Sexual awareness, definitely.

But not love. Love came later. Love only came with time.

She just hadn't realized how very little time it could take.

The night wore on, and Melanie tried to relax in the straight chair while staying alert enough to notice if Scruffy even twitched. The nurses came quietly in and out, checking and adjusting. A doctor appeared, looked askance at Scruffy, made his examination, and asked if they were Matthew's parents.

"No," Wyatt answered. "We're just here with the comfort team." He pointed at the dog.

The doctor started to answer and seemed to think better of it. He went out into the hall instead.

Wyatt said, "Doesn't Matthew's doctor even know his parents?"

"Of course—his main doctors do, at least. But this is a teaching hospital, and that young man is probably a second-year resident. His job is to monitor all the patients in this department and notify the senior doctor if there's any significant change."

"And that's what you want to do."

"Well—being a second-year resident isn't the height of my ambition. But it's a necessary step in the process."

She thought for a minute that Wyatt wasn't going to answer, but finally he said, "You'd do a better job of it. He's got a lot to learn." He looked directly at her, his gaze assessing. "Would you like a cup of coffee?"

"If you want an excuse to walk down the hall, sure."

"You look worn out, Melanie."

"I've actually gotten very good at relaxing in odd positions."

"Well, that's a talent that would come in handy if you pursued this idea." He went out, closing the door quietly behind him.

A talent that would come in handy if you pursued this idea…. Would… If… Pursued… The conditional twist of the words stuck out in her mind as if they'd been written in fire.

So Wyatt had doubts too. She wondered what his reasons were for questioning. Did he believe that she couldn't make it through the rigorous program? That she didn't have enough drive to succeed? That there wouldn't be money enough from selling the business to support her dream?

Or was it possible that he simply didn't want her to?

She allowed herself a brief vision of Wyatt begging her not to choose such a demanding life because it would leave no time for him. But the picture she conjured up fit so badly with reality that she couldn't even work it up into a good fantasy.

In fact, the choices she made about how to spend her life were none of Wyatt's business. Perhaps even more importantly, he wouldn't want them to be.

You may have fallen in love, Melanie, she reminded herself. *But that doesn't mean the feeling's mutual.*

He had kissed her—and he'd seemed to enjoy it. But he'd definitely had mixed feelings about it, or he wouldn't have hesitated before he kissed her. He wouldn't have made that remark afterward about Scruffy being the only one in the house who had any sense. He wouldn't have rushed away as if he'd had a swarm of bees after him.

And she couldn't fool herself that the kiss had been anything unusual for him, because a man who had no experience couldn't have kissed her into mush and come out of it himself no more affected than Wyatt had been.

She would be deluding herself if she thought his comment about her and medical school had anything to do with his own feelings. Clearly, he felt her dream was beyond her reach. But did he think she was incapable, or that the finances were impossible?

She might have asked him, but he hadn't returned yet when Matthew's parents arrived.

The child's mother gave a little shriek of horror when

she saw him, surrounded by machinery and tubes and wires. Matthew opened his eyes, and suddenly his face took on a wan, pinched look again, as if he was in pain.

Melanie couldn't blame the woman, because she'd been taken aback herself at the first sight of Matthew. Add in the love that Matthew's mother felt for her son, and perhaps a good dose of guilt for not being beside him when he'd taken a turn for the worse, and it was no wonder she was shocked.

Still, hadn't a few weeks in the hospital taught the woman to keep her emotions under control when Matthew could hear? The last thing he needed was his parents passing along their own fear.

After that initial exclamation, however, Matthew's mother seemed to pull herself together. She came over to the bedside and reached carefully for her son's hand. "Darling, we're here…" Her eyes widened. "What is that animal doing in his bed? I will not have a filthy dog next to my son when he's ill. The idea of all the germs—"

Scruffy raised his head, obviously curious about the fuss, and the mother leaped back as if she was about to be attacked. Melanie jumped up, shortening the leash and putting a hand on Scruffy's neck. No matter how solid his training was, if Scruffy felt that Matthew needed protecting, he might actually do it. As she'd explained to Wyatt, he was still a dog.

But even though she was watchful herself, she wasn't going to let this woman make disparaging statements about Scruffy. "He's not filthy, he's highly trained, he doesn't have germs, and he's been here for your son when—"

Wyatt spoke from the door. "We're happy to have helped Matthew relax until you got here. Now that we're not needed anymore, we'll let Scruffy have a well-deserved rest.'' He set two cups of coffee on the bedside table and shook hands with Matthew's father. ''Melanie, it's time to tell the mop he's off-duty.''

She snapped her fingers softly, and Scruffy tipped his head as if to argue that his job wasn't done yet. Then he worked himself out from under Matthew's hand and stepped carefully out of the bed.

Melanie leaned over the child. ''Matthew, Scruffy needs to go and rest now. But if you'd like him to come and visit again, you tell the nurses—all right?''

The child's mother sniffed.

Out in the hall, Wyatt said, ''I don't think you should count on a return invitation.''

''It's ridiculous. Some people just don't understand.''

''And they won't unless they're educated. Maybe that's where your strength really lies—in the compassionate end. Of course, you'd need to work up a more persuasive argument than you were using on Matthew's mom.''

Melanie sighed. ''I know. I'm tired, but that's no excuse. Thanks for rescuing me before I said something I would really have regretted.''

''Any time,'' he said lightly. ''I'm sorry I took so long to get back with the coffee that you didn't get to drink it, but one of the nurses hit me up to buy a raffle ticket.''

''I wish they wouldn't do that.''

He gave her a sideways look. ''Hit me up? Or sell me a raffle ticket? Oh, you did say you had a thing about gambling. What's the big deal?''

''It's the principle of the thing. Gambling is gambling. It usually starts small, but it doesn't stay that way. People are hurt, whole families are destroyed—'' She knew she sounded vehement, and she swallowed the rest of the sentence. But she knew she'd already said too much.

Wyatt was silent until they were in the car. "You're not just talking in general, are you?"

It obviously wasn't really a question, but she shook her head. "I'd be in medical school now if it wasn't for the slot machines and the blackjack table and the racetrack."

"You?" He sounded horrified.

"Heavens, no." She bit her lip, but now that she was started there wasn't anything to do but go on through. "My father. I was finishing my second year of college when he died. That's when we found out that instead of leaving my mother well provided for, he'd drained every asset and every resource. He'd borrowed against his business, his life insurance, even Mother's car. It was all we could do to salvage the house."

"But the junkyard survived."

"Probably only because he'd forgotten it entirely. Mother actually didn't know it existed until later, after everything else was finished and done with. Or perhaps he still owned it only because no one would loan him anything against it. It wasn't exactly a liquid asset." She sighed. "Of course, it still isn't." She shot a tentative look at Wyatt. "What do you think Brad Edwards's friend is going to say when you talk to him tomorrow?"

"I couldn't possibly guess. But he's not the only possibility."

He's not the only possibility. Well, that was pretty clear. He was trying to keep her from getting her hopes up, which must mean Wyatt had already concluded that the man wasn't a serious buyer.

"Maybe the reunion next weekend will lead to something,'' Wyatt went on. ''Don't fret about it, Melanie. We'll get it sold, and then we'll both be free.''

Free of the business. Free of the responsibility. Free of each other.

Yesterday, Melanie would have wholeheartedly endorsed that philosophy. Even a few hours ago, she would have agreed without a second thought. But now...

Now, she admitted sadly, she wished that Wyatt didn't sound quite so eager to be done with her.

They'd set the reunion and picnic up for Saturday, when the yard was open anyway and their customers were used to coming in—especially the ones who were painstakingly and slowly doing their own renovations. They were the ones, Melanie had explained to Wyatt, who were more likely to know someone who wanted to be in the business.

And since Wyatt had given up the idea of charging an admission fee and giving the money to charity, they'd simply passed the word along that everyone who was interested in old cars was welcome to come and bring their friends. It was easier than creating an invitation list, but a nightmare when it came to ordering food. Melanie finally took her best guess as to how many people might actually show up, called in an order to the catering department of the nearest supermarket, and went back to work. It took her two days to catch up on everything that had slid behind schedule because of her head cold and the extremely late start she'd had the morning after taking Scruffy to visit Matthew at the hospital.

When she got to work on Saturday morning, the guys had already strung up flags and bunting and moved all the cars that were awaiting renovation into a neat row off to one side of the lot in order to leave room for the customers to park. Wyatt and Robbie were filling dozens of balloons with helium from a tank strapped in the back of Robbie's pickup truck.

"I just hope somebody comes," she said, "or we'll all be stuck here eating hamburgers and hot dogs for weeks."

"You're turning into a grouch," Wyatt said. He put another balloon on the helium tank and opened the valve.

She had to admit he was right. The week had been busy as well as stressful, and all the unknowns were starting to weigh on her. If she knew for certain that there was a buyer somewhere in the wings, then she could begin to make plans and to prepare her employees for the changeover—and to reconcile herself to the idea that Wyatt would soon be going out of her life. If, on the other hand, she knew for certain that there wouldn't be a buyer, then she'd stop dreaming of the impossible and settle down to work.

And enjoy having Wyatt around, without being so fearful of how long the interlude would last, a little voice in the back of her mind whispered.

Either way, she could adjust. She had, after all, adapted to worse things. It was the fact that she didn't have an inkling which way things would go that was wearing her out.

One thing she needn't have worried about, however, was whether her customers would show up. By ten in the morning, they'd started to arrive in small groups with well-polished cars, and by noon they were swapping stories and admiring each other's work from one end of the lot to the other. A number of them were wandering around the row of cars which were awaiting restoration.

If nothing else, she thought, perhaps they'd sell a car or two today.

She was fixing herself a hamburger from the pile beside the caterer's grill when she spotted a half-familiar face in the crowd. It took her longer than usual to place it. In fact, she'd run through her mental list of the cars they'd restored twice before she realized this wasn't a customer at all. It was the man who'd bought their charity package at Erika's auction. Phillip, that was his name.

He must have just arrived, and he was obviously perplexed by the crowd. A moment later he spotted Melanie and made a beeline for her.

She felt a chill run down her spine. "Oh, no," she said. "Please tell me it isn't today that Wyatt arranged for you to go to Felicity's. Because if it is—"

Phillip laughed merrily. "That's not till tomorrow. Noon at our house, so we can go to the Sunday buffet lunch."

"Perhaps it's none of my business," Melanie said, "but for the extortionate amount you paid for a meal and taxi service, are you sure you wouldn't rather have dinner?"

He shook his head. "It's not the food we're interested in. We want to show off that glorious car in sunlight when everybody can see us, not hide it in the middle of the night." He looked around with concern. "You're not going to sell it today, are you? All these people—"

"I'll make it a point not to sell it till after you've had your ride," Melanie assured him gravely.

He grinned. "That's all right, then. Otherwise I might have had to buy it myself. Mind if I go look at it?" He seemed to take the answer for granted, which was just as well since Melanie was nearly speechless. "Uh—which direction should I go?"

She pointed toward the back of the building, and he wandered off.

With a single word, she could have sold the Cadillac... Of course, it wouldn't have been ethical to tell him she was negotiating a deal when she actually wasn't. Still, it wouldn't have taken much to talk Phillip into buying something he obviously wanted anyway.

She turned back to her hamburger, but she was still thinking about the Cadillac when she glimpsed Wyatt coming toward her, working his way through the crowd, shaking hands and greeting guests. Her throat tightened at the sight.

Once, she recalled, she had thought his face was interesting—even compelling—but not handsome. She remembered thinking that he'd be no competition for Jackson in a Greek-god contest. Technically, she supposed, it was every bit as true today, though she had trouble recollecting exactly what it was about Wyatt's face that she had thought wasn't handsome. Now when she looked at him, all she could think was that he was the most delicious-looking man she'd ever seen.

Even on that first day, however, she'd been smart enough to know that *interesting* was more important and more lasting than *handsome* could ever be. And as she looked back now, it was clear that from the very beginning some deeper level of her brain had recognized that this man was unlike any other.

He hadn't spent much time at the yard in the last couple of days—in fact, he'd stopped by only a couple of times since the night he'd taken her to the hospital to visit Matthew. She'd been very careful on the few occasions when she'd seen him, trying her best to keep everything normal, to react in just the way that a business partner should.

But she couldn't help wondering if he was keeping his distance because somehow she had given herself away. When she'd been hit by that sudden, blazing realization that she'd fallen in love with him, had he been able to see it in her eyes? Had he read her mind? Had he somehow figured out that his partner wasn't thinking of business when she looked at him?

"Hey, Mel," he teased as he came up to her. "You throw a nice party."

"Thanks, Bub." She kept her tone every bit as playful as he had.

Wyatt reached for a plate, a bun, and the ketchup bottle. "There's someone coming this afternoon you should keep an eye out for. Special treatment would be a good idea."

"Who?"

"Bryant Collins."

Melanie shook her head. "Am I supposed to know this guy? What does he look like?"

"I don't know. Remember Brad Edwards's friend? He wanted to see the place in action, so I invited him to come to the picnic." Wyatt put a hamburger patty on the bun and added a slice of tomato.

Melanie said carefully, "You're telling me this is the same friend who's thinking of buying the business?"

"I don't know what he's thinking—he didn't confide in me. But he said he'd like to look the place over."

Melanie felt herself start to do a slow burn. "So you invited him to come today? Dammit, Wyatt—"

"Why not? Bub and Mel's Used Cars is certainly looking better and busier today than it has in recent memory."

He was right, of course, and yet she couldn't swallow her fury. "It didn't occur to you to warn me about this?"

"What would you have done about it? I didn't know it myself till yesterday. That wouldn't even have given you time to take down all the old calendars off the office walls, much less clean up the weeds and the last row of cars back by the fence."

"I could at least have tried to straighten the place up!"

"When? Between two and four this morning? There wasn't enough time to do anything significant."

"You could have put him off."

"And missed the chance for him to see this?" He waved a hand at the closely-parked rows of classic and exotic cars which had turned the parking lot into a rainbow-colored patchwork quilt. "All you would have managed to accomplish if I'd told you yesterday would be to drive yourself crazy about everything that should have been done before a prospective buyer came to look. So I thought it would be better not to tell you."

She couldn't argue with him. Not that she didn't want to, but it wouldn't be wise while they were surrounded by customers and guests. At least half were people she'd never seen before, and any one of them could be Brad Edwards's friend. If he was to wander by and hear this argument…

"How's Matthew doing?" Wyatt asked.

He sounded concerned but casual—as if, Melanie thought, there was nothing more to be said about the prospective buyer. She decided that later—when it was safe—she was going to give Wyatt a very large piece of her mind.

In the meantime she tried to smother her irritation. "Janice told me just this morning that he's doing better."

"No more requests for the mop to keep him company?"

"Not yet. It should be interesting to see what happens tonight, though, on our regular visit." She caught a drip of ketchup from her sandwich just before it splashed on her T-shirt. "Darn it, I didn't think I'd put so much ketchup on this." *Of course right then you were dreaming of Wyatt instead of thinking about hamburgers. You could have put arsenic sauce on it and not noticed.*

"I'm sorry to break the news, but your boyfriend seems to have consoled himself with another woman," Wyatt said.

Melanie looked around. "Bill Myers?"

"He's right over there with a blonde."

She followed the direction of his gaze. "It'll never work," she said. "That's Angela Dawson."

"What's wrong with her?"

"With her, nothing. With her car…" Melanie gave an artistic shudder. "We're restoring a Cobra for her. Bill worships his Mustang."

"Personally, I'd say they make quite a pair." Wyatt smiled.

Melanie felt her heart turn over. It simply wasn't fair that he could do this to her, she thought, with nothing more than a smile.

Beside her, a short, stocky man with a mustache said, "Are you the owner?"

"One of them." She reluctantly tore her gaze away from Wyatt. "Here's the other one. What can we do for you?"

The man with the mustache ignored her and reached for Wyatt's hand. "Then you're Reynolds. Good to meet you. I'm Bryant Collins."

Wyatt gestured toward the grill. "Would you like some food first, or shall we show you around?"

Bryant Collins shook his head. "Neither, thanks. I've been here for a couple of hours—I've already given myself the tour. Is there a place we can sit down and talk?"

Sunday was warm and sunny, and Melanie and Wyatt put the top down on the Cadillac convertible before driving across town to pick up Phillip and his wife for their lunch at Felicity's.

As she started the engine, Wyatt said, "What do you think of the offer?"

She'd known the question was coming, because it was the first quiet moment they'd had to talk since Bryant Collins had drawn them aside yesterday. The reunion had still been winding down when Melanie had left to take Scruffy on his regular hospital round last night, leaving Wyatt to deal with the stragglers.

But expecting the question didn't mean she was ready to answer it.

"I don't know." She didn't look at him. "I mean, I'm glad he wants to buy it—that's reassuring. But there's something about him…"

"Him? I thought it would be the money that bothered you."

"It does," she admitted. "It's not nearly as much as I'd hoped for. And the way he just tossed a figure on the table without even asking how much we wanted for it—"

"That means he'll pay more."

"I suppose so. It just seemed arrogant to me, to put a value on it himself without even consulting us."

"And you're worried about how the guys will get along, working for him."

"Of course I'm concerned. You don't know them as well as I do, Wyatt."

"They'll adjust."

"That sounds as if you've made up your mind." She kept her voice level. It wasn't any surprise that he wanted to accept Bryant Collins' offer—even if he held out for a higher price.

"We don't have bidders standing in line, Melanie."

He was right, of course. And it was foolish of her to reject a solid offer, even if it wasn't exactly what she wanted. Especially, she admitted, when the real problem was that she wasn't quite sure what she wanted.

But she did know one thing for certain—and that was what she didn't want. She would not even try to keep Wyatt bound to a business he disliked, because to do so would be a recipe for bitterness. So if the business had to sell, and Bryant Collins was the only buyer…

"I know," she said. "So…make the best deal you can, and I'll sign."

It felt as if she was tearing out her heart.

Wyatt didn't seem to notice. "Look at this," he said, and she realized that the entire neighborhood had come out to observe Phillip and his wife go off for lunch. Some were mowing lawns or weeding flower beds, but the majority were frankly gawking at the car as Melanie parked it in the driveway beside the middle-class house in the suburbs.

Phillip was in no hurry to get started; he was obviously enjoying being at the center of attention. "Mind if I try out the driver's seat?" he asked. "Just to sit there for a minute, I mean. I know the rules about driving— Wyatt told me."

Melanie couldn't stand it. Instead of answering, she tossed him the keys.

Wyatt's eyebrows soared. "What happened to not letting anyone loose with this car?" he asked under his breath.

"I'm not letting him loose." Melanie knew she sounded defensive. "I'm riding along. But just take a look at him."

"Yeah, he looks like a kid who's just been handed a free pass to the carnival—including the bumper car track."

"You don't have to be involved."

Wyatt shook his head. "Oh, no. This I have to see." He helped her into the back seat.

Phillip held the door for his wife and got behind the wheel. "Everybody aboard," he called. "No necking back there, now, young ones."

"You have nothing to worry about," Wyatt said easily.

Melanie bit her lip. Did he have to make it so painfully clear that he wasn't attracted to her?

"We keep a Corvette especially for lovers' lanes," Wyatt went on. "It was Melanie's idea. So much more intimate, you know." And as Phillip cautiously worked the Cadillac into traffic, Wyatt curved an arm around Melanie's shoulders.

Phillip and Phyllis insisted that Wyatt and Melanie join them for brunch. "That's just because you want to leave the car out front to draw attention," Melanie teased, and Phillip laughed and agreed.

The buffet was the biggest and most elaborate she'd ever seen, so huge that simply tasting a single bite of everything would take hours. But Melanie knew it wasn't the memory of the food that would stay with her forever. It was the knowledge that this would probably be the last time that she would share such an occasion with Wyatt.

Even before she had given her approval for the sale, Wyatt had made his decision. So with the two of them in agreement and a buyer waiting, it was only a matter of working out the details—the exact price, the conditions of sale. But she thought, from talking to Bryant Collins yesterday, that none of those things were likely to be sticking points.

So it was only a matter of time before the deal was finished and the partnership was over, and they could go their separate ways. No more charity auctions, no more nightclubs, no more lunches at Felicity's.

No more Wyatt.

She told herself not to think about that right now. She'd enjoy what she had at the moment. There would be plenty of time for regrets later.

She was in the ladies' lounge, toying with her lipstick and waiting for Phillip's wife, when the door opened and Jackson's Jennifer came in.

But she's not Jackson's Jennifer anymore, she reminded herself, and wondered once more what had happened. Perhaps just finding out that Jackson had once owned half a junkyard had been the final straw for an obvious society girl like Jennifer. But she probably hadn't known that till after he'd sold it, so why would it have been any big deal? Maybe it didn't have anything to do with Classical Cars.

Jennifer drew herself up sharply, staring at Melanie. "You're the one who's with Wyatt," she said. "I think you should know what sort of a guy he is."

I do know, Melanie wanted to say. *He's the kind who brings chicken soup to a woman when she's sick, and buys her the kind of flowers she likes instead of the sort*

*that are easy, and steals a key so he won't have to wake
her up to deliver them.*

"He's the kind who takes advantage of people,"
Jennifer said. "The kind who pretends to be a friend and
then swoops in when they make a mistake and mops up
everything they have."

"You're talking about Jackson, I assume." Melanie
kept her voice level. "It sounds to me as if Jackson
didn't make a mistake, he committed fraud. He didn't
exactly level with Wyatt when he sold him the business,
so what Jackson has to complain about now is beyond
my understanding."

"Sold him the business?" Jennifer said blankly.
"Jackson didn't sell Wyatt the business."

Hadn't Jackson told her anything at all about the deal?
Probably only the part that reflected well on him.   And
yet…

I'm single and broke, Jackson had told her the night
of the charity auction. At that moment, Melanie had been
too busy wondering what had happened between him
and Jennifer even to consider the other half of the statement. Now she wondered how she'd missed it. It was
all so obvious—Jennifer had dumped Jackson because
he no longer had any money. But how could Jackson be
broke if he'd sold his business to Wyatt?

Doubt was gnawing deep inside her. "Then how did
Wyatt get it, if Jackson didn't sell?" Melanie's voice
felt shaky.

"Jackson put the business up as a stake in a poker
game," Jennifer said flatly. "And Wyatt walked away
with it."

Wyatt's words echoed in Melanie's head. When she
had suggested he go back to Jackson and void the sale
because he hadn't known exactly what he was buying,

he'd said, *It wasn't that kind of a deal.* And more than once he'd as much as told her that he hadn't paid Jackson's price….

The evidence had been in front of her all along, but now it all made sense. Wyatt couldn't void the sale, because there hadn't been one. He hadn't paid Jackson's price, because he'd scooped it up as part of a poker pot. He hadn't charged Jackson with fraud because to do so, he'd have to reveal his own illegal gambling…

"Phyllis," she called. "I'll wait for you outside." She didn't pause for an answer.

Wyatt was in the foyer, leaning against a wall with his arms folded across his chest. He pushed himself upright and said, a smile in his voice, "Phillip's already gone out to play with the car."

"I just had a chat with Jennifer," Melanie said. "No wonder you didn't tell me why she slapped you."

Wyatt drew a long breath, as if he was bracing himself.

Melanie didn't pause. "I think before we sell the business I have a right to know exactly how much you have invested in it. What did it take? A full house? Four of a kind?"

"Melanie—"

She cut him off, her fury building. "Or did you bluff Jackson with a pair of deuces, just for the fun of it?"

Wyatt's face was like stone, and his voice like cold steel. "I could have. That young man should stay out of poker games."

Melanie thought that Jennifer's announcement had hit her as hard as anything possibly could. But it wasn't until the last feeble hope shriveled that she realized she'd been holding desperately to the notion that Jennifer might have been wrong, that Wyatt might laugh and explain, and that everything might be all right after all.

Now she knew that nothing would ever be all right again.

CHAPTER TEN

MELANIE didn't know how she managed to stay on her feet. Sheer stubborn pride, she supposed, was all that kept her upright. Even if she could salvage nothing else from the chaos, she would hold on to her dignity. She was not going to let Wyatt guess how deeply this betrayal had stabbed her.

Being disappointed in a business partner was one thing. Acknowledging that she'd fallen in love with that business partner—only to find that he was nothing at all like she'd thought he was—was another thing entirely.

"You'll make sure that Phillip and Phyllis get home," she said. She didn't intend it to be a question, and it was clear that Wyatt didn't take it as one, for he nodded curtly. "I'll take a cab."

"Melanie—"

She stopped, but she didn't turn to face him. "I don't care to hear how you did it. It's really none of my business anyway—how you got your share."

"No, it's not," he said quietly. "So I'm not offering to explain. I told Bryant Collins I'd get back to him tomorrow. Do you still want to make a deal?"

"More than ever," she said. "Take whatever we can get. Just get it done as soon as possible." She pushed through the door.

The cab had taken her halfway across the city before she realized that she didn't have enough money in her pockets to pay the fare. She told the cabbie to take her to Classical Cars instead, so she could borrow enough from petty cash to carry her through till she could go to the bank on Monday.

She was still vibrating from the shock. How could she have been so wrong about Wyatt?

Because she hadn't wanted to recognize the signs, she admitted. But in fact, even though she hadn't wanted to acknowledge it, she had seen a resemblance between him and her father. She remembered thinking that the lack of common sense Wyatt had displayed in buying a business without quite knowing what it did reminded her of some of her father's odder deals.

Well, no wonder—because those deals of her father's had probably been negotiated over a poker table, too.

She'd always known that her father gambled. Other fathers played golf or told raucous jokes or went to church all the time; Melanie's father bet on races, on ponies, on football games. It was simply a part of him.

What she hadn't known until it was too late was how much of him the habit had consumed. It had seemed a harmless hobby, until he died and everything came crashing down around them. What had seemed to be a solid middle-class life had turned out to be no more real than a movie set, and like the false fronts of an Old West town, it had taken no more than a breeze to knock it down. She had watched her mother grow old in a matter of weeks…

When the cab stopped next to Classical Cars, Melanie was startled to see Wyatt's car in the parking lot, and it took her a moment to get her head straight and remember that Wyatt had left it there that morning when they'd picked up the Cadillac. With any luck, Phillip would be driving around Kansas City and showing off his borrowed toy for hours yet, and she'd have plenty of time to pay off the cabbie and go home before Wyatt came back to retrieve his car.

The petty cash box was buried at the back of the bottom drawer of her desk, and as she was digging it out she heard a rustle from the direction of the shop and then the creak of the door opening. Melanie froze at the sound of footsteps in the showroom.

Robbie stopped in the doorway. "Melanie? I heard someone moving around out here."

She eyed the enormous wrench he was carrying. "And you thought we had a burglar? No, just me, trying to scrape up enough to pay my cab fare."

"Cab fare? But I thought you and Wyatt were—"

"Long story, Robbie. And the meter's still ticking." She put the box back and started out to pay the cabbie.

Robbie was still lounging in the doorway when she came back inside, and for the first time, it occurred to Melanie to wonder why. "It's Sunday. What are you doing here?"

Robbie shrugged. "There's a lot to do. Yesterday was fun, but it didn't get us any further along on the Cobra or the Pontiac. And if you're going to be showing the place off to potential buyers, we'd better keep up with the workload."

"We're not going to be showing it." She caught herself. "I mean, I think it's already sold—all but doing the paperwork."

"To that guy who was poking around here yesterday?"

She tried to smile. "There must have been a hundred people poking around yesterday. Which one do you mean?"

"The one with the mustache like a walrus."

"That's the one. He said he liked what he saw."

"That covers it, then." Robbie's voice was dry. "Because he saw everything there was to see."

"There's no deal yet, but we talked about terms. He agreed to keep everybody on the staff."

The only real obstacles, Melanie reflected, had been the size of the check Bryant Collins was willing to write, and her intuitive sense that he wouldn't be easy to work for. But now, she was willing to take less money just to have the whole thing over so she didn't have to face Wyatt again. And as for her guys—

How do I know the next buyer who comes along wouldn't be even worse for them? But that didn't make her feel any easier about Bryant Collins.

Robbie seemed to hear the doubts in her voice. "Don't worry about it, Melanie. I'm sure if he buys it, the deal will work out all right. People who work on old cars are pretty much all alike, under the skin. We'll be fine."

Melanie wished she felt as certain as Robbie sounded. But then, she wasn't confident that Robbie was really convinced, either—she was pretty sure he was just trying to make them both feel better about the inevitable.

"You know," Robbie said slowly, "it was a big shock around here when Wyatt turned up."

That, Melanie thought, *is the understatement of the year.*

"We'd all kind of gotten used to Jackson not paying any attention and leaving everything to you. Wyatt's not a bad guy, though."

"We just don't know much about him." It hurt to admit, even to herself, that she had fallen in love with someone who was so completely a mystery. She didn't even know what he did, or where he lived. *South of downtown* took in a lot of territory.

"Anyway, that turned out all right. So I imagine this new guy will too."

That turned out all right.... Melanie felt her heart twist. *Not for me,* she wanted to say.

"There was something I wanted to ask you about the Pontiac," Robbie went on. "It'll just take a couple of minutes."

"I'm not in any big hurry," Melanie said, and followed him out to the shop.

A little later, with Robbie's question answered, she chose a white Corvette to drive home. That was another thing she'd have to take into account when the sale went though, she realized—she'd have to buy a car, because she would no longer have an unlimited choice to draw from. And then things like oil changes and tires and insurance wouldn't be part of the business's routine expenses. She'd be paying for all of those herself.

As she thought it through, the offer Bryant Collins had made was sounding smaller and smaller. But changing her mind now wasn't an option. She had given Wyatt the go-ahead to negotiate for her, and as long as he stuck to the deal she'd agreed to, she couldn't back out.

She'd just be very careful to read the papers before she signed anything.

She almost didn't notice, as she drove through the lot, that the Cadillac was parked neatly right next to the building, and Wyatt's car was gone. He must have come while she was back in the shop with Robbie—and perhaps he hadn't even realized that she was there.

But of course it would be no surprise to find that Wyatt hadn't wanted to talk to her any more than she wanted to talk to him.

Melanie was amused to notice that it was Bill Myers who delivered Angela Dawson to pick up her Cobra. He was driving his Mustang, though the blue driver's door hadn't yet been repainted to match the almost fire-engine red of the rest of the car. And through the open window of the showroom she could hear them arguing heatedly about the relative merits of the two brands.

Wyatt was right, Melanie thought. They do make quite a pair.

It was several seconds later before she realized she'd done it again—thought of him automatically, warmly, as if he were a friend and everything was fine between them. She wanted to kick herself.

She had thought that the longer he stayed away, the easier she would find it. Surely as the days went by, she would stop thinking about him. He'd be no more than an absent partner, as Jackson had been.

But Wyatt was anything but absent, because he was everywhere she looked. He was sitting in every car they'd driven together. He was lurking at the edge of every old calendar on the office wall. He was standing beside the coffee machine whenever she went to refill her cup.

Each time the door opened, Scruffy lifted his head and looked expectantly at the newcomer, and then drooped back into his basket again.

Melanie knew exactly how he felt.

She got the keys for the Cobra and went out to greet Angela and Bill. They'd moved on from the question of which was the better car and were discussing the relative merits of do-it-yourself versus professional restoration.

"I must say I'm on Angela's side here," Melanie said as she joined them. "Bill, you know the guys could have that Mustang of yours looking like it just came out of the showroom within a week or two. All you have to do is say the word.''

''It's the satisfaction that counts most,'' Bill said stubbornly.

Angela laughed at him and started up the Cobra's engine. ''I'll race you home,'' she offered. ''And you can have a head start while I sit here and write my check.''

From behind Melanie came a man's voice, low and full of humor. Wyatt's voice. ''Don't do it, Bill, or she'll never stop rubbing it in.''

Melanie's heart gave an odd little jolt. She turned to face him, trying to keep herself steady. It had been days since she'd seen him, but that didn't make any difference—except perhaps to make him look even more appealing.

Angela was in a hurry to be out on the road with her new toy, and so Melanie processed the paperwork at record speed. It was only a few minutes later that she put Angela's check under the chunk of Missouri limestone which served as a paperweight on her desk and turned to Wyatt, who was playing tug-of-war with Scruffy.

He stopped immediately, much to Scruffy's disgust, and closed the office door. The amusement he'd displayed as he talked to Angela was gone; the good-humored playmate had vanished. His face was chilly as he surveyed Melanie.

She sat up straighter. ''I'm assuming you're here because you have something to report about the sale.''

He sat down across from her. ''I've talked to Bryant Collins several times. He won't budge from his initial offer.''

''That's crazy. Nobody does business that way.''

"He says if we insist on conditions like keeping all the employees for at least a year, he can't afford to—''

"He said he'd keep them permanently. Now he's changing it to just a year?"

Wyatt said mildly, "If you'll let me finish, Melanie… You have to be realistic. That agreement is completely unenforceable anyway."

"Which he knows perfectly well," Melanie grumbled. She closed her eyes and rubbed her temples. She could take this offer, and have it over with. Or she could turn it down and continue this mismatched, unhappy partnership.

But they couldn't go on like this. The stress would do nothing but get worse, and she could feel in her bones— and see in Wyatt's face—the toll it was already taking. There was really no choice, and she knew it. "If there's no other buyer and he's not willing to budge, then I suppose…" Her voice trailed off. She couldn't bring herself to say it.

"There's one other possible buyer."

Melanie sat up straighter. "Why didn't you tell me that right away?"

"Because it's just about the same amount of money."

Melanie sighed. She'd been hoping for more, because she'd tried every way she could to make the numbers add up, and she didn't like the result. Her half of Bryant Collins' offer might get her through medical school. But by the time she finished school, she'd be scraping bottom—and she'd still be only halfway through her training. She couldn't live on the pittance paid to interns and residents, and there wouldn't be time for any other kind of job to fill in the cracks.

And if this new offer was no more, then she would still be in the same pickle.

"The sales price is about the same," Wyatt went on. "However, instead of paying it all up front as Bryant Collins would do, the buyer would make a one-third down payment and then pay the rest over a longer period of time."

"So what you're saying is it's really a worse deal, with the money trickling in like that."

"However, in return for the more generous time frame, we'd also get a small share of the profits."

"Having been in this business for a while," Melanie said, "I wouldn't count on there being profits. Why are you even telling me about this?"

"Because it also offers better conditions for your workers. I think we should take it."

She'd been opening her mouth to refuse, but that stopped her.

"If you disagree, I can go back to Bryant Collins and tell him there's another bidder," Wyatt said. "He might increase his offer."

Melanie pulled herself up short. "No," she said. "If this other deal is better for my guys, then that's what I want to do." Maybe if she put the house on the market and lived on canned tuna, she could make it. *I can always sell some blood,* she thought wryly.

Wyatt stood up. "I'll get the sales contract drawn up. It won't take long to go through, so you can make arrangements to start school right away if you want. You should have the first third of the money within a week."

"Who's this buyer, anyway?" Melanie asked idly. "And where did you find him?"

For a moment she thought he wasn't going to answer. "He found me," Wyatt said finally. "It's Robbie."

Melanie felt her jaw go slack. "*Robbie* has the resources to buy this place? He can't have been moonlighting to save up, because he's always here.... Oh, of course—that's why he'll need a lot of time to pay.'' As she got used to the idea, Melanie felt like dancing. ''It's perfect, Wyatt. The customers trust him, the employees will be pleased—''

''You'll have a regular income, and I'll be rid of an albatross 'round my neck.'' He pushed his chair back into place and was gone before she could respond.

An albatross 'round his neck. She wondered for a moment if he had been talking about the business—or about her. The business, of course, she told herself drearily. He'd do anything to get rid of this business. But Melanie herself wasn't important enough to Wyatt for him to consider her a problem.

When Melanie went out to the shop to congratulate Robbie, he had his head under the hood of the Pontiac. The engine was running, she noted—which was a major step forward, since the last time they'd tried to start it, it had screeched like a banshee. It was still pretty noisy, though—she had to tap Robbie on the shoulder to get his attention.

He killed the engine and reached for a towel to wipe his hands.

''I came out to say congratulations to the new owner,'' Melanie said.

Robbie's hands stilled, clutching the towel. ''You don't mind?''

''*Mind?* Of course not. Why would I mind?''

He shuffled his feet. ''I just thought... Wyatt didn't want me to say anything to you about it, so I thought you might be upset.''

Melanie frowned, remembering that odd hesitation of Wyatt's, the moment when she'd thought he wasn't going to tell her who the buyer was. But that made no sense at all. It was Robbie, for heaven's sake—not an old poker pal or a career criminal... "Why didn't he want you to tell me?"

Robbie shrugged. "Just being modest, I guess."

"About making a deal with you? I shouldn't think that would—"

"About helping me to swing it. Angie and I have always wanted to have our own business, but I never thought it would be possible. Even when I asked Wyatt about it, I thought it was a waste of time. I don't have the kind of money it takes to buy a place like this. But then when Wyatt said I could pay it off over a long time—I just couldn't believe it."

That's easy to explain, Melanie wanted to say. *He doesn't have anything invested, so whatever he gets back, no matter how little it is or how long it takes, is gravy.*

But she couldn't bring herself to wipe the worshipful look from Robbie's eyes. Not for Wyatt's sake, she told herself, but because it would hurt Robbie to discover that his hero had a flaw. If he found out that Wyatt had made that deal not for Robbie's sake but because it was coldly practical from Wyatt's point of view, Robbie would be devastated.

"Of course, he gets a third down," she murmured. "That's a pretty good chunk of change right there."

And there's no way that Robbie has that kind of money, she thought uneasily.

She knew exactly what Robbie earned, because she was the one who wrote his paychecks. She knew that Angie had quit her job when the baby was born and had been at home ever since. And she was pretty certain that neither one of them could have inherited a windfall without everyone at Classical Cars hearing about it.

So where was Robbie getting the money to make a one-third down payment on the car lot within a week?

There was only one answer, and Melanie didn't like it.

He'd do anything to get rid of this business, she had told herself just this afternoon. And she'd been right.

Robbie was shaking his head. "No, he doesn't get a big payment up front. He explained to me why you need money right away, and I think it's great, really—you going back to school. But I don't have that kind of cash. So when Wyatt offered to loan me that, too, and let me pay back everything I owe him a little at a time over the next ten years..."

That's the bit I missed, Melanie thought. *No wonder he was in such a hurry to leave, before I could put the pieces together.*

Wyatt was so anxious to get rid of the business that he was not only willing to take peanuts for it but he would wait years for the money. And he was so anxious to get rid of Melanie that he was willing to pay for the privilege.

Maybe she was more important to him than she'd thought. She must be even more of a nuisance than she'd realized, considering what it was costing him to be rid of her...

Doesn't it make you feel special, Melanie—being singled out for special treatment like that?

The office was too small to fit everyone in, so Melanie had the guys move the cream-colored Thunderbird out of the showroom and set up a table instead. Angie came in hours before the scheduled signing, her arms loaded with crepe paper and balloons, to decorate the room as if for a party.

Melanie retreated to the office and for the last time went through the motions of checking for orders, updating the records for each car that was currently under renovation, making entries in the computer ledgers. As soon as the papers were signed, this would be Angie's job. But though she'd been training her successor all week, and she was confident that Angie would do just fine, something inside Melanie insisted that she leave everything in perfect order.

So she was the last to join the group around the table. There were five of them—she and Wyatt, Robbie and Angie, and an attorney—plus baby Luke toddling around the room and entertaining himself by batting at each balloon in turn.

Melanie sat down across from Wyatt and signed in silence. It took very little time—much less than Angie had spent decorating the room—and then it was done. The three years she had spent in the car business were over, reduced to a few pieces of paper.

Robbie and Angie were hugging in the middle of the showroom. Luke, noticing that he was being left out of the embrace, tugged at his parents and babbled anxiously. The attorney gathered up his papers. Wyatt headed for the door.

Melanie intercepted him. "Can I talk to you privately, please?"

He looked reluctant.

"It'll only take a minute, Wyatt." She looked toward the office, and then realized that it wasn't hers anymore. "Outside, maybe?"

The wind was crisp as it whipped around the building, and she hadn't stopped to pick up a jacket. She shivered.

Wyatt said, "Let's sit in a car. Your choice."

The closest was the red Cadillac which had been part of the charity auction package. Melanie slid behind the wheel and then on across into the passenger seat, turning so her back was against the door.

"Have you signed up for school yet?"

She shook her head. Then she held out the check Robbie had given her just minutes before. "Here."

"What's this?"

"Your money back. You don't have to pay me off. I'm glad you arranged for Robbie to buy the business, and I'm willing to take the same terms you're getting. And don't be angry with Robbie. He didn't tell me, I figured it out for myself."

He didn't take the check. She reached across the car and tucked it over the sun visor right above his head.

"What about your schooling?" he said quietly.

"Maybe I'll go to nursing school instead—it's faster and less expensive. Or I might be able to get an actual job working with companion dogs. It doesn't matter—I can still help kids."

"That's not what you want."

"Well, I long ago learned that we don't get everything we want, so—"

"He really hurt you, didn't he?"

"My father, you mean? Yes, he did. But that is so far beside the point, Wyatt... You just don't get it, do you? Didn't it occur to you, when I told you how I felt about gambling, to tell me about the poker game?"

"No. I didn't see any reason to trash Jackson then— since he wasn't your partner anymore."

"Oh, that's rich. How about you? Didn't it occur to you that I might care how you'd got this place?"

"Why should it matter to you?"

The quiet question stopped Melanie in her tracks. If she'd been an ordinary partner, it wouldn't have mattered. It was only falling in love with him which had made this the worst thing that could happen to her...

He reached up and pulled the check from the visor. "Why won't you take this from me? Because it's tainted? It isn't, you know. I didn't win it at poker."

Melanie shook her head. "I just can't."

"Then that's it," he said.

It's over, she told herself. *You've done what you had to do. Now get out of the car and walk away.*

But she couldn't move. It was as if her brain had suddenly kicked into such high gear that her body was paralyzed. "It doesn't fit," she said suddenly. "You care too much."

Wyatt laughed, but there was no humor in the sound. "You're quite right, Melanie. I have a much bigger problem than gambling." He looked down at the check. "But you may have cured me." He folded the slip of paper into fourths and stuck it in his breast pocket. "You—and Jennifer."

Melanie was afraid to breathe.

But he didn't go on.

She said, softly, "You could have taken Bryant Collins' offer and walked away with cash, but instead you found a way for Robbie to have the business he dreamed of. You could have just sympathized with me about not being able to go to school—but instead you manufactured a whole scenario to make it possible. And you'd have kept both of those things completely secret if you could have pulled it off." She took a deep breath. "So you couldn't have watched Jackson toss his business onto the table and then taken it away from him with the turn of a card—it's not in your nature. But what did happen?'' She was asking herself, not him, and even as she said it, the answer began to take shape in her mind. ''You thought you were helping Jennifer. Didn't you?''

His eyebrow lifted a fraction, but he didn't comment.

''Tell me,'' she said firmly. ''Or I'll hunt down Jackson and Jennifer, and I'll find out what really happened in that poker game.''

''That would be a waste of time, since I wasn't even in the game.''

Melanie felt the world rock a little under her and then settle back into place, and she breathed a little more easily. *I wasn't wrong about him after all,* she thought.

He turned toward her and leaned against the car window. ''If I tell you, it goes no further,'' he warned.

She nodded, too afraid of breaking the momentum to speak.

''Jennifer's older brother is a friend of mine. He's been very worried about his little sister and the mysterious new man she's been dating. So when I saw Jackson join the high-stakes poker table at the Century Club, I kept an eye on him. He's an abysmal player, you know.''

Melanie wasn't surprised.

''When he offered to put his business up as a stake, I suggested he take a sure thing instead of a flyer and sell it to me. I figured when the hand was finally over and he saw the cards he'd been up against, he would realize he couldn't possibly have won, and he'd be grateful to have escaped with his teeth. He'd have learned a lesson, I'd have done my friend a favor, and Jennifer would find out what kind of a guy she was dating. And, incidentally, I assumed that as soon as he regained his senses, he'd tear up my check and keep his business.''

''What happened?'' she whispered.

"He tossed my check onto the table and drew a card, trying to fill an inside straight."

Melanie could see it as clearly as if she'd been in the room. "And he missed."

"Of course he missed. Have you ever tried drawing to an inside— No, of course you haven't. Sorry."

She nodded. "I have, actually. My dad taught me the rules, and how to figure the odds. So that's how you ended up owning half of Bub and Mel's Used Cars. No wonder you weren't very happy to find out we didn't deal in Lamborghinis."

"I was kicking myself that morning, yes. My Don Quixote impulse had cost me a cool two hundred thousand dollars, and all I had to show for it was a bunch of rusty Chevys and a redhead who was doing her best to make my life miserable."

It was a fair description, Melanie admitted. And it was still pretty much on target—though she wasn't actually *trying* to annoy him any more. Of course, if he was so frustrated with her, why had he gone out of his way to provide her with money to go to school? "Two hundred thousand? Is that all?"

"All?" He sounded stung. "You said yourself Jackson's share of the business wasn't worth what he wanted for it."

"Of course it wasn't—but I don't imagine Jackson would agree. I suppose that's why Jennifer insisted you hadn't bought it? Because they thought you hadn't paid enough?"

"I'm sure he'd have taken a second check if I'd offered it."

"I imagine so. What in heaven's name do you do that you can write a check for two hundred thousand dollars and have it taken as seriously as cash in a poker game? Those guys want the goods—pay or don't play.''

"After my grandfather sold the flour mills, he bought financial institutions.''

"You mean like banks? *Plural?* That figures—going straight from the riverbank to the other sort... Never mind. I suppose Jennifer thought you should either pay more or give it back, and that's why she slugged you?''

"She'd have been quite happy to have me take the hit for him.''

"You know, she's really not worth trying to rescue,'' Melanie murmured.

"Thank you,'' he said politely. "If I'd only met you first and had the benefit of your wisdom, none of this would have happened. Of course, then I wouldn't have met you at all.''

And you'd be a whole lot happier, Melanie thought. She took a deep breath. "I'm really sorry, Wyatt. I judged you without even listening.''

"And yet,'' he said, "you trusted me to make this deal.''

Her heart gave an odd flutter. She hadn't looked at it that way before, but he was right. Even when she'd thought the worst of him, it had never occurred to her that he might cheat her. Deep down inside, she had trusted him to do what was right. What would be best for her.

"Let me do this for you, Melanie,'' he said. He pulled the check from his pocket and held it out to her.

She looked at the future it represented, and slowly shook her head. "I can't,'' she said. "I can't owe you.''

"It's not a loan.''

"That's the problem.''

"I don't understand.''

"I'm not sure I can explain." *Not without telling you everything. Not without admitting I love you. Not without embarrassing myself past all redemption.* But then, what did it matter? If she saw him again at all, it would be purely accidental. So maybe it would be better if he knew the truth—because then he'd make sure there were no accidental encounters.

"You're too important to me, Wyatt," she said. "I can't put myself on the same level with Jennifer—being a charity case, needing to be rescued. Not when I want to be—more than that. So you see—"

She stopped suddenly. His eyes had gone suddenly shimmery, like sunlight on water.

She tried to swallow the lump in her throat, but it wouldn't cooperate.

"More—how?" he said softly. "Perhaps you'd like to show me." He moved closer.

Short of jumping out of the car, there was no place to retreat—and she didn't much want to, anyway. She didn't know if he pulled her toward him, or if she moved on her own, but she didn't care—suddenly she was in his arms where she'd longed to be, and he was kissing her with a tenderness that was more terrifying than force could possibly be.

When he finally stopped kissing her, he tucked her head under his chin and laid his cheek against her hair. "It was definitely good thinking not to choose a Corvette to hold this conversation in." He sounded hoarse. "Now tell me why you think I regard you as a charity case."

"Oh...Erika, for one. You seemed to think she wouldn't have bothered to steal my boyfriends."

He drew back and stared at her.

"All right," Melanie muttered. "I'm being silly, because all that was years ago and I'm grown up now. But you obviously believed that I couldn't attract anyone Erika would be interested in.''

''No, I thought that any guy who'd be susceptible to Erika wouldn't interest you enough to ever make it to boyfriend status. That's why she couldn't steal anyone from you—because if they'd be worth stealing, they wouldn't take a second look at her.''

''Oh,'' she said softly. ''I didn't know—''

''That when you laugh, it makes me want to tell jokes just to hear you do it again? That when you first wake up in the morning your voice is the sexiest sound on the planet? That I may be resistant to your viruses, but I sure as hell can't resist you? Dammit, Melanie, where did you think I was going when I started out that door this afternoon?''

''I don't know. I didn't think about it.''

''I was going over to your house to wait for you, where you'd have to talk to me.'' He moved enough to dig into his pocket, and pulled out a brass key, dangling it in front of her. ''There are advantages to doing favors for Robbie. He didn't have any scruples at all about stealing this from your desk.''

''I'll fire him.''

''You can't,'' he said against her lips. ''You're not the boss anymore.''

''That would make it difficult,'' she admitted.

''Melanie,'' he said. ''Will you marry me—and be Doctor Reynolds?''

''You don't mind? It means years of hard work, of long hours—''

''Of helping kids,'' he said. ''I wouldn't have you any other way. Just make sure to keep some time in there for me.''

She did her best to look as if she was thinking it over.

"I think I can manage that. Yes, I'll—I'll marry you, Wyatt." Her voice cracked, and the words felt ticklish.

"I'll start by bringing you coffee in bed every morning," he offered.

Melanie shuddered at the thought. "Please—spare me."

"All right," he said. "I'll just stay there with you instead."

"Now that," Melanie murmured, "is a *much* better idea."